ON
STORMY
SEAS

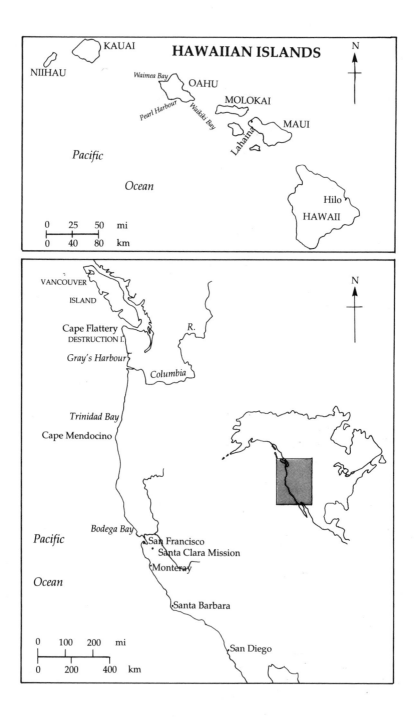

HAWAIIAN ISLANDS

KAUAI

NIIHAU

Waimea Bay

OAHU

MOLOKAI

Pearl Harbour

Waikiki Bay

MAUI

Lahaina

Pacific

Ocean

Hilo

HAWAII

N

0   25   50   mi

0   40   80   km

VANCOUVER

ISLAND

Cape Flattery

DESTRUCTION I.

Gray's Harbour

R.

Columbia

Trinidad Bay

Cape Mendocino

Bodega Bay

Pacific

San Francisco

Santa Clara Mission

Monterey

Ocean

Santa Barbara

San Diego

N

0   100   200   mi

0   200   400   km

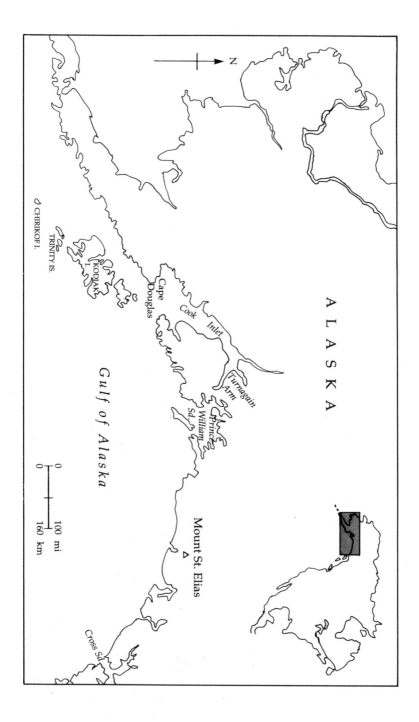

ALASKA

Gulf of Alaska

Cook Inlet

Cape
Douglas

KODIAK
I.

TRINITY IS.

CHRIKOF I.

Turnagain
Arm

Prince
William
Sd.

Mount St. Elias

Cross Sd.

N

0   100 mi
0   160 km

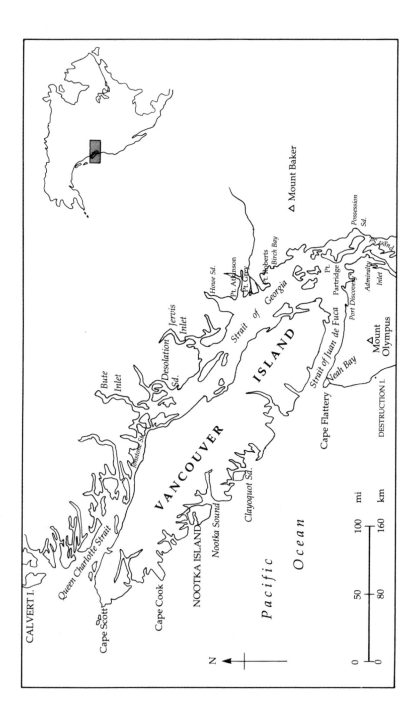

Mount Baker

Possession
Sd.

Whidbey
Island

Pt.
Roberts
Birch Bay

Pt. Atkinson
Pt. Grey
Howe Sd.

Strait of Georgia

Admiralty
Inlet
Port Discovery
Pt.
Partridge

Jervis
Inlet

Strait of Juan de Fuca

Desolation
Sd.

Mount
Olympus

Bute
Inlet

Neah Bay

Cape Flattery

DESTRUCTION I.

Johnstone Str.

ISLAND

VANCOUVER

Queen Charlotte Strait

CALVERT I.

Clayoquot Sd.

Cape Scott

Cape Cook

Nootka Sound

NOOTKA ISLAND

Pacific

Ocean

N

0   50   100   mi
0   80   160   km

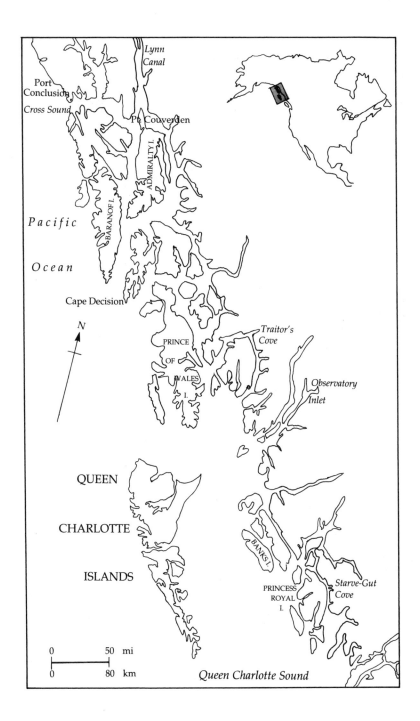

Lynn
Canal

Port
Conclusion

Cross Sound

Pt. Couverden

ADMIRALTY I.

Pacific

BARANOF I.

Ocean

Cape Decision

N

PRINCE

OF

WALES
I.

Traitor's
Cove

Observatory
Inlet

QUEEN

CHARLOTTE

ISLANDS

BANKS I.

PRINCESS
ROYAL
I.

Starve-Gut
Cove

| 0 | 50 | mi |
| 0 | 80 | km |

Queen Charlotte Sound

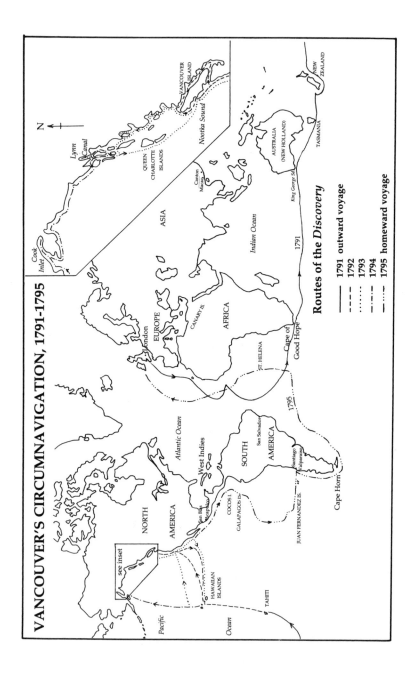

VANCOUVER'S CIRCUMNAVIGATION, 1791-1795

Cook
Inlet

N

Lynn
Canal

VANCOUVER
ISLAND

QUEEN
CHARLOTTE
ISLANDS

Nootka Sound

EUROPE

London

ASIA

Canton
Macao

CANARY IS.

AFRICA

Indian Ocean

AUSTRALIA
(NEW HOLLAND)

NEW
ZEALAND

TASMANIA

King George Sd.

1791

ST. HELENA

Cape of
Good Hope

1795

Atlantic Ocean

West Indies

NORTH
AMERICA

San Blas
Acapulco

COCOS I.

GALAPAGOS Is.

SOUTH
AMERICA

San Salvador

Santiago
Valparaiso

JUAN FERNANDEZ IS.

Cape Horn

see inset

HAWAIIAN
ISLANDS

TAHITI

Pacific

Ocean

Routes of the *Discovery*

——— 1791 outward voyage
– – – 1792
· · · · 1793
–·–· 1794
– ·· – 1795 homeward voyage

ON STORMY SEAS

B. GUILD GILLESPIE

The Triumphs and Torments
of Captain George Vancouver

HORSDAL & SCHUBART
Victoria, B.C.

Horsdal & Schubart Publishers Ltd.
4252, Commerce Circle
Victoria, BC
V8Z 4M2

Cover painting by Maurice Chadwick, Victoria, BC.

Chapter-head drawings by Brenda Guild Gillespie, Vancouver, BC.

Maps by Peggy Ward, Tsawwassen, BC.

Design and typesetting by The Typeworks, Vancouver, BC.

Canadian Cataloguing in Publication Data
    Gillespie, B. Guild (Brenda Guild), 1951-
        On stormy seas
        Includes bibliographical references and index.

    ISBN 0-920663-12-5

        1. Vancouver, George, 1757-1798.   2. Explorers—England—
    Biography. I. Title.
    G246.V3G85 1992   910'.92   C92-091154-4

Contents

Preface

Every history writer owes a primary debt to those who create source records and to those who keep them safe for the public to view. The scholars who research these records and, by their interpretations, continually pique our interest and renew our understandings play an important role as well. My first thanks is to these many, vital individuals.

I wish to thank the National Historic Parks and Sites Branch of Canada, for it was one of their historical markers on the crest of Spanish Banks hill in Vancouver, Canada, that started my long study of George Vancouver and his world. On a lovely fall day in 1979, I cycled up the hill and paused to cool off at the cairn, which read:

The Last Spanish Exploration
In commemoration of the first friendly meeting of the British and
Spaniards in these waters. Near this place, Captain George Van-
couver on the 22nd June 1792 met the Sutil and Mexicana under
Captains Galiano and Valdes—the last Spanish exploring exped-
ition in what is now the BC coast. The commanders exchanged
information, established mutual confidence, and continued the
exploration together. IT WAS DAWN FOR BRITAIN, BUT TWI-
LIGHT FOR SPAIN.
Government of Canada, 1929

The last, poetic line fired my imagination, from which dozens of
questions then tumbled: Who was George Vancouver? Why was he
here? And what were Spaniards—gypsies, to my mind— doing so
far from their spicy latitudes? Why was Britain on the way up and
Spain on the way down? I quickly got myself to a library, and the
rest is . . . well, history.

Not that history is a static, done thing. To wit: In March of
1984, the King and Queen of Spain became the first Iberian monar-
chs to visit Canada, and they spent several days in Vancouver.
Their tour naturally included a drive around the impressive Spanish
Banks hill, but what about that commemorative plaque? "It was
dawn for Britain, but twilight for Spain" would never do for regal
Spanish eyes; the plaque was hastily replaced shortly before the
tour, with the text diplomatically reworded and credited to the Historic Sites and Monuments Board of Canada, Government of Canada, 1929. Unfortunately, the shiny new plaque fit poorly over the
weathered old spot, but no matter: face was saved, and our royal
guests were well served.

I wished to know where the old plaque had gone, hence I queried
locally and was directed to write to the appropriate authorities in
Ottawa. I did, and in return, I received a telephone call—no letter,
nothing in writing—stating that the text had been replaced in 1976
and that the old plaque no longer existed. If it had been replaced in
1976, I asked, why had I seen it in 1979? Moreover, I had stood in

the rain early in 1984 to transcribe it for purposes of my own writing.

No, no, the *text* had been replaced in 1976; the plaque had been replaced sometime thereafter. Was it not interesting, I asked, that the new plaque went up just before the royal visit? Indeed, not. The change of text and the timing of replacement were coincidental, and what I saw was not at all the way it was. My questions were wrong and improper. Case closed.

My debt to the National Historic Parks and Sites Branch of Canada, therefore, comes from the happy knowledge that history is alive and kicking, here and everywhere, being written and rewritten according to the exigencies of the day, with the full authority necessary to keep it value-free and immutable.

I owe a great deal to John Vancouver, who wrote little—at least little that's survived—but, through his few words, left some telling clues to his nature and leanings. He was quick to decry injustice and long to bear a grudge. The former is evidenced by his 1796 book about the state of the poor, whose situation he felt could be remedied by the creation of worker- controlled pension plans, including such progressive measures as maternity benefits. The latter is evidenced by his quarrel with the Earl of Warwick, for whom he worked as agent from 1801 to 1804. As late as 1825, John Vancouver published a memoir vigorously refuting the Earl's charges against him. John's voice came through to me so clearly that much of my writing felt secretarial, hence I gladly give him most of the credit. As for any errors, we'll share those, although I suppose I'll have to answer for both of us.

To historian Dr. W. Kaye Lamb, a Vancouver scholar without equal, I owe something like five years of my life, for his researches saved me at least that much time, not to mention a lengthy trip to England, which I had neither the time nor money to make. For his kind attentions—reading and correcting my manuscript, while graciously accepting my storyteller's view of history—I am honoured and grateful. For his suggested title of *On Stormy Seas*, I am warmly and deeply thankful.

ON STORMY SEAS

I wish to thank my husband, Donald Gillespie, whom I met shortly after I began investigating George Vancouver's life and who, after more than a decade of supporting my history reading and writing habits, remains good-humoured when friends and relatives ask him if I'm still "sleeping with George." Since some of my best historical understandings and imaginings have occurred just as I drift off to sleep, who am I to tell old sailors and their Muses when to visit?

In assembling the illustrations for the body of the text, I received generous help from numerous individuals in Canada, the UK, US, Spain, and Australia. To Mrs. Caroline Bundy, Dr. Robin Inglis, Captain Desmond Fortescue, Lieutenant Commander V. Edwards, Captain D.G. Wixon, Count Nikolai Tolstoy, Dr. Thomas Brock, Mrs. Anne Yandle, Sanna Deutsch, Lynn Maranda, Benoit Cameron, Tara Steigenberger, and many others representing institutions who responded to my queries with unexpected interest, my hearty thanks.

My final thanks is to publisher and editor Marlyn Horsdal, whose enthusiasm for and understanding of the material struck a chord right away, and whose sharp skills and kind manner have kept us on course and on an even keel. She's the pilot, I'm the clerk, John's the agent, and George is ever the captain. I pray we've done 'the old man' justice.

B. Guild Gillespie
Vancouver, Canada, 1992

Lord Camelford's Bones

December, 1828   Southwark, Surrey

Strange are the things that vanish from this earth, completely
and without a trace. I, John Vancouver, have experienced
many puzzling disappearances over my 76 years, and with but one
exception, they have caused me unmitigated pain. As I am old, ill,
and about to vanish myself, leaving few enough traces of my existence, the time has come to record all that I know of certain missing items, beginning with the corpse of one Honourable Thomas
Pitt, the second Lord Camelford and Baron of Boconnoc.

Lord Camelford met his much deserved demise, at the age of 29,
at the hand of his best friend, who shot him dead in a duel in March
of 1804. It is pleasantly ironic that a man with so many sworn enemies, myself foremost among them, should be killed by a friend, but

the mad young lord forced the duel on a frivolous point of honour and finally paid with his life for his endlessly foolish rages.

It was his dying request that his mortal remains be buried on an island in the Lake of Bienne in Switzerland, near to where he had been schooled in his younger years. He professed to have found some peace during that time, taking leisurely refuge beneath the very tree Jean-Jacques Rousseau had favoured for similar purposes, which must have been his life's only respite from wishing to kill someone or destroy something for not bending to his every whim.

1804 was no year for a small cavalcade of snivelling relatives and sycophants to parade an English stiff through France to Switzerland, however. Travel to France was illegal, and even if it were not, Napoleon's troops would have had them all for breakfast, then afterward picked their teeth clean with Camelford's bones. The best that could be done was to embalm the remains and place them in the Church of St. Anne's at Soho, there to rest uneasily until war ended in Europe, following which the requested burial might take place.

Eleven years were to pass before Wellington's troops had Napoleon's for breakfast at Waterloo, thus paving the way for the little English funeral procession to make for Switzerland. Strange to say, however, the body had by then disappeared, entirely and inexplicably. It was more rumour than news, for there were few mourners left to care—and none enough to press the matter—but it was an oddity nonetheless. Vanished. Completely. Camelford would never know eternal peace, for nothing vexed him more than to be denied any and all he demanded. To have his final request thwarted would keep him in Hell forever, and I, for one, could not be more gratified.

I do not profess to know anything of the body's disappearance, and even if I did, I should not tell a soul. To my mind, an eternal sort of justice has been served, and should I be questioned at Heaven's Gate concerning the whereabouts of the remains, I should readily point out that, wherever they may be, the Devil has been given his due.

This is, therefore, the one vanishment of my life that has not caused me heartache; indeed, to the contrary, I view it as a small blessing. Small it is, because nothing—absolutely nothing—can compensate for the many and larger losses I have suffered. Most particularly, I am haunted by images of precious documents I once held in my hands, by telling words I once heard, by gross injustices I once witnessed, but which all now exist only in my memory, soon to be gone too. I lay the blame entirely at Camelford's feet—wherever the traces of those foul bones might be.

Were these losses private only, I should not bother to put pen to paper, struggling against physical incapacity and time itself to record what I know of certain missing items, echoing voices, and forgotten actions. The public record must be served, however, for the public must know what wealth it once possessed, but does not now hold and can never repossess.

Knowledge can be a more potent force than the material goods it represents, hence I propose to replace the lost items with what I know of them. They pertain entirely to my dear and much lamented younger brother, Captain George Vancouver, who gave his life to the service of expanding the farthest geographic limits of human knowledge, and who died broken in health and spirit by those considered his superiors, Lord Camelford prominent among them. By their callous treatment, they destroyed a brilliant man, yet he died certain that his public good works would shine through the centuries, untarnished by the unsavoury politics of the day.

In the 30 years that have passed since George died, the truth of this has been borne out, and handsomely enough. The full import of his discoveries likely will not be recognized for another century, perhaps another two. Of this, I am as certain as he was and, on this count, shall die a contented man. I should not rest easily, however, were I to take certain truths—and my own uncertain speculations—about George Vancouver with me to the grave. To know well the published record of his achievements has been one of my life's great privileges, one that remains open to those who wish to study George's own accounting of his remarkable voyage; to know

2
Young George

Had Camelford peered through a window at George as he lay dying—and I feared the miserable sneak might do so—the young and handsome wretch would have seen an old and ugly opponent, one he considered by looks alone to be well worth his consuming hatred. As I sat beside my brother and held his hand while he took his last breath, I too could plainly see what an unlovely wreck he had become; but dear God, how I loved him for all the beauty I saw in his faded eyes and tattered heart.

He had grown obese in his final years, topped with popping eyes and balding pate—symptoms of an unnamed illness that had plagued him for many years. He was a month and some shy of his 41st birthday, yet he looked to be 50, 60 . . . a shipwrecked man, tossed upon the most hostile shores he had yet encountered, and he had encountered many. Dear old England, that is, had failed to provide him with the faintest future hope, and he died bereft of her decent care and deserved reward for his years of arduous, faithful service.

In his pale and dying eyes—an image that remains deeply etched upon my conscience—I shall ever see the young boy I once knew. He was a pretty child, all silky wheatstraw hair and twinkling curious eyes, a quiet little fellow with interests and a humour all his own. He was lively, yes, but in a determined way, not one to run hither and thither without purpose. Indeed, he seemed born with a purpose and was resolutely unswerving from its fulfillment.

Where I and Charles would jump and play fancifully at the sea's edge, our little brother George would instantly lose himself in contemplation of the sea's horizon, his keen eyes intently reading the waves and clouds as if they were a book containing the answers to all mysteries. Those were lighthearted days at King's Lynn, when we lived as close to Heaven as one might be. Every necessity was fulfilled, and every answer appeared within our grasp, for did not the world lie at our feet? Did not all roadsteads lead to our door?

Our Father, John Jasper Vancouver, was deputy collector of customs at the port of King's Lynn. He was well connected and well liked—to him, the two most important perquisites of his employment at the Custom House. He was portrayed in cartoons carried by the local newspaper as rotund and busy "Little Van", a caricature he quite enjoyed.

Our Mother, Bridget Berners Vancouver, was his perfect partner, a handsome, cheery little woman who had birthed six children and raised five past childhood, with George the last of the brood and much loved by all of us.

George took to school instruction with particular ease, and he soon came along to the King's Lynn Grammar School with Charles and me, ever striving to keep apace and doing quite well at it, even without our indulging his lesser size and years. To keep the bullies at bay, we three boys developed a close and active teamwork, and thus, the sibling reliance fostered within our home was tempered and annealed by our mutual support in the larger sphere. This affection continued throughout our lives, until George died in 1798 and

Charles left me alone in the world in 1815. Thirteen years it has been since I have been in the company of a kindred soul of my own generation; I am quite ready to join them, I pray soon after this task is done.

Dear Mother died when George was 11 years old. Being the youngest and the most closely attached to her, he was irreparably shocked and desolated by her passing. Father carried on as best he could, but the heart was gone from our cosy home. Our sisters Sarah and Mary could not take her place, in part because neither was fully like her, and in part because their futures lie in marrying and making their own families.

It was then that George began drifting away on us, drifting away to sea, as if in his dreams he might comb the world's oceans and find Mother's spirit somewhere on his journeyings. He was not endlessly melancholic, however, because he was yet a boy; stories of exotic adventures at sea could still percolate through his grief, giving him welcome respite from the pall that settled upon us, Father in particular.

George read avidly about the travels of our most famous sailors, and he felt most keenly the thrill of Yorkshireman James Cook's rapid rise as England's star mariner. Cook had lived and first sailed not far to the northward of King's Lynn, adding an immediacy to young George's growing appetite for tales exemplifying the seeming rule of merit in life upon the sea.

He saw in James Cook the exhilarating promotion of a low-born man, through sheer will and unfailing competency, to every opportunity and reward his genius deserved. George knew well Cook's various exploits (surveying and charting the St. Lawrence River in Canada, leading to the capture of Quebec on the Plains of Abraham; the masterful mapping of Newfoundland; the improvement of navigation through studies of the transect of Venus), and when Mother died, Cook had just begun his first voyage of discovery around the world.

Such interests and yearnings sustained George through the first and most difficult years following our loss, honing his desires to the point that only a life dedicated to the king's naval service and to the advancement of knowledge would do. What a tall order! Only a handful of ships out of hundreds in the British Navy served such noble and peaceful purposes.

Our young George dreamed not only of being with Captain Cook; in retrospect, I believe that he adored the man, sight unseen, and, from the youngest age, wanted to *become* him. He could not see then, given a bit of string pulling and a lot of damned hard work, why he could not. Such naivety! And, bless his heart, he died unsullied to the core, still not understanding why it could not be so, for he had fulfilled his part of the bargain. Thus, he died a failure, if measured by societal recognition and reward, but worthy of sharing a piece of Heaven with his beloved Captain Cook, if measured by his merits.

When Captain Cook returned from his first circumnavigation of the globe, he was championed by all, from the king to the last lowly commoner. He was showered with accolades and soon commissioned to sail again. He was promoted to post-captain and given two well-appointed vessels of his own choosing in which to continue his exploits, in the name of science and in the peaceable service of the king, for the ultimate betterment of all nations, civilized and savage.

Fortune smiled upon George in his 14th year, for Father used every shred of influence he possessed to secure a posting for his youngest son upon no less a vessel than Captain Cook's ship, H.M.S. *Resolution*. Every lad with his eye on the sea would have sold his soul to be taken on as midshipman with the great captain, and our George was numbered among the lucky few to be chosen.

He accepted his prized placement with heartfelt joy, of course, but also with a most quiet and serious intent. If he was going to follow in the old man's [sailors' familiar term for their captain] shoes, he was determined not to miss a step through pointless, juvenile merrymaking. As he was young and fresh in appearance then, one could not so readily see how very old he was by nature, but time certainly brought this forth in good measure. He had always been a thoughtful, well-behaved boy, small for his age, and delicate in every feature. When he signed aboard the *Resolution*, his fine fair hair, smooth pink cheeks, and shy eyes made him appear to be a most amiable 11- or 12-year-old.

As it was usual enough for boys from well-connected families to begin their sailing careers at that tender age, he was not an oddity on board. He could easily have been overlooked, however, for none would have guessed that within his small frame beat a heart daring to dream of greatness. Overlooked I am certain he seldom was, for he had a quiet and pleasant way of putting himself in line for any and all services he could, that he might learn the ropes by climbing each and every one of them, in fair weather and foul.

When he returned from Cook's second round-the-world voyage, in excess of four years after his departure, my little brother had grown into a solid and confident young man of 18 years. Where he had left looking younger than his age, he now looked slightly beyond it, so rigorously had he driven himself to be equal to every challenge. By nature, however, he remained as I had always known him since his earliest days: quiet; sincere; sensitive to matters of the heart; driven to the perfect fulfillment of his destiny, putting service to king and country before all else.

He returned to King's Lynn laden with gifts from exotic ports of call for every member of the family. It was with great sadness, therefore, more easily imagined than described, that I informed him his gifts for Father were of no use, for the dear man was by then two years cold in his grave. If George had ever secretly considered a settled life close to the comforts of his natal home, they were completely dashed with this news. He was shocked and made desolate anew, almost as severely as he had been when Mother died. He was an orphan now, more so in spirit than I and his sisters were, for we had made homes of our own.

I had a wife and young children by then; we lived contentedly in Father's house, and I served in his position as deputy customer. Charles had become a wanderer of a different sort than George, travelling between England, our ancestral home of Couverden in Holland, and America, always intent upon some grand scheme or other, often of the scientific or philosophic variety. Charles was more ebullient, quicker to fill the silence with talk and laughter.

Still, both brothers seemed to need distant dreams and constant motion to fill their empty hearts.

My pleasure, therefore, was in welcoming them as warmly and as best I could whenever they came home. Martha and I would use every means possible to convince them to stay a while, if not permanently, but never with any success. We gave them a home, nonetheless—a permanent home. George, in particular, ever assured me that knowing this was of immeasurable value to him throughout his lonely life.

In August of 1776, George sailed again with Captain James Cook on his third voyage round the world—a seasoned, 19-year-old midshipman who would, upon his return, qualify handsomely for his lieutenant's papers. The purpose of the expedition was to complete Cook's survey of the Pacific Ocean, by exploring its northernmost reaches in search of the Northwest or Northeast Passage. All this is too well known for me to describe at length; my purpose is to reflect upon the import of various influences that gave shape and substance to George's own career.

Cook was nearly 50 years old then, and he was growing weary and cranky from his years of continual service. He very much wanted to stay home with his wife and children, of whom three out of six had survived past childhood.

Young Mrs. Cook had lived an unenviable life, alone and impoverished, while all England lionized her husband and conspired to send him away from her. That she was truly devoted to her husband was unquestioned, and it is generally supposed that were she to live her life over, she would have chosen none other for a husband, but what a price she paid for love! She lives yet at Clapham, a sad case, indeed. Her husband is nearly 50 years dead, and she has outlived her children by decades. She has no one: no grandchildren; few friends; no reason to live, yet she proudly survives. She is, after all, Mrs. James Cook.

Mrs. Cook was in possession of many personal letters sent to her, whenever and wherever possible, from her loving and faithful husband. (Indeed, George confirmed with admiration that the good captain was absolutely faithful to his wedding vows, never having considered another woman in all his days at sea, however far he might be from home and however tempting a siren might appear.) Mrs. Cook was much hounded by his admirers to release these letters, or portions she chose, for publication. To keep some part of the great man for herself, I suppose, she burnt every single word he wrote to her. Thus, the public man survives; the private heart has been reduced to cinders, lost forever in a hellish blaze.

Similarly, nearly every vestige of my brother's private life has vanished entirely, as if he had lived all his days without a personal history, without a face or a heart. I contend that Lord Camelford and kin were behind the destruction of many documents that offered proof of my brother's human qualities, in a desperate attempt to rub a great man's name from time's honour roll. The public has no portrait, not even a sketch of George's visage, to keep his memory alive—a circumstance that well suited his enemies.

Thus it is that I fairly ache for all the good and decent things that have disappeared through willful destruction and pointed neglect over the course of time. Perhaps it is folly to think that my simple words can replace a small part of them, but I must try, for I yearn to share something of my brother as I knew him, that he might survive in the record as a whole man.

That Captain James Cook had a heart—a large and full one—is well known, even without his letters to his wife. That Captain George Vancouver had a heart—an equally large and full one—is scarcely known at all, therefore I am impelled to right this misperception and reconstruct what I know of all that has been stolen and destroyed.

Before I continue my narrative of George's younger life, I wish to make another point about Captain Cook's wife and, by comparison, George's lack thereof. Naturally, George and I had discussed the possibility of his marrying, but he was extremely averse to putting a woman he loved through such trials as Mrs. Cook suffered. I pointed out that it was her choice to marry a wanderer and, blessed with his children, to await his return.

He asked me if I would leave Martha and my children. Would Father have left Mother?

Of course not, I argued, but that was different. To George, however, it was no different—not one whit so. He would never marry. He would never tempt a woman to love him sufficiently to ruin her life for him. He did not admire James Cook in this regard, and he vowed to take his lesson from this, the great captain's most selfish and dreadful mistake.

My, my, such strong words from the young fellow who worshiped the decks upon which Captain Cook walked and the seas upon which he sailed! I teased him about being terribly pure. He answered with complete sincerity that, indeed, he tried to be, leaving me with nothing further to say.

I write, therefore, both with joy and regret, that I suspect George found a woman to love him and, perhaps, to bear his child. If my presumption is correct, then I am joyful that he shared life's sweetest fruit, and that he may yet have a son who lives half a world from here; I have the bitterest regret that this may be at the heart of what killed him. That is, he could not be with her because Lord Camelford conspired to make his return to her impossible.

I am sorry, dear reader, that I keep getting distracted and jumping ahead of myself. I must rest a bit, gather my strength, and start afresh on the morrow. I am so very tired; I shall be grateful when this final, vital chore is done, and I shall fall gently asleep forever.

3
Captain Cook's Murder

In 1777, George was so fortunate as to visit the island of Tahiti for a third time. There, once again, he proved that of all Cook's men, the natives loved him best. Of my dear brother's many admirable traits, perhaps the most remarkable was his ability to judge a person on his own merits and to respect him first and foremost for a shared and common humanity. That is to say, he showed all necessary deference to rank, but was quick to establish a rapport based upon intelligent curiosity and genuine caring.

This is not an easy thing to describe, for one might question why George could not form some sort of respectful, workable relationship with young Thomas Pitt, before Pitt became the completely insufferable Lord Camelford. But I am getting ahead of myself again, which I must try not to do. Suffice it to say that George's rapport with the native Tahitians, men and women alike, was well recognized by all aboard Cook's ships and noted more than once in the journals of his commanding officers.

Whether or not George formed an intimate friendship with a young Tahitian woman, he never disclosed. If he did, and it was quite likely, I am certain his gentle ways and his concern never to harm those weaker and poorer than himself ensured that she was nothing but enriched for knowing him.

As Cook's two ships sailed northward from Tahiti to search for the legendary Northwest Passage, they happened upon what may be viewed as Cook's greatest discovery: the Sandwich Islands [now the Hawaiian Islands], an incomparable piece of paradise perfectly situated in the midst of the vast Pacific Ocean. They stayed but a short time during that first encounter, but once again, George instantly proved his uncanny understanding of native peoples. He left many an Indian[1] there with vivid, lifelong remembrances of him—as time was later to tell.

They were soon off to the northwest coast of America, where little was known of that lengthy shore from Spanish California to Russian Alaska—and little was known about those endpoints either. They first landed on American shores at the port Cook called King George's Sound, which soon became known as Nootka Sound, the name it has retained. The natives there were a different people entirely from those of the South Seas, requiring a more formal, distant interaction, which George managed with characteristic ease.

Nootka was not a port of paradise like Tahiti or the Sandwich Islands, but it served very well for timber to replace storm-rent sticks [masts and yards] and for the collection of sea-otter pelts. These latter had little value to the Englishmen, yet they indulged the natives' new-found love of metal goods by accepting them in barter.

After a difficult summer sailing to high Arctic waters, through Bering's Strait, Cook quit his search for the Northwest Passage in those ice-filled seas. He turned his ships to the Sandwich Islands,

---

[1] A misnomer loosely applied to brown-skinned peoples found inhabiting any and all newly discovered lands.

there to refit over the winter season. Ship's Master William Bligh, now renowned of *Bounty* fame, found a safe and impressive harbour on the island called Hawaii.

The natives welcomed Captain Cook as their god Lono. He was uncommonly tall—six foot, four inches—as were the aristocratic Hawaiian people; he had white skin; he rode upon huge white-winged vessels more splendid and powerful than any they had ever seen; he was intelligent and kindly disposed, yet fierce when crossed; and he was suitably aloof. For two weeks, while the Englishmen filled their bellies and their ships' holds to overflowing, they all lived as gods, Cook above all others. They sailed away contented in every want, adored by a nation of the most generous, happy heathens on God's good earth.

A wild storm soon conspired to damage the *Resolution's* masts. They were forced to limp back to the lovely bay they had so recently quit. What gods were these, the natives wondered, that their ships were so easily broken by a common storm? Perhaps their beloved Lono was mortal after all. The priests had said so, prophesying his death, and what they said always came true.

Thieving and other mischief by the natives rapidly escalated, while the lofty and weary Captain Cook's temper grew ever shorter. On February 13th, 1779, George witnessed the armourer's tongs being stolen, hence he and a master's mate leapt into the nearest boat—the cutter—and took after the native thief. A scuffle ensued near the beach, in which George and his companion were pelted with sticks and stones. The master's mate so angered the attacking natives that one warrior approached close enough to strike him with a paddle. George, seeing this, intercepted and bore the full brunt of a crippling blow.

George eventually made it to safety, much battered and bruised from his continued attempts to save his mate, and he fortunately spent the next days resting on board ship. Had he not been so dreadfully wounded, he may well have died in the fracas that ensued the following morning, which resulted from the theft of the ship's cutter.

The story of Captain Cook's murder is so well known that there is no call for me to expand upon it here. My purpose is to record the profound and lasting effect it had upon George, such that he ran his own ship with the memory of it ever fresh in his mind and, perhaps, by compensating for what went wrong that terrible day, he paid with his life in another way entirely.

That Captain Cook was stabbed, beaten, drowned, and thoroughly dismembered by the Hawaiian natives is beyond dispute, but that he could have been saved by his own men, had they acted appropriately, is still an open question. George had firm opinions on the matter, although he did not witness the horrifying deed with his own eyes. He was, and ever remained, a respectful friend of William Bligh's, and he took to heart Mr. Bligh's scrupulous accounting of the whole pathetic affair.

Cook had enemies among his officers and young gentlemen, as even the greatest captain is certain to have. Cook trusted implicitly that when the time came for a show of absolute solidarity among his company to repel a murderous attack, none would fail to protect him. This proved to be the fatal flaw that led to Cook's demise, for at the moment when one of his lieutenants, John Williamson, should have rowed to shore to save him, the officer chose to sit, hold fire, and watch the old man be torn limb from limb. That Williamson and Cook were at constant loggerheads was well known; that Williamson made no attempt to save Cook, despite the old man waving frantically for help, was unconscionable.

The head of the marines, Molesworth Phillips, was also in a position to direct his men to fire upon the savages who descended upon the good captain, who was proving to be very mortal indeed. Phillips failed to do so, choosing rather to turn tail and run to save his own skin. His men followed suit, naturally, although four of them were caught in the fray and murdered nonetheless. By Bligh's reasoning, Phillips, too, was a good candidate for a court martial and hanging from the yardarm for treason.

Williamson and Phillips suffered no such fate, however. Williamson used his well-greased connections aboard ship not only to save his hide, but to win a promotion for himself. Phillips was not promoted, but he escaped censure entirely. Mr. Bligh was nearly beside himself over this unbelievable miscarriage of justice and, for his efforts to correct it, won himself the condemnation of his fellow officers for the remainder of the voyage and the distrust of the Admiralty for the rest of his career.

Mr. Bligh eventually rose through the ranks by the sheer brilliance and doggedness of his nature, but the campaign to smear his good name and deeds continues to this day. Now, years after he has died, he is becoming one of the great villains of history. This must not happen to George, although the campaign to blacken his name has been carried on with vigour equal to that suffered by Captain Bligh.

The point of this present notation is to record that George's heart was as broken by the savage, senseless death of his mentor as by the deaths of Mother and Father. He vowed never to trust his officers and marines as Cook had done, for one of them was certain to fail him at a vital moment.

On George's own long journey, therefore, he remained more aloof than Captain Cook had been, and therein may lie some of the seeds of his demise. Camelford, or Midshipman Thomas Pitt as he was known then, could not and did not get the better of his commander throughout the voyage, tirelessly try though he did, but chose to wage his bitterest battle against George when both were safely back in England and had nothing but a civil relationship— civil in the legal sense, that is, for Camelford was anything but civil in nature.

Camelford used his every connection and charm against George, and formidable those connections were. (His charms were another matter, there being none I could see and few that even his best friends could long tolerate, but I understand that when Camelford was in a paying mood, he had charm enough to suit his fairweather friends.) His most powerful allies were the holy trinity of his two first cousins and his brother-in-law, who were, respectively: Prime Minister of Great Britain, William Pitt; William's older brother, John Pitt, the second Earl of Chatham, who served as First Lord of the Admiralty, then as Lord Privy Seal; and brother-in-law William Grenville, who served as Minister of State, then Minister of Foreign Affairs.

These connections afforded Camelford easy access to all manner of state documents, George's submissions to the Admiralty among them. One of this madman's acts of vengeance, in my opinion—although I have no means to prove it—was to obtain and destroy the journals George kept as a midshipman during his more than eight years aboard Cook's vessels. These documents were surrendered by George at the completion of each voyage, as were all the journals of Cook's officers and young gentlemen. I believe George's records are the principal ones of consequence to have vanished. Why this happened, and who perpetrated this monstrous act against the public record, is not difficult to surmise. The loss is unforgivable and irreplaceable.

Let the record stand, therefore: the observations and growing abilities of the young man, George Vancouver, who was to become Captain Cook's greatest follower, are now nowhere to be found and, I believe, never will be. The world is denied seeing how a boy's handwritten observations, made so scrupulously and diligently, matured to produce a journal of discoveries that will ever stand among the best published.

How I wish I could visit the Admiralty's collections and there request to extract George's earliest volumes for study and admiration, but a filthy scoundrel has precluded me or anyone from doing this. A few missing bones and no burial spot seem small justice indeed.

4
Completing Cook's Voyage

I have failed to mention, because it is so well known to me, that on George's second voyage, he did not serve directly under Captain Cook on the *Resolution*; rather he was midshipman aboard the smaller tender vessel, the *Discovery*, under Captain Charles Clerke. This arrangement was perhaps not ideal, but Clerke was an old friend of Cook's, and he was a competent commander in his own right.

He proved himself competent, that is, when in good health, but he had the misfortune of growing increasingly debilitated from the outset of the voyage, due to a tragic circumstance. Charles Clerke had a brother who was an officer in service to the British East India Company, and Charles put his name to a paper backing some financial scheme or other on his brother's behalf. His dear brother failed to make the requisite payments, skipped the country in command of an East Indiaman, and left Charles liable for his debts.

While Captain Cook prepared his two ships to sail on Britain's most glorious voyage of discovery to date, his second-in-command was being held on the King's Bench awaiting trial. Clerke's name was not cleared, and he was not released to undertake his prestigious posting, until several weeks after Cook had sailed for the Cape of Good Hope. Cook left instructions for the *Discovery* to proceed as soon as possible for the appointed rendezvous at Capetown, by this tactic speeding Clerke's release. Alas, Clerke had contracted tuberculosis while awaiting clearance, and from thenceforward, he was a condemned man.

The upshot of this was that a once-capable officer lost firm grip of his company and vessel in direct proportion to the inroads the disease made upon his health. The *Discovery* became a lax and inconsistent ship, hence it was no surprise that the armourer's tongs and the ship's cutter—both of which precipitated, ultimately, Captain Cook's slaughter—were stolen from that vessel.

The lesson George took from this, when the time came for him to sail his own ships on a voyage of unprecedented length and hardship, was to keep his rule firm and fair above all else, ever consistent in his application of praise and punishment. There were many times throughout his five-year voyage when he was deathly ill, but he never succumbed, as Clerke had done, to the easy path of giving his inferior officers undue authority. All official activities aboard ship remained under his watchful eye and unwavering command.

What efforts this took on his part, I can scarcely surmise, although I witnessed his monumental application of will over spent health during the years in which I helped him prepare his journal for publication. To do so aboard ship, on turbulent seas and in inhospitable climes, stretches the imagination to the limit.

Despite Captain Clerke's questionable ability to control his own people and vessel, he took command of the expedition following Cook's murder, that being the natural devolution of duty. He led both ships once again through Bering's Strait and into ice-bound Arctic waters, meeting with no more success at penetrating either the Northwest or Northeast Passage than had Cook. They retreated to Kamchatka, where, in sight of the crude Russian settlement of St. Peter and St. Paul, Captain Clerke breathed his last.

He had held on to life months past when the disease should have taken him, for it was his fervent wish to be buried on land. Something about the sea swallowing his shrouded body, there to sink to the darkest depths of Davy Jones's locker, filled him with dread and kept him alive until the mountains of Kamchatka were sighted. In this regard, I am ever grateful that dear George is buried in the churchyard of St. Peter's Church at Petersham, held firmly by dear England's soil, even if his memory is not held so firmly in English hearts. He suffered Charles Clerke's debilities and died but one year younger in age than Clerke, yet—and not to sully Captain Clerke's well-deserved good memory—rose above his pains and tribulations in a way unmatched by any British commander, save perhaps the much vaunted Horatio Nelson.

Following Captain Clerke's death and burial on Russian soil, so far from home, John Gore was promoted from captain of the *Discovery* to captain of the *Resolution* and commander of the expedition. Gore was 50-some years old, American born, and equal enough to the task at hand, which was to sail Cook's beleaguered vessels to China and thence home to king and country. He had some difficulty maintaining discipline aboard both ships, and I do not wonder but that George took some lessons from Captain Gore's command.

At Macao, Cook's people discovered that their indifferently gathered little hoard of furs from Nootka Sound and more northerly waters fetched outrageous prices—up to $300 [Spanish dollars] apiece—from the hong merchants at Canton. Apparently, top mandarins and the emperor himself fancied them for royal robes. After many months upon hard seas, with hearts despondent for many reasons, some sailors took with a vengeance to the possibilities this commerce might open up to them. There were rumblings of mutiny, that they might return to the northwest coast of America to gather systematically the much prized pelts, but Gore managed to contain their enthusiasm by appealing to their better judgement. Excepting two seamen who jumped ship to return to Nootka on their own, never to be seen again, Gore brought Cook's company home without incident.

Gore continued in Cook's shoes when he returned to England, taking up the post of captain in Greenwich Hospital, which Cook had held before he reluctantly agreed to sail again, and which he would have resumed had he lived. This must have been a bitter pill for Mrs. Cook to swallow, for her husband, more than any man, deserved a lubber's life, with his beloved wife by his side for the rest of his natural days.

George was 23 years old then, and he earned his lieutenant's papers immediately upon returning to England. This precious document does not now exist, another missing item for which I cannot account, except to infer that it was willfully removed from George's keeping.

Lord Camelford made himself thoroughly obnoxious by frequent visits to George's home at Petersham during the last years of George's life, when he trespassed with impunity and terrorized with glee. The house was never secure enough to keep Camelford out, and, as George was obliged at times to leave it unattended while conducting his business in London, all manner of personal documents were then at risk. George removed some papers to the keeping of a friend in Berkshire, but alas he could not send them all.

What anger, frustration, and heartbreak I suffer anew, when considering George's missing lieutenant's papers. How proud he was of that accomplishment! When I look yet into George's dying eyes, so clearly drawn upon my memory, I see in them the shy pride of our young lieutenant, once Cook's boy and now a king's man, well on his way to realizing his dreams. My, how handsomely did he wear his new uniform and tricorn hat, with crisp new papers in hand. I weep for that document now, for all the goodness and decency it represents.

Gone. Gone but for my memories, which remain so immediate, so real, I cannot quite believe that they must soon vapourize too, leaving only what others might conjure from these few words.

5
Serving War and Peace

In late 1780, when George returned home, England was at war with her American colonies and had been for several years. A pall was over us, a gloom that darkened more upon receiving advance notice—from Kamchatka via the Russian court—that Captain Cook had been murdered. The *Resolution* and *Discovery* returned with little fanfare, and those upon them were soon turned about, posted on warships and sent off to kill, or be killed by, our cousins across the Atlantic.

Once again, Fortune smiled upon our George, for he was posted to convoy duty in the English Channel and the North Sea, keeping him from the distant fray. He served in this capacity for over a year, then he sailed to the West Indies, where he remained until peace was declared in 1783. He saw little direct action during those years, praise God, and he returned in fair health to England.

During the profound peace that followed the American war, he was unemployed and on half-pay for 15 months—a most trying time for a young officer of his abilities and ambitions. When he was commissioned again, he numbered among the lucky few (rather, I should say, among the plucky few) who received appointments. By early 1785, he was back again in the West Indies, where he was to serve for over four years.

During those years, George sent me infrequent and affectionate letters, which are now missing, for my possessions have not been secure either. Damn their disappearance, curse their irreplacable loss! I must not expand upon this now, however, for I have much to tell of George's early service.

George's vessel was charged with preventing contraband commerce from occurring between England's cotton-and sugar-producing possessions in the West Indies and the newly independent United States of America. This fierce, fledgling nation had fought by every means, fair and foul, for independence, spurning all aid and direction from Mother England, hence it was vital they not cheat and find succour by illegal trade with our loyal colonies.

George's principal employment was patrolling our West Indies possessions, remaining ever vigilant of the smugglers' craft. It would have been a restful tour of duty, pleasant even, if his descriptions of the islands bear any truth, but it was difficult for him for two major reasons. In the first instance, it was generally routine in the extreme. This condition improved somewhat after Commodore Sir Alan Gardner arrived to assume command of the tiny fleet and to introduce useful sailing and surveying exercises. He took an immediate liking to George and swept him under his generous wing. Indeed, through years of instruction and patronage, Gardner ushered George through the ranks and, ultimately, secured his greatest command. Aboard Gardner's small West Indian fleet, George also befriended several devoted young officers—Joseph Whidbey, Peter Puget, Joseph Baker—who later served with distinction aboard his two ships.

Second of the difficulties George suffered while serving in Caribbean waters was a climate unhealthy in the extreme. Many, many of his shipmates died of yellow fever, malaria, the flux, the ague, and every pernicious form of disease known to man. George succumbed to several plagues there, all of which he survived, but his health became permanently damaged. A mysterious residual condition, of an insidiously destructive nature, found firm root, and I was much dismayed by the inroads it had made upon George's constitution when first I saw him upon his return to England in the fall of 1789.

He had grown prematurely old. His hair was thinning; his face was drawn; he tended to a pastiness of colouring, a lassitude of manner, and an unevenness of temper that had never before been his nature. He fought hard against these difficulties and, for the most part, he succeeded in maintaining a semblance of liveliness and well-being. His weakened physical state made him prey to every passing infection, however, against which he was forced to struggle and repeatedly rise; he endured and conquered more visitations by the demons of ill-being than any other ten mortals put together.

From George's tedious and trying years of West Indies service, I can happily report that his logs and surveys of Jamaica and environs have survived to this day, in the Admiralty's keeping. In particular, George's certificate of lieutenancy aboard the vessel *Fame* remains in family hands, and the prophesy it bespeaks gives me no small pleasure. Fame was to be my dear brother's lot—fame to last untarnished through the years; fame to long outlast a childish man's attempt to erase what the Fates had written. Fame of so real and enduring a nature that, with or without my words to confirm it, George Vancouver's name shall live on for millions to know, for centuries to come.

When George first returned to England from Jamaica, he was greeted by the most pleasant prospect of joining a voyage of discovery to the northwest shores of America, where Nootka Sound was yet the only officially known and named port between California and Alaska. The Admiralty's purpose was twofold: first, the expedition was to survey and chart all that Captain Cook had bypassed on that coast on his way to search for the elusive Northwest Passage in high Arctic waters; second, the expedition was to identify appropriate harbours for the establishment of penal colonies such as the one just founded at Botany Bay in New Holland [Australia].

Two ships were engaged for this service: the *Discovery*, newly built and named for the tender vessel of Cook's final voyage; and the *Chatham*, new also and named for the second Earl of Chatham, recently appointed First Lord of the Admiralty. Through Lord Gardner's influence, George was commissioned to sail as second-in-command under Captain Henry Roberts, a fellow midshipman from Cook's last two voyages. Roberts was a handsome, exacting fellow, well known for the superior quality of his sketches and charts. In fact, it was he who rendered most of the charts published in Captain Cook's journal of the third voyage, copying and replacing all of William Bligh's masterful work.

What a political stew that was! The Admiralty was so incensed at Bligh's continuing cries for justice with regard to Captain Cook's perhaps preventable death, they refused to publish Bligh's many surveys and charts of Pacific ports, although they were vital to illustrate Cook's journal, and they were of a quality surpassing even Captain Cook's remarkable draughtsmanship. The Admiralty assigned young Henry Roberts to rechart all Bligh's surveys, giving Roberts full credit, although it was commonly known who supplied the original work. Roberts had little choice, if he wished to progress in his promising career, and Bligh was paid off with one-eighth of the profits made from the sale of Cook's journal—a handsome sum, given the immense popularity and numerous reprintings of this publication.

Bligh did not blame Roberts, nor did Roberts attempt to trump up his career on these false pretences, for Roberts was, indeed, quite brilliant in his own right. Thus, George was greatly pleased to serve as first lieutenant under Captain Roberts, and indeed, a wonderful exuberance percolated through his poor health. As for Bligh, George was gratified to learn that the Admiralty had forgiven him sufficiently to give him command of a little expedition to Tahiti to gather breadfruit plants, for the purpose of transferring them to our Caribbean colonies for the improved feeding of slaves.

If George had grown deathly ill while stationed in Jamaica, living a civilized shipboard life, then the plight of the ill-kept, ill-used slaves was grave indeed. Mr. Wilberforce's battle to end slavery in the British empire was in its infancy at that time—a battle I supported wholeheartedly, for I was deeply mortified by George's accounts of the conditions under which the West Indies' slaves lived, and I cheered when George informed me of efforts being made to improve their pitiful diet.

Mr. Bligh was equally familiar with their case, for he had been employed for years as a captain of merchant vessels sailing to and from Jamaica. When the Admiralty offered Bligh the command of the breadfruit expedition—for a glorious purpose and pitiful wages—he leapt at the chance to do a good deed and prove himself to the grudging Sea Lords.

Thus, while William Bligh sailed the *Bounty* around the world for the betterment of one faction of suffering humankind, Henry Roberts and George Vancouver prepared to sail the *Discovery* and *Chatham* around the world for the betterment of another—that is, while seeking the Northwest Passage, to identify a suitable and distant home for the prisoners of Mother England.

In the spring of 1790, when George was nearly ready to sail from the Thames, Bligh returned unexpectedly to London and set all England agog—a hard-worn man with a shocking tale to tell. His lone little *Bounty* had been seized from him by his crew, who had mutinied near Tahiti, to trade all for the love of some South Sea beauties.

What a sensation this caused! None could understand why the leader of this insurrection, dashing and well-connected Fletcher Christian, who had the makings of a fine career before him, would do such a perplexing and dastardly thing. More impressive, however, was William Bligh's survival of the ordeal; he brought 18 loyal followers, packed into a 23-foot launch, to safety by navigating over 3,600 nautical miles of uncharted seas. Such a feat was not considered possible, yet Mr. Bligh returned to England in triumph, to be championed by all who had once reviled him.

In late April of 1790, while Bligh was the toast of the town, a man named John Meares arrived in London from Macao with news of another seizure of English ships—three this time, taken by the Spanish at Nootka Sound. Meares presented a memorial to the House of Commons regarding the capture of his company's vessels, and instantly, a crisis of frightening proportions blew up in England's face, a debacle known by remote little Nootka's name. All grand and peaceful plans were put to rest while we undertook the largest naval mobilization of our history. We quickly prepared to smash the Spanish Empire entirely, if necessary, to defend our wounded honour and abrogated rights.

What had happened? I shall briefly recall the events that threatened to precipitate the first war of global dimensions, and which now have faded almost entirely from national memory. Meares, a Royal Navy lieutenant-turned-Nootka-fur-trader, claimed to have bought land at Nootka Sound in 1788 from the presiding chief for the purposes of establishing a British fur-gathering factory; indeed, he resided there that summer and built a small vessel, the first to be launched on the northwest American coast. After wintering in China, where he merged his little company with a larger one, four of his vessels returned to Nootka for the summer trading season of 1789.

The commander of the expedition, James Colnett—an upstanding king's man, who had sailed with George on Cook's second voyage—encountered a hot-headed, drunken Spanish commander in port named Estevan Martínez, who laid claim to the entire northwest coast by right of a 1493 Papal Bull, which gave Spain all lands west of Brazil, from south to north pole. He also argued Spain's possession of Nootka by right of prior discovery and settlement, although he had no proof, and he boasted of instructions to repel foreigners with force.

Over several days, Martínez arrested and released several of Colnett's commanding officers, while detaining and releasing their vessels; Colnett tried to reason with this madman but finally, in a fit of frustration, called him a "God Damned Spaniard!" Instantly, Martínez shackled Colnett and took his people as prisoners of war and three of his ships as war prizes. When all valuables had been stripped from them, he sent the lot to San Blas, Mexico.

It must be noted that Meares was a charming scoundrel, who operated under the Portuguese as well as the British flag, when it suited his interests to skirt the law. He was known by the Nootka Indians as *Aita-Aita*, or a liar twice over, and the most informed directors of the company with which he merged in China held him in equal estimation. Naturally, he presented himself in England as a patriot in the extreme, and he was accepted as such, despite his shady dealings, for his plaint well suited Parliament's grander plans.

Since the 1783 Peace of Paris, Great Britain had been itching to take Spain to task for its part in the American Revolutionary War, which diminished our kingdom immeasurably, while they continued to expand their empire by the flimsiest of initiatives. Fortunately, Spain was slowly rotting from the inside out, and her closest ally, France, was intent upon self-destruction by means of a bloody, suicidal revolution. The time had come for the British lion to roar.

King George immediately ordered a general impressment of every able-bodied man throughout the realm, which was ruthlessly undertaken in the early hours of May 4th, 1790. Roberts and company were removed from their duties preparing the *Discovery* and *Chatham* for distant explorations, and George took up a lieutenancy aboard Admiral Lord Gardner's flagship in the channel fleet. Gardner promoted George to first mate at the first opportunity, then left George in charge while he attended Admiralty business in London, as all Great Britain prepared to trounce Spain.

Such a bullish front we had never shown before, as Spain struggled to mount an armada to fight us over the seven seas. Bless her timely weakness, however, for she could not rise to the challenge, and she capitulated before most of our warships left home port. We won every satisfaction demanded, and then some. Peace was achieved in October of 1790 through the Nootka Sound Convention, which was to be ratified at Nootka Sound the following year.

The *Discovery* and *Chatham* were perfectly situated to sail quickly for Nootka, and George was perfectly situated to take command, for Henry Roberts had been seconded for a peaceful reconnaissance of the West African coast, to search for new penal colony sites there. Lord Gardner pressed for George's recruitment in Roberts's stead, and his influence carried the day. On November 17th of 1790, George received a summons from their Lordships of the Admiralty to hasten from the channel to attend them at Whitehall [home of the British Admiralty].

This all happened with wonderful speed, and on December 15th of 1790, my dear little brother was commissioned to undertake the most plum assignment offered by the Admiralty since Cook last sailed. Indeed, Fortune had put him not only into Henry Roberts's shoes, but into the long-unoccupied shoes of Captain Cook himself. He was to follow in Cook's wake, to complete the work of England's greatest navigator by surveying the northwest coast of America from Russian to Spanish holdings, plus the Sandwich Islands.

He was also to represent Great Britain at Nootka for the concluding ceremony of the Nootka Sound Convention, there to meet a Spanish counterpart and receive back the land Spain had wrongfully taken. Through this act, British rules for territorial possession would be acknowledged and respected for the first time by Spain, thus laying a firm foundation for renewed expansion of the British Empire. Half of the North American continent now lay open to British interests, and by God, we were ready to stake our indisputable claim!

In total, George's commission comprised a perfect blend of scientific and diplomatic directives, which he was uniquely qualified to undertake. What a blessing the Nootka Crisis proved to be, for all loyal subjects of this sceptred isle, and for dear George as their honoured servant.

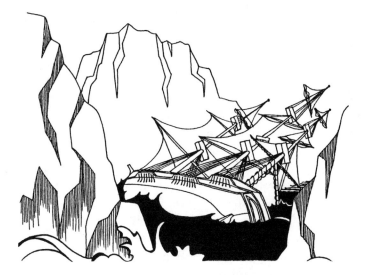

6
Welcome, the Honourable
Thomas Pitt

George was granted the usual privilege of choosing his own company, an indulgence the Admiralty deemed necessary to ensure that harmonious relations prevailed throughout a lengthy voyage on extremely crowded ships. The *Discovery* was to carry 100 hands over her 99-foot length, while the *Chatham* took on 53 hands over her 53-foot keel.

George had the pleasure of appointing, as his closest mates, a number of his West Indies' colleagues, who had recently served under him in the Channel during the Nootka Crisis. George was 33 years old at the time; all but one officer was younger, some by many years. Nonetheless, they had, in George's estimation, proven themselves equal to their commissions, and he trusted time would bear this out.

As with Cook's expeditions, the powers-that-be expressed great interest in securing placements for their young relatives, friends, and protegés, hence George was obliged to consider their influence and respect their requests. The result of this was that his authorized complement of nine midshipmen quickly swelled to 15, with the extra six being signed on as able-bodied seamen, or common hands. George could not limit these appointments by harking to his official restrictions, for the very men who had made the restrictions were asking him to waive them. The best he could manage was to assure these eager patrons that every lad would be rotated in service such that all would receive their due in requisite instruction and training time.

George had talked at length with Captain Bligh about the dangers of having too many high-born, over-indulged, lusty young men on board, for this appears to have been at the heart of what caused the mutiny of the *Bounty*. George was not pleased, therefore, with the numbers of young gentlemen he was forced to enlist, but he was determined that all would go well, by the judicious application of the lessons Captain Bligh had so bitterly learned. Constant, fair, and firm discipline would be the key; limited contact with South Sea society would preclude the formation of dangerous liaisons.

As George was ready to believe the best of his newly appointed officers and men, he welcomed the Honourable Thomas Pitt—son and heir of Thomas Pitt, first Lord Camelford and Baron of Boconnoc—with generous praise. Young Pitt came to George having survived a disastrous year of naval service under Captain Edward Riou, an esteemed shipmate of George's from days with Cook.

Riou's ship, with Pitt upon it, was sailing to Port Jackson[2] when, in the icy mists south of the Cape of Good Hope, it collided with a colossal iceberg and began to sink. In the resultant mayhem, only one overloaded boat of men got off the ship, leaving the others, in-

---

[2] Botany Bay in Australia was soon abandoned by the first settlers for the better conditions of nearby Port Jackson.

cluding Riou and Pitt, to drown in the frigid waters.

Four months later, news reached England that Lord Camelford's only son and heir had drowned on his first voyage, at which King George sent his personal and very heartfelt sympathy for the loss. Riou had not given up his ship, however; with good luck and hard work, he got her patched up well enough to hobble back to Table Bay at the Cape. One year after sailing from England, young Pitt returned safe upon home soil, begging to go to sea again. He was 15 years old and a hero in his family's eyes.

Pitt's placement on George's ship was sought by Lord Grenville, Home Secretary at the time, a favour he eagerly undertook for Lord and Lady Camelford. His motives were transparent in the extreme, for he wished to win Pitt's older sister Anne's hand in marriage. Grenville presented such a glowing portrait of the young future lord that George was most favourably impressed and, indeed, was prepared to steer him toward an enviable career.

George first met Pitt in March of 1791, just prior to sailing, and he recalled writing, in a letter to . . . whom, I can't remember . . . that, "I have found my Lord Camelford here with his family all very well. They have been waiting a few days with some anxiety for the arrival of the ship. I have as yet in course been able to see but little of my young shipmate; however, I cannot avoid observing that I was extremely pleased with his appearance and deportment."

As for appearance, Pitt was a tall and handsome fellow, fair of complexion, dark of hair, and well proportioned in every feature. One could not tell by looking at him that anything was amiss in his make up; indeed, when faced with such natural attractiveness, one's first inclination was to think well of him.

George was a good judge of character, although perhaps too much given to thinking the best of a person until shown otherwise—which accounts for his remarkable rapport with native peoples. Of England's native sons, he should have been more wary; we have centuries of high-bred corruption, championed through writings of its every form, upon which to perfect in our children every deceit of the wealthy and powerful.

Naively, George was worried only about the safe and proper care of his young charges when in distant and foreign ports, giving little thought to the increasingly rotten state of political intrigue from which they had sprung and had every expectation of perpetuating. I must not tar all George's midshipmen with the same brush, however, for there were good lads in the lot as well.

One such young gentleman was Robert Barrie[3], who was to become Pitt's bosom friend, yet also managed to serve George well and to retain his support and admiration. George's judgement may have been coloured by Barrie's relationship to Admiral Lord Gardner as "Uncle Alan"; nonetheless, George was not mistaken in his assessment of Barrie's good temperament and many talents. I recall George once saying to me that Barrie quite obviously had no use for Camelford when the two midshipmen first met one another, and Barrie even said that he had written to his mother something like, "I don't like his character, therefore sha'n't court his acquaintance."

To my mind, Barrie did Pitt two favours in this lifetime: the first was to instantly detect Pitt's defective nature, though the snake's charm unfortunately won him over; the second, for which I remain grateful, is that if Barrie had come to Pitt's call the day of the duel that finished our mad Lord Camelford, Barrie likely would have stopped the idiotic event and Camelford might yet be alive. Bless Barrie for being elsewhere than was supposed on that day; he finally and unwittingly removed himself from the acquaintanceship of a person he had judged correctly in the first instance.

The captain of the newly built *Chatham*, William Broughton, was cast upon George. He did not excite George's interest from first meeting, but George was willing to believe, by the man's glowing commendations, that he was equal to the task. Of greater interest to George was the appointment of his good friend from days with Cook, Richard Hergest, as agent [commander of a storeship] of a third vessel, a supply vessel called the *Daedalus*. He was to rendezvous with George either at the Sandwich Islands or Nootka Sound,

---

[3] For whom Barrie, Ontario, is named, in honour of his years of service in that area during and following the War of 1812.

to deliver extra provisions and additional instructions relevant to the final settlement of the Nootka affair. If only Hergest and Broughton could have exchanged positions, for Hergest would have brought greater experience, knowledge, and high-minded purpose to the expedition.

As it was, there were few men aboard either ship over the age of 30, and only one was married, as far as George knew. An old friend from the West Indies, Master Joseph Whidbey (with whom George had won high praise for their survey and chart of Jamaica's Port Royal) was older than George by two years, and was, I believe, George's oldest officer. In retrospect, one can clearly see that the overall youth of George's company made for a less than ideal situation, for a good measure of experience and wisdom are vital for tempering young men's passions.

The 1780's and '90's were the decades of young men, following William Pitt the Younger's rise to Prime Minister at the tender age of 24. He appointed many of his young relatives and friends to positions of high power, hence Parliament and Whitehall were dominated by callow youths, who presumed, whenever they saw fit, to override the judgement of more seasoned statesmen.

It is no surprise, therefore, that the crowd of young men George took on had very presumptuous notions of their self-importance and God-given rights. To their credit, young men bring an enthusiasm and freshness of view to their positions, and Great Britain certainly grew in strength and audacity during those years. Some credit must be given to King George III for leavening the green broth, for he had by then reigned for so long and so even-handedly that he brought some hard-won wisdom to bear upon his upstart and pushy young ministers of state. Imagine what dreadful mistakes might have been made had the king's frivolous and spendthrift heir, then Prince of Wales and now the little lamented King George IV, gotten his hands on the reins of power during those decades of young men playing at leading political roles.

To be fair, therefore, one cannot place all blame upon Camelford's shoulders for the state of the society in which he had been raised and the improbable expectations upon which he had long been fed. There was great unrest among all sailors in those days, partly the result of young men feeling their oats and rebelling against tradition and authority, and partly from just causes. There were despotic sea captains aplenty, only too willing to misuse and abuse their people to achieve their ends, caring not one whit who lived and died at their hands. George, conversely, was devoted to keeping all his people well used and in fine health, that he might return to England with the fewest lost to disease, carelessness, desertion, and the like of any ship that ever sailed. They could not have found a commander more dedicated to their common good; certain young men could not have done more, short of mutiny, to undermine his every effort.

As for mutiny, it was becoming increasingly common, at home and round the world. Captain Bligh's first mutiny (for he suffered mutiny several times over before his life was out), on the *Bounty*, was the most extreme, dramatic, and romantic of them all, yet it was but one of dozens during that decade and became, by the end of the century, but one of hundreds—indeed but one of many thousands, if the tally of all nations were taken.

Times had changed since Captain Cook had sailed. George had been away from home for so many of the intervening years, he poorly understood this. He might consider himself sailing in Cook's shoes, but certain of his midshipmen lacked the respect that George's generation had been raised to show, with never a question asked, never a finger lifted in defiance.

One might counter with the argument that Cook was murdered nonetheless, the result of too few lifting a finger in his defense. Indeed, in retrospect, one can see that Cook's fall marks the beginning of discipline's decline in all naval service. At the time, his shocking end appeared to be an isolated incident, one that demanded quick cover-up before it invited lengthy investigation and became general knowledge. To George's great credit, he held fast his command and vessels at a time when open rebellion was becoming commonplace. He suffered endlessly petty and dangerous opposition from the most brazen of his crew, with Pitt taking the lead, yet made a grand success of a voyage that could have fallen to ruin at every turn.

George was singularly unsuspecting of what trials lay before him when he escorted the Honourable Thomas Pitt to his midship berth. He had many, many things to tend to during the long, busy days in which he prepared the *Discovery* and *Chatham* to sail. One 15-year-old boy was the least of his worries.

Welcome aboard, therefore, the Honourable Thomas Pitt, future Lord Camelford and Baron of Boconnoc. For the record, George's conscience and heart were clear and well-disposed from first meeting; how could he know what a rankled, venomous spirit had received his generous embrace?

7
Sir Joseph's Grand Plans

During the hurried and exhausting weeks prior to sailing, George's greatest difficulty was with a third and unofficial mandate added to the expedition's purpose, one he did not welcome. The king, dear 'Farmer George', had long been interested in botany, a royal passion he shared with Sir Joseph Banks, President of the Royal Society, and advanced by the establishment of the Royal Botanic Gardens at Kew.

Young Mr. Banks had sailed with Captain Cook on his first global circumnavigation, making a thorough nuisance of himself due to his fanatical botanizing. He drove the company to distraction with his endless demands, including his preposterous insistence upon planting greenery here, there, and everywhere aboard ship. Cook restrained his famous temper, and Banks rewarded him for it by signing up for the second circumnavigation, with the *Resolution* to serve as his private floating conservatory.

As a 13-year-old midshipman, young George had witnessed Banks's grandiose and foolish constructs rise high over the decks, and he witnessed Banks's childish temper tantrums when the good captain had them torn down.

Banks was not yet Sir Joseph in those days, and he was new to the king's favour. His ranting and fuming, therefore, failed to override Cook's orders, and the Admiralty ignominiously struck him from the ship's roll. George was highly impressed, and totally in Cook's favour.

Now, nearly two decades later, Sir Joseph Banks had determined that some serious botanizing was in order aboard George's ships, and Banks had grown too fat and influential to be thrown over by a man whom Banks had known as a young snotty—the common derogation for midshipmen that Banks did not hesitate to use. Banks was not going to let one of Cook's haughty boys get the better of him this time, so be damned! Plant frames were brought on board and set up on deck according to Sir Joseph's instructions. Botanist and surgeon Archibald Menzies was given a cabin, and George was instructed to mind his every want, both professional and personal.

To the credit of Mr. Menzies, a serious, soft-spoken Scotsman, he wished to serve as ship's surgeon as well, that he might number among those enlisted, not among the supernumeraries. He was certified and had served several years as a Royal Navy surgeon; by this record, George should have welcomed him in that capacity. George had a stubborn streak when it came to matters of principle, however, and he would not bend on this matter. George had chosen his own surgeon, and that was that. Banks was not going to slip his man aboard in any official capacity, or Heaven forbid, the Lords at the Admiralty might add botanizing to their official instructions, and George would have three conflicting purposes to fulfill instead of two.

Conflicting purposes? George's hastily and belatedly draughted instructions required that, first, he acquire a more complete knowledge of the northwest coast of America and second, he receive from Spain the properties at Nootka Sound that rightfully belonged to British subjects. From the start, it was obvious to George that charting the coastline and waiting at Nootka Sound for a Spanish envoy were incompatible activities, especially since he had no instructions regarding the repossession ceremony itself, precisely what was to be returned, when the Spaniards would arrive, what to do if their understanding differed from his, and so forth. If he had to alter his schedule further, to allow Menzies to pick flowers at his every whim, God alone knew how the expedition would accomplish its ends.

The *Discovery* and *Chatham* did not, by George's adamant insistence, become floating conservatories. For this, he made an enemy of Sir Joseph, which was to have serious consequences when high society got its dander up about Camelford's accusations of ill treatment under George's command. Banks was ready to think the worst of George when he sailed; he was quick to spread malicious rumours when letters of the slightest complaint from the *Discovery* and *Chatham* arrived home from distant ports; he used every influence he could to humble George when he returned to England. Banks pulled many a string behind the scenes throughout his long career, most with an eye to increasing knowledge and bettering the human condition, but he disgraced himself over his petty and petulant secret campaign against George.

Had Banks chosen a botanist matching his own temperament, the voyage could well have been ruined from the outset. As it was, Menzies was an agreeable fellow, possessing such quiet good humour, intelligence, and patience that George was hard-pressed, from the first meeting, to dislike him. As George was ever one to judge the quality of a person separate from his position and associates—George's most redeeming characteristic *and* his undoing—he and Menzies were destined for a lively and fruitful relationship.

I saw the old surgeon recently, for he yet practises medicine in London, and he said to me something like, "What days those were!

A fine group of officers—a credit to the captain. He chose them all, except me. And those books that he wrote—strange that he could put so much of himself into the printed page. He was a great captain."

What words those were to me! If only all who read this might hold George Vancouver's memory as dear, such esteem would compensate for the privations he willingly bore to serve all humanity, and for the poverty he subsequently suffered to serve Camelford's petty ends. His final poverty of circumstance and spirit, that is to say, was—as all poverty is—a foul production of man's will. . . but I must not digress into the arguments I put forth in my lengthy publication of 1796 entitled *An enquiry into the causes and production of poverty and the state of the poor*. Suffice it to say that I shall rail against the injustice of poverty, which George encountered in its most pernicious form, until my tale is told and my life is done.

I have spent myself this day and soon must sleep. I shall begin the morrow by sailing with George on the first day of his great voyage, launching forth from the first entry of his journal, every page of which I helped prepare for publication. I shall be on firm ground— or on a worthy ship, more aptly—from henceforward, so intimately did we share every detail of those five years at sea.

He reminisced as we worked together, telling me details that his ever proper and private nature decreed go unmentioned or un-elaborated in his published accounting. It is these details I shall try to recall, as we progress through his journal, in order that something of what is missing from between the lines might be revived. Not that his journal is flawed or incomplete! No, it is a classical re-counting of all that matters to the explorer's eye, with little given to matters of the heart—as it should be. My wish is to reveal those aspects that discipline and modesty forbade George to mention, yet must be told if one is to understand the pattern and import of his life and death.

I shall try to remove myself from the telling, that the reader might sail as intimately with George as his writings and recollections will allow. Pitt, too, shall fade from the narrative as the business of the voyage rightfully takes precedence. The continual nuisance he created won little mention from George, who wasted little breath and ink on the incorrigible scoundrel. Come with me then, dear reader, on an incomparable

**VOYAGE OF DISCOVERY
TO THE
NORTH PACIFIC OCEAN
AND
ROUND THE WORLD**

in which the coast of North-West America has been carefully examined and accurately surveyed.
Undertaken by **HIS MAJESTY**'s Command
principally with a view to ascertain the existence of any navigable communication between the
North Pacific and North Atlantic Oceans;
and performed in the years
1790, 1791, 1792, 1793, 1794, and 1795
in the
DISCOVERY sloop of war, and armed tender CHATHAM
under the command of
CAPTAIN GEORGE VANCOUVER[4]

[4] This is the title page of Vancouver's published journal, first and second editions.

8
All Fool's Day

At dawn on April 1st of 1791, the *Discovery* and *Chatham* slipped their moorings from fair England's shore and sailed for strange and savage lands, with the *Daedalus* to follow in several months. That it was All Fool's Day did not escape notice, but this was cause more for concern than clownery. Prime Minister Pitt had recently called for the Royal Navy to intervene in the Turko-Prussian War, hence those aboard George's ships felt great apprehension about leaving England at her time of need. They were destined, in George's words, "to a long and remote exile, and precluded, for an indefinite period of time, from all chance of becoming acquainted with its result".

As George was not one to read omens into superficial alignments, leaving on All Fool's Day little troubled him. Leaving a fleet mobilization behind did, however, in part for national concern and in part because it echoed a fateful circumstance from years past. In August of 1776, when he sailed with Captain Clerke aboard Cook's vessel *Discovery*, he also left behind preparations for war, that time against our American colonies. For George, who keenly felt he was following Cook's footsteps, this uncanny resemblance to days long past appeared as an augury—good or bad, he dared not guess.

Naturally, memories of Cook's demise at the Sandwich Islands sprang to mind, and George redoubled his determination not to suffer any variation of the same fate. The key was to keep good control of his people, his young officers and midshipmen most particularly. There was treachery in paradise; even the gentlest women there had deadly charms, as Bligh had recently learned. If signs and portents had any meaning, they must be used to guide him safely home through a labyrinth of dangers.

By the end of April, both vessels lay anchored in the roadstead of Santa Cruz, Tenerife, there to take on wine, other refreshments, and much needed ballast for the *Chatham*, which had proved to be a very crank little vessel. A near fatal fracas took place ashore there, which George declined to mention in his published journal, for he saw it as a matter relevant to his personal command, not his public commission. It is worthy of recounting here, however, for the first inkling of trouble from Pitt occurred on the wharf at Santa Cruz, where the fray occurred.

It was Sunday, and George, along with several senior officers, was dining with an Irish resident of Santa Cruz, who offered them welcome respite from the sun's heat and what refreshments he could at an impoverished port. They wore cool, light clothing, having no need of their heavy uniforms for a private engagement.

While so occupied, George heard a distant commotion coming from the direction of the water. Instantly, he and his officers ran down to the wharf, there to find Thomas Pitt and several drunken seamen fighting a mob of Spanish guards, each faction intent upon killing the other. When George dashed in to break it up, the Spaniards paid him no heed—he cursed that he was not in uniform, for they failed to recognize his rank!—and threw him unceremoniously off the wharf into the water. One of the ship's boats fetched him, then picked up Pitt and several others who had jumped into the sea to save their hides.

What had happened? As near as George came to understand, Pitt was among a small party sent ashore to round up some men for their watch, but as they had spent their liberty on excessive quantities of cheap wine, they were in poor condition and of no mind to return to the ship. A quarrel ensued, and a Spanish guard stepped forward to keep the peace. A seaman tore the musket from the guard's hands, who then bawled for reinforcements. These men arrived promptly, and the confrontation reached fever pitch.

Many Englishmen were cut and bruised, even those who had interceded to restore order and made no attempt to harm the Spaniards as they did so. Several very narrowly escaped death by violent blows and bayonet strikes. George could not blame the Spaniards, however, for they did not originate the quarrel, and they had some reason to react as they did. That they *overreacted*, George found reprehensible, and he complained of this to the governor, who assured George that he would undertake appropriate disciplinary action.

What of Thomas Pitt in all this? At the time, George could see no way in which he was culpable, and indeed, even commended his efforts to contain and direct his drunken charges. Had George known the young man's character better, he might have guessed that Pitt was the root cause of the near disaster, but he was inclined to believe Pitt's accounting of the affair, discounting entirely the accused men's attempt to shift blame.

Pitt no doubt drew satisfaction from confirming the guilt of the two most contrary sailors, who were flogged forthwith, several dozen lashes each. His greater pleasure perhaps derived from hoodwinking George, inflating his desire to do so again at the first opportunity. George came to learn that Pitt had, since the earliest age, enjoyed creating a continual uproar, while exonerating himself. George had before him in Tenerife a perfect example of Pitt's devious and dangerous manner of conducting himself, and he failed to see it, so disposed was he to thinking well of the young man and giving him every benefit of the doubt. Damned fool, George could see in retrospect—the dupe of a damned fool young man!

Upon leaving Tenerife, one week into May, George was taken so ill that he believed himself to be within days of expiring. Cranstoun, the surgeon, offered no medications or advice of value, while credit goes to Mr. Menzies for successful intervention, possibly saving George's life. Menzies prescribed a nutritive diet[5] that had quite sudden and salubrious effects, but for this willing and competent service, he made no attempt to gain any advantage with George. Menzies was a patient man, certain that his expertise would be justly recognized and rewarded in good time.

Many officers and young gentlemen were far from so patient and so capable; they wore their ambition on their sleeves at all time, hence were quick to imagine what benefits would befall them should George die. William Broughton would become captain of the *Discovery* and commander of the expedition. George's first lieutenant, 20-year-old Zachary Mudge (a colleague from West Indies days and, worth noting, Pitt's family friend and protector), would become captain of the *Chatham*. All other officers would move up one notch accordingly—a pleasant prospect for all but George's most loyal officers. He was not to oblige them, however, not so early on in the voyage, and not much later, when he again took deathly ill. They would have to earn their promotions from him, not step over his dead body to take them.

It was slow going from Tenerife to the Cape of Good Hope, for the *Chatham* was still sailing poorly, even when ballasted with 23 tons of Santa Cruz beach stones. They crossed the equator on May 27th, whereupon all the usual ceremonies were performed on those

---

[5] The usual shipboard diet was salt beef, salt pork, hardtack (flour and water biscuits), peas, wheat, oatmeal, butter and cheese, sugar, olive oil, vinegar, suet, raisins, portable soup (bouillon), beer, wine, grog (spirits and water), and plenty of Captain Cook's cure-all, sauerkraut.

Cook believed that the captain must eat what his people do, to keep them faithful to his nutritive regime; Vancouver doubtless believed the same. His special diet likely consisted of salad greens grown on board ship, rob (extract) of lemon and orange, marmalade of carrots, sweet wort (thickened malt solution), mustard, and fresh bread. He likely also foreswore his everyday food, most particularly sauerkraut, which may have had the best remedial effect on his mysterious, undiagnosed condition. See the Epilogue for a possible modern diagnosis.

taking their first leave of the northern hemisphere. George was indulgent of this merrymaking, for it is a tradition that binds all sailors together, officers and seamen alike, a milepost in the making of a sailor, as he quickly changes from a soft shore lad to a hardened ship's mate.

Midshipmen who did not fancy having Neptune and his gang shave their heads, duck them, pierce an ear, and other such activities were allowed to trade their share of grog for peace from the gods-for-a-day. Aboard the *Chatham*, one of the gods got so very merry, he decided to return to his home in the sea and, with that, jumped overboard. As the *Chatham* was, for once, making good speed, this confounded fool was in every danger of drowning. The ship was instantly hove up into the wind, and the man, by chance, caught hold of a rope that was being towed under the chains [ledge-like structures high on the hull to which the shrouds, or mast-supporting ropes, are attached] and thus saved himself.

Sailors can be such Silly Billies[6], they would kill themselves and their dearest mates for the sake of a little fun. Like a stern parent, George was forbidden to appear amused by their antics, for so much as a smile upon his face would be taken as approval, and bedlam would have resulted, with deadly consequences. On crossing the bar, he had reason to be pleased with his company—despite the recent debacle on the wharf at Santa Cruz—so harmonious did relations appear to be between officers and men alike, for therein lies the greatest rub aboard ship. Pleased, that is, until the *Chatham* was forced to haul up, to save a drunken fool, and lose some hard-won distance, especially since his ships were taking longer than anticipated to make the Cape.

Nonetheless, it was a day full of good humour, especially when his young gentlemen—those who would not forego their allowance of grog to anyone, for any inducement—learned all manner of Nep-

---

[6] Prince William's nickname; he was King George III's fourth child and third son, who took to sailing as a career, but who was more intent upon drinking and womanizing than discipline and deserved advancement. As King William III (1830-37), he became known as the Sailor King. He was succeeded by his niece Victoria.

tune's tricks. There were happy days upon George's vessels, and plenty of them. A pity, it is, that one idiotic sailor could mar a rare day's merriment; that another idiotic fellow—Pitt, that is—could bring near-ruin to the entire adventure and tarnish the whole of it, even to this day, by puerile, vindictive behaviour.

During that early portion of the voyage, Pitt was still a wolf in sheep's clothing, and George was so deceived, he promoted him from midshipman to master's mate on June 1st. Rotation of duties was necessary among George's surplus middies, but promotions within those limited roles were judiciously given. Thus, Pitt became assistant to George's good friend and constant ally, Joseph Whidbey, an even-tempered, well-seasoned hand who could teach Pitt a great deal, were Pitt inclined to learn. George was then under the mistaken impression that, indeed, Pitt intended to advance by dint of mindful duty and hard work, not luck and the liberal application of influence.

Pitt continued to sleep and mess midships, hence he was still a midshipman in that regard—a young gentleman, that is, of similar status to the rest of the midships' rabble. His unofficial status, however, was that of spokesman for the young gentlemen, which was a factor of some import to George when he promoted Pitt. As proof of George's generosity, one can readily see that George did not hesitate to proffer a reward, *a priori,* for the future good services he expected to be rendered. Such repayment George received!

As master's mate, Pitt relinquished his charge of the timekeepers, a midshipman's duty. George put one Edward Roberts to this task, a likeable, 18-year-old fellow who came to George highly recommended by the old master astronomer himself, William Wales of Christ's Hospital. Wales had been George's first and most illustrious teacher aboard Cook's *Resolution,* from 1772 to '76, and even at his advanced age, he remained a most excellent instructor and good judge of character.

Regrettably, because of the overcrowded midships, George had had to sign on Roberts as an able-bodied seaman and berth this fine lad in the rough and tumble foc's'le, where he was obviously unsuited and unwelcome. He made the best of it, however, as did the other young gentlemen forced to suffer the same inconvenience. Until an opportunity arose for George to advance Roberts, the young man was little more than a servant boy to Third Lieutenant Baker, a misapplication George was eager to remedy.

With some satisfaction, therefore, George announced from the quarterdeck the latest rotation of midshipmen's duties, including Pitt's and Roberts's promotions, and he requested that his young gentlemen welcome their new messmate to the cockpit, as they call their quarters. Pitt took his promotion, naturally, with great pride, then—to George's astonishment—declared, as the midshipmen's spokesman, that there was no room for Roberts, therefore he was unwelcome in their mess.

The foc's'le men chimed in their refusal to have Roberts bunk with them, now that he was properly a midshipman and completely unsuited to their rude quarters. Poor Edward Roberts, so openly disgraced by the dishonourable protests of both messes! George was furious. In cold anger, he immediately ordered the carpenter to tear down the wall separating the foc's'le and midship berths, so that all would mess with one another, if neither would have Roberts.

The carpenter, Henry Phillips, was fool enough to voice his opposition to this task, and, to worsen matters, he made a poor job of it, earning himself a well-deserved flogging of several dozen lashes. George was wildly incensed with Pitt's impertinence, and he would have stripped him instantly of his promotion if it did not mean that Roberts would then lose his. George thus became acquainted with one of Pitt's many sly ploys: using his mates to secure his ends, by ensuring that another might suffer if he did. Pitt endured a severe lashing by George's tongue, but nothing more in this case, since Pitt had spoken for all those in midships, and George deemed that the combined messes provided punishment enough.

Pitt took promotion and punishment as readily as a duck takes water to its back, which is to say, his character appeared to be impervious to George's commendation or condemnation. Inwardly, however, embers of hatred were beginning to glow, stoked by the supposed injustices delivered by an irrational and despotic commander. As for George, he was beginning to see that the carrot he had dangled before Pitt from a stick engendered nothing but defiance and disrespect, hence George resolved, in the future, to firmly apply the stick itself, that he might win a grudging compliance and respect. Only when this was achieved would George soften enough to proffer reward when reward was due.

On the morning of July 9th, the Cape was sighted, and the next day, the ships came to anchor off Capetown, where they soon found their every need to be answered and for fair exchange. There, George encountered several Royal Navy ships and British East Indiamen, from which he found shipmates of old, hale fellows well met. All indicators at that port pointed to quick lading and complete restoration of rosy good health, to a man, by the invigorating effects of liberal shore leave and fresh provisions.

George was not to be in confident good spirits for long, however, for a large Dutch ship from the fetid port of Batavia [Jakarta, Java] arrived within days of his mooring, and it was a floating, stinking factory of death by dysentery. George's officers and men quickly fell to this plague, himself among them. His good humour was replaced with fear for his people's lives and great anxiety for the winds and tides to turn in their favour, that they might sail from there with all possible speed.

The barrier between foc's'le and midships was instantly rebuilt, to contain the contagion, but to little avail. Indeed, one of the hardest struck with the flux was Cranstoun, the surgeon, who also suffered a paralytic stroke that so affected his reason, he could not even tend himself. George was forced to humble himself and request the assistance of Mr. Menzies, who readily agreed.

Menzies could have insisted that this service go to the surgeon's mates, yet he responded in a swift and reassuring manner. George was grateful that Sir Joseph Banks had chosen this fine and capable gentleman for his botanical servant. Indeed, credit goes to Menzies for giving such solicitous good care to all hands that only one was lost to illness throughout the entire voyage.

Menzies was instantly amenable to following Captain Cook's tried and true prescriptions for the maintenance of good health, including drying and fumigating the ship by means of frequent fires between all decks, weekly baths for all hands, and the general application of vinegar to disinfect every noisome quarter. He took exception to the fires in sick bay, insisting that the smoke worsened his patients' condition, and George, being ever one to recognize and respect a reasoned argument, capitulated to Menzies's request to cease lighting them there.

George should never once have found quarrel with Menzies throughout the voyage, if he was not something of a fanatic about his botanizing—and worse, convinced that in such capacity he was answerable first to Sir Joseph and second to his commander. Preposterous! Captain Cook took fewer and fewer scientists upon each subsequent voyage, so presumptuous and disruptive did these self-appointed free agents become. They set a bad example for the rest of the company, and George was determined to have none of it. He succeeded for the most part with Menzies, and, despite some professional differences of opinion, George ever held him in highest personal esteem.

Menzies aside, and on the general topic of the people's health and good humour, George did not go to the extremes that Captain Bligh did to keep them up and working cheerily. Not only did Bligh apply Captain Cook's every prescription for good health, but he took a blind fiddler on the *Bounty*, that his people might dance each day, weather permitting. And dance they did, until they had such sport of it, they wanted it no more!

If one can imagine the gay sound of dancing on the decks to a fiddler's tunes, one might little understand how they came to hate such levity, simply because it was enforced. None complained when required to drink their daily ration of grog, and dancing to jolly music surely uplifted their spirits to an equal degree.

Seamen, however, are the most confounded lot of men upon God's earth, for when it is decreed that they partake of a little culture and that they sweat a bit to have their fun, they will do all they can to counter these measures, on principle alone. Most dedicate their lives to disavowing all refinement and sweating the least they can, at least on lawful and required duties, although they will work like slaves to swindle and cheat their masters for no more gain than a lick of rum—and a taste of the cat for all their efforts. Dancing, indeed! That is cause enough for mutiny in most sailors' minds.

When the *Discovery* and *Chatham* left Capetown, few aboard either vessel had strength to dance at all, as more than half succumbed to the flux. Those who might have danced were prevented from doing so by such fearsome storms, there were few hands up to steer the ship and man the yards. The *Chatham* fared better than the *Discovery* on the count of healthy men, having fewer infected, but her pitching and tossing in tempestuous seas nearly did her in several times over.

After weeks upon angry seas, George officiated over the gloomy business of burying a marine, who had, from the first, been the most violently ill of his people. George was much affected by this death, suffering from unspeakable fears as he took his people ever farther from civilized society toward unknown, savage lands. He was not alone in his melancholy; following the funeral, several hands who had appeared to be recovering relapsed to a state near death. George was made of sterner stuff, struggling against all odds to keep private difficulties from affecting his public duties, a façade he successfully maintained throughout the voyage.

The ships became so thoroughly sodden from mountain-high seas and torrential rainfall, the mind could more easily imagine sinking forever into that cold, wet hell than walking again on firm ground under clear, warm skies. For all George's years at sea, he never became immune to such morbid concerns; like all sailors, he felt his mortality as keenly through the last storm he suffered as he did through the first. Unless one has experienced the terrifying and torturous tedium of storms and the sickness they induce and compound, one cannot imagine how fine and fair life might be again, when safe upon a green shore.

9
Safe at the Southern Edge

Safe the southern coast of New Holland was when, late in August of 1792, George discovered a good harbour (which he named King George Sound) and uninhabited shores. The weather was most hospitable, and wild foodstuffs improved their diet considerably. The few native people who lived there had abandoned their wretched homes and few belongings, for reasons unknown.

George was relieved to be thus freed from the tiring and potentially dangerous business of interaction with the Indians. The emptiness of several villages and surrounding land was disconcerting, nonetheless. George was well versed in stories of frightened Indians hiding in the hills and woods, then attacking full force, hacking their hapless visitors to pieces. Captain Bligh lost one of his loyal supporters in this manner when he and his mutinied men landed their launch upon a South Sea isle. George had heard tales of a seemingly abandoned stretch of beach between Nootka and California suddenly coming alive with the horrifying whoops of several hundred savage warriors, who succeeded in tearing apart every stranger on shore.

And, of course, George knew intimately what price Captain Cook had paid for his trust in native peoples—as well as in his own people. Cook had been in many, many dangerous situations during his ventures onto strange shores; perhaps it was just a matter of time before the worst befell him.

Because of George's great caution on shore, he was regarded by certain of his company as being foolishly nervous of so much as a single Indian jumping out and saying "Boo!" That he might fear in any way the wretched souls who called this bleak land home was cause for merriment; indeed, it was cause for a little sport at a deserted village, which George toured with a small, armed party.

This crude encampment bespoke well the unenviable state of those residing there, wanting for most everything considered essential for the rudest of existence. Not only were they sadly lacking in tools and utensils, but their only weapons appeared to be crude spears with charred and blunted ends, which could not have been very effective either for hunting or for defense.

The tip of one spear had evidence of blood upon it, and fresh blood at that. In the eerie stillness of the abandoned encampment, George instantly ordered everyone to cock his piece, to be ready should any hostile Indians appear. This caused such stifled sniggers, George angrily demanded and eventually received an explanation: the blood was from a midshipman's cut finger, which he had wiped on the spear for the purpose of alarming George.

George did not gladly suffer their ridicule, and he made them well aware that, when recounting the incident in private quarters, their loud laughter would be the sound of jackasses braying. If his young gentlemen had such little respect for George and for his extensive experience visiting Indian nations, then clearly they would have no respect whatsoever for the native peoples themselves. George redoubled his resolve to keep his company and all native peoples at as respectful a distance from one another as possible, to prevent the disasters that inevitably befall those who lack the most fundamental of human virtues—respect for one another and for all creatures who share God's earth.

The young gentlemen's little practical joke thus resulted in short-lived hilarity and in long-term landing restrictions. Even after the shameful debacle on the wharf at Santa Cruz, George had given them generous shore leave, and for it, had won their derision through a juvenile prank. Naturally, Pitt perfectly enjoyed this attempt to humiliate George and, when upbraided for his ridiculous pleasure, smirked contemptuously. Indeed, since Pitt had escaped punishment for protesting Roberts's move to midships, he had grown ever more bold in his defiance of authority in numerous ways, most of them petty and all of them reprehensible.

Pitt's transgressions ranged from questionable private dealings to falling asleep on his watch, from impetuous actions to impertinent comments. George had not caught Pitt straight out and on his own yet, but he would in time, if Pitt did not mend his ways. His good luck and popularity could not protect him without fail.

In Captain Bligh's estimation, Fletcher Christian was an equally handsome and popular man aboard the *Bounty*, one who had employed a similar animal magnetism to serve his every whim, with disastrous consequences. Pitt was younger by half a dozen years than Christian, but his greater social status and wealth balanced this shortfall. George would have no Fletcher Christian on board his ship, in any guise.

That is, the problem with Christian and Pitt was one of roles, as well as of particular individuals. If the worst character is removed from a company of a hundred men, as likely as not another will turn renegade and fill the void. The part of 'leader of the opposition' among the junior ranks was open for the taking, and Pitt simply fell into it with devilish ease. George was determined to nip the problem in the bud by making an example of Pitt following his next serious offense. George was watching and waiting; he would use the first justifiable opportunity to flog the self-crowned princeling.

Such forethought was made in passing, for George was fully concerned with the well-being of his company and the progress of his commission. Despite the good effects of landing on the southern exposure of New Holland, close to half George's people remained somewhat debilitated by the dysentery. He felt it imperative to find a better shore for attending to their restorative needs, hence chose to make for Dusky Bay, New Zealand, a pleasant and commodious harbour where he had spent many weeks total in 1773 and 1777 with Captain Cook.

Time was also a consideration, for they had lost several weeks by slow sailing on Atlantic waters. George abandoned his plans for exploring the Tasmanian coast, where he wished to prove or disprove the speculation that Tasmania was an island. This was of little interest to his people, for they were intent upon realizing their own speculation, which was that they would make next for the new colony at Botany Bay. When it became obvious that they were not heading in this direction, some grew quite petulant over this supposed change of plans—although George had disclosed nothing of their route, landings, or indeed, any of his private instructions or discretionary orders for the voyage, even to Captain Broughton.

This was standard procedure, of course, but some of his cockiest young men felt privy to such information and rather righteous in their demands to hold sway. Of course, George paid them no mind, except to insist that they work cheerily, their dashed hopes be damned. There was surveying and charting work to be done at Dusky Bay, filling in parts of Cook's charts that the old man had puckishly named "No Body Knows What." George was ever conscious of his commission to extend and improve Cook's explorations, yet for it, he suffered ridicule from those who dared regard him as a poor, pint-sized, and deluded imitator of a great man. When he grew passionate chastising the perpetrators of such patent nonsense, they added that to their derision, as if George were making poor work of imitating Cook's famous temper.

In such instances, George was cursed for what he did and cursed for what he did not do. The best course was to keep his own counsel and his own company, for any shared reasoning or reaction would inevitably be used against him. There is no more difficult and lonely role to be served upon the sea than that of commander, particularly of two small vessels destined for the most remote corners of the world. Grudges were held, nursed, and compounded, until a certain few of George's company were entirely disposed to believe the worst, before he said a word or raised a finger. If he had given them nectar and ambrosia, the rabble rousers would have looked for a way to incite a riot over it.

Fortunately, George had far more good and reliable people than bad; and though much of this present recounting is, and will be, of his difficulties, this must not obscure the fact that George and his people had a majority of good and well-spent days together. He did not run particularly happy ships, that is certain, but he ran hale and hard-working ones, with all the rewards that good health and good deeds engender. Such recompense had always been enough for George. Indeed, as one who could not count good health among his blessings, he little understood the grumblings of those who had vibrant constitutions, honourable commissions, and time free each day from shipboard duty, yet felt cheated nonetheless.

George looked to Dusky Bay [now Dusky Sound] for the complete return of well-being to all hands. George knew his people had set their sights on Botany Bay, but every report from that little outpost was far from encouraging, so difficult was the site proving for even the most industrious souls—and there were few enough of those among the prisoners—to scratch out the barest living. All those lovely, strange plants that delighted Mr. Banks during the week he spent there in 1770 were useless, and worse, the soil yielded a poor harvest of European crops. Sir Joseph should have shown good faith and gone to live there himself, as governor or some such exalted station, if it was so confoundedly wonderful!

Dusky Bay, on the other hand, could answer the *Discovery*'s and *Chatham*'s every want, and George could also advance the purpose of his commission. By November 2nd, both vessels made New Zealand, after a gratifyingly quick crossing. Before bringing the ships into harbour, George deemed it expedient to reconnoitre the bay first by means of a ship's boat. As he did so, a small gale blew up, attended by heavy squalls, forcing the *Discovery* to seek safe anchorage at one harbour, while the *Chatham* found safe refuge at another.

George knew his young gentlemen were not pleased with this arrangement, for the distance precluded any communication between them, and, as Edward Bell[7] stated in his journal, "in this dreary place their Society would have added much to each other's Comforts." Oh, George's poor, lonely little midshipmen, cruelly prevented from the solace of each other's company! If they felt desolate upon the shores of Dusky Bay, George could not imagine how they would fare upon the more remote and wilder shores of northwest America, and for months on end, two or three summers running, with long, hard hours of survey work to attend, not just the labours of self-preservation.

Pitt and friends seemed to think their purpose was to forward their own adventures, and that George's uncaring about their entertainment needs was hard-nosed indeed. They were in for some rude surprises—later, if not sooner. When the weather broke and it became possible to anchor the vessels in the same harbour, George kept the ships apart; their situations were good enough for their purposes, and perfect for his.

They encountered no native peoples there and found few signs of any having been in the vicinity for years. With Captain Cook in 1777, George had met seven families there, and he wondered if contact with white men had led to their destruction, either through disease or through warfare with neighbouring tribes, who may have slaughtered them for the priceless trinkets Cook and crew had given them. George felt keenly the weighty responsibility that attends the privilege of discovering new peoples, and could plainly see, in every instance, all manner of irreparable damage done to previously self-reliant, cooperative societies. Decimation was common; total destruction was inevitable, in some instances, and he deeply mourned

---

[7] The *Chatham*'s clerk, credited with authorship of an anonymous journal. As per Admiralty instructions, Vancouver gathered up his officers' journals upon completion of his voyage and delivered them to Whitehall. He had access to them while he and his brother John prepared his journal for publication.

this. He was disappointed not to meet old friends at Dusky Bay, aggrieved to think he might innocently have played some role in their collective demise.

George immediately set his people to brewing spruce beer ashore, following Cook's own Dusky Bay recipe, which produced an exceedingly palatable decoction[8]. Few cared that it was an effective antiscorbutic and eased the symptoms of gonorrhoea; most simply enjoyed its good taste and liberal rationing.

Bird life abounded at Dusky Bay, as did legions of blood-thirsty sand flies. George made no note of these latter, so little did he think his personal discomfort to be of public interest. Rather, he noted the salubrious effects of the air and the abundance of necessary provisions, both for his ships and for his company. When his vessels quitted Dusky Bay toward the end of November, he boasted of all hands being restored to perfect health, save the surgeon and another who suffered chronic complaints, and two with minor wounds.

He also proudly pointed out that, "on the most trifling occasion of indisposition, no person was ever permitted to attend his duty." George wondered how he could be the tyrant Pitt and his followers insisted he was, when not one of them could dispute the consistent application of this policy. Indeed, if George had not been so tirelessly mindful of the good health of his entire company, and if they had suffered all manner of illnesses consequent to poor care, then he would have had a much easier time commanding them.

That is, sick men are easier to control than those in excellent health at the peak of their young manhood. Undoubtedly, Bligh's mutiny had something to do with his unceasing care of his people's well-being, hence there is a sad irony in all the good that Cook's prescriptions for diet and cleanliness on lengthy voyages have done. Commanders can now keep all hands hale and hearty, and with this blessing, the people see fit to threaten mutiny and, for the first time

---

[8] "leaves of the spruce tree mixed with Inspissated juce of Wort and Mellasses... [mixed] with an equal quantity of the Tea plant", boiled in giant cauldrons and vats, then fermented for a fortnight.

since men first sailed round the world, they have the strength to carry it out. Clearly, as health improved, the incidence of mutiny rose also, in direct proportion.

Nonetheless, the proper course is the one George took: to see to every person's perfect good health, and to take every action necessary to contain and direct the resultant vigour with which they tested every virile muscle. Thus, the weeks spent at Dusky Bay were beneficial to all, minor protestations to the contrary. Everyone performed his duties admirably enough, and George foresaw, in their splendid well-being, the makings of great success during their extensive and intensive explorations during the following summers.

10
Huzzahs for Tahiti

The last words Captain Bligh heard from the *Bounty*, as he and his faithful men were set adrift in the open launch, were "Huzzahs for Tahiti!", repeatedly and defiantly shouted by the drunken mutineers. They steered the ship for their beloved isle, where their women, many of them pregnant, awaited their return. George's men knew well this tale, and they shouted their own "Huzzahs for Tahiti" as they now made for that land of fabled beauties.

George had been there three times previously, yet none had ears for his sober appraisal of its virtues. As if to intensify each man's ardour, the weather conspired to make a difficult passage, which would only increase their gratitude upon landing in paradise.

The two ships soon separated and beat their way past an uncharted and hazardous group of small islands George named The Snares, in memory of a similar, nearby discovery Cook named The Traps.

To be following Captain Cook's trail so closely and to have spectres of past experiences suddenly rise up was unsettling, as the Channel fleet mobilization had been when George set sail. What coincidences might await him at the Sandwich Islands, he dared not think.

The *Discovery* next happened upon a mountainous island [Rapa Island, about 500 miles WSW of Pitcairn Island] inhabited by several thousand Indians, from which native men in canoes enthusiastically bade him come ashore, but George declined the opportunity. Atop the high and craggy mountains, fortifications could plainly be seen on six peaks, which led the midshipmen to speculate that George was fearful of landing, and for an odd reason, indeed. They contended that George considered the fortifications to be the handiwork of the *Bounty* mutineers and did not wish to take them upon his ship, as he would be forced to do, should this prove to be true. He was supposedly so very afraid of mutiny that to have a real mutineer upon his ships would set him to quaking in his boots. What nonsense, for George judged the structures to be of native manufacture, having seen similar ones on other South Sea islands. Further, as Bligh's mutineers were little different in kind from the very men who served aboard the *Discovery*, he would have been pleased to take them aboard and to deliver them to justice, that those deemed guilty might hang from the yardarm for their heinous crime.

In any case, his duty was to explore and chart the Sandwich Islands and northwest American coast, which would prove time-consuming enough. The continuing hard blow into which he sailed was slowing his progress significantly, without his looking for further delays.

Where they had expected to celebrate Christmas Day at Tahiti, they spent the holiday at sea, under gloomy skies. George ordered them to be fed as much as they could eat, but they agreed to save their traditional double grog allowance for making a toast at Tahiti.

So prevalent was talk among his people about what luxuries they might purchase for themselves from compliant Tahitians, George felt it judicious on Christmas Day to deliver his "RULES and OR-DERS for the guidance and conduct of all persons in, or belonging to His Majesty's Sloop Discovery and Chatham tender; enjoined to be most strictly observed in all intercourse with the natives of the several South-Sea islands." When they met the *Chatham* at Tahiti, he would give Captain Broughton a copy to deliver forthwith to his people.

The sole purpose of their brief stay at Tahiti was to provision themselves in preparation for the summer season upon the northwest coast of America. Four of the five conditions of the rules and orders, therefore, related to limitations on trade, for the following purposes: to keep it absolutely under George's control; to keep prices fair; to prevent theft by the natives; and to prevent embezzlement of ship's property by the crew. He also insisted most emphatically that everyone "use fair means to cultivate friendship in the different Indians, and on all occasions treat them with every degree of kindness and humanity."

George would not tolerate his people ill-using the natives, and he would not tolerate his people, through their own laxness or stupidity, being ill-used *by* the natives. Either case was sure to win swift punishment, as severe as the situation demanded, both to impress the offender and to ensure none other followed his example.

George thus dampened somewhat his people's "Huzzahs for Tahiti", yet they still had great hopes of winning favours from the Tahitian ladies in exchange for nothing more than the satisfaction of mutual desire. They had heard so much about the innocent and natural way with which all Tahitians approached the matter of conjugal relations, as if it were no different a bodily need than hunger or thirst, that they expected to find every pleasure imaginable, given the freedom to indulge themselves.

The *Discovery* made Matavai Bay by month's end, there to find the *Chatham* already two days in port. Following a happy reunion, marked by jubilant relief that all hands had fared well, Broughton assured George that he had been kindly received and attended by their friendly hosts. To preserve this good state, George promptly gave him a copy of his "RULES and ORDERS" to impress upon the *Chatham*'s men. There would be no casual visits ashore in Tahiti. There would be no unauthorized trading. There would be no loss or damage to any part of the ships' outfits. There would be no cause for conflict with the natives.

Broughton presented George with a narrative of his proceedings during their separate passages, parts of which displeased George. He learned that Broughton had landed at a small, uncharted, inhabited island not far from the one George had noted, but declined to explore. He was annoyed on two counts: first, Broughton had no instructions to explore such discoveries; and second, through his careless command, his men were forced to save themselves from a supposedly unprovoked attack on shore by shooting to death a native warrior and perhaps wounding several others.

Broughton was proving to be a very popular commander of his people, in part because he shared their over-confident and contemptuous attitudes toward native peoples, and in part because he had named many of his minor discoveries after the first of his people to descry them. George, on the other hand, had a well-known and respectful regard for native peoples, and in general, he named his various discoveries after their principal feature (eg. Bald Head, Five Finger Point, etc.) or after the great men who had patronized and forwarded his expedition. To name new lands after the seaman who reefed or furled the sails in accordance with his duties, hence had first view from on high, seemed to George to belittle the voyage's purpose, to discount those who had made it possible.

Seamen abounded—the so-called "lice of the sea"—and were more or less interchangeable, one with the other. Until any one of them distinguished himself beyond the call of duty, George would not name the smallest of geographic features after them; if and when one rose to his attention by commendable means, then he might bestow the man's name upon some landmark, if such reward suited the discoverer. If an extra tot of rum were more to his taste, then that would be his reward—and the one nearly every seaman would choose over posterity, so little did they care beyond their immediate comforts.

Proof of this assessment was evident from what George learned about the current state of the *Chatham*'s cutter, which had been severely damaged during a tempestuous rainstorm the first night of her arrival at Tahiti, due to the carelessness of those on watch. Those who served from the foc's'le and from midships would rather shirk their duty than get soaked in a storm, be damned the equipment's safety and integrity.

To name any landmark after such individuals who, without continual discipline, were likely to do something reprehensible just moments after being honoured for all time was foolish. Worse, Broughton was proving to be untrustworthy, and if he did not change his ways, George was secretly determined to find an acceptable means by which to relieve him of his command—not immediately, but when circumstances presented themselves, which George could not foretell.

The company's first taste of paradise was not quite as they had expected, for a continuing gale made Matavai Bay a poor anchorage with respect to sea and swell, tumbling them about upon the decks and preventing the island's famous beauties from swimming out to ease their eager anticipation.

The weather cleared by New Year's Day, although the surf still broke violently on shore. This continued to limit contact with the natives, although some young women braved the waters and made their way aboard. It being Sunday, George declared a holiday and ordered as much fresh pork and plum pudding as each man could eat, and "lest in the voluptuous gratifications of Tahiti, we might forget our friends in England, all hands... [drank] the healths of their sweethearts and friends at home."

Several of the women ashore were the spouses of Bligh's mutineers, each with a child as proof of their 'marriage'. George soon learned that the ship *Pandora*, sent from England to pick up the mutineers from Tahiti, had taken 14 Englishmen prisoners and quitted the island just eight months ago. Fletcher Christian was not among them, for he, a handful of mutineers, and some dozen or two dozen Tahitians had escaped to parts unknown. George could guess well enough what would become of him, however, based on the stories he learned from the natives about the lives of the 16 mutineers—two now murdered—who stayed at Tahiti.

First, however, a word about how this information came to

George. During his previous visits to Tahiti, he had become the best friend, or *taio*, of a young chief by the name of Tu. He renewed his friendship with this much aged, much mellowed man, who was now known as Pomare.

European weaponry had given Pomare the means by which to make himself king of all Tahiti—the first such absolute monarch, as their political system had previously been one of power-sharing by greater and lesser chiefs, with none being dominant over all. George regretted this and blamed Bligh somewhat and the mutineers yet more for destroying an ancient and peaceable system of government.

Through Pomare and his associates, George learned that the mutineers' lives had changed considerably when they became permanent members of Tahitian society. The Tahitian language caused them considerable difficulty. It is very fluid, with words constantly changing and being dropped, according to current taboos. Where the Englishmen's transgressions had been tolerated while they were guests, they were now expected to conform to every linguistic restriction, with penalties of death threatened for those who did not give their best effort to comply.

They also learned that sexual freedom is a privilege for the young only, and that upon procreation, there are strict rules of behaviour for the father and the mother to follow. Perhaps hardest for the mutineers to accept was that their chosen woman, their monogamously loved 'bride', was free to share her favours with her husband's *taio* and was, in fact, required to do so. The women were not without voice in these and many other matters, and their gentle compliance when first 'married' to Englishmen soon gave way to stubborn shows of strength in promoting Tahitian manners and modes of living.

One mutineer's *taio* was the principal chief elsewhere on the island, and when this chief died unexpectedly of natural causes, the mutineer became heir to his position, according to tradition. Another mutineer became so outrageously jealous, he murdered his shipmate, to the shock and disgust of the peace-loving, timid Tahitians. In a rare act of retribution, they killed the murderer.

Had the *Pandora* not picked up the remaining mutineers, George guessed that they would have wreaked such havoc upon themselves and the natives that all might eventually have met such ignoble ends. He surmised, therefore, that Christian and his little band of pirates and Tahitians would not last long in one another's company, even if they found a perfectly safe haven on which to spend the rest of their days.

Time was to bear this out. Numerous whaling vessels have visited the now-famous Pitcairn Island, with the first discovering the mutineers' hide-away in 1808. The eight mutineers who found their way to Pitcairn Island had waged such mindless and bloody war on one another that, by 1800, but one remained. Evidently, Fletcher Christian was among the first murdered, although there are many versions of exactly when, how, and why he and his mates died. George believed that justice would be served, one way or another, and that the rogue's life inevitably carries its own punishment. How true! If only he had lived to see the truth borne out in this instance.

Given the upheaval at Tahiti caused by the dangerous familiarity that had developed between Bligh's men and the natives, George had little choice but to severely limit shore leave, most particularly for his seamen. Among the common people, therefore, only the sick and those on duty spent time ashore, and then under close watch. Officers and young gentlemen were granted more generous leave ashore, provided they stayed within the encampment area and made no attempts, from this favoured position, to make any social advancements toward the natives.

George had been lenient in his allowance of women on board, in every quarter. This failed to satisfy his young gentlemen, who felt they could better take their ease with the ladies upon shore. George found several young gentlemen amusing themselves this way beyond the shore encampment, Pitt among them, of course. This blatant mockery of the rules had to be addressed, and not principally for the purpose of curtailing his young gentlemen's leisure with Tahitian women, but to prevent theft, embezzlement, and deeper entanglements, each with attendant difficulties.

George decreed that his midshipmen would be allowed on shore only if on duty. Their courting of the ladies would take place aboard ship, which was somewhat less than ideal, due to the stifling heat and close quarters in the midship mess, where any sort of privacy was impossible. When Pitt voiced the midshipmen's complaints regarding this arrangement, George quickly remedied the situation by forbidding women to visit their mess at all.

As if to add to the young gentlemen's troubles, the natives ashore entertained those watching from on board by staging celebrations called *heivas*, or wild dances of such an obscene nature that even the most chaste onlooker suffered considerably. George could not prevent the Indians from dancing upon their own lands, hence he was powerless to prevent this wanton provocation.

There was a great deal of grumbling from the shipstayed and frustrated young men, as one can readily imagine. George would not have imposed their punishment for long, however, had Pitt not chosen to follow his own foolish counsel and force yet greater punishment upon himself and continued denial upon his messmates. While he was on duty ashore, George caught him talking with a young woman and, upon closer examination, George discovered that he had offered her some iron in return for her favours.

Pitt denied that anything but a civil intercourse occurred between himself and the young lady, protesting as if George had not eyes in his head. Pitt held in his hand a piece of ship's property—a piece of iron hoop that had been fashioned at New Zealand into a zigzag shape to make a grid iron. George had made it abundantly clear, in his rules and orders, that embezzling any item of ship's property for barter with the natives would not be countenanced. At last, he had caught Pitt alone and red-handed. Punishment was in order.

George removed Pitt to the *Discovery's* cabin, and called for First Lieutenant Mudge and all midshipmen to join them there. The boatswain's mate was called as well and instructed to bring his whip. When all were assembled, George informed Pitt and company of the crime in question, namely the purloining of the ships' stores, which was punishable by the laying on of 24 lashes.

With that, Pitt was stripped to the waist and flogged accordingly. Mudge was much distressed, for he sailed under the patronage of

Lord and Lady Camelford, who had put their son in his care aboard ship. Mudge intervened after the first 12 lashes, requesting of George that, provided Pitt would promise to behave better in future, would he please remit the second 12 lashes? Pitt was too proud to have any of this, and he refused to give his word and thus be begged off. The remaining dozen lashes were applied, then all were dismissed, with the ban on women in midships to remain in place for the remainder of their stay at Tahiti.

Two points are worthy of mention here. First, George was purser aboard his ship, as Bligh had been on the *Bounty*—a new cost-saving measure introduced by the Admiralty that was having disastrous effects. Ships' suppliers are so notorious for shortchanging their clients, it is commonly said that, "A sailor's pound is 14 ounces." George's people were inclined to think that George himself was somehow cheating them of their full rations, that he might make a tidy profit by skimming from them. Some held the view, therefore, that George was angry at Pitt for purloining the ships' stores principally because the item in question would be docked from George's pay, and they considered him such a miser that he would stop at nothing to save a penny. Stuff and nonsense! George had Pitt flogged for official and justifiable reasons, not to seek private and petty revenge. He could take his case against Pitt to any flag officer of the Royal Navy and win it, without question.

Second, floggings of midshipmen were not common, but neither were they unheard of. By journey's end, more than half of the *Discovery*'s complement of 100 people had been flogged, including Pitt and two other midshipmen. Of the *Chatham*'s complement of 53 people, an equal proportion were likewise flogged, including one midshipman. Twenty-four lashes comprised the usual punishment; the range was from one to twelve dozen, depending on the severity of the offense and the number of previous transgressions. During Captain Cook's day, whipping was necessary less often and less severely, but since the messy American Revolution, the rise of young men to inordinate power, and sailors' increasingly good health, firm measures had to be taken to maintain order, particularly during long and tedious voyages upon small and crowded vessels.

The midshipmen's situation was soon made worse by the death of Pomare's old and much revered brother-in-law, which resulted in a taboo on trade of all kind between the Englishmen and natives, food included. In this land of plenty, all hands were forced back to ships' rations, which angered Pitt to such a degree that he disobeyed orders once again and secretly arranged the purchase, for a much inflated price, of six hogs to feed himself and his mates. Such a bold transaction could not be completed with any discretion, and when it came to George's attention, he seized the animals, kept them alive on board until the ships set sail, then fed the lot of them to the full company at one sitting. Pitt was livid! He believed George had stolen them from him, and he added this insult to his recent injuries.

George's instructions bade him make for the Sandwich Islands for the remainder of the winter, there to rendezvous with the storeship *Daedalus* and to prepare for the coming summer survey season. Since the *Daedalus* had sailed months after George's vessels quit England, there was little chance she would make the Sandwich Islands until late in winter if, indeed, she arrived there at all before George sailed thence to Nootka, which was their second and more likely place of rendezvous. There was no rush, therefore, to make the Sandwich Islands on that count.

Furthermore, George was apprehensive of spending too many weeks in the waters where Cook had been slaughtered, when he was able to supply all possible wants at Matavai Bay, among old and generous Tahitian friends.

Broughton was not as mindful as George of his people, or even his own person, and therein lay the cause of yet more difficulties for George, the worst of which arose during the last days spent at the island. First, three axes were given to native men for the purpose of cutting wood. As no wood appeared within a reasonable length of time, George rightly assumed these coveted articles had been stolen. No sooner had he set to retrieving them than Broughton reported missing a full bag of his linen, which the native women were washing. It contained a dozen shirts, which were prized by the Indians and absolutely irreplaceable so far from a civilized port.

George was furious. Of all the thefts that had occurred, and there were many of a petty nature, this was the worst. While George stormed around, in a mad rage calculated to cause such distress in the natives that they might return the stolen linen forthwith—for they were a self-confessed timid, fearful people, and this ploy had worked perfectly in the past—one of his company deserted ship and eloped with his new-found lady love, a young woman of royal Tahitian blood.

The deserter was no ordinary sailor, but a special passenger named Kualelo, a native of the Sandwich Island of Molokai who had sailed to England aboard an English fur-trading vessel and who was now being returned to his homeland. He was not a very capable or even very likeable fellow, being of low birth and limited intelligence, hence he particularly relished his princely reception at Tahiti. As he gradually gave away all his European treasures to his Tahitian princess, he achieved ever-greater status in her and her family's eyes. Because he was a supernumerary on board ship, and nearly useless in every capacity, many of George's men felt he should be allowed to make himself a new and prosperous home wherever he chose.

George could understand their sentiments, but he could not agree with allowing his charge to go free. His instructions clearly stated that Kualelo was to be returned to the Sandwich Islands, and it would set a dangerous precedent to let any man desert, for there were numerous Englishmen who yearned to follow Kualelo's lead. George had axes, linen, and an escaped man to retrieve before his vessels could sail and, as all was in readiness and all had gone smoothly for the previous three weeks, he was exceptionally frustrated and angered at these losses.

At the height of George's heated negotiation for the return of the missing items and man, Broughton decided to stroll ashore, alone and unarmed, in an unauthorized attempt to effect the return of his shirts. He suffered no harm, but his efforts were in vain. George grew angrier still. Eventually, two of the axes reappeared, as did Kualelo, who was obviously a heartbroken and much impoverished man.

Many an English sailor was heartbroken for him. That they could not partake fully of the island's bounties was a hardship, but that a poor and pitiful Sandwich Islander could not make a new life with his chosen lady was a harsher sentence still. In this instance, George did, indeed, seem to be a man of the hardest, most hateful spirit.

He was never one to put popularity ahead of duty, which was, of course, one of the reasons why he rose to the heights necessary to deserve and fulfill his commission, while equally talented colleagues from days with Cook had not. Besides, the dim-witted and foolish Kualelo was no more capable of fitting into Tahitian society than Bligh's men were; he would have encountered extreme and perhaps fatal difficulties when his initial period of grace wore off. He belonged on the Sandwich Islands, and there he would go.

His desertion could not go unpunished, yet his own foolish actions had provided penalty enough, thus George determined only to move him out of the gunners' mess, where he had bunked since sailing from England, and put him into the fo'c'sle with the common seamen for the remaining few weeks of his voyage. This seemed to be the most unthinkable injustice to Pitt and his friends, but George found no evidence that any of them put their money where their mouth was, for not one of the complaining young swains offered to replace the possessions Kualelo had lost to his fair-weather Tahitian friends.

It seems that no white man was destined to quit Tahiti without great yearning for love lost to a native woman, and if they lost none of their own, they clutched their breasts on behalf of another. Since Captain Samuel Wallis discovered Tahiti in 1767, it has been thus. Unfortunately, not many men returned as George had done, hence few could see what became of the legendary Tahitian beauties over the years. In George's own words, "Beauty in this country, especially amongst the women, is a flower that quickly blossoms, and as quickly fades: like the personal accomplishments of the Creoles of America, theirs soon arrive at maturity, remain but a short time stationary, and as rapidly decay."

The young women George had admired on previous visits had

become a shocking sight, so seriously had they declined to wrinkled, toothless obesity. He had aged prematurely as well, and none who knew him previously hesitated to note his own rapid decline. He felt such poignancy in these meetings, such a sense of melancholy that his eager young shipmates could not possibly understand, yet it would one day strike them, when they too returned to their young loves and found much in ruin. His duty was to make sure his lads had every opportunity to grow old and to gain this wisdom, a responsibility he took most seriously.

In terms of good health and safe conduct, their stay at Tahiti was an unqualified success. They sailed away on January 24th, 1792, with every man more fit than when he left England. Indeed, no greater loss had occurred than for Broughton's shirts to have permanently found new owners, who no doubt were overjoyed with the fruits of their thievery.

II

Lord Sandwich's Islands

Now, nearly ten months absent from England, George at last considered that his voyage had begun. For the first time, his vessels' heads were pointed toward the grand object of the expedition, but this was less an occasion for elation than for considerable regret over their poor progress to date. He had calculated that, by this time, he should be quitting the Sandwich Islands, which were yet nearly 800 leagues distant.

George had been with Cook in 1777 when he chanced upon the Sandwich Islands, which he named after the First Lord of the Admiralty and good friend of Joseph Banks, George Montagu, the fourth Earl of Sandwich, who is now best remembered for eating meat between slices of bread, so he need not leave the gaming table during his 24-hour gambling stints. That Cook had found those small islands in the midst of the vast, uncharted Pacific Ocean bespeaks the uncanny good fortune he had as an explorer; if there was land to be found, the Fates conspired to place it in his path.

The Sandwich Islands were an ideal place for trading vessels to provision and refit between China and the northwest coast of America, yet the dozen or more merchant ships that had visited there for such purposes had produced few charts, none of them reliable. George was to produce the first map of the larger islands, which appeared to be seven or eight in number.

He was under no pressure to begin surveying during his first winter there, for he would return the following year between summer seasons spent reconnoitring the northwest coast. He would then occupy his people with plenty of vigorous work, to keep them moving about and fully employed at a land of amorous delights and wicked intrigue.

On March 1st, George sighted the largest island of Hawaii, whereupon he read to his company the same rules and orders he had delivered prior to their arrival at Tahiti. They were none too pleased with this, but George viewed the distant shore with dread and determination. His mind was teeming with memories, some of which were colourful and pleasant, but all of which were darkened by the shadow of Cook's death.

By March 3rd, the ships were off Kealekekua Bay, where every sailor eagerly pointed out and ogled the place where Cook fell, enjoying the delicious shivers it gave them. George felt ill. He could hear the shouts of long ago, as hundreds of implacable warriors attacked Cook with rocks and spears, then, for good measure, drowned him in the warm, clear, aqua waters of paradise. He could see blood swirling in the water, and he could vividly remember what the few retrieved parts of his beloved commander looked like: head, with scalp and ears missing; torso, with heart cut out, the rest disembowelled; hands cut off, slit, and salted to preserve them; portions of arms and legs severed and charred; feet nowhere to be found. The Indians so thoroughly tore apart this giant of a man, his remains had to be buried at sea in a weighted coffin.

Several canoes containing native men came off to greet the ships, carrying fresh food for barter. George soon learned that in return they wanted either exorbitant prices, paid in metal, cloth, trinkets, etc., or they wanted arms and ammunition. They would hold out until George understood and complied. Understand he did, from the first instance, but comply? Never!

His vessel was next approached by a canoe carrying a tall, well-made native man who introduced himself as Kaiana, a name George recognized from reports by John Meares (the Englishman, called "Liar-Liar" by the Nootkan people, who played a key role in the Nootka Crisis). Meares had taken Kaiana to China in 1787, then to Nootka Sound for the summer of 1788 before returning him to the Sandwich Islands that winter. Despite this extended contact with Englishmen, Kaiana had forgotten every word of the English language he once knew except that for wine, which he requested of George the instant he came on board.

Using Kualelo as translator—and a poor one at that, for he had a rudimentary English vocabulary and abysmal enunciation—George learned that no vessel had been at the islands since the preceding autumn, which meant that the *Daedalus* had not arrived yet. This was extremely disappointing news to George, but Kaiana assured him that no ship appeared without it being communicated from Niihau to Hawaii within a day.

George enquired about some of the chiefs and other men he had known long ago at Kealekekua Bay, and he learned that much had changed. The old king was long dead, and his treacherous nephew, Kamehameha, had become the new ruler. Kaiana insisted he and Kamehameha were equals now, and George had no way then of ascertaining the truth of it, but if he remembered correctly the role Kamehameha had played in Cook's slaughter, this was not likely. Kamehameha had no equal—not in stature, physical abilities, cunning, intensity, menacing good looks, or any other attribute. He had been a singularly powerful young man; he was now on his way to becoming a singularly powerful ruler, if he had not succeeded in doing so already.

George had no desire to stay at Kealekekua Bay in any case, but word of Kamehameha's ascendancy was one more reason to look for water—the ships' only required provision—at Oahu or Kauai.

When he informed Kaiana of this, Kaiana asked if he, his wives, and royal retinue might sail on the *Discovery* to Kauai. George agreed, but was disconcerted by Kaiana's obsessive desire to ascertain the number of men on duty in the different parts of the ship and the abundance of arms and ammunition. He obviously wanted to make some use of these things. George assured him that all his people were highly trained warriors sent by King George of Great Britain to peacefully explore the islands, but they would defend themselves by doing formidable damage to any attackers.

Kaiana requested that George delay sailing until his attending party joined him. George complied and anchored overnight in Kealekekua Bay. Under black skies, he looked at the foreboding hills, remembering the fires that had burned on them prior to Cook's fall, a warning none had heeded. Worse fires burned afterward, when sailors defied orders and went on a rampage ashore, torching everything in sight, killing natives, then parading their heads about on pikes and on the boats' gunwales. Smoke and frightful wails had filled the air; blood had splattered and dripped everywhere.

By the next morning, messengers brought Kaiana news that made him decline, for undisclosed reasons, to accompany the ships to the leeward islands, to George's relief. Kaiana then hatched the plot that he become Kualelo's patron, offering him land, a house, and other handsome advantages if he would consent to this arrangement. Kaiana assured George that the confused state of affairs at Molokai, due to recent wars and current preparations for yet another, precluded Kualelo's happy return to his home island. George doubted Kaiana's motives, but, as the proposed arrangement received Kualelo's enthusiastic support, he agreed. What use Kaiana would make of the hapless Kualelo, George would see the next winter, then adjust the situation accordingly, if it proved unfavourable.

To the minds of certain young gentlemen, George could do nothing right for Kualelo. This time, they dared complain that Kualelo was put ashore like a convict to his place of transportation, with few belongings to ensure his comfort and well-being among strangers. George would hear none of it. He had fulfilled his duty to

the man; from henceforth, Kualelo was free to make his own fortunes and misfortunes as he saw fit. He returned to the Sandwich
Islands much elevated in status and possessing knowledge that
would stand him in good stead, if he chose to apply it.

On March 4th, the *Discovery* and *Chatham* set sail for Oahu.
That evening, as they stood along the Hawaiian shore, they were
much surprised to be haloo'd from a large canoe by a native man demanding, in broken English, to know who they were, to what
country they belonged, and politely requesting to come aboard.
Thus, George first met Jack, as this Indian introduced himself.

Jack had sailed for 20 months aboard the Boston traders *Columbia*
and *Hope*. He was a sprightly fellow, keen to join the *Discovery*.
George found his company and translating abilities so agreeable, he
signed him on the next day.

Two days following, the *Discovery* made Waikiki Bay at Oahu.
The *Chatham* was delayed by calm weather. The Waikiki natives
were distantly civil, and, although George wondered if this was a
peaceful veneer to cover their hostile intentions, he was pleased to
keep it thus, that he might collect water for his ships with the least
interference. Jack impressed the few men of authority at that port—
the greater chiefs were away preparing for war—that King George's
ships were manned and armed in ways far superior to the trading
vessels the natives were accustomed to serving, and no mischievous
nonsense would be tolerated. Small wonder, then, that George
continued to be coolly received!

While George and a small landing party took a well-guarded tour
of the watering place, which proved to be an inconvenient distance
from shore, he noted further the polite caution of the natives. This
caution extended to his ship, for the women refused to comply with
the sailors' repeated requests to come on board. This highly frustrat-
ing situation continued throughout the evening and night.

The *Chatham* arrived toward midnight of March 7th, to be greeted by women who, on learning she was the *Discovery*'s consort, similarly refused to climb on deck. Both companies had now been
nearly a week in view of available women, with no contact being
established. One can imagine how the likes of young Pitt felt about

this circumstance; he and his mates condemned the women for their cheeky refusal of service and considered the natives' caution to be entirely George's fault.

By the next morning, George had struck a deal to hire native men to help supply water to the ships. The women took courage from this agreement and soon found employment of their own. Mr. Menzies wrote that, "whoever might be inclined to censure the conduct of the ladies for with-holding their company from us on the preceding day, had now no cause to complain for they came off in large groups not only in the Canoes but on swimming boards with no other intention than that of tendering their persons to any one that would choose to have them, & those who were unsuccessful in their aim went away chiding us for our want of gallantry."

The work on shore did not proceed to George's liking, for the native men were given more to joking and cheating than to performing honest labour for honest pay. They found great humour in filling the calabashes with sea water, which saved them the long trip from the watering place to shore. Buyers who failed to taste the contents of every container and paid for them nonetheless suffered the Indians' amusement and derision. George did not long tolerate this form of thievery and, in short order, had all his people aboard and under way for Kauai, where he hoped to be more willingly served for fair barter.

The ships bore up to Waimea Bay early on the morning of March 9th, and by nine o'clock, were anchored. At one past noon, George made his way ashore to search for a ready water supply and employable natives to haul it. Both he found in short order, much to his satisfaction. A native chief also accorded him the use of two houses, one for his officers and one for his workers and guards to spend the night. The chief put a taboo on the water supply area and the buildings, that none might enter those sanctuaries without George's approval. The officers and men who envisioned a heavenly night ashore with the ladies were much disappointed, therefore, because no woman would disrespect the taboo, and George would allow none of his people to go where the women salaciously invited them.

George toured the shore and the inland plantations (principally of the taro plant, interspersed with some sugar canes and sweet potatoes), where he and his party were accosted by the most shameless women he had ever encountered in all his travels. Their licentious displays drew up his censure and dislike, disgust and aversion, offense and abhorrence, to use his own words on the subject. As he had no recollection of the women behaving this way on his former visit to the Sandwich Islands, nor of the native men being such avid partners in their degradation, he could only conclude that it was a result of contact with white men, who taught them the sad business of the flesh trade.

This pained George a great deal, to see a proud people, among whom wanton prostitution had been unknown, become such willing perpetrators of their own ruination, which certainly would result if the situation continued unchecked. Curse the crude men of every trading nation who tempted a simple people to sell their tenderest wares for gew-gaws. Curse those who traded in firearms and ammunition, that the Indians might war against each other till nothing of their former good order and harmony remained, till every ill of the white man's world reduced them to slaves at best and ashes at worst.

The disgust and aversion George felt during his first brief return to the Sandwich Islands sparked his desire to save them from further unregulated depredations by white men. Peace and order must be established, on every ship, every shore, and every transaction between. During this first reacquaintance, he had no time to effect any change, thus he wished to spend as little time as possible there. Where his men relished the thought of returning the next winter, George dreaded it, for he would have to negotiate peace with Kamehameha, his jealous allies, and his vengeful enemies. Until George could impress a solution upon the native chiefs, his ships full of randy young Britons simply added to the islands' dissolution.

Three white men were now permanent residents at Kauai, and George met the first of these on March 11th. Rowbottom, a young Derbyshireman aged about 17 years, paddled a large double canoe to the *Discovery* and introduced himself. He was in the employ of

1. John Vancouver

2. Captain James Cook

3. Mrs. Elizabeth Cook

4. *William Bligh*

5. *John Meares*

6. *Estevan José Martínez*

7. Spanish Insult to the British Flag at Nootka Sound

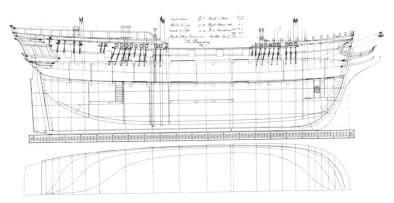

8. Elevation of the Discovery

9. Robert Barrie

10. Sir Joseph Banks

11. Archibald Menzies

13. Kaiana

12. Zachary Mudge

14. Robert Gray

16. Dionisio Alcalá Galiano

15. Interior of the Discovery's Cabin

17. Cayatano Valdés

18. "The Discovery on the Rocks in Queen
Charlotte's Sound"

19. Friendly Cove, Nootka Sound

20. Juan Francisco de la
Bodega y Quadra

21. Maquinna

22. Interior View of Maquinna's House at Tahsis

the American trader, John Kendrick. Kendrick, in command of the *Washington* and *Columbia*, had been at Nootka Sound when Colnett and Martínez came to blows, with Kendrick playing the Devil's advocate between them. George did not, therefore, hold Kendrick in any esteem, and he was equally disposed to think ill of Kendrick's employees.

Rowbottom and his mates were to establish a trade for sandalwood and pearls, but first they had to make their way with the natives, which was no easy task. Not until the island chiefs saw what use their guests might be to them as translators, particularly for the procurement of firearms, did their treatment improve significantly. Rowbottom professed not to be tired at all of his situation, although he confessed he had been unsuccessful in his principal purpose.

Rowbottom warned George to keep his people on constant alert, for George's suspicions that the natives keenly coveted his ships and weapons were well-founded. He illustrated by detailing the fate of the schooner *Fair American*, a tiny American-owned fur-trading vessel manned by only five hands. The captain was 18-year-old Thomas Metcalfe, son of New Yorker Simon Metcalfe, who sailed the larger *Eleanore* in consort. They left China together for Nootka, but were separated by a storm.

When young Metcalfe made Nootka, Martínez captured him and his ship, taking them to San Blas to join Colnett's three captured vessels. The Governor of New Spain quickly saw the absurdity of this situation and had the *Fair American* released. Metcalfe then sailed to Hawaii, which he made in February of 1790. His crew somehow insulted their Hawaiian hosts, who were, in any case, predisposed to laying their hands on a sailing ship and all her armaments.

Native warriors, led by a lesser Hawaiian chief, seized the opportunity, murderously attacked all aboard the *Fair American*, and took her as their prize. Kamehameha thoroughly disapproved of this action and, to punish the lesser chief, took the spoils for himself. By chance, one white man survived—just. Kamehameha took the sailor, Isaac Davis, into his care; he was nursed back to health and became an honoured prisoner. Davis still lived at Hawaii, along with

John Young, a friend who was somehow stranded from the *Eleanore*, which had continued in pursuit of the fur trade.

So emboldened were the warriors with their relative success, they soon attempted to take a brig at Maui, but fortunately failed. George's large complement of men and tight discipline would keep the natives from effecting a seizure, but they would search for every sign of strength and weakness, to make an attempt if an opportunity arose.

All this information played seriously upon George's mind. Kaiana's ominous curiosity about the ships' capacities and capabilities made sense now, and in precisely what way, George soon learned. Some lesser chiefs assured him that, had Kaiana come to Waimea Bay aboard the *Discovery*, he would have been killed the instant he landed, for although he had once been an ally of the Kauaian ruler, he was now a sworn enemy. These chiefs could scarcely believe that Kaiana had entertained the notion of coming to Kauai; George could plainly see what role his men and guns might have served had they been caught in the bloody fray between two warring factions.

On March 10th, with watering well under way, George toured the Waimea River, where he and his party were harassed by women who were, if possible, behaving more obscenely than those encountered before. The next morning, he met the other two men in Kendrick's employ, a Welshman named John Williams and an American named James Coleman, this latter instantly proving himself to be a degenerate and sarcastic fellow.

That afternoon, while George was taking a pleasant walk on the beach, he noticed fire on the hills to the east of the river, from on high down to the water's edge. Some chiefs explained that the fires were a usual agricultural practice, a view that Menzies upheld, for he had seen evidence of it on Oahu recently and during his previous visit to the islands in 1788. Other chiefs, however, said that the fires were to prepare for the arrival of a visiting high chief, who would come the next day. George was not inclined to believe either story, and he quickly sought safety aboard his ship, taking two midshipmen with him and leaving his armed, 20-man shore party to spend the night in the two houses under heavy guard.

The surf was running high, making a difficult offing for the native canoes employed to ferry the Englishmen to their waiting boats, and thence to the ships. George's canoe upset in the surf, an action he believed was deliberately taken by his native paddlers. Both midshipmen were washed back toward shore, and one who could not swim was in grave danger. George swam to the pinnace, which was manned, and he directed it to pick up the nearly drowned young gentleman.

The next morning, after an uneventful night, trade resumed and all appeared to be peaceful. George's renewed confidence was not to last long, however, for new fires were soon lit, and there was no sign whatever of any royalty arriving. That evening, George insisted that the shore party sleep aboard ship, although the surf was running higher than the previous day. Not surprisingly, the large canoe used to ferry the men, equipment, and arms upset again, this time nearly drowning several men and resulting in the loss of several muskets and working tools. On shore, some arms and a musket had to be abandoned, to George's great worry.

The morning of March 13th dawned uneventfully, and to George's great relief, an elderly chief and his young son arrived. Even more gratifying, everything left on shore was untouched, and several items that had washed from the canoe were returned. The natives promised to search for the remaining missing items and return them all—and, indeed, they did so. George looked more the fool to his officers and men, who were forming a good opinion of the Kauaian people. He was aware of their sneering assessment of his distrust, but would not rest his guard, choosing rather to suffer his people's certain ridicule than to suffer the natives' uncertain fury.

The old chief, Enemo, was now regent to his young son. He remembered George from his days with Cook and even insisted that George had given him a lock of his hair in friendship, although George had no recollection of it. He declined to fulfill the chief's request for a new lock of hair, and, by such a cool renewal of an old acquaintance, won the chief's equally cool welcome. To win the old man's favour by other means, George invited the chief and his companions to sup and sleep aboard the *Discovery*—a royal treat for these royal personages. The old chief happily agreed to this, but only on the condition that George leave a hostage on shore with some of the chief's party, to ensure his own safety on board.

This was quite sensible to George, and he chose Thomas Manby, master's mate, to stay with the small party left ashore, including the young prince. So seriously did Manby take his duties and the threat posed by his good-natured company, he recorded that for "Two hours I reveld in extatic enjoyment [with a] Royal female." That night, when he had returned aboard ship, he recorded, "I was surpris'd after dark by a Canoe paddling under the stern of the Ship inquiring for me by the name of Mappee [the best the natives could make of his name] and instantly knew the voice of the Stranger to be the Royal female that I'd pass'd some happy moments with in the early part of the day. She had deserted the residence of Enemo to say again farewell, bringing me some handsome mats and a few pieces of Cloth. [A]fter staying with me two hours she again took a sorrowful adieu and left the Ship with a heavy heart."

What a good laugh Manby, Pitt, and their mates must have had at George's ignorance of their activities, when they were entrusted to guard at all times the safety of Englishmen and Indians alike. These foolish young men could not believe that death and devastation lay so close at hand on those pleasant isles, that fear and greed could corrupt harmonious relations with shocking swiftness.

Further, none had seen the extent to which the islands had been laid waste in the 15 short years since Cook had discovered them. George estimated the population to be only two-thirds its former size, principally the result of continual war. Venereal complaints had taken their toll, as had other introduced diseases. The worst loss, however, was that of pride, as the new commerce with white traders made prostitutes of all the islands' peoples, from the chiefs who sold their souls for firearms to the women who sold their hearts for trinkets.

No, George's men were blind to the miseries of paradise, while George, who saw too well, could not get his people away from there fast enough. He sailed from Kauai, where his water needs were fulfilled, the instant a good breeze blew for an offing, which was at the inconvenient hour of three in the morning of March 14th. He would put in briefly at Niihau, where large quantities of yams were obtainable, then he would quit the islands entirely. This caused a scramble among upward of a hundred women on board, a few of whom swam ashore, while most chose to sail to Niihau, being only a few leagues distant and constantly traversed by native canoes.

After two days at Niihau, all was in readiness to sail, and all took leave of their ladies by six in the evening. George left two letters with Rowbottom, one to be delivered to Lieutenant Hergest of the *Daedalus*, whose delayed arrival was much regretted, and another to be forwarded to the Lords of the Admiralty. With that, the *Discovery* and the *Chatham* spread full sails to the wind and pointed their prows to the northwest coast of America.

The grand adventure was now more truly under way than when the ships left Tahiti, but George's exhilaration was dampened by multiple concerns: for the *Daedalus* and her safety; for the state of the Sandwich Island kingdoms; and for the ability of his men to rise to the hardships that lay before them.

George knew he had become an object of his young men's scorn, many seeing him as a prudish, posturing, timid little man, given to passionate, but irrational and heartless, displays of authority. He found comfort in the knowledge that his strongest critics were in for some surprises. There was none who could lead them on an intricate survey of the coastline from southern California to Alaska better than he, and by God, they would come to respect him for a vigour, discipline, and perfection of service unseen since Cook's day. Their time for play was coming to an end; their time to work—and work damned hard!—was nearly upon them.

He would sweat the contempt out of them, and when they learned to push themselves to the very limits of endurance, they would be proud of themselves and grateful to him for their good health—indeed, for their very lives.

12

Making Their Station

The *Discovery*'s people took their last view of the Sandwich Islands through the rosy glow of sunrise on March 18th, then quickly turned their attention to repairing the mainmast, which had sprung shortly after their departure. The carpenter, Henry Phillips, dared to disagree with George's particular directions and finished the work to his own satisfaction. His defiance angered George in no small measure, for Phillips had been a thorn in his side since June last, when he was flogged for impertinence and negligence of duty over removal of the barrier between foc's'le and midships. At present, rather than redo his handiwork as instructed, Phillips chose to argue with George, showing shocking disrespect.

Phillips had taken courage from the general air of contempt held for George and perhaps, as a journeyman, he felt justified in holding his ground. George was never one to be fooled by inferior work-

86

manship, however, and he was doubly angered to be told he was looking at good quality materials and work when clearly he was not. Further, he had reason to be dissatisfied with the stores in Phillips's keeping, which were in condition equal to the use he made of them, which was poor indeed.

George had had quite enough. The time had now come to remove entirely the source of irritation, that it might be a lesson to all his people. Much to Phillips's surprise, therefore, George had him arrested and confined prisoner in his cabin, where he was to languish until suitable transport could be found to send him home.

The sly, admiring glances Phillips's outburst had won him instantly vanished from every face, swallowed hard by young gentlemen and seamen alike. A carpenter's mate took over the carpenter's duties and set his long face to following George's instructions to the last detail. "And cheerily!" George demanded, for Phillips had suffered no worse treatment than he deserved. Every member of the full company knew the rules, and every member would earn his just reward by scrupulously following them. Compliance was the easy part, punishment the hard.

The remainder of the month taken to make their station—that is, to fall in with the northwest coast of America—was sporadically stormy but uneventful. On April 17th, the coast was sighted just above 39° north latitude, or approximately 115 miles north of the Spanish settlement at San Francisco. George had hoped to fall in farther southward, but the season was too far advanced to backtrack.

The shoreline from 39° to approximately 47° north latitude proved to be straight and unbroken, as George had expected, based on reports from English fur-trading vessels plying those waters since 1785. Before his ships lay a compact coastline of cliffs near shore and beautiful green hills in the distance. The weather was pleasantly cooperative, with the clouds and fog obscuring the land by night and clearing away by day.

There were few signs of habitation upon that immense and verdant coast, where native encampments doubtless were dwarfed by the great wilderness that surrounded and protected them. After a week of tracing the continent's edge, the ships finally encountered a few Indians, who spoke a language different from that George had heard at Nootka Sound in 1778. They had some knowledge of white men's trade goods, but contact had obviously been limited, for they had no understanding of firearms. They lived yet in an admirably natural state, and George recorded a generous assessment of their neat and cleanly appearance, their few crude belongings, and their honest attentions. Some of George's people were not so kindly disposed to the Indians, with Pitt among those who considered them filthy and stinking—"the nastiest race of people under the sun."

This attitude distressed George, and although he had no means by which to insist his people alter their opinions, he was determined to show every deference due their Indian hosts, leading by his example. As their purpose was not to trade, there would be little direct interaction between his company and the native Americans. George was relieved that this was so, but it was unfortunate as well, for the Indians' first and principal contact would then be with traders, who were an unscrupulous lot.

George's respectful but limited interactions with native peoples could not outweigh the misfortunes the Indians were certain to suffer from the attentions of white traders, and he feared the devastation underway in the Sandwich Islands would soon spread to northwest American shores. Indeed, his charts would make the countless bays and inlets more accessible to 'civilized' men, thus hasten the destruction. His best hope was that settlement would soon proceed in a well-governed manner, with British colonists—men, women, and children—working the fertile earth, introducing the gentle arts, and tempering the excesses of renegade merchants. In particular, unregulated trade in firearms for the purpose of intertribal warfare was incompatible with domestication, requiring that the first settlers make short work of this and every other unprincipled trade practice.

On April 28th, the ships were opposite a feature called Destruction Island [directly west, across the Olympic Peninsula, from the present cities of Seattle and Tacoma] by the English trader Charles

Barkley, the sight of which chilled every man's blood. In the summer of 1787, Barkley had sailed there from Nootka Sound in pursuit of furs. He encountered Indians near the island, which faced a river's mouth on the mainland shore. Barkley sent a boat carrying five men and trade goods up the river to search for native encampments, there to barter for furs. The five men disappeared and were never seen again. The next day, Barkley sent a strongly armed party to search for the missing men, but only mangled and bloody portions of their clothing were found, and no part of their bodies or boat. Barkley immediately set sail for China, leaving his five men for dead and bestowing the name of Destruction Island to mark the site of their ghastly demise.

George was not remiss in relating what he knew of these melancholy events, for he wished to impress upon his people what price may be exacted by the natives for injudicious behaviour, however innocently undertaken. Respect and fear are two sides of the same coin, and he wished his company to respect and to fear the natives in equal measure, that a civil harmony might prevent every sort of misunderstanding and misfortune.

Several hours later, after sailing past that grim island tombstone, the ships descried a sail, the first reported in eight months at sea. She raised American colours, and by six in the afternoon, they spoke her: she was the *Columbia* of Boston, Captain Robert Gray. George was astonished to have fallen in with the very person John Meares had credited with entering the fabled Strait of Juan de Fuca and sailing through it far to the northward, thus proving that Nootka Sound was situated on a very large island. George sent second mate Peter Puget and Mr. Menzies to Gray's ship, to question him about this remarkable feat, which the *Discovery* and *Chatham* had been sent to confirm.

While George awaited their return, he took great pleasure in the beauty that surrounded him, as the sun set on a singular and most spectacular snow-gowned mountain previously named Olympus by John Meares. George had not seen the original Olympus, but he had no doubt that *this* Olympus was among the world's outstanding landmarks. His people were equally transfixed by the sheer magnitude and majesty of the continental backdrop to the eastward, capped by Olympus, which reigned supreme over all.

At the time, George had difficulty finding words to convey his impressions of such beauty; later, his memories were nothing compared to the profound majesty of the features themselves. He could only conclude that for those who wish truly to appreciate it, the long journey must be made and the view taken in for oneself.

Puget and Menzies returned to report that Mr. Gray's supposed journey through Juan de Fuca's strait was news to him, for he claimed merely to have entered the strait, proceeded up it 17 leagues, then turned about and left by the same route. George was pleased at this disclosure, for if a way existed through the strait, the honour of being first to do so might still be his.

George already held John Meares in low esteem—despite being a beneficiary of the furore he had caused, by fanning the flames of the Nootka Crisis—and his opinion fell further still when he learned that Meares and Gray had met in the summer of 1788 at Nootka Sound, there to boast unreasonably about their every exploit and success. To counter Meares's inflated talk of the vast number of pelts he had obtained, Gray embellished native conjecture that Nootka was on a large island by declaring himself the first to sail through the inside passage. Meares gave yet more credence to this yarn by publishing in London an account of the discovery, complete with a crude map credited to Gray.

The current object of Gray's interest was a large river immediately to the southward, which George had noted as he sailed past its mouth the previous day but declined to explore, for his instructions required only that he chart such rivers as were navigable by his ships. Gray complained of having spent the past nine days trying in vain to enter this river, so strong was its reflux over a wide range of shallows. This proved, to George's mind, the correctness of his assessment. Gray had been dogged in his attempts to enter the river because he believed large numbers of Indians lived along its banks, which would provide him with a rich new source of furs for the China market.

Gray confessed he was no longer a popular fellow with the

Nootka-speaking tribes, and if George was not disposed to think very highly of him for his boastful deceits, then he positively disliked him upon learning the reasons he had worn out his welcome to the northward. Gray sent a warning to George to be mindful of the Indians, who were, he said, a sorry lot given to every dangerous trickery. To illustrate his point, he told of his encounter with the Indians of Clayoquot Sound, the next inlet southward of Nootka Sound. He wintered there in late 1788, and all appeared peaceful while he and his men built a small ship. The chief of the district, however, conspired to capture the *Columbia*, which Gray learned about early enough to foil the plan completely. To punish the Indians, he had his men burn their village, which he claimed to have been a work of ages, the finest of the Nootka nation.

George had no mind to dally in the company of such a heartless liar; quickly and without ceremony, he parted for the northward. Gray was so suspicious of the *Discovery* and *Chatham* as rivals in trade, he followed the vessels northward until they entered the Strait of Juan de Fuca, the exploration of which George had claimed to be his sole objective.

While Gray kept watch, Indians came off in some numbers to the ships, but George established no communication or trade with them. George took the opportunity to acquaint his company with a strict policy of not trading when in sight of any merchant vessel. Gray was soon satisfied that George did, indeed, command ships of discovery, not commerce, and he made off to the southward, to beat his way inland via the large river he was to name after his ship and claim for his young, expanding country.

George had second thoughts about passing up this outlet, for upon closer consideration of its latitude, he realized it might be the entrance thought by the Spanish to connect overland near to the Mississippi's headwaters. If it was in such flood as Gray described, there was likely a navigable channel by which to sail inland a considerable distance, and George now regretted that, if this were the case, the honour of first discovery would go to Mr. Gray and the United States of America. (The Spanish, who knew its approximate location, had surrendered any claim on two counts: first, by signing the Nootka Sound Convention; and second, by refusing to publish accounts of their discoveries and settlements[9], which precluded the establishment of reliable dates.) He had no time at present to correct his possible misjudgement, however. He would survey and chart the river when his summer's work was done to the northward, prior to making his way to the Sandwich Islands for the winter.

George's present object, the entrance to Juan de Fuca's 'fabled strait, lay before him, if any reliance could be placed upon Indians' stories and traders' boasts. It must fall just beyond Cape Flattery, named by Cook in 1778, where he had flattered himself he might find much needed anchorage to restore his ships and people, George among them. As thick weather prevented close scrutiny, Cook's two vessels continued northward. When the clouds eventually lifted, they found secure anchorage at the now-famous port of Nootka Sound. There, Cook and company spent a memorable month refurbishing their outfit, exploring the area, and trading for the sea-otter pelts that would, to their surprise, turn into gold at China.

Of Cape Flattery, Cook wrote, "It is in the very latitude... where geographers have placed the Strait of Juan de Fuca, but we saw nothing like it, nor is there the least probability that iver any such thing exhisted." He had a sixth sense for ascertaining geographic realities and puncturing geographic myths, but George was to prove over the next few months how wrong Cook was in this rare instance.

---

[9] Spain's long-held policy of secrecy dated back to the days of Sir Francis Drake, for he had read their accounts of the lucrative trade route between Mexico and Manila, to exchange gold for spices; he sailed to Pacific waters knowing exactly where to pluck the plums of Spanish commerce.

13
Beyond Cook's Flattery

In 1592, an adventurer named Juan de Fuca claimed to have discovered an inland sea between 47° and 48° north latitude on the western coast of the Americas. De Fuca was a Greek from Cephalonia, his real name being Apostolos Valerianos, who served 40 years as a mariner and pilot on Spanish vessels. His assertion regarding a possible Northwest Passage was much disputed during the intervening centuries, leaving George with no more reputable claim than de Fuca's own, made in 1596, when he told his tale to Michael Lok at Venice, Italy:

> ...the said Viceroy of Mexico sent him out againe Anno 1592, with a small Caravela, and a Pinnace...to follow the saide Voyage, for a discovery of the same Straits of Anian[10], and the passage thereof, into the Sea which they call the North Sea,

which is our North-west Sea. And that he followed his course in that Voyage West and North-west... untill he came to the Latitude of 47 degrees, and there finding that the land trended North and North-east, with a broad Inlet of Sea, between 47 and 48 degrees of Latitude, hee entered thereinto, sayling therein more than twentie dayes....

And that at the entrance of this said Strait, there is on the North-West coast thereof, a great Hedland or Iland, with an exceeding high Pinacle, or spired Rocke, like a piller thereupon.

And he also said, that he being entred thus farre into the said Strait, and being come into the North Sea already, and finding the Sea wide enough every whère... hee thought he had now well discharged his office, and done the thing he was sent to doe.

If there were such a passage, George expected to find a tall pinnacle to mark its entrance, but he saw no such noteworthy rock midst the many islands that dot those waters. His people pointed to this isle and that, claiming it to be de Fuca's famous pillar, but George failed to see what excited them. Third Lieutenant Joseph Baker and Mr. Menzies at last claimed to have seen the definitive structure, a singular island standing approximately 150 feet tall and 50 feet across. It had been visible for a few minutes only, and it lay closer to the mainland than anticipated—hardly the great landmark de Fuca claimed it to be, although George conceded that de Fuca's tiny vessels likely sailed much closer to the shoreline than the *Discovery* and *Chatham*, and, from that view, it may have loomed before him quite dramatically.

Past that point, there was no denying that a broad passage existed between 48° and 49° north latitude. George wondered why de Fuca had misplaced it by a full degree, when latitude measurements were relatively accurate by his time. Nonetheless, as de Fuca had

[10] Named by Sir Francis Drake in 1578, when he raided Spanish holdings on the Pacific coast of America. He boasted that his Strait of Anian *was* the Northwest Passage, but his intent was to intimidate the Spaniards with this claim, not to substantiate it. Drake perhaps explored as far northward as Cook's Cape Flattery, but no positive proof of this exists.

claimed, it led to a "very much broader sea than was at the said entrance, and that he passed by divers Illands in the Sayling."

George and his entire company were astonished by the grand vista that greeted them on the clear and pleasant morning of April 30th, when they sailed into Juan de Fuca's strait, a name George retained for the waterway. A gentle breeze billowed the sails above, while all around was majestically calm, as the ships skimmed over a glassy sea. So enchanted were the companies, they gaped in awe, moved to exclaim only in reverent whispers, when words came at all.

To the northeast, Lieutenant Baker descried a distant mountain, so lofty and white as to appear quite unreal, which George named in his honour. This was the first of several such lone and lovely peaks George named while reconnoitring the remarkable waterway he had just entered. He had known that the straight and compact northwest coastline broke up into uncounted inlets and islands north of Cape Flattery, but as he stood poised to begin the first of his detailed explorations, he had no inkling how complex and difficult his commission would be.

He was already firmly committed to working his young men hard during their summer surveying seasons, but he was unprepared for the extent to which the land itself would impose the greater challenge. Had he and his people known as much during the first, enthralling day they entered the labyrinth, their high spirits would have been tempered considerably. As it was, they had just opened the cover of a great book, and so compelling was the first page of the first chapter, all were eager to begin a close reading of its promised wonders.

The first order of business was to find a safe anchorage, that the ships and their men might renew themselves for the adventures ahead by watering, wooding, inspecting, repairing, and so forth. On May 2nd, both vessels sat snug in a bay George called Port Discovery, where, he was fully convinced, they were the first civilized people to land within the strait. They now stood upon the threshold of the very doorway by which they might attain everlasting fame for bringing an entirely new region to the world's attention.

As if the Fates smiled upon this exhilarating prospect, the weather continued to cooperate to the utmost, adding dimensions of pleasure and gratitude to those of awe and worthy ambition. The close and contentious days of Tahiti and the Sandwich Islands were swept clean from memory by the calm, cool solitude of lands that reminded all eyes of dear England when she had lain, in eons past, as a wild, virginal bride—a sleeping beauty awaiting civilizing husbandry.

During the next busy, lighthearted days, a few natives appeared, obviously closer in habits to the brute creatures of the wilderness than to the industrious Englishmen they cautiously approached. As proof of some ingenuity, they wore woollen garments of their own manufacture, apparently made principally from the hair of dogs they tended and sheared for that purpose. They readily traded their weapons and implements for knives, trinkets, etc., then, much to George's consternation, they offered to sell two children, each about six or seven years old, in exchange for a small sheet of copper. This he peremptorily forbade, expressing as best he could his great abhorrence of such traffic.

George later learned that Spanish traffic in young children was common, with some of their vessels carrying dozens of native boys and girls, all purportedly rescued from slavery and cannibalism. That cannibalism occurred within and between the various tribes George could not absolutely refute, but he had numerous opportunities throughout his explorations to share meals with native peoples, and, while they were often convinced that white men eat human flesh, his questions to them about eating such meat themselves invariably earned their vigorous disdain.

The Spaniards' universally renowned zeal for saving pagan souls compelled them to buy young Indians, that they might bring God's lost children into Christendom and potential salvation. They no doubt put their young charges to good use from day to day and, in some cases, throughout the night as well, thus perpetuating the slavery they professed to be stopping, but in the name of God this time, not a heathen chieftain's ease and pleasure.

In any case, George made clear his displeasure in human traffic and got on with the business of preparing three boats[11] to explore the surrounding shores. On May 7th, at five in the morning, he set out with one of three small parties (each comprised of officers, midshipmen, and seamen) to begin surveying the continental shore of northwest America. His intention was to become sufficiently knowledgeable about the region that he might further reconnoitre it aboard the refitted *Discovery* and *Chatham*.

They carried provisions enough for five days, and, as the weather was pleasant during that time, they travelled in relative comfort and ease. To George's chagrin, he soon discovered that they had entered a maze of islands and inlets to either side of a waterway he named Admiralty Inlet, which frustrated their progress. Their enjoyment of fresh provisions and the pristine beauty that greeted their every twist and turn provided a measure of compensation for their difficulties.

The land was not entirely an innocent paradise, as evidenced by the discovery of two tall, rudely carved upright poles, each bearing a human head, recently placed there. The hair and flesh were nearly perfect, but they were thrust upon the poles with such force, pieces of cranial bones and scalp were borne some inches above the rest of the skull. No native people came forth, and no clues were found to explain the macabre scene.

As the morning of the sixth day dawned, provisions were exhausted, and all hands were much affected by their strange and savage surroundings. An ominous silence enveloped them, broken only by the croaking of ravens, the bark of seals, the screaming of eagles, and the sinister rustling of the wind through giant, creaking trees. Mosquitoes and sand flies pestered them mercilessly, yet George would not lead his men whimpering back to the ships, like

---

[11] By the 1770's the number of boats carried by a ship-of-the-line had increased to six: launch, barge, pinnace, yawl and two cutters of different lengths. They ranged from approximately 16 to 26 feet in length and were rigged with one to three masts, depending on the boat size and function. Vancouver's favourite boat was the *Discovery*'s beamy, three-masted yawl, which was 25 feet long, rigged with a lug sail and rowed double-banked with eight oars, four to a side, with two rowers sharing each thwart.

children crying for their mother, when so much work remained to do. He resolved to continue despite their privations, and continue they did for another three days, until continual rain set in, obscuring the land under cloud and fog.

When the three boats belatedly returned to the ships, their waiting shipmates had grown anxious for their safety, having imagined all manner of gruesome endings for them. They expressed welcome relief that nothing untoward had happened, while the returning parties were equally relieved to find the ships in good order, nearly ready to sail.

Not all reports regarding the ships and their people served to warm George's heart, however, for his apprehensions of leaving them to Broughton's care had proven well founded. Broughton reluctantly reported that the *Discovery*'s binnacle glass had been broken—although quite by accident. When pressed, Broughton revealed that Pitt had caused this misfortune, but it could have befallen any number of the midshipmen. George was instantly in a rage. What did Broughton mean? That so many midshipmen were cavorting about the quarterdeck recklessly, any one of them could have done the damage? That was no defense, but a worse indictment!

George summoned Pitt forthwith, and the cocky young man readily confessed to his crime—for the willful destruction of a vital piece of ship's equipment *is* a crime—with not one whit of contrition evident in his words or manner. He had been romping with another midshipman and yes, it was he and he alone who had caused the binnacle glass to break.

The first order of business was to identify the other midshipman, for whom George guessed Pitt might be taking the blame, which was somewhat noble, but insufficient to protect him from receiving just punishment. In short order, the Honourable Charles Stuart, 16-year-old son of the old Earl of Bute, was implicated as the attending party, which further annoyed George, for Stuart served aboard the *Chatham* and had no business romping about any part of the *Discovery*.

Upon questioning Stuart, George readily discerned that the lad was more interested in avoiding the shame of a flogging than matching Pitt's 'nobility' and taking equal share of the blame. Stuart was a decent enough young fellow, lacking Pitt's hardheaded ways. His father was an old man, then nearing 80 years; in fact, unknown to Stuart, his father had died that very spring.

Bute had been the king's oldest and dearest friend, and though George did not shy from punishing his young gentlemen and seamen as they deserved, to whip Bute's son based on any but incontestable evidence would have been foolhardy indeed. Stuart's punishment, therefore, was a visit to the masthead for a prescribed time, a place by now familiar to him, for he had had his share of questionable little misadventures. Whatever injustices Stuart felt he suffered by going there, he never said, for he bore this punishment with patience and dignity.

Pitt alone was culpable. If George's first lengthy absence from the ships was taken by Pitt and his young followers as an opportunity to cavort without restriction, George shuddered to think what worse damage might occur in the future, for doubtless there would be many more surveying expeditions in the months to come. He must make the supremacy of his rules and orders well known. Swift, hard punishment was the only answer, and punish Pitt he did, with another flogging in the cabin, exactly as before.

From henceforward, George decreed that there be no communication between midshipmen on separate ships when he was absent on surveying expeditions. They were welcome on each other's vessels only by invitation, that George might continue his habit of dining, on a rotational basis, with each of his young officers-in-training, as he had done since first sailing.

Unfortunately, so influential was Pitt among his peers, and so aggrieved were they by Pitt's second flogging, all but one declined George's future invitations to share his table. Young John Sykes alone, son of George's London agent, continued to follow his own advice and sup as he saw fit. George was wounded by his young gentlemen's misplaced loyalty to Pitt, for good officers are as much made by the informal lessons enjoyably taught over a pleasant meal as they are by formal lessons taken above and below deck.

Quite apart from the furore of Pitt's second flogging, there was much for the reunited boat parties and ships' people to discuss, most particularly their encounters with native inhabitants, both living and dead. Of the many dozen living inhabitants encountered, all hands were impressed with the poverty of their circumstances. Most Englishmen were quick to condemn and despise, applying no further thought to their prejudices. George was not enamoured of the Indians' filthy, squalid habits, but he was never one to dismiss out of hand. He gave deep and measured consideration to the bestial state of the native peoples in a beauteous, bounteous land.

George was particularly concerned with the numbers of Indians who bore smallpox scars, which eloquently bespoke the ravages of this European disease. The survivors appeared to be in deep decline. So poorly did they tend to themselves and their crude homes, their villages were characterized by an overgrowth of weeds and by a repulsive stench. The effort needed to relieve themselves in the woods or nearby streams seemed so great to make, they lived dispiritedly in unspeakably fetid conditions.

Pride and decency were not lacking entirely, and George found them to be courteous and honest during trading encounters. The women, in particular, were shy and chaste, as George had recalled their Nootka neighbours to be. They were not by physique or dress considered attractive to the English eye, yet they suffered numerous attacks of gallantry made on them by the sailors. The greater contrast between them and the Sandwich Islanders was not in beauty, however, but in behaviour, for solicitations of their tender affections shocked their modesty to such a degree, many of them burst into tears. Further, some even endeavoured to hide themselves in the bottom of their canoes, where they crouched in an extreme state of uneasiness and distress.

George was not pleased with reports of such assaults upon the sensibilities of the native women, but he was pleased nonetheless that his men would have no easy time forming attachments or introducing venereal diseases to the fair sex upon those lengthy shores—and not by his prohibitions, but by the ladies themselves.

As for dead Indians, the severed heads on pikes were far from the only evidence of the natives' mortality. Numerous corpses and bones were found throughout the land: in the woods and meadows, shallowly interred; in the trees, hung in canoes and baskets (these latter likely the final resting places of royalty); on the beaches, littered about, some partially buried, some dismembered and strewn promiscuously, many more poorly cremated in fires.

Menzies chided George for his supposed obsession with the subject of Indian depopulation, which appeared obvious to George, from Tahiti to this desolate shore. Menzies asserted that he had been on the northwest coast and at the Sandwich Islands four years previously, and he noticed no change whatever. He contended that the Indians were merely nomads, migrating seasonally and abandoning their encampments when they became too fouled and infested for even the beastliest savage to tolerate.

George was not convinced by this argument, but he did not argue his case with Menzies. Migration, firearms, and disease likely all played a role, which only proper study by trained scientists would disclose. Officially, he suspended his judgement as best he could and made note of what he saw. In private, he contrasted his present impressions with those formed 15 years previously, and he seriously doubted that the present marks of depopulation were more apparent than real. Time would tell—if it were not too late.

On May 18th, the ships sailed through Admiralty Inlet, and, over the next three weeks, they made a thorough examination of a remarkable and intricate waterway that stretched southward nearly a hundred miles. George honoured his tireless second mate by naming the inner waters of the inlet Puget's Sound, and he named other features principally in honour of great patriots and worthy patrons.

George guessed that Puget's Sound was but the first of many, many convoluted waterways they would encounter. He was, therefore, "thoroughly convinced, that our boats alone could enable us to acquire any correct or satisfactory information respecting this broken country; and although the execution of such a service in open boats would necessarily be extremely laborious, and expose those so employed to numberless dangers and unpleasant situations, that might occasionally produce great fatigue, and protract their return to the ships; yet that mode was undoubtedly the most accurate, the most ready, and indeed the only one in our power to pursue for ascertaining the continental boundary."

This observation and determination is worthy of quotation, for George never wavered from the correctness of this assessment. To his dying breath, he knew that by the method he chose[12], he had completed a survey of a magnitude and accuracy unequalled in all history—and never to be duplicated, for there does not exist in the world another uncharted stretch of coastline so extensive, so complex, or so fraught with navigational dangers.

As George was so thoroughly familiar with the means by which he surveyed thousands of miles of intricate coastline, he thought no more of describing his methodology than explaining how one rows a boat. For the uninitiated, however, questions abound. Alas, little was said and less was written about this aspect of the voyage, hence the general reader can only surmise the basic pattern by which George completed his grand undertaking.

The *Discovery* and *Chatham* found shelter at an anchorage that offered wood, water, and suitable ground for setting up the observatory and making spruce beer. From there, one or two boat parties set forth to explore the adjacent continental shore. Each party consisted of two boats, each manned by an officer, a midshipman or two, some marines, and a rowing crew; each was armed with swivels, muskets, small arms, and sporting pieces. They were provisioned for ten days to a fortnight, and they carried a generous variety of trade goods and gifts for encounters with native peoples.

They worked from four past midnight till dusk, taking their meals through the day during short landfalls, cooking only when ashore for the night. The men usually slept in tents and the officers in mar-

---

[12] There is no evidence that Vancouver received either surveying instructions or the special book of record, suggested by Sir Joseph Banks to the Admiralty, in which he was to record latitude, longitude, bearing of headlands, height, direction, and course of tides and currents, depths and soundings of the sea, shoals, rocks, etc. He probably used the 8th edition of *The Practical Navigator and Seaman's Assistant*, by John Hamilton Moore, published in 1784, although he was guided chiefly by his own experience with Cook and later with Whidbey in the West Indies.

quees, although they occasionally slept together in the boats—a detested ordeal.

The purpose of landing was to take bearings, which they did as often as occasion required and allowed. The commanding officers of each boat party—most often Joseph Whidbey and James Johnstone—made sketches as they proceeded, which they gave to Lieutenant Baker upon returning to the ships. He added their findings to a fair sheet, from which the final chart was composed.

George's own keen observations and orchestrations ensured that the quality and quantity of the boat surveys never fell below his exacting standards. He kept copious notes of every navigational point of interest, for his reputation, and his alone, rested on the perfection of his company's work.

We may thank Providence that the results of George's great survey exist complete and intact, published many times over as the master chart of his vast explorations. Fortunately, also, he included some of his chronometrical and astrological observations—vital to ascertaining the accuracy of his survey—in his printed journal, for the bulk of these fundamental notations have disappeared. We may thank the Devil and his earthly helpers for this inestimable loss to the science of navigation; 'tis a sad world, indeed, where petty politics eclipse the advance of knowledge, but there you have it: another vanishment for which we might all weep.

By Sunday, June 3rd, the ships had worked their way to the bottom of the sound and back up it, and both had come to anchor in a comfortable port. To reward his weary people for their exertions, George declared a well-deserved holiday, with a double allowance of grog for the purposes of toasting King George III's birthday. While ashore, he took possession for king and country, calling this portion of the waterway Possession Sound and the whole of it the Gulf of Georgia [now Strait of Georgia].

The Honourable Charles Stuart imbibed rather too much grog that day, drinking excessively to the health of the king, perhaps attempting to impress George with the inviolability of this connection, regardless of the quality of his service. No doubt also playing on his mind was Pitt's recent punishment, recalled anew by the flogging the previous day of a seaman from the *Chatham*, who earned three dozen lashes for negligence of duty. (The man had announced fake soundings, in consequence of which the vessel grounded. Fortunately, the bottom was soft, and she floated free unharmed, but had the bottom been rocky, she could have suffered serious damage.)

With all present at the day's celebration, the very drunken Stuart took a razor from his waistcoat pocket and, showing it to George, said, "Sir, if you ever flog me, I will not survive the disgrace. I have this ready to cut my throat with." George did not doubt Stuart's sincerity, and he cursed the anguish Pitt caused his so-called friends. Heaven help anyone who became Pitt's enemy—a fate George would come to know only too well.

On June 5th, the *Discovery* and *Chatham* sailed clear of Possession Sound, having taken nearly six weeks to advance not one degree northward since entering the Strait of Juan de Fuca. With nearly 15° latitude of coastline yet before them to survey and chart over two or three summers, all rumoured to be equally labyrinthine, George felt hard pressed to make the most of each day. So much remained to do before making for Nootka Sound, there to meet the *Daedalus* and to play out his diplomatic role.

14
Spanish Company

On June 6th, George passed the northwest point of Admiralty Inlet, which is characterized by a high, white, sandy cliff, with verdant lawns on either side of it. He named this lovely spot Point Partridge, to commemorate dear Martha's maiden name—a touching gesture that shows his thoughts were often close to home, however far he sailed.

Captain Broughton proposed that the ships' next rendezvous be at Strawberry Bay [on Cypress Island], which he had scouted by boat, named, and declared to be a commodious and safe harbour for the ships to moor while the boats surveyed the continental shore. He promised a good supply of fish there as well.

George arrived first and put his ship in with little difficulty, although the bay was greatly exposed to the winds and sea. Alas, the approach proved so treacherous that Broughton lost a stream anchor—the only one he carried—when he attempted to gain anchorage, to George's high annoyance. Moreover, when George set his men to fishing, they repeatedly hauled the seine to no effect. From foolish antics ashore to damnably foolish negligence aboard ship, combined with unreliable powers of observation, was there no end to Broughton's carelessness?

Apparently not, for the next day he requested of George some oil for painting the *Chatham*, since he lacked sufficient of a single colour to complete the work. George said no. When the vessel left England, she carried enough for the purpose, hence the shortage was yet another case of Broughton's mismanagement. He would have to make do.

There was much grumbling among the *Chatham*'s people about George's meanness when they set to 'making do', which meant leaving one side of the vessel yellow and painting the other half black. George little cared what they thought, but in retrospect, while preparing his journal for publication, he was forced to consider all the events, major and minor, that coalesced into unforgiving hatred by Camelford and his supporters. Every measure George took to protect the expedition and to punish offences that might scuttle it was seen as petty, petulant, stingy, and unjust. The painting incident was just one of many.

By June 11th, the ships advanced northeastward to a large, pleasant, and safe port, which George later named Birch Bay. The following daybreak, George set out aboard one of two surveying boats, each provisioned for a week. Six days later, they were 114 miles north of the ships, having explored nearly every inlet and outlet of the continental shore. George bequeathed dozens of names to prominent features, from Point Grey to Point Atkinson, from Howe's Sound to Jervis's Inlet, thus honouring good friends and great Britons alike along their arduous, dreary way.

George was impressed in a melancholy way by the countryside, much of which rose up before him to stupendous, foreboding heights, cloaked in dismal, gloomy forests from shoreline to snowy peaks. The weather continued serene for the most part, but this did little to counter the oppressive loneliness he and his people felt, surrounded by a monstrous, silent wilderness.

They encountered Indians occasionally, but they lived so close to nature's ways, they did nothing to alter the Englishmen's sense of alienation, which increased as the boat parties rowed ever farther from their snug little vessels. On the morning of June 19th, when they set out at their usual hour of four in the morning, George directed them to take a welcome southerly course, heading back to the ships. They rowed so eagerly that by evening, George estimated they were 84 miles from 'home'.

Not only did they start each surveying day at daybreak, but they rowed till the last glow of twilight faded. Thus, they continued after their evening meal on the 19th, with Lieutenant Puget joining George, leaving Thomas Manby, master's mate, in charge of his own boat. As usual, George kept his boat to the continental shore, a position he had so consistently taken, he thought it no longer bore mention.

As darkness fell, Manby lagged behind George's boat and eventually lost sight of it. Rather than stay by the continental shore, Manby followed the channel by which Puget's boat had entered Jervis's Inlet, which lay separate from the mainland. He had no compass, no food, and only a musket for protection and hunting. George had no idea where to look for him, so riddled with islands and inlets was every part of that vast waterway. They could play an endless game of wild goose chase there, with nothing to be gained for it and a great deal to be lost, hence George continued as planned, heading toward the ships.

Three days later, they still had not reunited. June 22nd marked George's 35th birthday, unbeknownst to his people. He contented himself with thoughts of a hearty breakfast ashore at Point Grey, a prominent headland where he had some hope that Manby's boat might readily see and join them—a perfect gift to alleviate his concern for their well-being.

As they rowed southward toward Point Grey, George was astonished to descry not the launch, as he had hoped, but two small vessels anchored near the tip of the point. He would have company, and plenty of it, for his little private celebration! The ships, each no longer than 50 feet, raised Spanish war colours. In short order, George met Señor Dionisio Galiano of the *Sutil* brig and Señor Cayetano Valdés of the *Mexicana* schooner.

Fortunately, Señor Galiano spoke passable English; had he not, little would have been learned from one another, for no one else spoke the other's language. He informed George that they had sailed from Acapulco, Mexico, for purposes of exploration. They had made their way first to Nootka Sound, which they had quit 17 days earlier, and they had entered the Strait of Juan de Fuca by the same route George's vessels had taken. They spoke to Broughton, in charge of the *Discovery* and *Chatham*, on their way northward, hence they were expecting to meet George's boat parties.

George, on the other hand, was greatly surprised, and he "experienced no small degree of mortification"—his own words, and perfectly put—when he was informed that two Spanish ships, under Quimper in 1790 and Eliza in 1791, had reconnoitred the exact same waters he had just quit and that Eliza had sailed a short distance beyond his turnaround point. When they compared charts, there was no disputing this claim. Further, Quimper and Eliza had even used Discovery Bay to refit, exactly as the *Discovery* and *Chatham* had done.

For all George's efforts to date, nothing new regarding the Northwest Passage had been discovered—a tremendous disappointment. Puget's Sound was impressive, of course, but led nowhere. George's only other claim was that his charts were obviously far superior to those the Spaniards had produced, and in that, he took some comfort. They also had not sailed through the strait and around the great island to the west; George could still be the first to do so, and he strengthened his resolve to that end.

Galiano informed George that the Spanish emissary to Nootka Sound, Commandant Don Juan de la Bodega y Quadra, had made that port late in April and anxiously awaited George's arrival, that they might negotiate the restoration of the disputed territories to the British Crown. Pressure was upon George to finish surveying for the season and get on with his diplomatic mission, but he refused to be rushed. He would not give up a single day of exploring during the short summer season to undertake what he guessed would be an impossible task at Nootka, due to the hasty, half-baked instructions he had received just before leaving England. He very much hoped that the *Daedalus* carried some definitive directions for the Nootka settlement, but Galiano said this vessel had not yet made Nootka. That being the case, and the survey taking precedence, Señor Quadra would simply have to wait.

Galiano and Valdés were polite, friendly, and obliging to George, providing pleasant company for his birthday breakfast. Better, he thought, to have fallen in with refined explorers than ruffian fur-traders, regardless of their nationality and the tidings they brought. Before parting ways that day, they agreed to George's suggestion that they explore farther northward together, rendezvousing in the gulf between Point Roberts and Burrard's Channel [Burrard Inlet], as George had named these two prominent features after Navy friends of old.

By midmorning of June 23rd, George returned to his vessels, which sat very prettily in the waters of Birch Bay. A welcome sight they were, a port that his people later agreed was the most pleasant along the entire coast. George was much relieved to see the *Discovery*'s launch as well, meaning that Manby and crew had arrived before them. Better yet, all of them were well and little the worse for wear.

Manby was not relieved to see George. He was fuming with anger pent up over the difficult days and nights he and his people had suffered on their return to the ships. George was astonished! He was also exhausted, for he and his boats had covered upwards of 330 miles in the course of 11 days—a commendable feat for healthy young men, and a remarkable trial for George, who was never fully well at any time throughout the voyage. How dare Manby accuse him of deliberately rowing out of sight, leaving him without a compass or provisions! No compass? Was he not put in charge, made responsible for ensuring he had all necessary equipment? And hungry? Yes, they all were hungry, damned hungry. They would have to conserve their provisions better and become more proficient at finding wild food.

Manby complained of the voracious feed of mussels he and his people had eaten for an evening meal, immediately after which they became violently ill, saving themselves only by repeated disgorgements until the nausea and fever passed. George returned that it was damned foolish to make a Roman feast of unfamiliar foods, containing God-knows-what poisons.

But mussels are a very familiar food, Manby protested. With that, George fairly exploded in anger, pointing out to Manby that nothing, absolutely nothing, was familiar upon these strange shores and nothing, absolutely nothing, should be taken for granted there!

Manby dared counter, that did not George take for granted that he knew the route by which the lead boat would disappear into the night? Yes, by God, George's boat would always follow the continental shore, as best he could, and none would now forget it! George grew so incensed at Manby's insolence, he spit out every epithet he knew to describe an impertinent fool. He was determined that such a worrisome, needless separation should never again happen, staging a show of complete fury to impress upon all his people the seriousness of his intent. Manby took great offense and, from that day thence, closely nursed his resentment of George, not understanding that George, like a scolding parent, was acting out of benevolence, not malice.

George's extreme anger and foul language in this and other instances were not entirely justifiable, however. It must be noted that ill health continued to plague him, and when he was near to collapsing from exhaustion, he lost control of his temper with terrible ease. This distressed him further, thus aggravating his condition and compounding his frustrations, until he ranted like a man possessed.

This is written with great sadness, for one wishes, when singing the praises of a great man, to show the unquestioned correctness of his every action. Alas, this cannot be done in George's case, for he suffered from an increasingly debilitating condition and, as the disease progressed, he occasionally fell far below the exacting standards he set for himself as a rational and reasonable man.

To worsen matters, George was much too stubborn and proud ever to apologize, even in private. He was also fearful of showing any weakness—of health or of character—for he knew that some aboard his ships would twist it to their every advantage and his every disadvantage. Thus, Manby now numbered among those who felt deeply wounded by George, and George could only hope that future service together would slowly ease the tension between them and eventually erase Manby's anger. Neither would forget this incident, but George was ever ready to forgive. Manby was a good hand and a good man; in time, he might understand and forgive.

There were too many such as Pitt fanning the flames of hatred, however. Manby did not stand a chance to let bygones be bygones, hence George did not stand a chance to let time heal the rifts. Worse, he could not control his temperamental outbursts, and he could not educate his people sufficiently to keep them from doing things that drove him to distraction. It was a recipe for disaster at every turn, and greatly to George's credit, he managed well enough to bring home the most splendid piece of surveying and charting ever done, anywhere or by anyone, and he kept more men alive aboard his ships than would have survived had they lived those years as landsmen in England.

Thirty-five years old he was that June, with less than six years left to live and much, much more left to do. Poor health kept him in continual fear that his work would outstrip his days. If only Pitt, Mudge, Broughton, Stuart, Manby, and their ilk could have understood how this black dog hounded George. Would they have cared? Would anything have turned out differently aboard ship? Or would Pitt simply have moved in sooner for the kill?

15
The Inside Passage

The *Discovery* and *Chatham* joined the *Sutil* and *Mexicana* on Midsummer Day [June 24th], and they sailed directly to the turnaround point of George's recent explorations, there to continue their northward survey. The landscape continued to impress George with its stupendous and empty aspect; he sprinkled his journal pages liberally with such words as dreary, forlorn, gloomy, silent, deserted, and so forth. Desolation Sound was the name he chose for the wide basin immediately northward of Jervis's Inlet.

The English and Spanish companies collaborated well together, with George taking all surveys of the continental shore, for his charts had to be correct in this regard and verifiably so. His purpose was to show conclusively the existence or, as he suspected, the nonexistence of the Northwest Passage, and he would take no expedition's evidence but his own. The responsibility was his, and he hoped the renown would be too—if he lived long enough to earn it and to enjoy it.

As they progressed northward, they saw many whales, which increased their certainty that the Gulf of Georgia connected with Queen Charlotte's Sound [Queen Charlotte Strait], so named by an English fur-trader in 1786. George kept the name, for it would be a perfect union of waters, just as King George and Queen Charlotte had been blessed with a long and faithful union of marriage.

George and his people also noted an impressive rise and fall of the tide, which more than once flooded their shore camps, washing the men out of their beds and deep slumbers. This unpleasant circumstance could have only one pleasant outcome: they would sail clear through to northern Pacific waters, saving them a long and tedious return journey via the Strait of Juan de Fuca.

Beyond Bute's Inlet, with Stuart Island at its mouth, lay the narrowest, most dangerous riddle of passageways yet encountered. The Spaniards parted ways with the Englishmen thereabouts, on July 13th, for they wished to continue northward by their own route. Following an exchange of good wishes and expressions of mutual satisfaction, Galiano assured George that a cordial reception awaited him at Nootka Sound, where all had been put in the highest order of readiness for delivery into British possession.

Several days later, George visited a large native village at which muskets were common possessions, having been bartered from Nootka natives. The Indians discharged their pieces without hostile intent, and the chief was hospitable. His people were anxious to trade with their unexpected guests—their first opportunity to obtain, first-hand, civilized man's much coveted domestic articles. George, of course, would permit no exchange for firearms or ammunition. In return, George's people took more than 200 sea-otter pelts, which they hoped to send by fur-trading vessel to China and eventually reap a tidy profit for their small efforts.

Strange to say, the greed that motivated some of George's company to collect pelts with unseemly passion was then rumoured to motivate George also. Naturally, he took furs in payment for the goods he offered, but he was not intent upon stockpiling any large number, as was thought by his critics. His people continued to impute great miserliness to him in meting out the ships' stores, that he might make a profit as purser, and they likewise accused him of avariciously acquiring furs, that he might further increase his fortunes at their expense.

What a miserable lie this was! What a nasty assault upon his character, for though he was necessarily thrifty on a voyage of such long duration, he had lived a wholly impecunious life in the king's service and had no want, whatever, to do otherwise. Royal Navy captains made less than £100 per year; most merchant captains made above £500, and many made thousands. Clearly, had profits motivated George in the least, he would not have chosen naval service, and most particularly not peaceful naval service far from civilized waters, where there was no chance of enriching himself by capturing enemy vessels as prizes of war.

Here again, an innocent and honest action on George's part was deliberately misconstrued, that his reputation might be further tarnished. He was powerless to redress the rumours—and too proud, besides, for he would not stoop to countenance or counter any malicious whisperings, which would have conferred a certain legitimacy by recognition and protest. From George's silence, Pitt's deluded case against him continued to mount.

Fur-trading success in those dangerous, uncharted waters was the least of George's concerns. Navigational success was his absolute priority, so difficult were the passageways closest to the continental shore. With clear weather, advance boat parties, and constant soundings from the ship, he had every hope of guiding his vessels through the narrow, rocky gauntlet that stretched before them, working the sails with a precision his people had never before attempted. George's ship turned and tacked exactly as he bid her; his abilities in this regard were second to none in the entire Royal Navy.

George was severely distressed, therefore, when the *Discovery* hit a bed of sunken rocks at four o'clock in the afternoon of August 6th. How had this happened? That morning, a thick fog and absolute calm had greeted them, and no soundings could be gained. The ship was at the mercy of the currents and tides. By noon, the fog had dispersed somewhat, and George chose to continue tracing the continental shore aboard ship, rather than sending the boats out ahead. He foresaw a tricky bit of sailing, but with utmost attention, he expected to avoid every danger.

Alas, he had misjudged! The tide was near flood, meaning it would take many long, harrowing hours to reach full ebb, at which time the *Discovery* would be perched, very perilously, high upon the rocks—if she did not fall off entirely. Instantly, every effort was made to heave her free, assisted by the *Chatham*'s boats, but to no avail. After half an hour, she fell, with a terrible crash, onto her starboard side. George had the yards and masts struck to keep her from tumbling farther. In this increasingly stressful situation, the best George could do was to have her shored up with bracing timbers, then wait and hope—that the braces would hold and that the high tide would float her free.

By eight o'clock that evening, an hour before low water, the *Discovery*'s head slipped off and, as Mr. Puget so aptly wrote, "it was then thought all was over, & that she would immediately upset but providentially the Shores of a projecting rock . . . brought her timely up." By nine o'clock, the *Discovery*'s head end was just barely in the water.

Slowly, oh so slowly, the tide rose and righted the little *Discovery*, and, at two past midnight of August 7th, she washed off her rock without apparent injury. Imagine, then, the hearty cheers and heady sighs that accompanied this blessing!

By noon, the hold was restowed, and the sky cleared sufficiently for George to ascertain the latitude of his near-disaster: 50° 55′ [likely near Ghost Island in Richards Channel]. He determined to continue up the narrow, dangerous channel, there being no other or better route by which to keep with the continental shore. In this tense situation, she proceeded until five o'clock, when she made somewhat wider, deeper waters. George would not breathe easily, however, until the *Chatham* completed the gauntlet and joined his vessel from astern.

George's worst fears were soon realized. The *Chatham* fired a distress signal to announce her precarious position aground on a ledge of sunken rocks. After an exhausting and anxious night spent freeing the *Discovery*, the prospect of another long night of calamity was nigh unbearable. Fortunately, the *Chatham* suffered no initial damage, and her trial could not be of long duration, as the tide was nearly at half ebb when she struck. But would she float off unharmed? Only time would tell.

A thick and gloomy fog ushered in the morning of the 8th, completely obscuring the *Chatham* from view. George remained in a most painful state of suspense until about nine in the forenoon, when he had the satisfaction of seeing her loom through the lifting fog, under sail and ready to proceed in consort through the channel.

What luck they had! Both vessels could have been lost and the expedition sunk, yet each had floated free without harm. It was a sobering lesson for George. He could not berate Broughton for sloppy navigation, for he had suffered the first and worst predicament. George was humbled, and he won little sympathy for it.

Since leaving England, he had suffered great and continuing anxiety about the safety of his vessels and people; now he was plagued by vivid, recurring memories of the bone-jarring thud the ship made when striking bottom, followed by groans and cracks from complaining timbers as the hull rose from the water, sagging under her own ponderous weight, punctuated by the most horrid crashes when twice she fell.

The *Discovery* and *Chatham* continued northward to approximately 51° 30′, where they put in at Safety Cove on Calvert's Island, a convenient and aptly named retreat, from which boat parties could reconnoitre the continental shores. The good weather that had attended their expeditions from first making the northwest coast now gave way to uninterrupted cold grey wetness, delivered by varying mixtures of fog and rain. George explored "as desolate, inhospitable a country as the most melancholy creature could be desirous of inhabiting."

His surroundings perfectly matched and magnified his own despondent state. The season for effective surveying and charting was done. At midnight of August 14th, George and his extremely exhausted boat party returned to the ships, where they waited for the remaining two boat parties to come back from what would be the last surveying expedition of the summer.

On August 17th, a brig came into view and raised dear England's colours—a welcome sight! The *Venus*, Captain Henry Shephard, greeted George with good news: the *Daedalus* was in port at Nootka. George was relieved and heartened, but for a moment only, for Shephard brought terrible news too. Three of the *Daedalus*'s company had been senselessly slaughtered at Oahu: Lieutenant Richard Hergest, the ship's agent; William Gooch, the astronomer destined to join the *Discovery*; and a Portuguese seaman. George was stunned and much aggrieved: Hergest had been an unequalled friend for many years; Gooch was an important, eagerly awaited addition to the expedition.

George was furious, too, that his people had dared to ridicule him for his suspicions that mortal danger lurked about every Sandwich Island. Now they would understand his fears and appreciate his caution, but what a ghastly price to pay for this lesson. Damn! Hergest and Gooch dead! George instantly resolved to bring justice to the perpetrators of this dastardly crime when he returned to Oahu the coming winter, to teach both his own people and all the Sandwich Islanders something about the price of innocent misjudgement and murderous folly.

The next day, both boat parties returned to the vessels, very tired and discouraged by hostile climes, boisterous seas, and forbidding shores. What happiness they experienced upon learning that they were making forthwith for Nootka was tempered by news of the unprovoked murders at Oahu.

As the ships got underway from Safety Cove on August 19th, the weather cleared briefly, adding a little sunshine to their mixed feelings of satisfaction for a job well done and weary melancholy engendered by desolate surroundings, topped with horror and grief over the bloody news from their winter paradise. George's still-hoped-for achievement of outstripping Galiano and Valdés in the race to prove the insularity of the huge island upon which Nootka sat brought little joyous forethought. What mattered now was that Nootka's relatively safe shores were in the offing, and that the *Daedalus* awaited their welcome company, on this vast, forlorn rim of the known world.

16

The Island of Quadra
and Vancouver

The great island on which Nootka sat required a name, which provided George with a pretty puzzle for several weeks. Mr. Menzies meddlesomely gossiped that it must be named for the king, especially since King George's Sound, named by Captain Cook, was now universally known as Nootka Sound. There was some merit to his argument, but it was also presumptuous and polemical. George had named a vast tract of land on the southern coast of New Holland after the king, and the Gulf of Georgia now bore his name. Dear God, was there to be some kingly reference every few leagues? Worse, such a name might infuriate the Spanish, who, when push recently came to shove, had already ceded a great deal to Great

Britain. No, George would name the island as he saw fit, be damned what Menzies thought!

The outer coast of the island required only cursory surveying, since George had just proven it separate from the continental shore. Ever the mapmaker, however, he sailed as close to the land as prudence allowed, and he plotted what he could make of it whenever the fog lifted and the rains lightened. He recognized certain features such as Cape Scott and Cox's Island from the ill-made maps of the first two English fur-trading ventures upon that rugged coast. With some pleasure, he sighted the prominent headland Captain Cook had called Woody Point [now Cape Cook], which signalled that he was once again sailing in the old man's wake.

Cook had named only a handful of major features along the shore as he searched for a safe harbour, an honour that fell by chance to Nootka Sound. Had the weather cleared a day earlier or a day later, another port would have shown itself to be adequate, so blessed was this land with bays and inlets to serve every need. Nootka was now firmly etched upon the world map, as dozens of vessels plied their way to her door. What a legacy Cook had left, when all he sought was a place to wood, water, and fix his longitude.

What difficulties Cook had left too, for he and subsequent English venturers presumed they had the right to make port wherever they chose north of San Francisco, Spain's northernmost settlement. Cook's company also inadvertently discovered the potential of the fur trade with China, which was certain to interest informed merchants of all nations. Cook's journal, published in 1784, triggered the race for northwestern shores. It was then merely a matter of time before the prime contenders for Nootka's riches came to blows over whose flag should fly there.

When George made Nootka Sound under clear skies on August 28th, Spain's red and gold colours waved high over the principal anchorage at Friendly Cove. On the promontory sat numerous Spanish buildings (where once the Indians had built their summer village), complete with gardens, livestock compounds, and other signs of domesticity. The Spanish brig *Activa* stood in the roads, bearing the broad pennant of Don Juan Francisco de la Bodega y

Quadra, commandant of New Spain's principal naval port at San Blas. The *Chatham* and *Daedalus* were also at anchor, in company with a small English fur-trading vessel, presenting in total a tranquil, civilized, and most welcome sight for the weary sailors.

The *Discovery* and the *Activa* exchanged a 13-gun salute, then George went ashore to meet his Spanish host. Señor Bodega y Quadra instantly showed himself to be a gentleman of rare intelligence, refinement, and generosity. George knew something of his past record from a recent translation of his narrative regarding his explorations of 1775, which revealed a man possessing great courage and stamina as well.

In that year, Señor Quadra (as he wished to be addressed, by the unusual choice of his mother's family name) had sailed on a voyage of discovery northward of Nootka Sound, claiming for King Carlos III a large bay at 55° north latitude. He completed this survey in a 36-foot schooner, with a crew of 13 men, half of whom were ill. Worse yet, before sailing northward under such duress, seven of his men had been slaughtered by Indians near Destruction Island, where Barkley's five hands were to meet a similar fate 11 years later.

Quadra had won George's admiration sight unseen. Faced now with this venerable Spaniard, aged near 50 years, who showed every mark of a highly civilized as well as daring man, George was honoured, indeed, to make his acquaintance and to be, by diplomatic appointment, his equal. He was determined to rise with dignity and humility to his commission. By the manners and deeds of Quadra, he had also to rise to the standards set by this Peruvian-born nobleman, who would have been an ornament to any country's crown.

From the first day onward, Quadra and George alternately shared one another's table, usually breakfasting aboard the *Discovery* and supping on shore. Another important dignitary resided at Nootka Sound as well, one George did not graciously receive at first, to this man's insult and distress. He attempted to come on board the *Discovery* on the morning of August 29th, but as he appeared to the officer and seamen on watch to be just another rag-tag Indian, he was rebuffed, as per instructions.

Maquinna angrily stormed ashore to apprise his good friend Quadra of this unforgivable breach of etiquette and, by Quadra's patient explanation and kindly escort, soon found himself properly introduced to Captain Vancouver. Needless to say, George was much chagrined, for he prided himself in giving native peoples every appropriate measure of respect. He had failed miserably in this instance and felt keenly his obligation to make amends with the chief, without overstating his case and giving away the ships' stores to do so. With this intent and Quadra's cooperation, he hoped to right matters with Maquinna in good time.

Quite separate from these pleasant and unpleasant events of the first full day spent with Quadra, the whole of it was not one of easy conversation, for neither George nor Quadra spoke a word of the other's language. Quadra had a servant who could speak English, but he could not read or write it. For everyday purposes, his services were adequate, but to settle their official business, they needed a literate translator.

Their negotiations were to be conducted by an alternating series of written communications, to provide a complete record for their respective courts. That Lord Grenville and the Admiralty had made no provision for an able translator was a ridiculous oversight. Broughton could speak and write French, as could Quadra's naturalist; they might proceed in this third language, but the possibilities for making errors due to double translation were manyfold.

Much to George's relief, a midshipman from the *Daedalus* stepped forward and demonstrated his verbal and written fluency in English and Spanish. George immediately transferred Thomas Dobson onto the *Discovery* and awaited Quadra's opening letter, that the Spanish flag might be struck from these shores and the English raised in its stead.

George had no great hope of reaching easy agreement and quick settlement, for the *Daedalus* had carried not one document, among the paltry few she delivered to him, that clarified the situation or provided procedural instructions. George had no authority to exceed the vague intent of the Nootka Sound Convention, which in no way spelled out *how* the transfer of territory and attendant rights to it were to take place.

On September 1st, Quadra delivered a lengthy letter for Dobson to translate. While he was doing so, the *Sutil* and *Mexicana* arrived from their circumnavigation of the great, unnamed island—to George's relief, for now the honour of proving its insularity most certainly went to his expedition, by a narrow margin of just four days, to the glory and gain of Great Britain.

George and Dobson pored over the translation of Quadra's transmittal, distilling each point raised to its very essence. George included Broughton in this and every activity pertaining to the negotiation, to act as his witness and as his second, should events preclude him from completing the task. As George had feared, the dual purpose of his commission was untenable, for he could not chart a complex length of coastline whilst also negotiating the final settlement of the Nootka Convention. By careful consideration of Quadra's present words and recent actions, George deduced that the Spanish knew this and were well prepared to take advantage of it.

Quadra had arrived at Nootka Sound in late April and expected George to arrive shortly thereafter, to forego explorations upon the coast until the Nootka land claim was settled. Quadra spent the summer overseeing the establishment of a new garrison called Fuca [now Neah Bay] at the entrance to de Fuca's strait, and he sent out Galiano and Valdés to make a hasty survey to the northward of Fuca, to verify Nootka's probable situation upon a very large island. By these accomplishments, he expected to press an audacious demand upon George.

Quadra's letter argued that, given the true circumstances of Meares's exaggerated and duplicitous claim (the details of which he had learned from Robert Gray of the *Columbia*, who had called at Nootka that summer and who had witnessed Meares's shabby little Portuguese operation in the summer of 1788), Spain had nothing to deliver up to England, nor damage to make good. Nonetheless, Quadra was ready to cede to England, in good faith, the houses, offices, and gardens of Nootka in exchange for recognition of a fixed point delineating Spain's northernmost possession. He proposed that the boundary be set at Fuca and that both nations have free access and use of territories to the northward, upon which future establishments might be formed only by permission of the respective courts.

No wonder Spain had been in such a hurry to build an establishment at Fuca! No wonder Galiano and Valdés were sent out that summer to complete their survey to the northward of Fuca before George could do so, thereby laying Spain's claim to the entire island upon which insignificant little Nootka sat, as well as to the adjacent continental shores! Fortunately, George had scuttled this clever plan by choosing to explore first and negotiate later. Without question, England could now make the very claims to which Spain aspired, and by her own rules—right of prior discovery.

George had to read Quadra's letter very closely, indeed, while considering who had called at the port, why the fort at Fuca was necessary, and who was sent to explore what and why, to figure out exactly what Quadra was proposing. The point of his letter appeared to be that Spain would not relinquish her *claim* to the area, but would transfer *title* to the tiny spot where Meares's shack had stood. Further, Spain would only do so if George agreed to cede all the lands south of Fuca, while leaving all lands north of it open to Spain's future claim, presumably based on the Galiano-Valdés reconnaisance (now neatly foiled by George's unexpected preemption!)

When George fully understood Quadra's strategy and its implications, he quickly drafted a reply: he had not been empowered to undertake such a negotiation and settlement. He could only attempt to make good the first and fifth articles of the Nootka Sound Convention of October, 1790, which stated that he was to receive the disputed Nootka territories and to be assured that Spain would not interfere with the rights of British citizens to free access to all ports north of San Francisco.

Quadra's reply was prompt and to the point: first, he was pleased to say that he derived the greatest satisfaction from finding a person of George's character, with whom he was to transact the business of delivering up Nootka; second, he would accept George's offers; third, when the transaction was completed, they could sail away together or agree to rendezvous at San Francisco or Monterey. He asked George what plans he had for occupying Nootka that winter, and he concluded by inviting George to tour the premises, that he might fully appreciate what Spain was leaving to British care.

George instantly devised an *ad hoc* plan for winter occupation of Nootka, sent it off to Quadra, then met him on shore for the proposed tour. The Spanish settlement had cost King Carlos a good deal, for it consisted of several well-constructed buildings in good repair, a new oven (used to bake fresh bread for George's people, delivered every morning throughout their stay), thriving gardens, and livestock facilities containing poultry, cattle, pigs, and goats. George was suitably impressed, but uneasy about Quadra's hasty agreement to settle. Had he been hoodwinked? He would have to wait for Quadra's next letter to better judge this.

Quadra sent a brief reply on September 2nd. Unfortunately, Dobson's writing arm had been injured and, for several days, he was unable to transcribe this letter or pen George's answer. Dobson read the letter to George, who "did not conceive it required any immediate reply," because it was simply a succinct reiteration of Quadra's original proposal: he still wished to strike a deal George was not empowered to make.

George and Quadra could do no official business until Dobson rallied, hence they spent the next week attending to their separate concerns, while continuing to dine together on a daily basis. Quadra suggested they join Maquinna, who had just removed to his winter home some 30 miles up the inlet, and regale him with a pleasant repast. George readily agreed. On September 3rd, they set out on an enjoyable boat journey, past shores George had seen as a midshipman with Cook in '78, that time hard at the working end of the oars.

Quadra and George laid on a splendid feast for Maquinna in his great longhouse, complete with silver cutlery, dinnerware, and European foods for native royalty. "The rest of the Natives entertained themselves at a Mess not less gratefull to their palate. It consisted of a large *Tunny* and a Porpus [tuna and porpoise] cut up in small pieces entrails & all into a large Trough with a Mixture of Water blood & fish Oil, & the whole stewed by throwing heated Stones into it"—in Menzies's words.

Maquinna had never been so well fêted by white men, nor had any chief upon that coast. He was proud to an extreme; to show his pleasure and prowess, he took a very active part in several dances and mimes performed to entertain his Spanish and English friends.

Following the native displays, George's and Quadra's men contributed songs, accompanied with fifes and drums, and they did reels and country dances. They left before nightfall, that they might find a suitable overnight campsite en route to Friendly Cove. All participants parted company well satisfied with the efforts of the day. George had redeemed himself; his memories of that day were vivid and fond, indeed.

The next morning, George, Quadra, and respective companies enjoyed breakfast together, as they made leisurely progress back to the ships. In conversation during this little excursion, Señor Quadra had very earnestly requested that George name some port or island after both of them, to commemorate their meeting and the very friendly intercourse that had taken place between them. George, taken by a rare moment of unfettered happiness, proposed a perfect name for the great island he had circumnavigated: the Island of Quadra and Vancouver [Vancouver Island], in honour of their friendship. Quadra was highly pleased and instantly agreed.

Not all of George's people were so enamoured of Quadra's many good characteristics, most particularly his treatment of the Indians. Many complained that Quadra was too good to them, for his house was open to them all and he fed a considerable number each day. How could he teach them subjection this way? How could any white man be secure in those territories with those savage, inveterate beggars ready to take every advantage of their natural superiors? George perfectly agreed with Quadra in this matter, hence he also fell subject to his people's condemnation. He shrugged it off; Quadra was the man to heed, not one, nor even one hundred, ignorant sailors.

About that time, George took the opportunity to transfer a number of people to the *Daedalus*, for a variety of reasons. First, from among the *Chatham*'s officers, he chose a new agent for the vessel, subsequent to which he appointed the still-smouldering Thomas Manby to serve as the *Chatham*'s master. Manby rejoiced at the posting, not because it was a minor promotion—indeed, he claimed he would have refused it had he been in England—but because the move cleared him of George, whom he steadfastly refused to forgive since their falling-out at Birch Bay.

George arranged to ship three of the *Discovery*'s people to Port Jackson on the *Daedalus*. The first two, Dr. Cranstoun and the boatswain, were chronically ill and would likely never recover to full health. To fill Cranstoun's place, George requested that Menzies officially sign on as the *Discovery*'s surgeon, an appointment Menzies was reluctant to take, on principle alone. When George insisted Menzies put in writing all his reasons for refusing, he could see how untenable his position was, for he had willingly served as ship's surgeon since leaving Capetown. Further, George and Menzies had formed a friendship of sorts, grudging in some respects, but admiring in others. At last, Menzies achieved the position that Sir Joseph Banks had proposed for him and, indeed, that the Fates had decreed.

Phillips, the carpenter, who had been under arrest since leaving the Sandwich Islands, was also transferred to the *Daedalus*. He would proceed via Port Jackson to England, there to await trial by court martial upon George's return.

These transfers marked the beginning of a number of neat despatches and shuffles George effected over the next few months, in part because they were necessary and in part to dismantle the tinderbox of hatred that, unless defused, was sure to ignite and explode one furious, ill-fated day.

By September 10th, Dobson was able to translate and transcribe Quadra's short third letter: he recognized George's limited commission; he agreed to lay the matter before their respective courts to resolve; he would leave to George "possession of what Mears [sic] occupied"; he would also leave the houses, gardens, and offices at George's command (without surrendering them); and he would re-tire till a clear and authentic decision was made.

George had sailed half way round the world to accept the 100-foot triangle of land Meares used for his shore operations? Not like-ly! On September 15th, George wrote to Quadra that, unless the whole territory was ceded, he must decline further correspondence. Quadra bowed to this impasse. The Spanish flag would continue to fly over Nootka Sound, and the matter would be reported to their respective courts for future settlement.

That same day, a most horrific event took place, altering the warm relations that had existed between the Spaniards and the In-dians. Quadra's servant boy, a likeable lad of some 15 years, who had disappeared two days earlier, was found in a cove not far from the ships, with his head nearly severed from his corpse, his calf muscles cut out, and other bodily parts barbarously wounded. When Quadra demanded of Maquinna that the murderer be given up—for he presumed an Indian to have perpetrated the crime—every native inhabitant of the sound beat a hasty retreat, thus prov-ing their guilt to those inclined to make narrow, presumptuous judgements.

Quadra was not of this sort, yet he markedly cooled his generous assessment of his Indian friends and was reluctant to look for the murderer among his own people. The Spaniards favoured the story that the boy had been enticed away from the settlement and into a canoe occupied by three Indians, two girls and one man, on the promise that he would enjoy one of the girls. At the height of his pleasure, he was murdered by the Indian man—an unthinkably bru-tal act!

The Englishmen, who had a more detached view, noted that a black man of most infamous character had deserted from the *Activa* about the time the boy was first missed, and further, there were nu-merous Spaniards, especially those from New Spain, who had ferociously savage dispositions. Some thought the body had been hastily and strangely mutilated to fix blame on the Indians.

No real or suspected culprit emerged from the wild rumours that circulated, and the boy was laid to rest with little hope of justice ever being done. Another sort of justice, applied to the group rather than to the person, was certain to be enacted in the months to come, however. Quadra sailed from Nootka Sound on September 22nd, and with him went the Indians' best chance for fair treatment on their individual merits. On October 2nd, Salvador Fidalgo arrived to take over command of the Nootka settlement for the winter. His first officer had recently been killed by Indians at the new de Fuca colony, hence he took a very dim view of all native peoples and was sure to exact payment from all to atone for the presumed guilt of one.

With Quadra, George sent numerous papers regarding his transactions at Nootka, which Quadra agreed to forward from California to New Spain, and thence via Spain to the Lords of the Admiralty. That this packet arrived safely in England is evidenced by there being one document—and the only part not written by George—in the Admiralty's keeping, but the rest have vanished. More mischief on Camelford's part? Who else would take these pages and uncounted others, selecting only those penned by George? Strange, it is, and not entirely a mystery.

George had continuing reasons to be dissatisfied with Pitt's behaviour, which had improved only marginally since he was flogged at Discovery Bay. Naturally, in George's report, he made mention of various officers and men, most notably those despatched, promoted, or otherwise deserving comment. Pitt was not up for favourable review, and George did not shy from briefly stating his case against the young man, that evidence might be filed well before any major disaster such as desertion or mutiny might occur.

Zachary Mudge, as Pitt's guardian, continued to be a stubborn nuisance; George happily devised a plan by which to rid himself of this disappointing first mate. He gave Mudge the exalted duty of serving as messenger to the King's Court at St. James, which is to say, he put Mudge aboard a fur-trading vessel bound for China carrying a packet of papers containing the whole of the present Nootka Sound negotiation, extracts of George's journal, and a copy of the survey. From China, Mudge was to make his way to England with all haste, that some final resolution to the Nootka stalemate might be devised. By this means, George hoped to receive further instructions come the next summer and thus satisfactorily complete that part of his commission.

At Canton, Mudge could also sell his shipmates' furs, which were expected to generate a tidy profit for each hopeful trader. George, too, had a small stake in this China barter, but he cared little about its success, contrary to what his acquisitive detractors believed. It is so common for the worst offenders to ascribe their own embodiment of deadly sins to their betters that it is, indeed, axiomatic. Greed, in this case, was seen to motivate George, who would gladly have given away all his pelts, and twice over, to be rid of Mudge.

With Mudge removed, George promoted his faithful allies, Puget and Baker, to first and second lieutenant respectively, and filled in each consequent vacant junior post with reliable hands. Broughton remained something of an annoyance, but he could be removed at some logical, useful juncture in the future—the near future, if possible. With this major reorganization of senior personnel, George felt considerably relieved.

No sooner had George completed arrangements for removing four of his people from the *Discovery* than Fate determined to give him two new charges—and unusual, useless ones at that! A small fur-trading vessel, the *Jenny* of London under Captain Baker, arrived at Nootka on October 7th carrying two young women from the Sandwich Islands. As Baker was bound straight for England by the Horn, he asked George to transport the women back to their home island of Niihau. What could George say?

He agreed, of course, but he was not making a direct run for the Sandwich Islands. He had yet to survey the northwest coast from where he had first sighted land southward to 30° north latitude, and he had also to rendezvous with Quadra at Monterey. He would be months sailing to the Sandwich Islands—months, that is, with the unsettling influence of young, provocative women on board.

The likes of Pitt were certain to make every use they could of the circumstance; George was equally certain, from the start, to keep a tight rein on his people and a close eye on the girls. He had just dispatched four known problems, then had two unknown and potentially much worse ones visited upon him. Relief and rest were obviously not to be his lot.

The *Discovery*, *Chatham*, and *Daedalus* sailed from Nootka Sound on October 12th, with all hands happy to take leave of a port grown cool under Fidalgo's administration and cold under stormy winter skies. They would continue in company to California and the Sandwich Islands—in pleasant, trouble-free company, George fervently hoped.

17
Romantic California

The two Sandwich Island woman introduced themselves as Taheeopiah and Tymarow, these spellings being the best George could make of their names. For reasons undisclosed, Taheeopiah changed her name permanently to Raheina shortly after boarding ship. Tymarow was about 20 years of age, while Raheina looked to be 15. The younger woman surpassed the older in pleasing appearance, deportment, and quickness; as well, she was from a family of some consequence, while the older was related to her, but of lower birth.

George still had aboard the *Discovery* the Kauaian man called Jack, and the two girls were delighted to find in him a native companion and a very able translator. Through Jack, George was able to learn something of the girls' plight, that he might determine the reason they had been kidnapped and judge the treatment they had received.

American traders had industriously circulated rumours about British traders stealing Sandwich Island natives to sell into slavery on northwestern shores in exchange for furs. The Spanish officers, Quadra even, were inclined to believe these speculations. The two young women expressed surprise at George's query in this regard, for they had never entertained the notion that they might be sold.

Captain Baker of the *Jenny* had protested vigorously against having such designs, claiming that he put to sea unaware of their being on board his vessel. He had appeared most anxious to find transport home for them, and he had expressed his sincere solicitude for their future happiness and welfare. When George asked the girls about any ill usage from Mr. Baker, they replied that they had been treated with every kindness and attention whilst under his protection.

Tymarow's and Raheina's own accounting was that they boarded at Niihau with several countrywomen. When the vessel was ready to quit the island, the others were sent ashore, while Tymarow and Raheina were confined down in the cabin until the vessel was some distance asea. They were taken very contrary to their wishes and inclinations, and totally without the knowledge or consent of their friends and relations, but they imputed no foul purpose on Baker's part.

However innocently they came to their misfortune, and however well Baker treated them, George felt strongly that justice had been poorly served. Mr. Baker's subsequent conduct did not vindicate him from the original, highly improper crime; their seduction and detention on board Mr. Baker's vessel were inexcusable.

Despite the disruption the young women caused on board the *Discovery*, George was pleased to help right a fundamental wrong and, further, to show his people by example the respect, care, and caution all native persons deserved. As well, there was something civilized about having a feminine influence on board, under his avuncular eye and paternal wing.

George deemed their native clothing and borrowed vestments to be singularly unladylike, especially on a ship teeming with ungentlemanly men. He set the sailmaker to stitching dresses for them, and he also set to teaching them proper manners, with the whole effect being so remarkable, he wrote most tenderly:

> They seemed much pleased with the European fashions, and in conforming to this new system of manners, they conducted themselves in company with a degree of propriety beyond all expectation. Their European dress contributed most probably to this effect, and produced, particularly in *Raheina,* a degree of personal delicacy that was conspicuous on many occasions. This dress was a riding habit, as being best calculated for their situation, and indeed the best in our power to procure. Its skirt, or lower part, was soon found to be intended as much for concealment, as for warmth; and in the course of a very short time, she became so perfectly familiar to its use in this respect, that in going up and down the ladders that communicate with the different parts of the ship, she would take as much care not to expose her ancles, as if she had been educated by the most rigid governess . . .

Acting as a Platonic sort of Pygmalion to two young ladies provided a pleasant diversion for George, and one might rightly suppose that this task enhanced his enchantment with them, Raheina in particular. More of this, however, as the journey progresses.

His official task, and one of comparative ease, was to complete surveying and charting the coast south to 30° north latitude, making note of Spanish settlements within that range. The great port of San Francisco, with its 16-year-old presidio, was to be the *Discovery's* and *Chatham's* next rendezvous, while the *Daedalus* was to make directly for Monterey.

En route to California, the *Chatham* was employed exploring the inner reaches of the river Broughton called the Oregon, previously known by various Spanish names and ultimately called the Columbia. At Nootka, Quadra had supplied George with Captain Robert Gray's sketch of the river, which showed that Gray had succeeded in penetrating some 50 miles inland following George's brief encounter with him in late April. Obviously, if it was navigable that far and perhaps much farther, it behooved George to explore its innermost reaches, that his superior survey and chart might preempt Gray's claim[13].

Broughton traced the river inland over a hundred miles, taking possession at his turnaround spot, which he named Point Vancouver. He guessed that the river originated several hundred miles inland, but did not support the speculation advanced by some of his people that the headwaters might originate near the great lakes and rivers of Canada. If they did, fur-traders might penetrate halfway across the continent by eastward drainages, then continue to the Pacific Ocean by this westward drainage—a sweetwater Northwest Passage, that is, and a very exciting prospect for daydreamers and armchair geographers.

George was neither of these things, nor was he an overland, freshwater explorer. For him, it was enough to know that small, sea-going vessels could scarcely penetrate the formidable bars and breakers at the river's entrance and could make no headway at all beyond a few leagues inland. Fur-traders from Canada or the new American nation might make something more of the river, but further exploration of it was not within George's commission.

The *Daedalus* explored Gray's Harbour [Grays Harbor] to the northward of the Columbia River, which they found to be a landlocked basin. The remainder of the coastline from Cape Flattery to San Francisco was unbroken in aspect and unsettled by Spaniards. During those weeks in transit, the scurvy reared its dreaded head, thus adding an urgency to making San Francisco, where a much vaunted, supposedly sumptuous manner of living prevailed.

It is perhaps worth noting that the origin of the name 'California'

---

[13] Vancouver's exploration was too late. Gray's prior discovery and claim formed the basis by which the border dispute between Canada and the United States was settled in 1846. The British argued their right to all territory southward to the mouth of the Columbia River, and the province of British Columbia was so named to strengthen this claim. Had Vancouver spent a few days in late April of 1792 exploring, naming, and claiming the river, Canada might now include most of Washington state and perhaps even some of Oregon.

is known to most sailors, for it embodies their most lascivious dreams. When Cervantes wrote *Don Quixote*, many such picaresque novels were fashionable, one of which described fantastical adventures in a faraway land called California—'cali', the Greek word for good, and 'fornia', the Latin root for arch, entrance, and fornicate. California was, therefore, a most romantic place by definition. As no English vessel had before visited California, Spain might be, for good reason, keeping well an enviable secret.

The *Discovery* turned into San Francisco's commodious bay at four past noon on November 14th. There were no immediate signs of a noteworthy settlement, nor did any appear as night fell, when George expected the lights of the presidio and town to guide him to the best anchorage. In deepening twilight, the *Discovery* groped for adequate mooring in a deserted cove, from which only a few distant fires were apparent.

The next morning revealed little in the way of human constructs, although, in George's words, "The herds of cattle and flocks of sheep grazing on the surrounding hills were a sight we had long been strangers to, and brought to our minds many pleasing reflections." The Niihau girls were delighted by this view, so odd and wonderful was it to them, which amused George and added to his enjoyment of their company.

A Spanish army sergeant and a Franciscan father were first to greet their English guests, then the acting commandant of the port, the venerable Ensign Hermenegildo Sal (resident at San Francisco since its founding in 1776), rode from the presidio to extend his official welcome. Tymarow and Raheina were fascinated by the horses—a most novel means of transportation. Two days later, Señor Sal sent horses to carry George and his officers to the presidio; the girls stayed on the ship, no doubt yearning to follow them ashore, that they might put their feet upon firm ground or even venture to sit upon a horse's back.

The presidio proved to be a disappointment, so small, crude, and ill-appointed was it. So this was the great Spanish settlement at San Francisco: a mud wall enclosing small mud houses with thatched roofs and a small neat church! Even Señor Sal's apartment lacked most civilized amenities, yet his wife and children displayed such an educated manner and dignity that they quickly took all attention from their crude surroundings.

The presidio tour was completed nearly as soon as it began, so little was there to see. Sal offered to provide horses for a tour, on the morrow, of the Santa Clara mission, 18 leagues to the southward, which George readily accepted. He asked if the Niihau girls might accompany the party, thinking that the venture might please them.

Tymarow and Raheina were thrilled by the proposed ride, and they instantly accepted. No sooner had they landed than they mounted their horses and kept their seats throughout the journey, without showing the least sign of fear—indeed, riding with as much ease and apparent satisfaction as if they had been brought up to it from their infancy.

While the girls rode prettily to the Santa Clara mission, many of George's officers suffered a trying day, mistakenly prepared for a journey of 18 *miles*, not leagues. The weather was serene; the hour spent lunching in the midst of an oak grove—an "imaginary park" to George—was extremely pleasant and, if one might speculate, romantic as well. The singular sight of two lovely young women, dressed in their European garb and picnicking in a most ladylike manner, must have been touching, indeed. That George grew increasingly fond of them, with Raheina as his favourite, is little wonder, given such an agreeable setting and circumstance.

The Santa Clara mission proved little different in size and construction from the presidio, while the few Spanish friars and soldiers provided an equally hospitable welcome and tour. When George and saddle-sore retinue returned to the presidio two days later, the *Chatham* was at anchor and both she and the *Discovery* were nearly ready to sail for Monterey.

To conclude his business, George requested of Sal an accounting of the refreshments and provisions supplied to his ships and people, that he might settle this debt. To George's distress, Sal refused to provide a tally and, further, refused to accept George's payment according to his own estimate of the amount owing. Sal insisted that these were Señor Quadra's orders, for he had covered every expense and would settle the debt at Monterey. The best George could do was to leave numerous gifts with his hosts—supplying them with various domestic articles and implements, some bar iron, church decorations, and several sorts of wine and liquor.

Quadra's generosity, so amply displayed at Nootka Sound, was evidently boundless, and George was unable to repay it in goods or in monies. This great Spaniard's kindness was placing George in a difficult position, one he was firmly resolved to put aright before leaving Monterey, for fear their respective courts might use this indebtedness as leverage against one another in subsequent negotiations. George could not then foresee how the British court might hold this debt against him personally, but there was much he could not foresee during those pleasant, romantic days at California.

After ten days at San Francisco—a port boasting great riches of nature and great poverty of cultivation—George directed his ships from the harbour, sailing away with his people's health and spirits much renewed, and his own heart much enlightened by temperate climes and excellent company.

18
Rendezvous at Monterey

The *Discovery* and *Chatham* took but one day and one night to reach the port of Monterey, where they were greeted by the *Daedalus* riding at anchor with several Spanish vessels. Señor Quadra waited ashore midst a pleasant Spanish company. By eight o'clock in the evening of November 26th, George's two vessels were safely moored, and George landed to pay his respects to the governor.

Señor José Arguello was in charge of the Monterey presidio as acting governor, but Quadra had boldly usurped his position—quite improperly, but for admirable purposes. He wished that his good relations with George might continue, to the mutual benefit of their respective nations. Thus, Arguello temporarily lost his interregnal authority and was none too pleased about it, but he could not hold sway over Quadra's natural and good leadership capabilities.

George confided in Quadra his desire to send word to England of his progress to date, possibly by despatching the *Chatham* for that purpose. This design quickly became known to the *Chatham's* people, most of whom were delighted by the promise of enjoying England's fair bounties in seven or eight months time. George also suggested to Quadra a possible alternative to this drastic measure, that of sending Lieutenant Broughton through New Spain to Spain, thence onward to England, if Quadra could help arrange it. Quadra immediately embraced this plan, offering to take Broughton with him to San Blas, where he would provide him with money and every requisite for his journey.

Naturally, this arrangement suited George perfectly, and he happily accepted. The hopes of the *Chatham's* people were miserably dashed, their dreams of seeing England in bloom next summer were replaced by prospects of drudgery and dreariness beyond measure for one, and likely two more surveying seasons. These tiny Spanish outposts were the closest they would come to civilized society for several more years. Little wonder, therefore, that every Englishman formed a tender attachment to the California settlements, and most particularly to Señor Quadra, who did everything in his power to ensure their contentment while in his care.

The Niihau girls took ill with stubborn colds, but they were plucky enough to partake of several entertainments held aboard the *Discovery* and ashore. They attended a dance and dinner held at the presidio on the evening of December 3rd, following George's pleasant tour of the San Carlos mission [Mission San Carlos Borromeo at Carmel].

The entertainments were scheduled to begin at seven, but the Spanish ladies had such unusual preparations to make that they did not arrive till near ten. They danced some country dances, including their favourite, the exhilarating Spanish dance called the fandango. It was performed by a man and woman, dancing either to the guitar alone or accompanied by voice, who traversed the room with such wanton attitudes and motions, such leering looks, sparkling eyes, and trembling limbs as would decompose the gravity of a Stoic.

Following this astonishingly lewd display, George requested that the two Niihau girls exhibit their manner of singing and dancing, to which they readily agreed. Alas, this form of entertainment did not amuse the Spanish ladies, who thought George had introduced a crude imitation of their favourite dance, and they soon departed in a huff.

Poor George! He was mortified that his young ladies, properly dressed and well-mannered, had suffered such humiliation. Perhaps their native way of dancing could not be fully appreciated outside of its native context, but the more obvious fault lay with the affectations and hypocrisies of the Spanish wives. George retained painful memories of their petty display, but by it, he came to appreciate his tender young charges the more for a lesson hard-learned from supposedly civilized society.

Señor Quadra, of course, was distressed by his ladies' poor manners, and he was desirous that George return himself and the Niihau girls to their good favour. To do so, George hosted a dinner aboard the *Discovery* the following evening. The ladies remained intransigent, however, and immediately complained about the ship's slight motion, which was so terrible in the ladies' estimation that they were very soon obliged to retire—greatly to George's disappointment, as one might imagine.

Disappointment was but one of George's humours, for he felt anger and disgust to a greater degree. In contrast to the Spanish women, his lovely Niihau ladies seemed all the more admirable, so open were their natures and sweet their temperaments. It is not to be wondered at that George leaned ever more toward enjoying the honest enthusiasms of native society, where his every civility was returned in kind.

George had little time to devote to such reflections, for he had many charts to prepare for Broughton's delivery to the Admiralty. After working on these for one long week from dawn through to the midnight hours, George requested and received Quadra's approval to stage a dinner, dance, and fireworks display ashore. Fortunately, this event was a particular success, to George's satisfaction and relief.

Discounting certain vexations, George found much to admire in the Spaniards' little society and its potential for betterment. With greater industry—for the Spaniards and Indians alike appeared to be surprisingly indolent—their tracts of fertile land, small homes, and the beneficent climate might produce the most enviable state of existence in the world. George could readily envision himself settled upon such a new world estate, living in harmony with the native people and allowing only the best of European civilization to find root in this Utopia.

Many of his people could as easily imagine an idyllic life as well, and a seaman from the *Discovery* deserted, no doubt for just such purpose. He was quickly apprehended by the Spaniards, but they would not return him to the ship until George promised he would not flog the man while in port. George agreed reluctantly and simply put the man in irons, a punishment so soft that George feared it would not deter others intent upon desertion. In fact, it would only increase their determination not to be caught, for they knew their hide would be flailed off them when they put to sea.

At month's end, the *Daedalus* sailed for Port Jackson, with instructions to return to Nootka Sound the following summer, bringing a year's provisions and stores. So handsomely had Quadra provided livestock for the new Australian penal colony that George was determined to settle his account at that juncture. Quadra would have none of it; he insisted that the only settlement in which he could possibly engage was that of seeing his guests accommodated to the extent of their wishes.

George later learned that Quadra had given Señor Arguello bonds worth $1,800 [Spanish dollars] to cover every expense, and all from his own pocket. Quadra refused George's offers of money, vouchers, or any other acknowledgement, but he did not forbid George from delivering many useful gifts to Arguello, to be divided as he saw fit. This George did as lavishly as possible, hoping it would defray some of his considerable debt, but unfortunately, the friars and officers soon became disgruntled with Arguello's distribution, proving that method of payment unsatisfactory.

What was George to do? Quadra's largesse was deeply appreciated, but might have serious consequences should this great man not be at Nootka or California the following season. Those working in his stead would have grievances galore to hold against George and company, unless the debt was quickly and completely paid. George might anticipate such difficulties, but he could not cross that bridge, as it were, until he came to it. Neither did he wish to con- template returning to this coast without Quadra being there—a lonely thought, indeed.

In early January of 1793, the *Chatham*'s armourer and a marine deserted. The former was a very ingenious mechanic who would be sorely missed, if he were not found and returned. Rumours circulat- ed that he had been enticed away by the Spaniards, who promised him $40 per day for his employment, but the Spanish officers made such great exertions to find him, these speculations seemed un- likely.

By mid-January, when the *Discovery* and *Chatham* were ready to sail for the Sandwich Islands, the two men were still missing. To as- sure George that the Spanish played no part in their desertions, Quadra promised to imprison them and send them to Nootka should they be caught. He also suffered George to take the port's only smith in the armourer's place, and so great was George's need for this service, he reluctantly agreed. The Spaniard in question was much more than reluctant, and he had to be delivered to the *Discovery* under guard.

That same day, January 13th, George's packet for Broughton's delivery to England was in complete readiness. It was a fat, hand- some thing, containing several letters, 19 charts and sketches, nine Spanish charts, 39 drawings, a report on the state of the *Discovery* and *Chatham*, and a copy of George's journal from April 1st of 1791 to the conclusion of 1792.

On the morning of January 14th, George's ships weighed anchor and sailed. They were joined that evening by three Spanish vessels heading for San Blas. They sailed in consort for several days, but at last and alas, George could sail no farther southward. The time had come to part.

On their final day together, January 18th, George reviewed the contents of the packet he entrusted to Broughton's care. Two of the enclosed letters were addressed, respectively, to Lord Chatham, who was yet First Lord of the Admiralty, and to Lord Grenville, newly appointed Secretary of Foreign Affairs (unknown to George, of course, who addressed him in his former capacity of Secretary of State). A third letter was addressed to Evan Nepean, Under Secretary of State. The first two of these three letters have disappeared entirely, while the third has, by chance, survived—or perhaps not by chance at all, given Camelford's connections to Chatham and Grenville.

George's letter to Nepean is a long one, essentially a polite beration of the government's failure to instruct and supply him adequately for settlement of the Nootka transaction, to his embarrassment and, he hoped, to his credit for taking the most cautious approach. A postscript George added on January 18th is, to this present writing, of more interest than the body of the letter, for George states, "Nor can I at last avoid saying that the Conduct of Mr. T. Pit [sic] has been too bad for me to represent in any one respect." One might readily imagine that similarly stinging comments graced the other two letters, which have conveniently vanished as a result.

With numerous letters, charts, sketches, and a copy of the journal in good order and placed in Broughton's care aboard the Activa, George, Quadra, and attendant officers shared a last meal aboard the Discovery on the evening of the 18th. George wrote touchingly that "the serenity of the sky and smoothness of the sea prolonged my pleasure on this occasion until near midnight... while the prospect of never again meeting Señor Quadra and our other friends about him, was a painful consideration."

Quadra and company finally returned to the Activa and took their leave. George's company voluntarily lined the yards to salute the Spaniards with three hearty cheers—and most particularly to honour Quadra, whom they held in highest esteem and veneration. Imagine them, like rows of sparrows perched on high, singing their huzzahs to the starry heavens, in praise of a great man. The Spaniards returned the salute in kind, in cordial praise of George and company, then each vessel pursued its respective voyage with all sails set.

. . . with all sails set. Ghostly ships slipping into the night. How profoundly that parting affected George's tender heart. How he loved Juan Francisco de la Bodega y Quadra, a sailor and a gentleman without equal!

19
Hawaiian Winter

From the tender, civil business of bidding Quadra adieu, George turned to the hard, brutal task of punishing his deserters. The prescribed 12 dozen lashes were applied; as this could kill a man, George divided them into two separate and equal sessions. This may seem a small mercy, but it was the best he could arrange to satisfy the law, serve swift punishment, and spare two lives.

Three days into the run for Hawaii, one of the carpenter's mates disappeared. He was last seen opening the gun-room ports and, as he was never seen again, it could only be assumed that he had forced himself through a porthole and purposefully flung himself into the sea. He was a good swimmer, the sea was smooth, and the decks were quiet; had he wished to be saved, his shouts would certainly have been heard.

Suicide it was then, for what else could it be? He was a man of gloomy, religious cast, hence the dark and gloomy weather attending his demise and funeral perfectly fit the company's bleak remembrances of his nature. George was so solicitous of his men's wellbeing and so desirous of their harmonious relations (thus hated Pitt's continually disruptive influence), he naturally considered what blame he might take for this needless loss of life. The man had been punished with three dozen lashes for theft the previous August, which perhaps played deeply upon his pious sense of guilt and shame, but if a deserved flogging was reason enough to jump ship, half the crew would by now be food for sharks.

George was not one to contemplate such mysteries at length, which is, indeed, why young Camelford's inability to let go of any disappointment or grievance puzzled and frustrated George no end. To his thinking, in life's checks and balances, when something is done and over, it is done and over—and on to the next thing, please, applying the lessons learned and shaping a straight course in the future.

George's present task was to prove or disprove the existence of a group of islands called Los Majos, long touted by the Spaniards to be eastward of the Sandwich Islands by some 10° longitude. George conducted a search of "indescribable caution"—in the grudging admiration of Thomas Manby—and found nothing. The words of the great French explorer, the Comte de la Pérouse, who searched in vain for those same islands in 1786, spring readily to mind, for he held that ancient navigators and their interpreters have "laid down islands which do not exist, or which, like so many phantoms, on the approach of modern navigators, instantly vanish." Science and industry have laid to rest many a phantom, with George well placed among a rare company of discoverers determined to shine light into every dark corner of the world.

The *real* Los Majos Islands—the Sandwich Islands, that is, which the Spaniards so seriously misplaced as to forfeit any right of possession by prior discovery—came into view on February 12th. George's purpose there would be threefold: first, to employ himself "very diligently in the examination and survey of the said islands", according to his instructions; second, to see that justice prevailed following the unprovoked murders at Oahu of Hergest and Gooch of the *Daedalus*; and third, to attempt establishment of a lasting peace between rival chiefs, that their once prosperous islands might again flourish.

A fourth and unofficial goal, one George was very desirous of perfectly attaining, was to return the Niihau girls to comfort and safety upon home shores. How fond he became of them, Raheina in particular, he never disclosed. Nonetheless, one must have lived entirely without love not to read something most tender in the description he penned of her—and even proclaimed by publication in his journal! To wit:

> The elegance of *Raheina*'s figure, the regularity and softness of her features, and the delicacy which she naturally possessed, gave her a superiority in point of personal accomplishments over the generality of her sex amongst the Sandwich islanders; in addition to which, her sensibility and turn of mind, her sweetness of temper and complacency of manners, were beyond any thing that could have been expected from her birth, or native education; so that if it were fair to judge of the dispositions of a whole nation from the qualities of these two young women, it would seem that they are endued with much affection and tenderness. At least, such was their deportment towards us; by which they gained the regard and good wishes of, I believe, every one on board, whilst I became in no small degree solicitous for their future happiness and prosperity.

One might better understand his profound interest in the Sandwich Islands by understanding his admiration of the people there, formed in large part by his attachment to the interests of the two Niihau women, one most of all. He approached those dreaded islands, where he had lost his beloved Captain Cook and now would seek just retribution for two equally senseless, brutal murders, with a passionate desire to stop all the killings, that all might live and trade in peace, Raheina among them.

The most formidable chief, who had caused the worst destruction by his rampages, was Kamehameha of Hawaii—the "dark-skinned, lonely one", according to his name. For his part in Captain Cook's murder and dismemberment, he earned the universal reputation of being a most ferocious, avaricious, capricious man. By looks alone, he was frightening, for he was well made and stood above six foot, six inches tall. His countenance was an assembly of quickness, cunning, dark humour, and ambition, playing across features gorilla-like in form and strength. If George was to negotiate peace, his work would necessarily begin and end with Kamehameha.

George's first two weeks at the Sandwich Islands were principally in Kamehameha's company at Kealekekua Bay. George's belief that a capable person of any nation, when treated with appropriate caution and courtesy, will respond in kind was handsomely borne out by this great and savage king, for he and George quickly formed an admirable understanding of one another and, by extension, of one another's societies.

Appropriate caution, in this case, meant strict limitations on all intercourse between ships and shore, as well as faithful abidance by George's well-known rules and orders regarding trade. The midshipmen, one might imagine, were highly displeased once again to be forced to hold court with the ladies in their overcrowded, sweaty little berth, an injustice they perhaps doubly resented knowing that George slept in a private locker astern, with his precious Niihau ladies close at hand.

Appropriate courtesy for Kamehameha and his people was more difficult for George to determine, for attention and gifts had to be meted out judiciously among the various chiefs and their ladies, if all were to feel favoured in keeping with their real and presumed status. That George did this perfectly can be seen in the civil and harmonious relations he insisted upon, hence engendered, from which great mutual benefit ensued.

It is worth a small note, perhaps, to say that Kualelo, whom George had transported from England and had left in the treacherous Kaiana's care, had fared well enough in his new Hawaiian home. He had been made a minor chief, which gave him standing well beyond his natural abilities. He continually pressed George for gifts of every sort, and George was again accused of extreme mean-ness for refusing to give this ambitious, rude man any more than he deserved—which was little, indeed.

Except for Kaiana and Kualelo, the islanders came quickly to hold George in high regard, for he was first, foremost, and always a man of honour—a King George man. In contrast to the greedy, fractious traders who fuelled internecine feuds for personal gain, George exhibited exemplary behaviour and demanded the same in return. Such a pleasant, decorous society instantly formed that all who forwarded it could not but be pleased with their efforts. Kamehameha, in particular, extended his generous opinion of Cap-tain George to King George himself and, as proof of this, gave in sa-cred trust to George the most splendid full-length yellow feather cape yet seen on the islands to deliver personally to the king, for him *and only him* to wear.

While pressing for peace, George put to Kamehameha the possi-bility of uniting the islands under King George's banner. Surpris-ingly, Kamehameha was not averse to the idea, except he believed, quite rightly, that a British vessel must remain at the islands to pa-trol and protect them. George could find no quarrel with this argu-ment; the great puzzle was how he could effect cession of the islands to Great Britain's care and fulfill this requisition. It was then far too early to think so grandly; time and circumstance would perhaps present him with the means by which to achieve that noble end.

Upon departing, George won from Kamehameha and his chiefs their promise to forward new peace proposals next winter, when he returned. In the interim, he could only hope that no already-planned warfare or new fomention would occur.

At Maui, George found shocking devastation caused by the pre-ceding 11 years of intermittent warfare. No battles had taken place for two years, but only because there was little left to fight with or for. Kamehameha's attacks, in George's words, "had so humbled and broken the spirit of the people, that little exertion had been made to restore these islands to their accustomed fertility by culti-vation."

During George's week at anchor in Lahaina Bay, he accomplished several aims to his satisfaction. His first priority was to talk of peace to the old king, Kahekili, who reigned over all the islands to the leeward of Hawaii. This George did with the same flawless skill he had employed with Kamehameha and court, thus winning Kahekili's promise to help devise a permanent disarmament the following year.

Kahekili's brother Kaeo, also a powerful chief, vividly remembered George from their meeting years earlier, although both men were much changed in appearance. George, to his humiliation, recalled nothing of Kaeo. Nothing! Kaeo now looked to be 40 or 50 years of age, while George had only a vague recollection of befriending at Maui a robust man aged about 18 years. Could this be the same person? George, too, had grown prematurely old and, of late, quite stout as well, since supping so finely with Quadra, then Kamehameha. He was becoming like Father, rotund and busy "Little Van".

To prove a loyal friendship that spanned the years and the globe, Kaeo produced a revered lock of hair George had given him, which matched so perfectly in colour and texture, George could not deny its origin. When Kaeo spoke fondly, with perfect recollection, of events and conversations they had shared, George was further humbled by this man's fidelity to an old friend. Such sincerity, warmth, civility; George could only love these people the more for the love they retained and returned.

George's second aim while in Kahekili's company was to enlist his aid with regard to finding and punishing the men who had murdered Hergest and Gooch at Oahu. He had heard rumours at Hawaii that Kahekili had already executed three of the criminals, and Kahekili spontaneously confirmed this. He also volunteered that three or four guilty men had escaped punishment by hiding in the Oahu mountains, only to reappear later, when the tragedy was all but forgotten.

George made it clear that passage of time would never wipe the injustice from King George's mind; punishment of the guilty was necessary and inevitable. George requested that Kahekili send a deputy—a reliable, respected chief—to sail with him on the *Dis-*

covery to Oahu, there to locate the men and bring them to trial.

George's third priority at Maui, as at Hawaii, was to explore and survey its perimeter. To his satisfaction, this peaceful labour was completed safely and successfully, albeit with a hair-raising adventure or two upon wild seas; by March 17th, all was in readiness to proceed to Kauai.

That evening, standing off the Lahaina roads, the wind and waves were so prodigious that George's dinner guests, Kahekili, Kaeo, and other chiefs, insisted they could not paddle safely to shore. Contrary to George's strict rules, therefore, he agreed to let them sleep on board ship. George got little rest that night, so intent were his guests upon talking at length about the fireworks display he had provided, and, to make matters worse, in the morning, Raheina complained of having had a hair ribbon stolen.

Damn them! Damn them for taking advantage, even so small an advantage! And of a fine, civilized young lady, no less! Much to the chiefs' astonishment, George flew into a fit of rage. Kahekili fled the cabin and jumped ship through the nearest porthole, which happened to be in Mr. Menzies's cabin. Kaeo was not so easily frightened and did not instantly flee, but the depth of George's passion over so trivial an item was shocking and comical—unless one is prepared to make a connection to Raheina that George took pains to conceal, even from himself.

Soon enough, normal relations were reestablished; parting gifts were exchanged, and the remaining chiefs took an affectionate leave of the ship. By noon, the vessels were under way for Oahu, where they made Waikiki Bay by mid-afternoon of March 20th.

Kahekili's deputy immediately set to rounding up the brazen, craven men who had murdered Hergest and Gooch. The next day, he brought three suspects aboard the *Discovery* for identification and trial, to be followed by execution at the hand of their Oahu chief, should they be found guilty beyond a reasonable doubt.

George's careful, two-day inquisition did, indeed, result in the execution of the three accused men, performed in as solemn and as awful a ceremony as possible, under full witness of the ships' companies and those few natives who dared to watch. Again, George's

words are spare and eloquent: "The criminals were taken one by
one into a double canoe, where they were lashed hand and foot,
and put to death by *Tennavee*, their own chief, who blew out their
brains with a pistol."

Rumours quickly circulated that three innocent men had been
selected, ones who bore bodily punctures—tattoos of a sort—
similar to the guilty men, that these sacrificial lambs might satisfy
George's thirst for blood. George was horrified by these idle accusations, for he believed he had conducted this business with indisputable fairness. He had provided the court for staging the trial, but
left judgement, sentencing, and execution entirely in the chiefs'
hands. The chiefs had no doubts about the correctness of their deci-
sions and actions, from which George took courage and dismissed
his detractors' malicious gossip.

The next two days were spent exploring the immediate harbour,
which was large and richly endowed with pearl oysters [Pearl Har-
bour], and a smaller bay, which was fronted by a village known as
Honolulu. The island had been laid to waste to a lesser degree than
Maui, but the land and people were in serious decline nonetheless.
As sweet water was not easily obtained there, and fresh produce was
in limited supply, George sailed for the lush island of Kauai, there
to complete his requirements for water and provisions.

If George dared wax tender describing Raheina, then he was
equally bold in penning his impressions of Kauai, an island he had
visited twice before, but had never seen so lovingly as when
Raheina was at his side.

> ... the country presented a most delightful, and even en-
> chanting, appearance; not only from the richness of its verdure,
> and the high state of cultivation in the low regions, but from the
> romantic air that the mountains assumed, in various shapes and
> proportions, clothed with a forest of luxuriant foliage, whose dif-
> ferent shades added great richness and beauty to the landscape.

Delightful; enchanting; romantic... these were not common
words to George. The writing of his journal was, from the outset,

"calculated to *instruct*, even though it should fail to *entertain.*" His journal is, indeed, a most disciplined exercise—dry reading, that is, for those with limited imaginations.

One need not possess great imaginative powers, however, to envision the Niihau girls standing at the ship's rail with George and expressing their unbounded pleasure at beholding beloved, familiar shores (for people of Niihau and Kauai travel readily between islands), which they had long doubted ever seeing again. Who would not feel the joy they professed and, by it, love them the more for their happiness and gratitude? No doubt, this pleasure was heightened by the necessity of soon parting, for is not "romantic air" also laced with such poignancy? Scented by the fleeting nature of beauty and affection?

As it was nearly the end of March, George was under increasing pressure to sail for the coast of America; he was driven by the need to make the most of the summer season and by the faint hope of completing his northwest survey come fall. George had little time to forward his survey of Kauai or to extend his peace negotiations there, but he made full use of the few days available to him.

George renewed his friendship with the old regent, Enemo, who had suffered a most shocking decline during the intervening year. Enemo pushed himself to the limits of pain to enjoy George's company, a flattery George took as a most serious obligation. Enemo confirmed rumours from Hawaii that Niihau had suffered a drought of unmatched severity; no produce was available, and no natives now lived there. Raheina and Tymarow must be settled at Kauai, but where? And would they be safe?

They were much changed by their year abroad, and they were, by certain of their experiences, in mortal danger. Women of the Sandwich Islands lead lives quite separate from the men, each having her own house in which to go about her daily business. They lie with one another elsewhere, for they are forbidden from entering into one another's houses, sharing living facilities, or even eating together.

Raheina and Tymarow had been favourably impressed by the pleasant community European men and women enjoy together, so much so, they quickly adopted it as their own. Sandwich Islands law held this crime to be so heinous that punishment was death; Raheina and Tymarow might become the first civilized ladies to be murdered there. How strange that Raheina might share her personal favours with George as she pleased, without fear of any but nature's repercussions, yet for sharing food at his table, she could be killed. My, how she and George had sinned together!

At Maui, Kahekili and Kaeo had assured George that they accepted the innocence of the Niihau ladies and would protect them. At Kauai, Enemo, the young prince, and Kauai's lesser chiefs agreed to abide by these declarations. George proposed purchasing a house and a small portion of land for the girls, but the island chiefs refused him. Instead, they agreed to give each girl an estate, which George insisted be vested in him, "that no person whatever should have any right in it, but by my permission; and that I would allow Raheina and Tymarow to live upon the estates."

Surprisingly, the chiefs agreed. On March 29th, George became a trustee landholder at Kauai, with Raheina and Tymarow as his permanent tenants. What man who loves a woman cannot see the happy potential of this arrangement? To augment George's pleasure, the chosen, contiguous estates were in size, beauty, and value far above his most sanguine expectations. The one nearest the sea and the most extensive was allotted to Raheina, no doubt in recognition of her higher rank, although the natives perhaps wished to honour Captain Vancouver's particular interest in her as well.

Nothing more remained for George to do at Kauai at that pass. Peace was in the offing next winter; the ships were fully watered and well provisioned; the survey of Kauai was in good order; Raheina and Tymarow were safely settled on their new lands. In words that belie little emotion, George simply wrote that Raheina and Tymarow, "attended us to the beach, where they took an affectionate leave, and we embarked for the ship . . ."

Aboard the *Discovery*, George bade farewell to native friends still employed procuring supplies, and, as they took their payment and leave, their final words were promises to George "to pay every attention, and afford all possible assistance and protection, to their countrywomen whom we had just landed, and in whose future happiness and welfare they knew we had great interest." We? Which we? One need not think too hard.

At ten that night, George put to sea. What of Raheina then, as she watched the ships' lights flicker and fade, riding under white wings into the night? And what of George, as he dined in his cabin without her sweet company for the first time in many months? As he stood at the rail, under cloak of darkness, gazing at the receding black mountains and verdant plains, a part of which was now pledged to him?

He would return. Surely that was a comfort. He would return.

20

Second Survey Season

All Fool's Day came round, for the second time since leaving England, just as Kauai dropped from sight. To mark the anniversary and to fill the sharp sadness George felt anew at leaving shores and friends he might never see again, he gathered his officers to sup on the best cheer his dear Sandwich Islands could afford.

For the people, he ordered a double allowance of grog to commemorate the day. To which sweethearts they drank this time, in their hearts if not by their words, one need not ponder: England's fair beauties were now as remote as dreams; their Sandwich Islands 'wives' felt yet as near and real as their rum-warmed bellies.

As if to match the chill grey state of George's spirit, the weather suddenly turned cold and gloomy. And, as if to match his own slow decrepitude, the *Discovery* was falling into premature old age, through overwork and limited opportunities to mend her properly.

She began shipping water at the bows shortly after leaving Kauai, and the cause could not be determined, nor the fault repaired, while on the high seas. Continual bailing was necessary to keep her head up—a tiring, tedious chore fuelled by all hands' unspeakable fear of joining the ghosts of sailors whose screams were silenced as they slipped to the black, briny depths, their fates unknown, their tales untold.

Despite the men's best efforts, the water was gaining on them. The pumps were set to good use, but the leak outstripped their labours, growing in pace just beyond all efforts to contain it. Fortunately, it was a slowly rising influx; chances were good they would make American shores sodden, but safe, if the timbers held and the crossing was swift.

The crossing was not swift, however, for the weather was against them, extending the usual three to four week run to the northwest coast by several weeks. The relentlessly growing leak, with water gushing into the forward hold at above one foot each hour, made it imperative to land at the first opportunity, thus George steered for Cape Mendocino, near 40° north latitude, rather than the appointed rendezvous with the *Chatham* at Nootka, near 50° north.

Even when in such a worrisome state, George was ever the explorer, for his vessel's slow undoing now afforded him the opportunity to reconnoitre a bay laid down on Spanish maps in 1775 by Bruno de Hezeta, with whom Señor Quadra had sailed in consort. Trinidad Bay appeared, from first approach on May 1st, to be less handsome than Quadra had recalled to George. Upon anchoring there on May 2nd, George's initial disappointment was confirmed. The roadstead was unprotected and unsafe; the beach was unsuited for careening. The necessary—perhaps even vital—repairs could not be made there. Damn the Spaniards' sloppy charts and empty boasts! And bless Don Quadra's many other graces, by which he redeemed himself from ready contempt.

The *Discovery* quit Trinidad "Nook", as George thought it better named, shipping ever more water as she pushed through the waves. By May 10th, for the first time since leaving Kauai, the sea smoothed its ruffled breast sufficiently for a close inspection of the bows, and Heaven be praised, the leak was discovered and temporarily patched. Now, it was straight to Nootka with all speed, for the five-month surveying season was already decimated and would be twice-over by the time they picked up where they left off the previous year.

As expected, Spanish colours still flew high over Nootka's shores, but the red and gold now also flew high over a new fortification erected on Hog Island, where 11 small cannons guarded the entrance to the sound and to Friendly Cove. Commandant Salvador Fidalgo and his men had been busy that winter, entrenching Spain's settlement there, despite the insecurity of her claim.

A Spanish vessel and two English traders were in port; the *Chatham* was not among them. Señor Fidalgo received George hospitably and quickly informed him that the *Chatham* had arrived on April 15th, much in need of repair and with many of her men in poor health from a tumorous condition. He had supplied Captain Puget and company with every assistance and amenity available, which were applied with such success that all were restored to good order, and they had sailed just two days ago, on May 18th. Captain Puget left a letter for George, detailing his progress to date. His departure was according to George's instructions, should the *Discovery* not make Nootka Sound by mid-May. Their next rendezvous would be at the channel where they quit last season's survey.

Fidalgo's solicitous care of his English guests convinced George that the new fortifications were, as the Spaniards claimed, to repel ships of other nations. George felt that they "added greatly to the respectability of the establishment" and further, "[Fidalgo] very justly considered employment as essentially necessary to the preservation of his people's health, which began to decline towards the spring. . . . " Indeed, Fidalgo complained of having passed a most irksome winter, characterized by incessant rain, punctuated in February by a severe earthquake and in April by a violent storm. A man and a boy died of the scurvy; work and wild vegetables saved the rest.

Where George admired the new breastwork and the industriousness it bespoke, most in his company took it as an affront to English claims and of such poor handiwork and small stature, it would merely annoy, not repel, foreign vessels. Once again, George stood alone in his judgement, refusing to fabricate a sinister scenario from a few sickly Spaniards' employment, and once again, his people thought him a fool for respecting Fidalgo's presumptuous, pitiful efforts.

George did not hold Spanish charts in any esteem, however, an opinion strengthened by Puget's report of the dangers he had met in early April when attempting to retrace the shores of Nootka Island using a chart supplied by Señor Quadra. (Not only is Nootka Sound situated on a very large island, but the port itself is at the southern tip of a much smaller island.) All hands aboard the *Chatham* agreed that their hair-raising misadventures through a narrow channel, fighting a deadly riptide, had been due to the shameful inaccuracy of the Spanish chart.

George's contempt for these useless documents was matched by pride in his own fine survey; the more disreputable Spain's efforts proved to be, the more certain he was that Britain would reap the rewards of his labours. Further, he hoped that no sailors of any nation would ever be led by his charts into inescapable danger and thus curse him from their watery tombs. Such a responsibility this is, extending well beyond the grave, and by this alone, George ranks among those rare visionaries who see life beyond their own short span.

A second Spanish vessel made Nootka soon after the *Discovery*, bringing Señor Ramon Saavedra to replace Señor Fidalgo as commanding officer of the port. Saavedra brought several letters for George, one of which was from Count Revilla Gigedo, Viceroy of New Spain and a most enlightened gentleman. His Excellency informed him of Lieutenant Broughton's safe conduct through Mexico and extended "the most flattering assurances of every support and assistance that the kingdoms of New Spain were capable of bestowing." How reassuring this promise was, and how unsuspecting all were of its hollowness. George and company had such pleasant anticipations of visiting Californian ports again come autumn, it was perhaps as well that they laboured hard for the summer under false hopes.

Another equally welcome letter was from the beloved commandant of San Blas, Señor Bodega y Quadra. Accompanying his letter was a well-chosen variety of gifts for George and his officers, proving that "this good man's kindness was not confined to us when only before his Eyes, he always said he ever should remember us, and I believe he was in earnest."—penned by Edward Bell, the *Chatham*'s clerk. Ah, Don Quadra—every interchange with him was pleasant and poignant in equal measure, bringing tears of joy and yearning to George's eyes. He prayed, with letter and presents in hand, that he might see that noble man again, if just once more before they must part forever.

George despatched a letter to the Admiralty in Fidalgo's care, to be forwarded from San Blas. His accounting of the winter's activities made its way home and remains yet in the Admiralty's keeping—perhaps too dry a report to warrant its destruction, but more likely not filed where a vindictive young lord and his accomplices might lay hand to it. George made no mention then of Mr. Pitt's continuing unruly behaviour, so consistently and tediously did this young man attempt to vex his very soul. Another summer of surveying work, gruelling beyond last year's foretaste, might remove a little stuffing from Pitt's shirt. George could only hope—and faintly, by then. So faintly, in fact, George was of a mind, when next he rotated his midshipmen in their duties, to demote Mr. Pitt to as junior a position as possible. He regretted his promotion of Pitt to master's mate two years previously, an error in the first instance that could be corrected easily enough.

There was not a moment to waste on the scoundrel, however; indeed, there was not a moment to waste for any purpose except surveying. Hasty repairs were done on the *Discovery* at Nootka, whence she sailed on May 23rd to join the *Chatham* in Burke's Channel. Three days later, the ships were in consort, and three days beyond that, George set out in one of two boat parties to begin surveying the continental shore. He was ill, miserably ill. The weather was wet, miserably wet. Before them lay a stupendous and desolate land, made drearier still by endlessly riddled waterways certain to cost them three miles of rowing for every mile charted.

Their food and drink were more generous this season (George sent an additional quantity of wheat and portable soup, to supply two hot meals per day, and an additional quantity of discretionary spirits), and their boats and gear were much improved, with better raincover and smaller tents for camping on narrow beaches. Cold rains mocked these clever measures, falling so incessantly that all were thoroughly sodden for days on end. As well, few wild foods could be found to supplement the ships' stores, which, while adequate, were base and boring. These sufferings did not hinder their progress, however, as they slaved from first light to last.

They encountered numerous Indians along the way, to whom George extended a respectful commerce. His people found ready trade in sea-otter skins and, being equally interested in examining young ladies' skins, made known their gallant wants. Imagine what disappointment greeted them, therefore, when the objects of their desire stood before them and appeared so hideous that even the keenest members withered at the sight.

The females upon that stretch of coast mutilate their faces by cutting a wide slit beneath their lower lips, which they stretch about a large, polished wooden labret. Even Thomas Manby, famous among his mates for his enchantment with all womankind, reacted to the labrets with disgust and abhorrence. Until he met these ladies, he had found no other fault with the heavenly sex than want of cleanliness, which soap and water soon remedied, hence he had not suffered a monkish existence the previous summer. This year, however, young Casanova seemed foiled at last.

Manby coaxed one fair maiden to remove her labret, hoping she might regain some beauty by so doing, but he was even more greatly repulsed at the result. "O' Woman, lovely Women," he lamented, "I did not conceive it possible that any woman, in any shape, could assume a loathsome appearance, but so it is." In repose, the labret was ugly enough; in motion, it was both unsightly *and* absurd, as Bell noted:

As may readily be supposed, this beauteous ornament affects their Speech—or rather their articulation—in a very great degree, and it is droll to observe this enormous Trencher wagging up and down at every word the wearer says, and this it does with a most extravagant motion very often, for the Women of this part of the world, like many other parts, wear the Breeches, and are not only great Scolds, but great Orators, and the vehemence and violence with which they speak, gives ample play to the Trencher.

The worst privation, to most but Manby's mind, was lack of native food, for greens were scarce in that season and fishes nigh impossible to catch. All hands were cold, wet, stiff, and craved fresh provisions for nine of the 11 days the boat parties were out; they were merely stiff, exhausted, and hungry for the final two days, when the weather finally turned pleasant.

A retrospective note is required here, for during that excursion, George surveyed a head of land that appeared no different from countless such features on that vast coast, yet was soon to gain a significance George could not guess. Indeed, he died without knowing how close he had come to meeting another great British explorer there, had he been in those waters but six weeks later.

Alexander Mackenzie forged his way across the North American continent to the Pacific Ocean in the spring and summer of 1793, the first white man to do so by a route north of Mexico. From his journal, published in 1801, these words fairly leap from the page:

Sunday, July 21 . . . Under the land we met with three canoes, with fifteen men in them. . . One of them in particular made me understand, with an air of insolence, that a large canoe had lately been in this bay, with people in her like me, and that one of them, whom he called *Macubah*, had fired on him, and that *Bensins* had struck him on the back, with the flat part of his sword. [By his troublesome nature], I do not doubt but he well deserved the treatment which he described. He also produced several European articles, which could not have been long in his possession. From his conduct and appearance, I wished very much to be rid of him. . . .

Macubah can only be Vancouver, although there is little likelihood George fired *on* him; George may have fired over him, to impress upon him the absolute superiority of firepower over brute force. Bensins? Menzies? Not likely, for Menzies was not in George's boat, and further, he was not a man given to striking anyone, excepting perhaps to save his life. Since Menzies makes no mention of an altercation in his journal, and George had no recollection of a violent meeting with natives during that excursion, one must cast a sceptical eye on the report of a disgruntled warrior.

Nonetheless, there the greater truth is: George was disproving the existence of the Northwest Passage by salt water on the one hand, while Alexander Mackenzie was proving it by sweet water on the other. By God, if they could have met! Two halves of the world would have come full circle at that instant, bringing east and west together at last, closing the book on the last great geographic mystery. Such are the joys of the armchair geographer, at leisure to imagine the impossible, while our real explorers suffer every privation in their attempts to *do* the impossible, nearly missing all manner of wonders and horrors in their quest.

June was George's birth month, marking the end of his 36th year. The 22nd dawned clear, a boon for the next surveying expedition, which set forth that day at sunrise. George was too ill to go, and he was in a mournful state, not principally from self-pity for his own declining health, but because of a recent and most dreary mishap.

On June 15th, Mr. Johnstone's boat party had made a breakfast of roasted mussels, which was their usual practice wherever these tasty morsels were found. Within an hour of eating them, several men suffered from numbness, sickness, and giddiness. Three became progressively paralysed, despite all exertions to keep them mobile, and one died several hours later. (Manby and his boat party had gorged on poisoned mussels the previous year and suffered sufficiently for all to have been given fair warning, but clearly, the lesson of cautious moderation when eating this native food was ignored by this year's hungry crew.)

George was informed that, "His death was so tranquil, that it was some little time before they could be perfectly certain of his dissolution. . . . From his first being taken his pulse was regular, though it gradually grew fainter and weaker until he expired, when his lips turned black, and his hands, face, and neck were much swelled."

Four men in George's care were dead now: one drowned in the Channel before leaving England; one succumbed to the flux; one took his own life; now one was poisoned by mussels. Each death weighed heavily on George, in part because he needed all hands to complete an arduous task, but his grief was not that cold. Each life has its own integrity and sanctity, and he reflected painfully upon how he might have saved his young charges from expiring, if he could have been at all places at all times, and all things to all his people. Untimely death filled George with a profound sense of failure, especially as he increasingly felt the grim reaper's presence, shrouding his own undertakings in morbid doubt.

Mussels were now a forbidden food, reducing all hands to a poor diet, indeed. The bay where George had passed his birthday was nicknamed Starve-Gut Cove, and to worsen matters, unpleasant weather quickly closed in again. None of this slackened the survey's progress, for only the convolutions of the land itself slowed their dogged northerly push.

At the ships' next moorage, the best bower anchor broke at the palm, "to our great surprize and mortification. . . The anchor appeared to have been composed of very bad materials, and to have been very ill wrought. . . .

"Such were the anchors with which we were supplied for executing this tedious, arduous, and hazardous service . . . A loss of confidence in the stability of these our last resources, must always be attended with the most painful reflections that can occur in a maritime life."

The most painful reflections? Strong words! Is this simply the voice of a melancholy man, or is it the plaint of a master mariner? It is some of both, no doubt, but more the latter than the former.

George had been frustrated numerous times past by the Admiralty's oversights, but for them to give short shrift on such vital equipment as anchors was frightening and unforgivable. They had willfully punished William Bligh on the *Bounty* by cutting corners and costs at every opportunity, which contributed handsomely to the difficulties of his command. George had never been in Whitehall's disfavour, yet they treated him just as cavalierly, as if to say that everything and everyone on his expedition was of lesser import than their own well-lined pockets and comfortable ambitions. Damn them all, for putting 150 men's lives at risk to save a few guineas on equipment prone to failure should "we be driven to the cruel necessity of resorting to them as a last resource."

By July 10th, fishes were caught in welcome numbers, and berries were ripening in useful quantities. On July 20th, George ran in with three English merchant vessels, under the command of the unscrupulous William Brown, with whom he spent the day before parting company. Brown had recently shot several native men at a village to the northward, where the tribes were growing increasingly bold and hostile. Their war canoes were longer than the *Chatham*, and their desire for firearms apparently overcame all fear. George had been warned, therefore, but he put little stock in any trader's words, so disposed were they to cheating, lying, bullying, and earning the Indians' treatment in kind.

George's health rallied sufficiently for him to lead the surveying expedition that set off on July 24th. The weather was splendid, and wild food was abundant. The natives he encountered did, indeed, appear menacing, with painted countenances and threatening postures, but George trusted that his policy of cautious respect and honest dealing would keep all parties on good terms.

On August 12th, George's yawl and accompanying launch were 140 miles from the ships, and it was in this remote location that tragedy reared its terrifying head. On calm seas and under hazy skies, George directed his boat to separate from the launch and make for the high, rocky shore, that he might take some requisite angles. Several natives paddled toward the yawl in two small canoes in search of good-humoured barter. While on shore, these Indians grew increasingly clamorous, halooing to four large, distant canoes to join the fray, which they did. The largest canoe was under the steerage of an old woman, with a remarkably large labret, who urged the warriors on with a steady harangue.

Upon returning to the yawl, George saw that the natives were in a very thievish, turbulent mood. He ordered his men to quit the shore with all haste and head for the launch, but the native canoes surrounded his boat and held her fast by the gunwales, oars, and lead line. The old vixen redoubled her scolding; a young warrior jumped onto the bow of the yawl and donned a threatening wolf-faced mask; another warrior dared snatch a musket.

The clamour and treachery surrounding George was frighteningly reminiscent of Captain Cook's last moments; in an equally unsettling parallel, the launch was too far distant to provide succour. George stepped forward with musket in hand to speak to the chief, which caused more than 50 Indian daggers and spears to bristle at him from all directions.

From this harrowing position, George had some success convincing the chief to belay his people's evil designs, but the old woman "put forth all the powers of her turbulent tongue to excite, or rather to compel the men, to act with hostility towards us." The likelihood of attack slowed and surged several times over the next ten minutes, with several more firearms falling into native hands, but finally, the old woman's words won out, and George's destruction seemed inevitable.

George's failed negotiations had won sufficient time for the launch to arrive within pistol-shot and, as he had no other choice, he gave the order to fire. Fire they did (unlike Williamson's shameful refusal when Cook waved for such aid), and the effect was astonishing, so quickly did the natives scatter overboard and make for shore. The tragedy of the event was that a number of native men were killed—estimates ranged from six to 12—and some greater number were injured. Two of George's men suffered serious, but non-fatal, injury.

Again, unnecessary and untimely death rendered George despondent. He blamed himself principally; he had foolishly relaxed

his guard against the natives, so peaceably had all previous encounters proceeded. He instantly tightened his own strict rules and orders, adding the condition that all firearms be kept close at hand
and in perfect readiness to fire at all times.

This information, and in much greater detail, can be got by any
reader from George's own journal, yet there is a further purpose for
reiterating this melancholy event upon these pages—a speculative
purpose of some import. Camelford complained of being flogged
three times upon George's ship, yet only the first two instances are
fixed in time and place (by Menzies's recounting), the first more
certainly than the second, and the third not specified at all. There
is some likelihood that he was flogged on board ship shortly after
the deadly confrontation with natives, or so one might guess from
Menzies's mention of distressingly hard punishments being inflicted
in the latter half of August, 1793. Who was whipped and for what
reason, he did not say, nor, indeed, does any record exist.

Floggings were mentioned sporadically in the officers' journals,
but George often banned their written notice—for the benefit of
his men, not to cover his own backside, that their poorest service
not overshadow their best, and thus dog them for years to come.
Floggings were to right past wrongs and put an end to the matter;
the captain's word, not the written record, would get each hand his
just reward.

Might Pitt have done something to precipitate the attack, such
as taunting the haranguing old woman? Or angering the warriors by
cheeky trading early in the encounter? Or failing to fire when
George ordered all able hands to do so? Perhaps, but nowhere is this
information now available, and at no time would George discuss information best put before the courts. Did the officers' journals that
are missing contain damning references to Pitt and the behaviour
that earned him his final flogging—behaviour so incontestably foolish or foul, he was compelled to destroy the evidence before it came
to trial?

All that remain are three facts: first, some unspeakable punishments took place soon after the tragedy; second, about that time,
George stripped Pitt of his position as master's mate retroactive to

June 1st, the second anniversary of his promotion to the post; and third, George bequeathed a strange, perhaps telling, place-name for the site.

Thomas Manby refers to the site as Skirmish Bay and the headland Cape Skirmish, likely because George called them that at the time. George placed them on the map, however, as Traitor's Cove and Escape Point [still named Traitors Cove and Escape Point]. It appears that he changed his mind about the names sometime after the initial dubbing, which he did occasionally. The word 'traitor' is a puzzle, for George was not one to consider the native people as traitors for attempting to steal what they could not get by trade or to seek revenge upon one group of white men for ill-treatment they might have received from another. 'Skirmish' seems altogether the more appropriate name for George to apply, yet Traitor's Cove won out. Why?

Such speculation brings one to the very verge of memory, making one want to grasp beyond life itself, shake the dear departed from their eternal slumbers, and press them with questions that should have been asked before time ran out. In lieu of that, one searches in vain through a haze of recollections, trying to sort out exactly what was said, when and why. Did George ever speak of Pitt's demotion? Allude to his third flogging? Traitor's Cove... Traitor's Cove...how the name teases the unknowing, unremembering mind.

There were ample opportunities throughout the voyage for Pitt to follow his own counsel and earn a flogging for it; one must be contented knowing that he moaned loud and long about having been whipped three times, and George did not deny this count. Enough of Traitor's Cove, therefore, whatever George intended by it.

Four days later, the yawl and launch arrived back at the ships, having covered 700 geographical miles in 23 days. To George's great frustration, they had advanced the tracing of the continental boundary only 20 leagues, or approximately 60 miles, northward of the ships. For such little gain, he had pushed himself too far, too hard; he was too ill to lead the remaining boat parties that summer.

Of seven anchorages total, he left the ships on surveying excursions only twice.

The northerly press continued, through a gauntlet of dangerous waterways and unpredictable natives, along the inside passage of Prince of Wales Island, until September 21st, when the days had grown too short and the weather too inclement to continue. Nearly all hands had worked to the utmost of their abilities for so long, under such trying conditions, George was anxious "that the vessels should retire to some milder region, where refreshments might be obtained; and where such relaxation and ease . . . might be given to those under my command, whose zeal and laborious exertions, during the summer, had justly intitled them to my best thanks and highest commendation."

George's men, with few exceptions, were the finest, hardest-working lot of sailors ever put together, and George was not remiss in conveying his approbation. They would repair to Nootka for the briefest possible stay, for the storms there were as fierce as those some six or seven degrees to the northward, where their summer's work concluded. Then they would be off to California, where warm weather and an equally warm welcome were assured—or so they thought. Such promises would spur them on: warm, alluring, empty promises.

21
California Revisited

George and company turned their backs to latitude 56° 30′ (that being the farthest northward the boats had plied) with keen regret that the damnably intricate archipelago stretching from Cape Flattery to this point had slowed their northerly progress and now necessitated a third season of surveying—a hardship for all hands and a possible death sentence for George, if his health did not improve at California and the Sandwich Islands.

George tried to lift flagging spirits by reflecting that the most arduous part of their task was now done, according to Spanish claims that the coastline above 56° 30′ was unbroken and intact. Next season would be easier—dear God, may Spanish charts for once be trustworthy!

Admiral Bartholomew de Fonte's pretended discovery of a Northwest Passage in present latitudes could now be laid to rest.

The time and place had come to decide, absolutely, that both de Fuca's and de Fonte's old chimerae were dead, hence George named the turnaround promontory Cape Decision, lying just southward of Conclusion Island.

To complete his instructions to the letter, George had two further tasks to attend: he must complete his survey of the outer coastline southward to 30° and northward to 60°; and he must settle the irksome Nootka business. To his own thinking, he had a third task as well: to bring peace to Hawaii, if possible by its cession to King George.

En route to San Francisco, the ships lost time along the outer coast of Queen Charlotte's Islands, which George was determined to fix with some accuracy upon his great map and, by so doing, he proved once again that the charting efforts of Spanish explorers and English traders alike were contemptible. Nonetheless, for every vaguely recognizable feature, George retained the name conferred by its discoverer, regardless of nationality, thereby paying tribute to their brave ventures onto unknown seas.

The ships were further delayed at Nootka, where George had hoped to rendezvous with the *Daedalus*. She was not in port, nor, indeed, did the presiding officer Saavedra report having much company all summer. The odd little trading brig had straggled in, most flying American colours and in pathetic condition, beyond Saavedra's capacity to serve. He suffered a brief flurry of excitement when a large French vessel, *La Flavie*, stood in Friendly Cove—excitement he well wished away.

The Frenchmen were mutinous, and not for the first time. They had successfully overthrown their commanding officers at St. Peter and St. Paul on the Kamchatka peninsula, where the primary business of their voyage was to exchange European goods for Russian-gathered furs. The mutineers capitulated following that uprising, but the reinstated officers were so fearful of the rabble on board staging their own little French Revolution, they dared not punish the perpetrators sufficiently well to kill the yeast in a bitter brew.

Saavedra was on board when the second insurrection arose, which his hosts barely managed to quell. To his dismay, they again refused to punish the ringleader, though they had him in irons. So vocal and adamant was Saavedra that they flog him, he had the satisfaction of seeing this vile man brought to justice and, he hoped, to his knees. Saavedra had no great hope, however, that her spineless captain had seen the end of his troubles, for as *La Flavie* set sail for China—to trade her furs for teas to take home—the crew was shouting about bringing their ill usage before the National Assembly.

For Saavedra, it was enough that the feverish vessel was gone; the taint of mutiny left a noxious smell in the air, the winds of which were now circulating the globe. George concurred. He made little and light mention of this news, for mutiny feeds voraciously on gossip, and he would have none of it. His own ships were running satisfactorily, since he had reorganized his people the previous year; only a few troublemakers were under his sharp eye, that he might catch and punish them swiftly and firmly, to prevent their crimes from mounting and spreading. The (dis)Honourable Thomas Pitt headed that rare company, *summa cum laude*, but his days were numbered. One more transgression, and he would be in chains, dismissed and awaiting transfer to a suitable transport vessel. Would that *La Flavie* were still at Nootka; Pitt would make a worthy mate aboard that ship of hot-headed, hell-bent fools.

The *Discovery* and *Chatham* were three days only at Nootka, taking on extra wood and water. All hands enjoyed the company of Saavedra and his small garrison, who generously shared what few civilized pleasures and wild foods were at their command. On October 8th, George happily saluted his Spanish friends and sailed for San Francisco, where he naively expected a similar welcome.

Fifty miles north of San Francisco lies a harbour known as Bodega Bay (named for Commandant Bodega y Quadra), which Spain was rumoured to be settling that summer. George directed the *Chatham* to reconnoitre the area, whilst the *Discovery* made directly for San Francisco, where they would next rendezvous.

On the evening of October 19th, the *Discovery*'s anchor found bottom in San Francisco's bay. The old commandant of San Francisco, Ensign Hermenegildo Sal, came off to welcome George.

Over supper in the ship's cabin, Sal graciously offered his services and hospitality, and he brought word of European affairs to men starved for news for nearly a year. Shocking stuff! In Sweden, King Gustavus III had been assassinated in the Stockholm Opera House. In France, King Louis XVI and his family had been routed from Versailles, taken to Paris, and imprisoned in the Tuileries. All France was in an uproar, bleeding from within and without. She had declared war on Austria, Prussia, and Sardinia; French troops crossed the Rhine, took Brussels, and conquered the Austrian Netherlands. To what madness would the *Discovery* and *Chatham* return? George had sailed home from Cook's final voyage to find all Europe sucked into the vortex of the American Revolution; now, it seemed he would return from his own monumental voyage to find all Europe being consumed by the beastly French Revolution.

George was further disheartened the next morning, when two letters arrived for him from Señor Sal. One letter requested that George acquaint him in writing of his arrival at the port, of the supplies he should want, and of the time he intended to remain in port, that Sal might forward this information to his superior at Monterey. The other letter stated that Sal was under orders to insist that no Englishmen come ashore, except to procure wood and water; only George and one officer might pass to the presidio.

What the Devil was this? George was perplexed and chagrined, indeed! The meaning was clear—"These restrictions were of a nature so unexpected, ungracious, and degrading, that I could not but consider them as little short of a dismission from St. Francisco..."—but why was this year's reception so very different from last? To his credit, Señor Sal appeared to be an unwilling partner in this nasty business, forced upon him by the governor who had replaced Arguello. José Joaquín de Arrillaga was behind the rebuff, and George determined to sail at first opportunity to Monterey, to see this monstrous man in the flesh.

Unfortunately, he had to wait for the *Chatham*. She arrived on the 21st, with news that Bodega Bay bore no trace of settlement. Then George had to wait yet longer while the tedious chore of watering was accomplished. In this humiliating circumstance, his people dared complain that he was a shameful milksop, complying too readily with every restriction, when he should have stormed off in a huff and made instantly for Monterey, to have it out with Arrillaga. This was neither possible, for water was too serious a want, nor would it have been fair to Señor Sal, who had showed his true colours the previous year and was now making the best he could of a regrettable circumstance. Thus, George suffered in fuming, wounded silence, forced to wait out the slowly passing days, while holding in his anger at Spaniards and Britons alike.

On October 24th, his vessels sailed free from one frosty reception bound for the next, which was certain to be icier still. The trial for George was to keep his head cool and his heart warm, rather than the reverse, but he was determined to do so, to show that martinet Arrillaga how a gentleman conducts himself, be damned what anyone, ally or foe, might say.

Fortune was not entirely against George, for the *Daedalus* appeared the day after he quit San Francisco, thereby alleviating the *Discovery*'s and *Chatham*'s sorry state of provisions and stores, goods for which George was loath to beg at any Spanish port, and most particularly Monterey.

As expected, George's arrival at Monterey on November 1st received a curt welcome from Arrillaga, who insisted all business be conducted in writing. He then sent two letters, in content similar to those from Señor Sal. George complied with Arrillaga's punctilious requests for information, but in the most vigorous terms defended his purpose, in so doing upbraiding the arrogant governor for his narrow, mean view: "... That the voyage in which we were engaged, was for the general use and benefit of mankind, and that under these circumstances, we ought rather to be considered as labouring for the good of the world in general, than for the advantage of any particular sovereign, and that the court of Spain would be more early informed of, and as much benefited by my labours, as the kingdom of Great Britain. That in consequence of these instructions, I had exchanged some charts with Señor Quadra, and others were ready for his reception. That I had not only been treated on my former visit here with the greatest friendship, and unbounded hospitality; but had received from his Excellency, the viceroy of Mexico, the strongest assurances, that these attentions had been shewn in compliance with the desire of his Catholic Majesty..." and so forth—a lengthy expostulation that earned a pinched reply, delivered on November 4th, complete with a reiteration of the severe restrictions under which George and his people must labour while in port. This was too much! The despicable governor was not even worth George's thunderous ill humour, a man whom he described to the Secretary of the Admiralty as having a "sneering, forbidding and ungracious stile... degrading and humiliating to the character and situation in which I am placed...." Fortunately, that letter survives, although the accompanying chart is missing.

George instantly declined any further correspondence and refused the sour assistance proffered by Arrillaga. He determined to retire as quickly as possible to the Sandwich Islands, where he trusted that the uneducated inhabitants of Hawaii and its neighbouring isles would cheerfully afford him every accommodation that had been unkindly denied at San Francisco and Monterey.

Yes, his dear Sandwich Islanders would greet him enthusiastically and fête him royally. Savages, indeed! In Arrillaga's third letter, he had dared call George ingenuous, a mantle he wore with pride, so sick was he of the unwarranted treachery of supposedly civilized nations. Even without Raheina and Tymarow by his side this year at Californian ports, he loved their people the more by contrast—and, might one venture, loved Raheina the more for missing her during those difficult days? California was not the same without her; indeed, California was not the same at all.

On November 5th (Guy Fawkes Day, with no doubt about who should be the Guy and burned in effigy), George's three spurned vessels sailed from Monterey and turned their attention to charting the 6-and-some degrees of latitude remaining of their southern probe, before earning sweet respite on Hawaiian shores.

Happily, George received cautious but kindly receptions from the commandants of the ports of Santa Barbara, Buena Ventura, and San Diego. The holy fathers also extended their gracious hospi-

24. A Young Woman of Queen
Charlotte's Islands

23. Kamehameha

25. Joseph Whidbey

Discovery Nootka Sound October y.e 2.d
1794

Dear Sir.

By the jenny of Bristol which sails this
night or tomorrow morning I take the opportunity

Thus you see my good friend I am once more entrap'd in
this infernal Ocean, and am totally at a loss to say when
I shall be able to quit it, and not having it in my
power, to communicate any particular information re
-specting our voyage I shall only further add that
your Son and all your friends in these Vessels are
in perfect health though greatly mortified at our pre=
sent detention from a more active station, which would

would be more congenial to our wishes than remaining
here in a state of unpleasant inactivity.
A few days after our arrival here I had an opportunity
of writing to my brother by way of New Spain but in
case that letter might miscarry be good enough on the
receipt of this to inform him of my welfare &c.
And believe I am with sincere wishes for
the happiness of your self Mrs Sykes & Family
yours with great truth
& friendship
Geo: Vancouver

26. Details of a Letter by George Vancouver

27. "The Town of Valparaiso on the Coast of Chili"

28. Prime Minister William Pitt

29. *John Pitt, Second Earl of Chatham*

30. A Caricature of Thomas Pitt, Lord Camelford

31. William Grenville

32. Anne Pitt

33. The CANEing in Conduit Street

34. The Discovery as a Convict Hulk at Deptford in 1828

35. Captain George Vancouver (?)

tality, despite the shore restrictions Arrillaga's orders imposed. Through these good people, George came to understand something of the role he had played in fashioning this year's reception.

It seems that George had muttered something the previous year about surveying Bodega Bay, which was relayed to the governor, thence to the viceroy, as a British plan to settle and fortify the area. Worse than the alarm this caused was the threat posed by George's excellent reports and charts, which would disclose to all the world California's enviable natural wealth, so poorly developed and defended by Spain as to render it exceedingly vulnerable to attack. George's openness and ingenuousness were not separate from the issue at all; they *were* the issue.

The Nootka Crisis had called into question Spain's time-honoured tradition of territorial possession by right of prior discovery, which England threw over for the more substantial rights of subsequent claim and settlement. George was now destroying Spain's time-honoured tradition of primary defense by secrecy; his three summers of peaceful exploration and subsequent publication might begin the process by which Spain's vast and weak dominions would be dismantled with frightful ease by any nation with a warship to spare.

Secrecy was never the English way, however, hence George had no sympathy for Spain, although he now understood Arrillaga's stance. The Spanish had yet to learn that even settlement of land is not enough to hold it; their self-righteous indolence would eventually lose them some of the most blessed soil on this good earth. He guessed that the current turmoil in Europe would delay the undoing of the Spanish empire, but he also guessed that it was inevitable, by the very behaviour Arrillaga and his soldiers displayed to defend it—pompous, prickly, lazy little men all.

Mail from Europe had arrived at Buena Ventura while he was in port, but there was nothing for George. Specifically and most disappointingly, he received no further instructions from London about the Nootka settlement, leaving him to trust that word would arrive at the Sandwich Islands or Nootka in the coming year, by which he might satisfactorily complete that portion of his commission.

The Spanish officers and priests who showed George favour, who followed the letter but not the spirit of their orders, won his affection, which he expressed in several ways. First, from San Diego, he forwarded to Señor Quadra copies of his latest survey, plus a private communication protesting his treatment by Arrillaga. A lesser man might have withheld the charts, in retribution for Spain withholding her assistance, but George was a man of honour, who lived and died by a code of unfailing fairness and decency.

Quadra was no less such a man, but—unrevealed to George by the arrogant Arrillaga—dear Quadra was presently rendered powerless by deathly illness. In retrospect, George lamented that he had burdened his great friend during his darkening hours. Had Arrillaga taken courage from Quadra's imminent demise? Uncharitable thought, but Arrillaga was a singularly uncharitable man.

Second, George expressed his gratitude by naming a handful of unidentified landmarks after the Spaniards who had served him well, Arrillaga definitely not among them. And third, to one of the dearest holy fathers, he parted with the barrelled organ he had kept—indeed, cherished—in his cabin. It was in good order and repair, after nearly three years of being tossed upon some of God's hardest seas.

Father Lasuen said he would take it to the seat of government at Monterey, and there deposit it in the church, where it would be carefully preserved as a memento of George's visits to California. George could not have been more gratified. His wildly generous gift so thrilled the good father that he would bless George at every opportunity. The pious Arrillaga would be vexed by this constant praise and would wince at the sound of the organ's every joyous note. [It is now at Mission San Juan Bautista, founded in 1797.]

At last, by mid-December, the ships sailed south of 30° north latitude, marking the end of their season's explorations. George had now charted from 30° to 56° 30′ in just two summers, a most remarkable feat! All eyes now turned toward the Sandwich Isles' fair shores; all hearts now yearned for their sweet embrace. Ah, precious Hawaii, "... where I could firmly rely on the sincerity of *Tamaahmaah* [Kamehameha], and the professions of the rest of our *rude uncivilized* friends in those islands, for a hearty welcome, a kind reception, and every service and accommodation in their humble power to afford; without any of the inhospitable restrictions we must have been under from the *civilized* governor at Monterrey."

22

Aloha Hawaii

Uppermost on George's mind, as his three ships cleaved through grey seas and skies toward Hawaii's colourful shores, was his desire to bring peace to all the Sandwich Islands, if possible by their cession to Great Britain. Such an agreement would require the posting of a warship to protect and patrol the islands—something George had done for years in the West Indies. Could he picture himself upon such a vessel? With a sumptuous tract of land on Kauai awaiting his residence? Dare he dream of governorship?

Dare one speculate on such matters? With the benefit of hindsight, indeed, it seems obvious: George would sow the seeds of peace that coming winter, and he would gather the seeds of allegiance to deliver to England. Would the old king, half-mad Farmer George, accept them? Tend to them, as he did his rare plant collection at Kew Gardens? Send George back to the Sandwich Islands, to nurture the tender, entwining roots of two very distant, very different nations?

What private hopes impelled George, he never revealed; what fruit of his arduous and loving labours might have sustained him, we shall never know. It is clear, however, that he sailed to Hawaii for the third time with great prospects in mind, shadowed only by fears that time was too short to realize them. As for his dreams, one must look between the lines, for nary a word escaped his pen or lips.

Kamehameha waited for George to arrive at Hilo Bay, as planned, where he kept British colours flying over his home and an English pennant adorning the masthead of his boat. When the three ships hove into sight mid-morning of January 9th, 1794, he and his people thronged in joyous welcome.

Hilo Bay's rich soils produced a cornucopia of fresh provisions, but alas, the roadstead was too exposed for safe mooring. George must sail to Kealekekua Bay—to Kamehameha's disappointment, for a taboo prevented him from leaving his present, and very pleasant, situation. Nonetheless, it was imperative that Kamehameha attend George, if trade and peace negotiations were to be successful.

By the artifice of questioning the sincerity of Kamehameha's friendship, which mortified and wounded the king not a little, George won the day: Kamehameha made an unprecedented decision to defy the priests and quit Hilo Bay aboard the *Discovery*. George was not only touched by such loyalty; he was deeply aware of the responsibility it carried. If he failed to strengthen Kamehameha's crown, he surely would weaken it, perhaps fatally.

Kamehameha was accompanied by many chiefs, women, and children, but his stunningly beautiful young wife, Kaahumanu, was not with him this year. Rumours of her unfaithfulness with Kaiana had caused him to cast her off, although he was in much pain and doubt about the entire circumstance. George was so fond of them together, and he was in such an uncharacteristically romantic frame of mind, he expressed his wish to help fashion a reconciliation.

Kamehameha brusquely refused, stating the islands' political affairs were open to George's benevolent interference, but personal affairs were none of his business. Now George was the one to be mortified and wounded, and not undeservedly. They had each risked something of themselves for the other, and by such means, the bonds of friendship were cemented.

At Kealekekua Bay, George again put his rules and orders into place, and again his midshipmen put up a howl of protest about their restricted shore leave. They had done nothing over the past months to prove their trustworthiness, however, nor did any but Sykes deign to visit George's table, although each was sent invitations in regular rotation. Until they responded to civility in kind, they would be treated as they behaved, which was as a mob of young delinquents best held in close quarters under close watch.

Mr. Thomas Pitt finally did himself in, and trust his black heart, he tried to share the blame with Sykes, as if this one true young gentleman might save him. Pitt's transgression was usual and trifling enough, but it was a punishable offense, and George had caught him fair and square. At last, Pitt's jig was up; George would suffer no more from his endlessly defiant and devious ways.

Pitt's last watch was with Sykes on the fo'c'sle. Pitt stretched out to sleep, which the young lord took as his blue-blood privilege, with the request that Sykes rouse him at log-heaving time[14]. Sykes let him sleep and hove alone, and it was this curious situation that George espied from the quarterdeck. "Mr. Pitt!" George called, but received no reply. "Mr. Thomas Pitt!!" he called again and made for his scrambling quarry.

By looks alone, Pitt's guilt was obvious, though he dazedly and desperately denied it. Sykes stood by his mate, but to no avail. If Pitt wished to sleep on deck, then sleep he shall—and wake and eat and sit and sleep again. George instantly had Pitt put in bilboes [shackles attached to heavy iron bars, fixed to the deck just abaft

---

[14] An hourly activity to determine the ship's speed in 'knots'. The officer of the watch held the log-reel on which a line knotted at 42-50 foot intervals spun off astern, while another held the log-glass to time the number of knots run out in a half-minute.

the mainmast], with a fo'c'sle man at each side for company.

There he stayed day after humiliating day, hopelessly un-repentant for ten days or a fortnight's duration, after which George had him released. Released entirely, that is, for George discharged him from his duties, without further examination or punishment. In early February, Pitt was transferred to the *Daedalus*, which would take him to Port Jackson, where he would be free to seek his passage home.

George heard no end of threats from the boy, but they little wor-ried him, for if Pitt's hue and cry about justice continued until they met again in London, a court martial would certainly clear George's good name and forever keep this nasty little hornet from buzzing about His Majesty's ships.

Pitt was not the lone thorn—or stinger, more aptly—plucked from George's side; his good friends and fellow midshipmen Thom-as Clark from the *Discovery* and Augustus Boyd Grant from the *Chatham* were likewise relieved of their duties and removed to the *Daedalus*, which sailed on February 8th. Good-bye it was then, both to the *Daedalus*, which George dismissed from future storeship duties, and to three inveterate scoundrels stripped of all honour and now blessedly sailing away—far, far away.

George had taken provisions and stores from the *Daedalus* suffi-cient for upwards of a year at sea, by which time his survey would be done, and he would be home, or nearly so. With the most worri-some shipboard business concluded, he took up a pleasant abode ashore and devoted his full attentions to his host's needs and plea-sures.

Kamehameha was like a child with a new toy, for George had given him something that preoccupied and delighted him without end. The *Discovery*'s and *Chatham*'s carpenters were building him a 36-foot schooner—a thrilling gift of immeasurable value. He in-tently watched every detail of construction, and he talked about lit-tle else.

George was elated as well, most particularly because the little vessel would serve to protect and patrol Kamehameha's kingdom until a larger vessel could be sent from England. She had a name already: the *Britannia*. The quicker she became seaworthy, the sooner and more readily would the principal chiefs cede Hawaii to the British Crown.

In gratitude, Kamehameha took George closer into his confidence. George was allowed the unprecedented privilege of attending a sacred ritual within the priests' precinct, as a respectful observer of all taboos and rites. The second and final day of the ceremony fell on February 14th, which marked the 15th anniversary of Cook's murder on those very shores. George felt the day keenly, although much had changed, perhaps enough so that a unique union might be effected between two cultures whose first encounter had been so tragic. Annexation appeared to be at hand; then, perhaps, the old man's death would serve a noble purpose and Britain would be compensated for the loss of her greatest navigator.

When this ceremony was done, Kamehameha returned his greatest attention to the *Britannia*, which quickly took form. Despite his avid interest in the vessel, he remained despondent about his lost love, Kaahumanu. George again dared offer his assistance in fashioning a reunion, and this time, Kamehameha accepted.

On February 17th, George invited Kaahumanu and attendants to the *Discovery* from her distant hideaway, inducing them to come with promises of plentiful gifts for all. Her father, Keeaumoku of Kona, the second most powerful chief after Kamehameha, desired a reconciliation, and he encouraged her to venture forth and accept George's valuable offer.

She and her party were soon being royally regaled by George in the ship's cabin, where many presents and much laughter were the order of the day. After a time, George said he really must send a handsome gift to Kamehameha, for it was not right that so much wealth be distributed with none going to the king. In jest, he proposed sending no more than a scrap of paper elaborately wrapped. This was so ludicrous, and so in keeping with Kamehameha's love of practical jokes, everyone, including Kaahumanu, encouraged George to do this.

Unbeknownst to them, George and Kamehameha had planned it all. Kamehameha had given George *two* pieces of paper: the markings on one meant Kaahumanu appeared to favour reconciliation; the markings on the other said she did not. George wrapped the former and sent it ashore.

In an apparent state of hilarity over a fine joke, Kamehameha rushed aboard and into the cabin to acquaint George with his happy approval of such nonsense. There, he feigned complete surprise at seeing Kaahumanu, while she stood truly shocked. For a moment, she appeared ready to turn her back on him; no one dared move or breathe.

Kamehameha headed quickly for the cabin door to escape, but George had strategically placed himself to catch the king by the hand. He then took Kaahumanu's hand and brought the two together. With that, the awful silence and tension were broken, and the handsome couple embraced in tearful reunion.

Kamehameha was completely overjoyed, while Kaahumanu was cautiously happy. She expressed her weighty obligation to George for his clever intervention, and she asked George to make Kamehameha promise not to beat her, which at first George took in jest. Her eyes told the truth, however, to George's mortification. Kamehameha readily agreed to this injunction, but Kaahumanu was still uncertain. She insisted George escort them ashore and oversee her restoration to all her former honours and privileges. At that, she appeared as overjoyed as her king; George could do no more, except hope and trust.

George had another reconciliation to effect before the business of cession could be forwarded, and this one was not as easily or happily accomplished. Ideally, all six chiefs who ruled over the island should be party to the agreement, but two were missing. The chief of Hilo was preoccupied with the defence of his district and would not send a deputy. Kameeiamoku, chief of Kohala district, was also prevented from attending, but for different reasons entirely.

Kameeiamoku had led the attack against the *Fair American*, killing her young captain and his three mates. The fifth victim and only surviving crew member, Isaac Davis, was still subject to Kamehameha's good care and growing esteem. Kameeiamoku was also rumoured to have been the first to stab Captain Cook, making him doubly disgraced and so hated by the many islanders who re-vered Cook and by all Englishmen that he rightly feared for his life at Kealekekua Bay.

George was not entirely in a forgiving frame of mind, but he rea-soned that the time had come to demonstrate peace, not just talk about it . He sent an absolute pardon to Kameeiamoku, on the con-dition that he come to Kealekekua Bay. George's people were out-raged; Kameeiamoku was a pirate and a murderer, protected only by his rank. George was painfully aware of the hypocrisy of his deci-sion, for had Kameeiamoku been a common man, he certainly would have been routed out and shot. Kameeiamoku was not a common man, however, nor would he ever be one. His special rank accorded him special treatment, although George wrestled hard with his conscience before resolving to let political expediency hold sway over blind justice.

Kameeiamoku came cautiously toward Kealekekua Bay, taking several long days and sending numerous advance messengers to as-certain the sincerity of George's offer. He made a grand entrance with more than a thousand canoes—an impressive array, but evi-dently no more than usual attending this proud, fierce, slippery-looking man.

Upon meeting George, he also appeared to be a most remorseful, shameful, and terrified fellow. At the first opportunity, he apolo-gized for attacking the *Fair American* and presented his reasons for doing so, the principal of which was revenge for ill treatment by Si-mon Metcalfe (of the *Eleanore*), the young captain's father. Kameeiamoku promised exemplary behaviour in the future, with sureties from several chiefs. George shook his hand, gave him some useful gifts, then all joined in a gala dinner celebration.

Kameeiamoku was unaccustomed to spirituous liquors and took to them with great gusto, despite warnings that he was certain to get very sick from his liberal imbibing. Indeed, he soon passed out, which greatly alarmed his many ferocious warriors, who believed that George had poisoned him. Fortunately, warm water revived him, and he returned to the table in surprisingly good form. Had he died from this innocent misfortune, which could easily have happened, what hellish retribution might have been exacted is beyond the imagination. George was under no illusions: the fury that had finished Captain Cook was still burbling beneath the surface, however flawless the present veneer of civility.

George wished to begin cession talks the next day, that he might settle the matter and sail immediately thereafter, for he had other pressing business in the offing. No doubt, Kauai was on his mind, where he might reap a tender harvest from the estates tenanted by Raheina and Tymarow. As well, he had yet to finish surveying the leeward islands, and he was determined to make an early start for northern waters, to quickly conclude his grand survey and hurry home.

The priests declared a taboo, however, delaying all negotiations for five full days. George's growing frustration was dispelled somewhat by his attendance at and active participation in a second and different sort of sacred ritual, an honour surpassing the first.

The extra days gave the carpenters time to bring the *Britannia* near to completion. When they sailed, the few remaining tasks could easily be done by the handiest of the 11 white men who now lived at Hawaii—the jetsam of merchant vessels from various civilized nations.

Finally, on the morning of February 25th, the five chiefs joined George and several senior officers in the *Discovery's* cabin. Kamehameha opened the meeting with a speech explaining the reasons for cession, to which all agreed. Each chief stated his interests in swearing allegiance to Great Britain, which were discussed, modified, and accepted. Kaiana advanced the following conditions: first, that some Englishmen, duly authorized for that purpose, should reside on shore by way of guards; second, that a vessel or two would be requisite to defend them by sea; third, since the Hawaiians had difficulty telling white men apart, most particularly the English and Americans, that some on board George's vessels, who were known to belong to King George, should return to Hawaii with the succours required. Again, all agreed.

Ahhh! So therein lies the very dream George may have fancied for himself. The Hawaiian people insisted that a familiar and trusted face return to them. Who better than their beloved Captain Van? George would present to King George the splendid yellow feather cape from Kamehameha (entrusted to George the previous year), and King George in turn would bid George return to Hawaii with royal blessings. How wonderfully simple, and indeed, why not? Hawaii is the fiery gemstone of the Pacific Ocean, a precious jewel fit for any king. That it might be got for a ship and a familiar face was a bargain without equal.

George and his officers agreed that Kaiana's terms were reasonable, and the five chiefs bade that the cession ceremony begin. In turn, beginning with Kamehameha, they declared themselves no longer people of Hawaii, but people of Britain. This was instantly made known to the surrounding, approving crowd. Several officers went ashore to plant the British flag and declare possession of the island. A salute was fired from the vessels, after which an inscription on copper was deposited in a conspicuous place at Kamehameha's residence. It stated that on the 25th day of February, 1794, Kamehameha and the principal chiefs of the island assembled on board the *Discovery* in Kealekekua Bay and, in the presence of George Vancouver and other of his officers, unanimously ceded the island of Hawaii to His Britannic Majesty and acknowledged themselves to be subjects of Great Britain.

George distributed gifts to the principal chiefs, their favourite women, and various attendants. Of this great day, George wistfully wrote: "Thus concluded the ceremonies of ceding the island of Owhyhee [Hawaii] to the British Crown; but whether this addition to the empire will ever be of any importance to Great Britain, or whether the surrender of the island will ever be attended with any additional happiness to its people, time alone must determine."

Time . . . George had so little of it, and so much yet to accomplish. He was now free to leave Hawaii, something he was both anxious and loath to do. He promised his Hawaiian friends he would try to return, but he knew that his *trying* was the only certainty; his return was perhaps a pipedream—sweet-sounding, but hollow, so many were the factors beyond his control.

George's ships left Kealekekua Bay on February 26th, to coast along the northward shore searching—in vain—for other good an-chorages. Kamehameha and his queen stayed on board the *Discovery* till near midnight of March 2nd, when at last all excuses for delay were played out. Such a tearful scene it was! George gave them each their parting gifts, then, to George's surprise, Kame-hameha demanded a small piece of red fabric, large enough to make a loin cloth.

George refused to comply with this ungrateful request: he had lit-tle red cloth to spare; he had other chiefs at other places to favour with it; Kamehameha had plenty of it already. No, he had bestowed many handsome, valuable gifts upon the king, and he could give no more. Kamehameha departed in an apparent huff, with not a tear in his eye.

To George's people, his mean-spirited denial of a last, trifling gift soured a touching farewell. Kamehameha's final request was entire-ly in character, however, as was George's reaction. They each had a role to play: Kamehameha's was to stride from the *Discovery* in a manly fashion; George's was to stand firm in tearless farewell. They understood and loved each other. Half a yard of red cloth was noth-ing, a mere prop. George would give it to him when he returned, and they would laugh uproariously in fond remembrance.

George did not land at Maui or even at Oahu, although Kahekili was at Waikiki. From shipboard, George simply finished the last de-tails of his survey, then made for Kauai, excusing himself because a storm was brewing off Oahu and time was too pressing to put in along the way. Perhaps he knew that peace talks with the chiefs of the leeward islands were useless: the Hawaiian chiefs were prepar-ing to make war on them, and George was powerless to prevent it. Perhaps it would be best when Kamehameha ruled over all the is-lands, in King George's name. There would be peace in union, near and far; Kamehameha and the new governor would oversee the re-turn of prosperity to all.

George spent nearly six days at beautiful Kauai, where he found his two Niihau women, each living happily under the care of a prin-cipal chief. Tymarow had married the chief of Waimea, a man young enough to fulfill all his husbandly duties. Raheina had married ancient Enemo, now known as Wakea. He was pathetically emaciated and scurfy, a condition brought on by the intemperate use of ava juice. Was he properly Raheina's husband? One must sincerely doubt it, although George never spoke of such private matters.

George had left Raheina to fend for herself, and she had done well. Most of her European possessions had been dispersed, as was expected, but her liberality with them ensured her good standing and safe landholding. Unfortunately, crops there and everywhere upon the island were poor that year, to George's disappointment. He could not supply his ships as handsomely from Raheina's and Tymarow's fields as he had hoped.

Raheina suffered no privations and would not as long as Wakea was her ally. Whether the old chief was her husband in name or in fact, George could only be grateful for his care. In the past year, Wakea had declared independence from Kahekili and Kaeo of Maui, supported by arms bought from the unscrupulous Kendrick of the American brig *Lady Washington*, who had been at the Sandwich Islands for many months, including at Hawaii and Kauai most of George's final stay. Kahekili sent a chief and some of his men to question Wakea's intentions, but no sooner had they come ashore than they were slaughtered. Kahekili next came himself and, surprisingly, he and Wakea reached a peaceful compromise. The island was tranquil at present, but Wakea would not live much longer, which naturally caused George great concern, for reasons readily imagined.

George could stay no longer among his Sandwich Islands friends, to help them further, if, indeed, he had helped them at all. Time would tell, but his time there had run out. The melancholy this induced, compounded by his chronically depressed health, made his farewell painful beyond words. He had only to complete his survey of Niihau, which was still abandoned due to drought conditions, then he must sail away; he must trust his beloved islands and their people to the Fates, for several years at least.

On March 12th, George said his good-byes to the Kauaian chiefs, who "all took their leave (excepting one or two who proposed to accompany us to Onehow [Niihau]) with every expression of the most friendly regard and attachment, and with repeated solicitations for our speedy return."

From between these lines, one might glean two pieces of information that George would not write or say: first, as the Kauaian women aboard ship had previously accompanied the vessels to Niihau, one can be certain they did so again, to spend the last possible moment with their English lovers. Did Raheina and Tymarow follow suit? Likely they did, for George had enjoyed their good company too often in the past to forego the opportunity to share his table again with his gentle ladies. They had sinned this way before, and often; they could be none the worse for doing so one last time, with Wakea's kind forbearance.

Second, there were "repeated solicitations for a speedy return." These, George states, came from the chiefs, but would the women not voice the same wishes? As the Sandwich Islanders hold fast to their friends and are quick to shed tears, surely Raheina wept as she pleaded, "Come back soon. Oh, please, you must come back soon."

On the evening of March 14th, the *Discovery* and *Chatham* quit the Sandwich Islands, saying a last "Aloha" to treasured shores and rare friends. To these loyal people, aloha means good-bye *and* hello, for they cannot bear the thought of parting forever. Indeed, neither could George, who cherished their bittersweet greeting and the promise it held.

Goodbye, then, until we meet again. Aloha.

23
The Last Mile

No sooner had the *Discovery* and *Chatham* got under way on March 15th than they lost sight of each other; as the weather turned dark and gloomy for the next ten days, there was little chance they would reunite on their deep-water traverse. They would meet again at the appointed rendezvous of Cape Douglas, at the eastern entrance of Cook's River [Cook Inlet], there to recommence their survey eastward, then southward, to Cape Decision.

Both ships were in delicate repair, not for want of attention, but for want of new materials—masts, yards, ropes, canvas, and so forth. The most dangerous surveying work, due to icy conditions, lay before them, in vessels scarcely equal to the task. George's health was as frayed as his ships' rigging and sails, with no promise of respite or restoration, only of further wear and tear. To worsen matters, very heavy seas broke the *Discovery*'s only marine barometer, which naturally aggravated George's rising anxiety and falling spirits.

By month's end, the temperature dropped below freezing; ice formed on the scuttle cask [container of fresh drinking water] on deck for the first time in the voyage. April blew in with a blizzard of snow, casting the rigging in lovely, deadly ice. Three years had now passed since the ships sailed from dear England's shores; how long ago, far away, and impossibly comforting did she now appear.

George passed a small and dreary snow-covered island on April 4th, then drew in with the Trinity Isles the next day. A young native man and a girl came off in a canoe, by words and gestures informing him that there were six Russians on shore and that the great land beyond was called Kodiak—Kodiak *Island*, George later ascertained using Russian, Spanish, and English charts.

On April 12th, the *Discovery* entered Cook's River, which welcomed them with heavy snowfall for three days. After years at sea, the men's clothing was reduced to rags and tatters, which they wore layer upon layer in a futile attempt to stay warm. Fingers must work freely, however; ears must hear, and noses must breathe, making frost-bite unavoidable. In this weather, George could not keep his people idling at Cape Douglas waiting for the *Chatham*, nor could he afford to waste a day if he was to complete their arduous service before winter set in again. He decided to proceed up river, therefore, to search for the answer to the greatest and most tantalizing geographic puzzle Captain Cook left for others to solve. George had been elected to do so, and he was determined to put it to rest for all time.

Captain Cook had traced the so-called river that bore his name a great distance inland without seeing any clues as to its terminus. It did not narrow significantly, but its water became brackish; *ergo*, Cook reasoned, it must be a river. He grew so impatient with that wide, icy waterway, upon which days were awasting to no apparent end, that he concluded his explorations at a point he called Turnagain and sailed away, contented with his conjecture.

Unfortunately, many an armchair geographer seized upon this supposed river as the St. Lawrence-of-the-Pacific, by which ships' passage might be made to a vast interior lake lately discovered by fur-trader Peter Pond. The requisite symmetry of God's plan ensured that Cook's River led to a western set of Great Lakes, and it simply remained for Great Britain to reveal and claim it, to her everlasting glory and growing good fortunes.

The *Discovery* bumped and bashed through dangerous drift ice, and she grounded more than once on submersed pinnacle rocks, making her way to a position just a few leagues beyond where Cook had turned round. There, to George's surprise, the waterway ended very abruptly in two narrow, dead-end channels. No river was in sight; ice break-up and snow-melt accounted for the freshening of the salt water. The greatest hope and challenge of George's survey was done, freeing him much sooner than expected from this icy hell, but his discovery cast a shadow upon Captain Cook's previously unequalled reputation as a master surveyor.

The old man's impatience had got the better of his genius; he had grown sloppy and presumptuous, where he had once been meticulous and cautious to a degree that George had ever wished to emulate. Now, the pupil's standards and skills had outstripped the teacher's. George found little pleasure in this; to the contrary, he suffered pangs of disappointment in his revelation, made worse by the knowledge that he must publicize it.

Poor George! He wished to extend the great, good captain's work and do credit to his name, not pencil in two little cul-de-sacs and discredit him by so doing. George was in a woeful state already, due to morbid fears regarding the condition of the ship and his own constitution; he was further distressed to realize that his great mentor had let his work slip below even mediocre standards, that age (and attendant debilities), impatience, and arrogant overconfidence had taken precedence over a job well done. George was truly alone now—alone and ill, without Cook's star to guide him.

On May 7th, the day after Cook's River earned its proper name of Cook's Inlet, two distant guns were heard, then—joyous sight— the *Chatham* sailed up to join the *Discovery*. All hands were well; the little tender was intact. Mr. Puget reported meeting several Russians and visiting their encampment recently, a pleasure George soon experienced on their way from the inlet.

So closely did these Russian traders follow the native way of life, they could best be told apart from the Indians by their lack of face paint and grease, for they adopted every other fashion of native clothing and habitation. Their personal cleanliness was found wanting, while their homes were surrounded and filled with such putrid, liquified offal that the stench was unbearable. Indeed, the smell choked civilized sensibilities to such a degree that no Briton could swallow the food that their Russian hosts generously provided from meagre supplies.

The more significant difficulty, however, was the inability to converse with the Russians. Once again, Whitehall had failed to provide a translator, although those who had drafted George's sealed instructions knew he would encounter Russians at this pass. Where George might have learned a great deal about Aleutian and Alaskan geography, and yet more about the extent of Russian-American commercial activities, he was reduced to guessing what the Russians' words and gestures meant, while putting very little stock in his crude understanding.

From Cook's Inlet, George made for Prince William's Sound, which he surveyed and charted from mid-May till mid-June. Though the season had advanced considerably, bringing warmer temperatures and rapidly lengthening days, the waters were no less dangerous. Drift ice from spring break-up and calving glaciers constantly rammed the bows, ripped the copper sheathing, and frayed the anchor ropes; hidden rock pinnacles caused several groundings (mercifully, without material damage); tidal flows were prodigious in height and speed, pulling the ice-worried anchor cables taut to near-breaking.

More Russians were encountered in these waters, commanded by Gregorii Ismailov, whom Captain Cook had met at Unalaska Island in October of 1778. Cook had judged him to be a most capable young fellow and, indeed, it appeared he had proven his mettle during the intervening years. George's frustration mounted: here was a Russian explorer, settler, and trader, clearly a cut above the rest, with whom he could converse no more readily than with the lowliest, crudest of the lot. The best George could ascertain was that there were 400 Russians employed in northwest American waters, and by his own judgement, they lived in relative safety, ruling over the native tribes.

George spent his 37th birthday en route from southward-facing Prince William's Sound, above 60° north latitude, to westward-facing Cross Sound, at 58° 20′ (which Cook had named in 1778 as he sailed past at some distance from shore). June 22nd of 1794 was a dismal day—indeed, part of a dismal week, so poorly could the ship ply against contrary winds. All was grey to George: grey skies; grey seas; grey land in the offing; grey health, tending more to fade than to brighten with each passing day. He could well guess that his years were numbered; so ill had he become with a "violent disposition, which terminated in a bilious cholic," he feared his life might better be measured in weeks or days.

On July 2nd, George ran in with Mr. Brown of the *Jackal*, whom he had met previously in command of three vessels. One had now returned to England, while his little tender had separated from him on their way from China. Brown brought news from Europe, which did nothing to lift the spirits, so rapidly was the French 'disease' infecting the continent and now the British Isles.

King Louis XVI had been guillotined on January 21st of 1793. George cast his mind back to that day: Where had he been? What had he done? He was making his way to Hawaii, just three days after bidding farewell to his dear friend Señor Don Quadra, who had behaved with perfect civility in savage lands, while those in civilized lands were apparently behaving more and more as savages.

The terror in France continued, as did her war against half of Europe. Mr. Brown brought word that she had declared war on England, attacking from without by force and from within by intrigue. Spies abounded. English malcontents adopted French doctrines and worked to subvert the inestimable British constitution, hard-won by regicide and blessed restoration[15] over a century before.

---

[15] King Charles I was beheaded in Whitehall on January 30th of 1649; the monarchy was restored under Charles II in 1660.

Brown's unwelcome and unexpected tidings, "breaking as it were from a cloud upon the minds of persons so little prepared to receive them," further weighted George's sagging disposition and health. All hands reflected most seriously and painfully upon the news, keenly feeling the utter remoteness of their loyal hearts, which ached to defend their dear homeland and loved ones.

By July 7th, the ships made Cross Sound, there to anchor for several weeks while boat parties reconnoitred the surrounding shores. George sent out one party in three boats, instead of the usual two parties in two boats each, so concerned was he for their safety in the ice-filled waters and amongst native people who appeared from first contact to be aggressive and wary, likely with good cause, of all foreigners.

In the hope that a short excursion might improve his health, George ventured into a boat on July 14th, to examine nearby shores. Alas, by noon, he was seized anew by a most violent colic, which confined him to his apartments for several days.

George very nearly died. Nothing less would compel him to make mention of his private condition in his public accounting. Even so, he devoted but one sentence to describe the most hellish days he had yet suffered aboard ship, every moment praying for release—be it by returned health or by welcome death. Not coincidentally, he named those features surveyed by the boat parties while he lay in deep decline after places and a person very close to his dying thoughts: Point Couverden, seat of the Vancouver ancestral home in Drenthe, Holland; Lynn Canal, after his natal home, King's Lynn; Point St. Mary's, after Mother's birthplace at Wiggenham St. Mary, a few miles from King's Lynn; Berner's Bay, after Mother's maiden name; Point Bridget, after her Christian name.

When George applied these names, he had returned from death's door, yet they illustrate clearly how he longed for home and for dear Mother during his days of crisis. He could not speak of such things; he would never admit how morbid his thoughts had been. He was ever a man who believed we are better known by our actions than our words.

Why then, one might ask, did George write such a lengthy journal?—half a million words, more or less, from a very private man. The principal purpose of his journal is to explain his surveys and charts so thoroughly that, by showing his expedition's day-to-day employments, all speculation regarding a sub-Arctic Northwest Passage might be permanently retired and, of more practical importance, future navigators might safely follow his lead, forewarned of known dangers and unavoidable oversights and errors. He wanted no life that relied on him lost, for he was exceptionally tender regarding the subject of death, perhaps because it had touched him so deeply as a child and so closely as a man. Thus, he found intolerable the reckless and death-defying antics of young men, and he zealously nipped in the bud every disrespect for life and every disregard for its sustenance.

Death was not a subject for discourse with George, however. All yearning for Mother was left unsaid; her memory was best served by placing her names squarely on the world map for all time, where he knew exactly their significance and where the curious, caring reader might discover it.

The boat parties returned after 16 days in dangerous, ice-fraught waters, where their worst fear was of attack by menacing Indians, armed with muskets, blunderbusses, and daggers, intent upon plunder and murder. In one instance, Mr. Whidbey's boats were forced to fire above, then at, some native canoes, with the consequence that some warriors were seriously, perhaps fatally, wounded. The boats then rowed all night to stay clear of any pursuers.

The survey suffered due to this unprovoked and regrettable confrontation; by retreating, Whidbey could not determine with any certainty which of many channels defined the continental shoreline. He would have to backtrack now—an unpleasant prospect, not only because of vengeful natives, but because the boats had been within 20 leagues of Cape Decision and, with that end so near in sight, it was doubly hard to recover lost ground.

August 1st was a pleasant day, made so by the ships putting in at Port Conclusion [at the tip of Baranof Island, south of Conclusion Island in Keku Strait], as George later named the final anchorage of the survey. They had but 1° of latitude remaining to chart, a task all believed would take a week, although the two boat parties were provisioned for a fortnight.

Those remaining with the ships refitted their rotting, much-patched wooden homes as best they could; they brewed spruce beer, the best of the voyage; they hunted, fished, and gathered greens for vital fresh food. Strange to say, they had not one native visitor during their entire stay at that port. This was an unprecedented and most eerie circumstance.

A fortnight passed, and the boat parties had not returned. Were the Indians avoiding the ships because of a deadly encounter with the boats? Such black worries plagued George's every thought, that he had hazarded his little boats once too often.

Each day's passing, with no sign of boats *or* canoes, increased George's anxiety to a fever pitch. How unspeakably miserable it would be to have surveyed thousands upon thousands of miles of intricate, treacherous coastline, only to lose the best of his people on the last few miles. Fifteen days passed... 16... 17... 18...

August 19th dawned through a deluge of rain, driven by powerful winds. The silence, but for the sounds of nature and the groans of the ships, pressed hard upon all hands, who dared not voice their darkest fears. What dismal news did they await, while they sat powerless to reach out and save their courageous mates? In such foul conditions then, "we had the indescribable satisfaction of seeing the four boats enter the harbour together from the northward. The parties soon reached the vessels, all well, and communicated the glad tidings of their having effectually performed the service, and attained the object that had been expected from this expedition."

From misery unfounded to joy unbounded in an instant! One can scarcely imagine the satisfaction—indeed, the very thrill!—that burst forth from the hearts of all the company. George ordered an additional allowance of grog, sufficient to produce the merriest of festivals. This soon prompted mutual congratulations between the two vessels, expressed by three exulting cheers from each.

Can you hear it then? The grog flowing freely, till all were spinning with it; the gleeful congratulations; the singing, dancing, whoops of joy; the dreary, grey, rain-soaked hills echoing with huzzahs bawled as loudly as 100, then 50, sets of healthy lungs can muster. There was never a company of men so deservedly proud of themselves as on that day, and George loved them all as sons—as a stern, devoted father loves his every son.

As with all families, they had suffered many differences and difficulties, but in that moment of utter triumph, all hands were united as brothers forever. Many might bear permanent grudges against George, but by God, they respected him and would bless him too, for forging them into a crew of sailors without equal. They were Vancouver's lads now, tried and true, and it would ever stand them in prideful stead.

Mr. Thomas Pitt would never taste this unimaginably sweet plum, by which the bile that choked him might have lost much of its bitterness. George had known that Pitt, more than the rest, needed to savour this fruit of his labours, yet he dared not keep Pitt for the third season. He could not risk putting Pitt in the boat parties amongst the Indians, who were better armed and growing bolder each passing year. Indeed, George believed that his survey was conducted just in time, as the Indians would have had the firepower and daring necessary to overwhelm his boat parties just one year later—or perhaps that very year, had Pitt still been in contemptuous service.

As it was, Pitt cum Lord Camelford later flew about England like a mad hornet, trying his best to get George's former officers and men to make public their every grievance against him, but none would do so: they remembered too well that remarkable day—the 19th of August, 1794—when they cheered and laughed and cried together in the rain and became family, with all the honour that implies.

Bad weather held the ships captive till August 22nd, giving George time to chart the latest surveys. The reason for the boats' last, over-long venture on the coast was clear: the continental shore lay farther to the eastward than expected, and coastal waters were more riddled with giant islands and passageways than any previously explored stretch of coastline.

George's hope the previous year for unbroken shores from Cape

Decision to Prince William's Sound could not have been more miscalculated; Cape Decision looks northward upon one of the world's most daunting archipelagos. That now known and so heroically discovered, all backs turned to it and all eyes looked southward from Port Conclusion toward home: 150° of latitude to the Horn, then nearly that much again to Land's End. At last—at long, long last—they were homeward bound.

24
Homeward Bound

Home, yes, but Nootka first. The business there, which was the voyage's secondary purpose, was still unsettled. George had high hopes that word from London had arrived at Nootka by then; sufficient time had passed, since Lieutenant Broughton had made his way home through New Spain, for instructions to be sent back via the same route. Broughton himself may be waiting at Nootka— a most pleasant prospect, despite George's past difficulties with him.

Such hopes were forced to percolate through George's crumbling health and, on August 24th, they were overshadowed entirely by a tragic misfortune. So dangerous was the offing from Port Conclusion, due to the rocky shore and pounding surf, the boats spent two days towing the ships to open ocean. When the ships were finally safe at sea, the boats were taken in. During this operation, one of the cutter's crew fell overboard, striking his head upon the gunwale as he did so. Thus knocked out, heavily clothed, and unable to swim, he sank instantly and irretrievably.

Isaac Wooden had been a good man, active and cheery on the boat excursions, highly regarded by his comrades, and well praised by his officers. The worst George feared had come to pass: the hardest work of the voyage was just done, and a man was lost after so much toil, with no respite or reward for his arduous service. How bleak life could be; how heavy its pall; how sad the hard, grey meanness of it.

Melancholy had long been George's constant companion; now it seemed bent upon pulling him ever closer to its suffocating bosom. What heartache and disappointment lay in store for him next? Would his hard-worn men and ships make it home? Dare he even hope that an English envoy awaited him at Nootka? Yes, he must hope, for surely he would expire in Melancholy's embrace if he did not.

On September 2nd, under fair skies blushing at sunset, the *Discovery* and *Chatham* came to anchor in Friendly Cove. Nootka's snug roadstead was abristle with the masts of three Spanish vessels, two English traders, and John Kendrick's Boston brig. No English envoy; no Lieutenant Broughton; no word from London, despatched or delivered in any form. Damn! Now what was George to do? He must hope, of course, that instructions were on their way, and he must await their arrival. Hope and wait. Wait and hope. How familiar this state was to become and for how long, George could not guess, and thank goodness for it. He had a number of hopes to sustain him then, of lesser and greater magnitude, and of lesser and greater likelihood, although he held to each one in succession as if it were his lifeline, until every fibre of hope was played out—or cruelly cut.

Another thread of hope was lost when George learned upon arrival at Nootka that Don Juan Francisco de la Bodega y Quadra had died at Mexico City on the previous March 26th. George's sweet hopes for a future meeting with this dear friend were dashed; eternity was now the appointed rendezvous.

As with previous bad news, George's thoughts slipped back to where he had been on that grievous day. What had he recorded in his journal? On March 26th of 1794, he was 11 days out from the Sandwich Islands, making for Cook's 'River'. A week of dark, gloomy weather and very heavy seas had given way to clear skies and smooth sailing; George had noted that the *Discovery* was within 15 leagues of Captain Cook's track of 1778.

What ghosts we carry with us! Was it mere coincidence that George's thoughts were of dear Captain Cook the very day the equally great and esteemed Commandant Quadra died? The rational man would answer yes, but if there is comfort in making such connections, then we must take comfort where we find it.

There is also consolation in knowing we will eventually join a good company of cherished souls; for George, dear Mother, Father, Captain Cook, and Don Quadra now awaited him. Despite poor health and its concomitant melancholia, however, George was in no hurry to attend them. Bright hopes, coloured by pleasant ambitions for the Sandwich Isles, and dreams of glory, merited by work done "with a degree of minuteness far exceeding the letter of my commission or instructions," kept him fighting to remain on this side of the grave.

The untimely loss of Don Quadra cast a long shadow over the entire west coast of the Americas, from his southern birthplace at Lima, Peru, to the northern limits of his remarkable explorations. Nootka was different without the promise of Quadra's arrival, although the present governor, Don José Manuel Alava, graciously offered every hospitality that was within his power to provide. Alava was awaiting his instructions for the Nootka settlement to arrive aboard a vessel from San Blas. If word did not come by October 15th, he and George would rendezvous at Monterey, where an envoy was certain to appear.

George hoped against the latter circumstance, for if it came to that, he must then ply northward to Nootka, perhaps even to winter there before the territory could be ceded to Great Britain. If his instructions arrived before mid-October, he could make the settlement at once and get his weary people home by next spring.

While George grew increasingly anxious to see a Spanish sail in the offing, he put the six weeks of stalling at Nootka to good use, refitting his nearly worn-out ships as best he could for the journey home—and it was this promise alone that kept his men on task. The weather was very changeable, with each storm blowing in more fiercely than the last, as the autumnal season advanced. The idea of wintering there was nearly unthinkable. His people were becoming restless and unruly; a fracas ashore between English and Spanish seamen erupted shortly after their arrival, forcing George to curtail shore leave. Fresh food was hard to find; the Indians had little to sell. How could he tell his men, after years of tedious, trying, triumphant service, that they were not homeward bound? Please, he prayed, dear lords of Parliament and Whitehall, send instructions and send them in time.

George and Alava distracted themselves and their officers by visiting Chief Maquinna at his winter home in Tahsis, a repeat of the visit George had taken there with Don Quadra. For George, somber reflections replaced the joy of the former occasion, although the second outing was as successful as the first. En route, he explained to Alava that the wild and inhospitable region they were traversing stretched hundreds of dreary leagues to the northward, which "occasioned Señor Alava frequently to express his astonishment, that it could ever have been an object of contention between our respective sovereigns."

A ship arrived on September 29th: the English *Jenny*, the same vessel that had carried Tymarow and Raheina to Nootka two years before. She was a trader; she carried no word from the king. So great was George's disappointment, he penned to his London agent and friend, James Sykes, that "I am once more entrap'd in this infernal Ocean, and am totally at a loss to say when I shall be able to quit it." Another ship arrived on October 5th: the English *Jackal*, late from China, with whom George had spoken recently in northern waters. Mr. Brown was no king's messenger.

No other ships arrived. At midnight of October 16th, George put his vessels to sea, heading for Monterey—there to rendezvous with Señor Alava, who set sail the next day. Alava promised him a welcome reception, assuring him that the viceroy had addressed and remedied the unfortunate misunderstanding of the previous year. Quadra had forwarded George's letter of complaint, which then had the desired effect. Praise be that great and good officer and gentleman, whose inimitable service extended beyond the grave. The restitution of harmonious relations was heartening news, but saddening also: all the Californias—even at their friendly, romantic best—lost much of their appeal without the prospect of meeting the good Don there.

The most furious storm of the voyage, excepting perhaps those encountered at and off New Zealand in late 1791, battered the *Discovery* and delayed her arrival at Monterey until November 6th. Foul weather or fair, there had been no need to hurry, for nothing from England awaited George's arrival. Alava, who arrived on the 8th, was also without word from his court. George wrote that, "I could not help feeling very great disappointment, anxiety, and concern. I was not, however, totally destitute of hope, that some letters might have arrive at St. Diego." Hope! How long the powers of England fed George a diet of waiting and hoping. Little did he know then that he had yet scarcely tasted their slow poison.

George did receive one letter, this from the viceroy concerning Broughton's safe and swift passage through New Spain to Madrid, and thence to London. Broughton had arrived home in good time then. Where, pray tell, was the return post? Word could have made Nootka, or California at least, with many months to spare—and most certainly if duplicates were separately despatched, which was expected procedure for such important business. Clearly, it was no longer important, as all Europe had lost sight of the world beyond France's paroxysmal state. George had been sent on a vital, pressing mission; now it scarcely mattered. Still, he must wait and hope. Hope and wait.

On the evening of November 11th, an express arrived from Mexico—good tidings, at last! Indeed, yes, but none for George, and the emissary dashed his hope of any arriving from San Diego. Alava received his instructions for the cession of Nootka to Great Britain, but George was empty-handed: "The embarrassment I had been long under was now very materially increased, and I was greatly at a loss as to what measures were best to be pursued."

Fortunately, the kindly Señor Alava confided part of his instructions to George, which stated that the respective courts had reviewed the negotiations held at Nootka in 1792 and settled them very nearly on the terms that George had repeatedly offered to Señor Quadra. His long-standing fear of having wrongfully held his ground—or rather, Great Britain's ground—was vindicated, to his relief.

The Spanish instructions also stated that a fresh commission from the Court of London had been issued for the final settlement of the matter, which apparently meant that George was relieved of this duty. George was mortified at being so unceremoniously replaced; the lords must have been displeased with his conduct, despite endorsing his stance.

George carried this weighty disapprobation until he returned to England, where he learned that the fresh instructions were addressed in the first instance to him, to be enacted by another only if circumstances prevented him from carrying out the commission.

In retrospect, this misrepresentation best served George and company, for had he known that instructions were forthcoming to him, he would have waited for them, either at Monterey or at Nootka. Since he had apparently been replaced, he need not wait a day longer on that account. He now had only two tasks to delay him: to prepare copies of his latest surveys for the viceroy of New Spain, in keeping with his promise to Señor Quadra; and to ready his outfit for rounding the Horn.

George also took the opportunity to prepare a second set of his surveys, that the viceroy might forward them to England. Some of those charts were copies of ones sent to England from the Sandwich Islands on the *Daedalus*. George's fear that these packets might be delayed or lost were well-founded, for the one he sent from Hawaii arrived in England after he had returned (and is now missing the enclosed letters), and the one he sent from California in 1794 is missing entirely.

What of Camelford's role in these disappearances? Can all losses be placed at his door? Of course not; distant postings quite regularly go astray. The pity is that, although some of George's documents were bound to be lost in transit or seized by jealous foreign powers, many more have disappeared than chance alone could take. One cannot make a case against Camelford for missing documents sent from afar, but this is no matter; one can make a case enough for those gone missing from under our noses.

At Monterey, the fear of tragic vanishments preyed upon George's mind, as he worked hard against future losses, be it of his surveys or of his people's lives on the dangerous voyage home. At last, on December 2nd, all was ready, and the winds were fair. The refitted, restored, but still beleaguered *Discovery* and *Chatham* quitted Monterey Bay, heading out to sea for the Cocos and Galapagos Islands.

The winds blew fair for weeks. Seafood was abundant and, excepting a few days of oppressive heat, the air was perfectly light and warm. Their situation would have been entirely pleasant were not all hands keen to press hard for home—George in particular, so feeble and debilitated had he become.

Christmas Day, the fourth since leaving England, was celebrated with plenty of fresh beef, mutton, poultry, fish, and turtle to eat, although fresh greens and fresh water were at a premium. Grog was the drink of the day, and plenty of it, that all might "call to their recollection their friends and favourites at home; on this occasion, though perhaps the circumstance may appear too trivial here to be noticed, yet as the sentiment arose spontaneously from the gratitude of the crew, I am induced to mention it; the memory of Señor Quadra, and the health of *Tamaahmaah* were not forgotten."

If anything was calculated to bring a tear to George's eye, this touching salute to two great friends could not have been better chosen. The crew had found fault with nearly everything he had determined and done; that they whole-heartedly endorsed the friendships he had pursued was a reward sweeter than any might have guessed.

The isle of Cocos rose up on January 20th, 1795. The 23rd to 27th were devoted to taking on as many tons as possible of fresh water, firewood, and coconuts, all of which abounded there. George made only one foray ashore and that with great difficulty, so weak had he become. He found some evidence of European traffic, including a note, dated January 1793, left in a bottle by James Colnett of the *Rattler*, a whale ship, the very English naval commander (and George's respected superior officer from Cook's second voyage) arrested by the Spanish at Nootka Sound in 1789, thus precipitating the Nootka Crisis. The note simply reported that Cocos Isle supplied them well and all hands were healthy when they sailed.

One cannot but be struck by the smallness of the sailors' world, for upon the vast high seas and off little-known coasts, their paths cross with surprising frequency. The same names appear again and again, as the same few sailors repeatedly venture forth—rare and hardy souls who open great new tracts of sea and land for the timid millions waiting at home to reap the benefits. Bless them all; and bless their commanders who, like George, use their people well and bring them safely back to the motherland.

Whilst at the Cocos Isle, many of George's company took to that ancient sport of sailors, shark-baiting. Never before had they encountered such numbers of sharks, nor roused them with their own blood to such fury, making for amusement aplenty by encouraging their cannibalistic feeding frenzies. Soon, such immense numbers of sharks had been attracted to the gladiators' arena, the path between ships and shore was a frightful gauntlet through which the boats must pass. George could bear no more: ". . . I thought proper to prohibit all further indulgence in this species of entertainment; which, independently of it being likely to be attended with serious consequences, was in itself of too cruel a nature to be witnessed without pain."

So here is the monstrous captain, again curtailing his men's every enjoyment without a care! They groused, as well, about the method George chose to gather coconuts: some wished to scamper up the trees like monkeys, while he insisted, for reasons of safety, that they fell them. By this means, they also collected a tolerable wood supply that would regenerate itself quickly.

In such matters, George may have fared better in his people's estimation had he explained his demands, but this is a preposterous thought, one that would never have crossed his mind or, indeed, the mind of any captain, of any service or any nationality. Those men who could read or cared to understand would find numerous explanations in George's published journal, occasionally stated and more often given between the lines—and clearly so in this latter case.

The Galapagos Islands, first seen on February 2nd, presented a very dreary and unproductive appearance compared to the lush Cocos. The principal island of the group received an afternoon's attention, on February 6th, from a single boat party; all hands but one reported nothing to excite further interest. The dissenting view came from Mr. Menzies, who was undaunted by the island's complete lack of fresh water and useful vegetation. The fauna and flora fascinated him, for it is a queer mix of tropical and polar species. Upon return to England, he continually and strenuously pressed the Royal Society to send a botanical expedition to that barren, lonely outpost. It has led to naught, for all exploration necessarily ceased during and following the dreadful war with France, but perhaps something will yet come of his seemingly frivolous exhortations[16].

On February 9th, as the equatorial Galapagos sank beneath the northern horizon, so too did the entire North Pacific Ocean, in the centre of which sit the tiny jewel-like Sandwich Islands. George looked back with great sentimentality, despite the many hardships he and his people had suffered over three long summers, for he knew that he likely would not return. The state of the world and his health precluded it, but even the most certain knowledge cannot overrule the yearning heart. He could wish; he *would* wish, from his last aloha to his last breath.

March blew in like a lion, bringing the first squalls experienced in many months. Alas, the worn out, rotten masts and yards were

---

[16] In 1831, the *Beagle* was finally commissioned to visit the Galapagos for just such purpose, with the young botanist Charles Darwin aboard to assess Menzies's enthusiastic report.

not up to it; the *Discovery's* mainmast, in particular, was badly sprung, and the main-topsail yard had been carried away. Lashed-up repairs resulted in a considerable reduction of canvas, with attendant loss of progress. George could only hope that the next port of rendezvous, at the Juan Fernandez Islands[17], would answer his pressing need for new spars.

To heighten George's worries, the scurvy again reared its head amongst the crew, and, in rapid succession, ever more hands fell prey to its ravages. How did this happen, when George had been so meticulous and strict in applying Captain Cook's antiscorbutic measures? Was this proof, after all, that they did not work over the long term? What a disappointment this realization would be, as painful as correcting Cook's survey in Alaskan waters.

After several anxious days, the cook came forward and confessed, with the utmost sincerity and contrition, that he had been giving the boiled salt-beef skimmings to the men, despite strict orders to the contrary, for some of them had convinced him that fat is an excellent antiscorbutic.

George, that beastly, mad-dog captain, instantly forgave the cook, punished him not at all, and sent him away satisfied with his absolute promise never to disobey orders again. If George's other men had been as forthcoming and honest about their transgressions, sparing him their determined sloth, pride, and insolence, they too would have earned such forgiveness, sparing themselves a taste of the cat. Any man who gets his bare back up against his commander is bound to have it whipped; George had no more choice in the matter than they, or he would not have been their captain in the first instance.

The *Chatham* had lagged behind the *Discovery* after crossing the equator, but she caught up to her hobbled consort one day north of the Juan Fernandez Islands, on March 20th. Mr. Puget reported having fallen in with a Spanish vessel several weeks earlier, from

---

[17] Best known as Robinson Crusoe's islands, made famous by Daniel Defoe's retelling of Alexander Selkirk's marooning there from 1704 to 1709.

which he learned that the anchorage at Juan Fernandez was bad. The far better alternate port, should they be in want, was Valparaiso, Chile.

George was under strong injunctions not to visit any Spanish settlement north of 44° south latitude on the South American coast, excepting in absolute necessity. Resorting to standard procedure in such instances, George put his desire to make for Valparaiso to the vote of his senior officers, and they supported him unanimously. Four days later, on March 24th, both vessels gained a distant view of the lofty Chilean coast. The Andes mountains, clothed in perpetual snow, gave it a bold and barren appearance, with no greenery in sight. Where would they get their new sticks, if this first impression of treelessness proved true?

Upon closer approach to Valparaiso Bay, a house and some smaller habitations gave the country a less sterile and forbidding aspect, but still, no trees were evident. Closer yet, upon rounding the southwest point of the bay, the country suddenly opened up, and the town of Valparaiso spread before them—a most pleasing array of buildings scattered about the adjacent hills, clearly without trees among the withered greenery.

Nonetheless, civilized man cannot approach a civilized town, after an absence of several years, without feeling excitement stir in his homesick breast, trees or no. George's ships anchored among eight sails in port and soon learned that an English whaler stood among them. This ship's captain greeted George cheerily, although he had nothing but disturbing news from Europe; he confirmed the lack of mast material; and he complained of a poor reception at this port.

George's heart sank. Welcome to Valparaiso, then. Welcome, indeed. With disappointment promising to heap upon disappointment, dashing hope and health at every turn, he wondered if he might perish there.

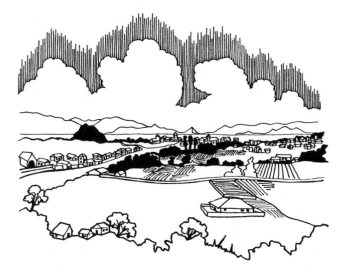

25
Hero's Welcome

In a sense, George did perish at Valparaiso. Some three years later, he prepared his journal for publication to March 28th of 1795—four days after arriving at Valparaiso—before hope and health failed him. He died too exhausted to contemplate reliving the rigours he had suffered while at that port and too disheartened to reflect upon his reception there, which contrasted sharply with his reception at home.

Despite the whaling captain's gloomy estimate of Chilean hospitality, George met with every civility and generosity from first contact with the port's governor, Señor Don Lewis Alava—none other than the brother of Señor Don José Manuel Alava, whom George had met recently at Nootka, then Monterey. The present Governor Alava offered George every amenity and assistance available at the port, subject only to President Ambrosio Higgins de Vallenar's approval. Alava immediately despatched a courier to the capital of Santiago, 90 miles inland, to announce George's arrival, purpose, and needs; he also requested permission to serve his English guests. While awaiting Higgins's reply, officers were given free run of the town; markets were open to them; water and fuel were available. George purchased fresh beef, greens, grapes, apples, and onions for his crew, which quickly eradicated all traces of the scurvy. George's own enfeebled condition was not so easily treated. Governor Alava graciously provided shore accommodation for him and several accompanying officers, with the hope that this arrangement, plus a restorative diet, would prove beneficial. Indeed, they did, and Alava's kindness and good company had an equally salubrious effect upon George's flagging spirit.

The whaling captain, whose grim reception at Valparaiso proved roundly deserved by his company's drunken and disorderly conduct, was not wrong about the availability of new timber for the *Discovery*'s rotten spars. To George's disappointment, nothing large enough for a new mainmast could be got anywhere in the country, forcing him to order the old one fixed by turning it end for end and securing it by the addition of 'fishes' [long wooden splints]. To be making such lash-up repairs in preparation for rounding the Horn was worrisome in the extreme, doing nothing to dispel the cloud of morbid doubt under which George perpetually operated.

On March 28th, the courier returned, bringing President Higgins's ample confirmation of Governor Alava's offers and an invitation for George and officers to visit him at Santiago. George could not decline this unprecedented opportunity, ill health be damned! Yes, he and five officers would travel by horseback over the mountains to Santiago—a vigorous outing that he hoped might hasten his return to well-being.

Back the courier went, post haste, to inform the president of George's grateful acceptance. The honoured party would set out after acknowledgement and further instructions were received from Higgins, which gave them time to forward ship and shore business sufficiently to allow for up to a fortnight's absence.

I, John Vancouver, must here intrude upon my narrative of

George's great voyage, for it is here, whilst I helped him revise his notes for publication, that my dear, dear brother breathed his last. So weak had he become, I feared he might expire at any point while recollecting the journey beyond Monterey, yet he clung to precious life until he reached this juncture—and, I believe, he might have rallied and lived many more years, if numerous misfortunes had not compounded to make him prefer death to hard, hopeless life. I, too, am now at death's door, although I have strength yet to rail at the injustices that robbed George of his due rewards, and thus, of his will to live.

Enough of vague allusions! Let me spit it out, and get this bitter taste forever from my mouth. I contend that Lord Camelford destroyed many of George's papers, and that, by so doing, he destroyed a great man himself. The final theft that George could not bear was the disappearance of the pages describing the Santiago tour, from its outset to its conclusion. These were separated from the rest of his notes—for they described the structures and workings of a kingdom previously unknown to the British Crown—that the king's counsellors on foreign matters might study them closely. They were thus more accessible to the young lord's rampages than the rest of the journal, which George kept constantly at hand and under close guard.

What proof have I that Camelford stole these notes? Or, indeed, any of George's notes? None, beyond circumstantial evidence, for the brutish lord was too smart to get caught—or caught by any who would tell, I should say. His high-placed relatives, by whom he had access to all manner of documents, would never have turned him over to blind justice, even had they caught him red-handed.

Honour among the privileged is akin to honour among thieves, although, to Lord Grenville's credit, he made a few faint efforts to contain and control his mad brother-in-law's malicious words and behaviour. But take action against the scoundrel? Never! The best punishment available was simply to find Camelford a naval posting abroad and send him away. His removal was a blessing to George, naturally, but the damage he had done was irreversible and unforgivable. Lady Justice, indeed—a whore to the rich, in this fair land!

Camelford's allies had so emasculated me, by the impregnable fortress they built round him, that I could only meekly state in my "Advertisement from the Editor" prefacing George's journal that, "The notes which he made on his journey from the port of Valparaiso to his arrival at St. Jago [Santiago], the capital of that kingdom, were unfortunately lost, and I am indebted to Captain Puget for having assisted with his observations on that occasion."

"Unfortunately lost"—how I choke yet on those two foul words! The 'loss' of George's Santiago notes was so poisonous to him that he could not live with the numerous realizations they forced upon him. First, of course, their disappearance made painfully clear how hopelessly corrupt and immoveable were the forces of high society against him. Second, he was obliged to retrace his steps to Santiago using Captain Puget's journal as a guide, which was adequate, but only if used as a means of reliving those trying days, to revive his own memories and words. Puget tended to lengthy and colourful descriptions of his various privations and pleasures, which would neither stand future visitors in good stead nor inform our court of Chile's domestic and military capacities.

Further, George had been in serious decline before trotting on horseback over the steep terrain to Santiago, and the pains he suffered on the journey did nothing, contrary to his dearest hope, to improve his condition. To be faced with moment-by-moment recollection of this enervating hardship was impossible for George. He could not climb those hills again; he could not bear the heat and dust and filth, even in memory. Without his notes, without his health, without any hopes for the future, he departed this life with unspeakable regrets and left to me the completion of his journal for publication.

He left little enough for me to do, for he had finished 50 chapters of 51 total. He refused to die until his commissioned work was entirely done and adequately described; upon reaching Valparaiso, in reality and in print, those commitments were fulfilled. The *Daedalus* had delivered to him additional, discretionary instructions to chart the South American coast from 44° south latitude to the Horn, but these were issued in such thoughtless haste and George's ships were now in such delicate repair, he determined to take his men directly home and not risk their valuable lives one day longer than absolutely necessary in Pacific waters.

At Valparaiso then, having made this determination, in large part because Higgins confirmed that new masts were unavailable, his commission was finished to the best of his ability. He was free to take his people safely home, report their monumental and splendidly successful undertaking, and offer the Sandwich Islands to the king as the shining plum of the voyage—a wonderful windfall for the price of a warship and a governor to sail her. Thus, despite his illness at Chile, he did *not* perish while there, for he had much yet to do and cherished rewards to reap—or so he could hope, and not unrealistically.

Henceforth, I shall continue and complete the narrative of George's voyage by intruding upon the telling, for I had the melancholy task of bringing his venture home to England, using Captain Puget's and George's notes. I foreshortened them as best I could, for much in the latter was described in fractured terms, and I had not the means to fill them in or to flesh them out. The lengthiest section of the concluding chapter was borrowed from Captain Puget's description of the Santiago tour, although his report differed from George's in style and content. I could not, however, do Captain Puget the injustice of cutting his work too sharply when, without it (and his kindly personal assistance), that valuable section would have been missing entirely from the published journal.

George made Santiago, in tattered health and ragged clothing, for even his best uniform was frayed from years of service, as were his officers'. A mile from town, they notified President Higgins of their imminent arrival. He sent them high-bred horses, richly caparisoned with gold and silver trim, on which to ride slowly to his palace. This opulent cavalcade, complete with four regal military escorts, brought forth huge, curious, cheering crowds from this city of 30,000 souls, which much affected George's sensitivities. He had wished for an unpretentious reception, but he was deeply touched, nonetheless, by the recognition these kind strangers—traditional enemies of England, no less—gave him and his fellow adventurers.

President Higgins perfectly understood George's modesty, hence, after orchestrating the grand entrance and hero's welcome, he devised many private, informal gatherings at the palace and the homes of friends, where he and George conversed (in fluent English, for Higgins was Irish-born, although he had been in the service of Spain for over 40 years) as if they were intimate friends of old. This was the welcome George craved—not the gaudy show, but an easy acceptance into the homes and hearts of his superiors. He was ever their humble servant and, as such, wished to serve them in their inner chambers with what knowledge he might impart to inform and enlighten them.

Foolishly, he foresaw treatment in England at least equal to that which President Higgins extended to him. He knew that, with England at war, there was little chance of a hero's welcome through the streets of London, but that was of no consequence. Tragically, the sort of reception that mattered to him proved to be of no consequence either—no consequence, that is, to those Englishmen who owed him their interest and a show of common decency, if not decency of a higher order.

When he died, with his Chilean welcome vividly in mind, he could clearly see his every perceived failure at home, his every suffered injustice, his every dashed hope for the future. The pain was unbearable; death at Chile was preferable to life in England. He trusted I would complete his journal and bring him home, for he could not face in memory the open, cheering crowds of Santiago or the secretive, jeering society of London.

26
England Ho!

George returned to Valparaiso on April 16th, refreshed in spirit and health from his resoundingly successful tour of Santiago. He found ship and shore business well advanced, with the *Discovery*'s mended mast ready to be installed. Unfortunately, this operation revealed that the main yard was also badly rotted and sprung, necessitating further lash-up repairs and at least a fortnight's delay.

At noon of May 6th, George's fortified vessels and people took leave of their gracious, generous hosts, with a 13-gun salute and a hearty hurrah. Their next rendezvous would be the mid-Atlantic island of St. Helena, some 16° south of the equator—if they survived the tempests of Cape Horn.

The weather soon fulfilled every expectation of its fury, bringing heavy, stinging snowfall as the ships doubled the Horn. On May

29th, they reached their southernmost latitude of nearly 57°; five days later they were a full 10° northward of this and could congratulate themselves on having survived the most dangerous stretch of their homeward journey.

George was not about to relax and enjoy an easy cruise, however. He seized the opportunity to explore a little—an irresistible impulse, wherever conditions permitted and a geographic enigma existed. Mr. Alexander Dalrymple, Hydrographer to the Royal Navy, had charted Isla Grande some 6° or 7° north of the Falkland Islands, although this speck of land had been reported once only, in 1675. George criss-crossed the designated area, but found only birds and seaweed, not a bump of land in any direction. Fortunately, the clouds had lifted sufficiently for him to see clearly, hence conclude firmly, that there was no Isla Grande where Mr. Dalrymple had placed it.

The Chatham was still in sight then, but with the Horn behind them, the work of staying in consort by constant signalling was too difficult and wasteful (using precious wood for false fires and powder for shots) to continue. Thus, they lost sight of one another on June 9th, each putting their tiny, fragile craft to the lone mercy of the elements.

George's 38th birthday fell as the Discovery reached midway between the Horn and St. Helena. The weather had become comfortable and serviceable, but George had a gloomy day of it nonetheless. At 5:30 the previous forenoon, seaman Richard Jones had fallen overboard from the main chains. A grating was instantly tossed overboard for him, but the ship was making such good speed, it took nearly a mile to get her turned about. Jones's cries could be heard through the darkness, but he could not be located.

George did not order the cutter—the only boat readily available—lowered to search for him, which to some must have seemed monstrously neglectful. It was in such leaky condition, however, it was more likely to sink the rescuers than to save Jones. George had to decide quickly how many men he wished to lose, and since he praised Mr. Jones faintly in eulogy, he obviously chose to lose one contentious hand over several better workers. The ship searched till the cries ceased, then resumed her northward thrust.

June 22nd could only be a melancholy day, as the dead man's effects were auctioned for the benefit of his kin, at the usual generous prices for every worn-out, near-useless article. Six men had died since the voyage began, and all from the *Discovery*. This operated grievously upon George's mind, so dearly had he wished from the outset to return without any losses at all. Bit by bit, he feared he was failing, failing. . . .

Failing, that is, by his own strict standards, for his accomplishments were outstanding in this regard. Never before had such a lengthy voyage into uncharted seas returned with so few hands lost, and only one to disease. As George was not given to reflecting upon his successes, at least until they were irrefutable, Jones's death increased his anxiety about delivering his company safely home. If his outfit was too weak to save one man following a minor catastrophe, how could he possibly save them all? Averting disaster was the only answer; he must not let ship's discipline slip for a moment, although he would be remembered as a hard captain to the last.

St. Helena appeared on July 2nd, to the great excitement and relief of all aboard the *Discovery*. To heighten their pleasure, the *Chatham* appeared in the south-eastern quarter at sunrise, and a joyous reunion was soon effected. Together, they made for port, the first British soil seen since leaving Falmouth. Talk of home and ease of communicating with England from St. Helena worried George; he and his people were under orders from the Admiralty not to divulge where they had been until permission was given to do so. He enjoined all hands, therefore, to respect this edict. Further, since he was obliged to gather all log books, journals, charts, and drawings when the voyage was complete, he demanded that his officers, petty officers, and young gentlemen surrender these to him now. Their work was done; further observations were unnecessary.

All but three journals officially end as of early July, 1795: George's, naturally, continued; Mr. Humphrey's, master's mate on the *Chatham*, was appended with the notes he kept following the surrender of his journal; Mr. Menzies brazenly refused to comply with George's demand. He relinquished his surgeon's daybook only, arguing that his extensive journal, kept for botanical purposes, could only be submitted to Sir Joseph Banks, who was his superior, not George. Tempers ran high; Menzies threatened to despatch his journal to Sir Joseph from St. Helena if George tried to seize it. George was incensed at Menzies's impertinence, but he did not press the matter, for Menzies was intractable; more importantly, he could be trusted absolutely to keep his knowledge secret until Whitehall approved its disclosure. Menzies had best not cross George again, however, on any matter that was entirely and unquestionably subject to his command.

As both ships approached the bay of St. Helena, George was distressed to see a large fleet of British ships standing out for the northward, no doubt heading for England. How he wished his vessels were sufficiently seaworthy to sail with them, for his people would be much safer in their company, not only to aid the *Discovery* should she founder, but also to protect her should enemy vessels be encountered. His need for new spars outweighed his wishes, however, hence he turned his eyes to the business at hand, which began with paying his respects to Governor Robert Brooke.

Brooke was abuzz with news from home. He confirmed that France was still Britain's principal foe, but Holland, which France had recently taken, was now a declared enemy as well. Rumour had it that France planned to take the Cape of Good Hope from the Dutch, which would interfere with English vessels plying the India and China trade. King George and court determined, therefore, to take the Cape first. The fleet George had seen leaving St. Helena was the first offensive returning to England, which included a number of Dutch prize ships. Another fleet carrying 3,000 troops now waited at San Salvador for orders to sail to the Cape and launch the definitive attack.

As George and the governor spoke, a beleaguered Dutch ship made port, unaware that England was now against her. A hapless fly had wandered into the spider's web, and George instantly recognized his duty. With Governor Brooke's blessings, he took to his boat, boarded the vessel, and seized it as a war prize. He met no resistance and, to his great pleasure, he found that the nearly derelict

Macassar carried a valuable cargo of spices, worth at least £90,000 in Holland, plus a good deal of money. George would escort her to England and, after the Crown tallied the full value and took its share, he should be granted the usual privilege of dividing the remainder among himself and his people.

·Now he had three ships to repair for the home stretch. In short order, the *Discovery* had her new mainmast and yards, her leaks were plugged, and she was ready to sail. George put the *Chatham*'s master, James Johnstone, and 17 hands on the *Macassar*, to patch her up and sail her to England. As resources were limited at St. Helena, which was suffering from an extended drought, George despatched the *Chatham* to San Salvador, where Captain Puget was certain to find every article and aid necessary; equally important, he would find a company of English ships with which to sail safely home.

George had planned to wait at St. Helena for a convoy from the Cape, for he was fearful of sailing unescorted and being captured on the high seas. Not only would he and his people languish in French or Dutch prisons, but every journal and chart would fall to enemy hands, likely never again to see the light of day. Fragments of these records despatched from California and the Sandwich Islands might survive, but the whole of his work, performed for the benefit of all nations, would be lost forever. Dare he sail with the *Macassar* and risk such tragedy?

Or was it such a risk? George had recently heard rumours that the National Assembly of France decreed that the *Discovery* and *Chatham* should pass the seas unmolested by French cruisers, notwithstanding the existing wars. Not only was this heartening in itself, but it echoed an identical order issued nearly 14 years earlier that granted Captain Cook's ships, under Captain John Gore, immunity from attack by American Revolutionary War forces. George had sailed much affected by eerie coincidences between his voyage and Cook's, and it appeared they would continue to the last.

At present, he understood that if he sailed for England unescorted, he ·could not take the *Macassar* with him. He could scarcely claim neutrality with a Dutch prize in tow. She would slow him considerably as well, while there was a good chance the *Discovery* alone could catch up with the convoy that had recently left St. Helena.

George also considered that his people would little tolerate an uncertain delay and, indeed, he was equally impatient to make England. He had sailed for years in a well-worn ship and on uncharted seas; surely he could get her home on the well-plied Atlantic, particularly if the French respected his neutrality. For three days following the *Chatham's* departure for San Salvador, George weighed these considerations. Finally, he concluded that the risks were not extraordinary, given immunity; furthermore, fear had never been his master, nor ever would be. On July 16th, he directed the *Discovery* to unmoor and set sail. Johnstone, in the *Macassar*, would follow when her repairs were complete.

On July 25th, George crossed the equator for the last time; the day was pleasantly marked without incident. Fair weather aided a speedy northward progress, with nothing worse than intermittent downpours to slacken the pace. George was determined not to be lulled by such easy sailing, however, hence he kept all watches fully posted and active. He was short the 17 hands transferred to the *Macassar*, which forced him to assign the seaman who worked for Mr. Menzies to stand his watch rather than idle about the plant frame on deck.

On July 28th, while Menzies's aide was on duty, a heavy rain fell on the uncovered frame, and many rare, delicate plants, tenderly nurtured over many months, were destroyed. Menzies flew into a rage at George on the quarterdeck, blaming him entirely for the loss. George responded with equal passion, earning Menzies's accusation of insolent behaviour unbecoming a commander. This, coming from an inferior officer! George insisted Menzies retract these harsh and improper expressions or face the full, legal consequences.

Menzies refused to do so. He said he preferred a charge and a court martial, and with that utterance, all conversation ceased: George put him under arrest and had him removed to his cabin for the remainder of the voyage.

Mr. Menzies could have apologized to George and won forgiveness at any time during his detainment, but he steadfastly refused to put rules and reason above his rage. George was agitated, naturally, by the loss of Menzies's good services and company, but he was also supremely confident that the Admiralty would uphold his right to man his ship as he saw fit for safe passage. Menzies could not possibly win his case, although his bitter disappointment at losing so many irreplaceable young plants was understandable, and Sir Joseph would support his not-so-humble botanical servant to the limit of his political and societal powers.

Sir Joseph was in for a public come-uppance, if Menzies persisted in his hot-headed folly. Perhaps when the good doctor realized that, he would make his private apology and be done with it. There was time yet for a reconciliation; George was hopeful one could be effected, while being prepared to go to whatever limit Menzies forced.

George made note of this confrontation, of course, but it was not for the public record. Of the time between crossing the equator and the 5th of August, when one of the Cape Verde Islands was seen, therefore, George simply told his readers that "nothing worthy of remark occurred."

On August 21st, the *Discovery* fell in with the British convoy, as George had hoped, which crept at a snail's pace due to the wretched condition of several Dutch prize ships. George was happy to join the 24 sail and enjoy a leisurely, safe passage to home. With great relief, he put himself under commanding officer Captain Essington's orders. He and all hands found sufficient pleasure in the company of countrymen and old friends to compensate for their delayed arrival.

On September 1st, Essington ordered a Dutch wreck in deplorable condition abandoned and set afire. One of the *Discovery*'s fragile boats was recruited for the task, which she completed successfully, then was returned on board. Whilst being hoisted in, she was accidentally stove entirely to pieces. George could scarcely believe his eyes; she was gone, irreparably gone.

I take full responsibility for retaining the following paragraph of George's journal, which he most certainly would have removed had

he lived to complete the final chapter. It is a touching tribute, however, that reveals the sentimentality of a supposedly cold, hard
man:

> I do not recollect that my feelings ever suffered so much on
> any occasion of a similar nature, as at this moment. The cutter
> was the boat I had constantly used[18]; in her I had travelled very
> many miles; in her I had repeatedly escaped from danger; she had
> always brought me safely home; and, although she was but an in-
> animate conveniency, to which, it may possibly be thought, no
> affection could be attached, yet I felt myself under such obliga-
> tion for her services, that when she was dashed to pieces before
> my eyes, an involuntary emotion suddenly seized my breast, and
> I was compelled to turn away to hide a weakness (for which,
> though my own gratitude might find an apology) I should have
> thought improper to have publicly manifested.

It was as if the whole of George's part in the expedition was
dashed before his eyes. This was the boat that had ferried his friends
Quadra and Kamehameha upon distant Pacific waters. Raheina had
sat sweetly in it, as the wind played with tendrils of her hair.
George had travelled many a mile in it; at night, he had slept in it
and under it. Now she was lost forever, and all that she had embod-
ied shattered and scattered with her—insignificant flotsam on the
wide, deep sea.

Her demise signalled the beginning of the end for the entire outfit. Soon all hands would be posted to other ships, then other ships
again. England was at war: how many of George's lads were certain
to die soon? Which ones? The *Discovery* would fall to pieces one
day, as would George, and likely much sooner than his dear old
ship. The grand journey was done, and only the glue of words could

---

[18] In Vancouver's published journal, he only mentions using the yawl, although he
likely meant the pinnace, according to his officers' journals. Also, given his extreme reaction to losing his favourite boat, one can safely guess that John Vancouver misnamed it here.

hold it together, keep it alive in memory and in imagination; enough words might preserve the entire, noble adventure, between the covers of a grand book. George was compelled, for numerous reasons, to put his last life and breath into preparing his journal for publication, but surely the need to keep his expedition intact was at the heart of what drove him.

The convoy was now nearing the British Isles, expecting to land within a fortnight on the western coast of Ireland. George was in a tender frame of mind, as his boat's undoing exemplifies, and he dared reveal as much in his shipboard writings. He likely would not have included such thoughts in his public accounting, without first draining them of passion, for he knew that his hopes and fears would be ridiculed by his detractors as unseemly weaknesses. Since he died devoid of hopes and fears, I could see no harm in showing that he had a few for company in the lonely privacy of his cabin:

". . . as our distance from England every day and every hour decreased, so our happiness became augmented in the grateful anticipation of once more breathing our native air, once more reposing in the bosom of our country and expecting friends. Every breast, as may be naturally imagined, was alive to sensations of a most pleasant nature, inseparable from the fond idea of returning home, after so long an absence, in an adventurous service to promote the general good. . . . In the midst of these agreeable reflections, however, presages of a melancholy cast would frequently obtrude upon the mind, and damp the promised joys in contemplation. Few of us had been blessed with any tidings from our family or friends since our last separation from them; and in the course of such a lapse of time what changes might not have taken place, what events might not have happened to disappoint our hopes; rob us of our present peace; or cloud the sunshine of our future days! These were considerations of a most painful nature, and tinged our joyful expectations with solicitude and apprehension!"

When George had arrived home from his first voyage with Captain Cook, he was shocked to learn that Father was two years dead. Clearly, his present anticipation of imminent and joyous reunions was shadowed by painful remembrances of that devastating event. Please, he fervently prayed: let all our family and friends be alive and well, changed only by the happy addition of new members.

On September 12th, the coast of Ireland was sighted, and on September 13th, the *Discovery* moored safely at the Shannon. Captain Essington ordered George to repair without delay to London. George quickly relinquished command to Lieutenant Baker and, with journals, drawings, and charts in hand, he took leave of his officers and crew.

This parting was difficult for George, and impossible for him to describe. He loved his bedraggled old ship, and he loved his company, the finest crew who ever sailed the seven seas. Not only had he kept nearly 100 hands healthy for four years, eight months, and 29 days, he had demanded the best of them and got it. He had shown them what sailors they could be—and, by God, as he bade them adieu, not daring to look backward lest they see his tears, WHAT SAILORS THEY WERE!

27
The End Begins

George arrived in London within a few days of leaving the *Discovery* at the Shannon. He went directly to Whitehall and deposited his papers, his own great journal with them. Word of his ship's safe return spread like wildfire throughout our small isles, and I made all haste to find my dear brother at his usual London lodgings at 142 Bond Street.

What a shock I had when first I saw him: dear God, he was a wreck! That he had been grievously ill for years was plainly and painfully obvious. His skin was puffy and pasty; his hair was thin and lifeless; his grip was feeble; and worst of all, his eyes were haunted by the deepest, darkest, saddest sorts of reflections. Upon seeing me, he could not have been happier to embrace an angel of God than myself, holding onto me as if I were life itself.

When I told him that all close family members were alive and thriving, and all good friends were equally well, he was relieved beyond words. Tears welled up in grateful joy, tears he knew he need not hide from me. He was a fragile man, no less so than his boat had been before she was dashed to bits. I could not let him be shattered by the vagaries of misfortune, hence I instantly vowed to give him what time and energies I could, for as long as necessary, to help him regain his health.

My children were sufficiently grown to require little care by Martha or support by me; they would have to manage as best they could without me, until George was sound again. Bless her heart, Martha always understood my great affection and devotion to my brothers, George in particular. I would fetch Charles from his perpetual wanderings and dealings, to help me tend to George and to protect him from the thrusts and parries of life, until he was well enough to fend for himself.

George was with us again! Praise God, and pray that Charles and I could bring him fully back to life, to enjoy every favour and reward his arduous service deserved. A new beginning was at hand. We had much to do and much to gain. Praise God; George was home!

He wanted to know every scrap of news I could tell, from the most trivial family circumstance to matters of utmost national importance. He could not, in turn, tell us much about his adventures, for he was still under orders of secrecy from the Admiralty. Not until he began preparing his journal for publication, with me for his amanuensis, did I learn how singular and splendid his achievements were.

Private talk of his officers and crew was not forbidden, hence George discussed a number of incidents, both good and bad, that punctuated the voyage. Mr. Menzies was much on his mind, for he had been forced to apply for a court martial immediately upon landing. He dearly hoped it did not come to that; he held Menzies in the highest esteem and would accept the weakest apology from him at a moment's notice rather than carry his ridiculous, hopeless case before the Admiralty.

George had little to say about the Honourable Thomas Pitt. The young scoundrel had become the second Lord Camelford and Baron of Boconnoc when his father died in January of 1793—a full year and some before George put him off ship at the Sandwich Islands. The extent and worth of Pitt's inheritance was staggering: he would sit as a member of the House of Lords, of course, upon reaching his majority; he was master of the extensive estate of Boconnoc in Cornwall; he owned Camelford House in London (his mother's principal residence) and Petersham Lodge near Richmond, the old Star and Garter district; both mansions were fully appointed and staffed to serve his every whim; to top it all, he had an annual income above £20,000 [over $1,000,000 US today].

The 'Honourable' Thomas Pitt had learned of his good fortunes at Port Jackson, but rather than hurry home with his good name in disgrace, he attempted to exonerate himself by taking up a position at Malacca on His Majesty's vessel, the *Resistance*, Captain Edward Pakenham. London was abuzz with gossip regarding Pakenham's toadying letters to Camelford's high-placed relatives, singing his highest praise for the young devil. Pakenham immediately raised Camelford to acting-lieutenant, a position he expected to be confirmed by August or September of 1795.

George was incredulous; was there no end to Camelford's conniving tricks, and no end of sycophants happy to prostitute themselves for him? Nonetheless, George had no further case to make against Camelford, having dealt with him adequately as circumstances demanded, then completely severed all ties in early 1794. He expected to see or hear nothing of Camelford in the future, even when the young lord returned to England, as he was certain to do. Since Camelford appeared to be winning his lieutenancy, despite years of unacceptable service and an ignominious discharge, George hoped never again to cross paths or words with this arrogant, undisciplined, unscrupulous cur.

As for Pitt's relatives, little had changed: his brother-in-law, Lord Grenville, had moved from Secretary of State to Secretary of Foreign Affairs; his cousin, Lord Chatham, remained First Lord of the Admiralty; Chatham's younger brother, William Pitt, still led the Tory government. As our father had long been an active Tory, with powerful connections in Norfolk, George had every expectation that our family's good Tory name would stand him in good stead.

George was not one to wear his political stripes on his sleeve—a role unbefitting his commission—but he believed his tacit support of the reigning Crown and ruling Court would ensure his welcome to society's inner circles. It was just a matter of time until the powers that be, though fully engaged in war, found time to entertain Cook's remarkable successor and until George was well enough to accept their invitations.

Such excuses, at any rate, were of some comfort to George. Upon landing, his greatest fear was that his handling of the Nootka settlement had displeased the government. He was relieved, therefore, to find that instructions had been sent *in his name* to effect the final transfer of Nootka to the British Crown, after which Britain and Spain would mutually abandon the site. As George had been expected to stay in Pacific waters for two summer seasons, and he had invoked his discretionary powers to stay for three, none faulted him for declining to stay a fourth.

The government was annoyed over the Nootka affair, nonetheless. In particular, George was informed that he would have saved the Crown a lot of bother and expense had he hoisted British colours over the little tract of land Quadra offered, after which England would have straightened out Spain's misunderstanding without need of a return emissary. Events in Europe were rapidly reducing the entire Nootka Crisis to an historical footnote, and it was a damned shame that a ship, officers, and men necessary to the war effort were being wasted half a world away.

Two separate parties had been sent to finish the Nootka business. The first was commanded by Lieutenant Broughton, with Zachary Mudge as his second, both of whom George had despatched to England with word of his difficulties at Nootka. Seven months before George's return, Broughton sailed the *Providence* (which Captain William Bligh had lately taken round the world, successfully completing his failed commission on the *Bounty*) to Pacific waters, for two purposes: first, to take possession of Nootka, if this had not already been done; and second, to justify his voyage by making the first survey of the coasts of Japan, Tartary, and the like.

The British Crown had also sent a lone deputy, Spanish-speaking Lieutenant Thomas Pearce of the marines, to Nootka via Madrid and Mexico to undertake the final restoration and abandonment ceremony. While George had been in the attentive care of Governor Alava of Valparaiso on March 28, 1795 (also the date to which George prepared his journal for publication before expiring), Pearce and Commandant Alava of San Blas were at Nootka, despatching this lonely little duty. George's work was truly done; his commission was fulfilled, from the last action to the last word. His efforts could cease; the pen could fall. . . .

Upon returning to London, however, George had much to do and much to tell. The Admiralty wished him to prepare an account of his voyage for publication, from which they hoped to turn a tidy profit, as they had done with Captain Cook's journals. By their lordships' cool reception, George understood that this request was not to flatter him, but he was still naively hopeful that, upon studying his charts and journal, they would be impressed with his unprecedented navigational achievements and would belatedly welcome him home and *into* their homes.

The *Chatham* put into the Thames on October 17th, followed by the *Discovery* on October 20th. George hurried to Long Reach the next day, happy indeed to see his ships and those who sailed them. He moved the *Discovery* up to Deptford, the final port of disbandment. It was a sweet reunion and sad parting, more readily imagined than described. As every officer and man was in splendid health and was vital to the war effort, they would be quickly scattered throughout the service. Some had been pressed onto other ships already.

George and Mr. Menzies were face to face again, and neither could completely suppress the pleasure of seeing one another again. George had the regrettable task of informing Menzies that he had filed a request for a court martial. Menzies had cooled off sufficiently to see the impossibility of his situation, and he offered an ample apology. With relief, George accepted it, and they shook hands as friends of old. On October 24th, George withdrew his request for a trial.

Another court martial was pending, which George most certainly would pursue: Henry Phillips, the carpenter, had returned to England via Port Jackson and was awaiting trial, as he had done since his arrest north of the Sandwich Islands in March of 1792. This would take place mid-November of 1795.

From Deptford, George forwarded numerous letters to Whitehall, strongly recommending promotions for his deserving officers and young gentlemen, and he also wrote favourably on behalf of several seamen, to secure them good postings. Certain of George's people may have nursed their grudges against him, but George was never so inclined in return. Whatever difficulties had been experienced throughout the voyage, every sailor who rose to his duties (regardless of the incentives and punishments required to effect proper service) received George's warmest and sincerest praise, in private to their succeeding commanders and in public to the Admiralty.

On November 3rd, the *Discovery* was paid off; the next day, George was put on the usual half pay of inactive officers. Half-pay, indeed! Since George had not been paid for a day since he joined the *Discovery* on December 16th of 1790, he might wonder if he had ever been on full pay. He had many creditors, and he owed a large and growing sum to his agent, Mr. James Sykes, who had generously and unquestioningly supported him throughout his service. To be put on half pay, though it was standard procedure, seemed absurd when five and a half years of full pay were owing. George could only politely request that the Admiralty attend to this pressing matter, then hope that he had not long to wait. Hope and wait—his old companions were back. How familiar they were to become, he could not possibly guess.

Phillips's court martial was held on November 17th at the Nore, exactly six years to the day that George had been summoned from the Channel fleet to Whitehall to receive his great commission. This November 17th served only to mock the command he had been given, for their lordships found "unproved" George's charges of inattention to duties, neglect of stores, and disobedience, while upholding only the charges of contemptuous and disrespectful behaviour. Phillips was 'broke' as a carpenter and reduced to serving on whatever ship the commander-in-chief of the Nore put him.

What mortified George in these unprecedented, unacceptable, and indisputable findings was that Lieutenants Puget, Barrie, and Ballard (the latter two having recently qualified for their lieutenancies, following George's highest commendation) acted willingly as his witnesses and completely corroborated all five of George's charges. Phillips pleaded on his own behalf, and his word was taken against his former commander and three superior officers. In retrospect, one can clearly see that the lords were setting a precedent for a far more important court martial that might follow, when a certain disgruntled young peer returned home.

George was stunned and defeated. This was his first inkling of what was to come, and what he saw struck fear in his heart—fear quite separate from considerations of Camelford. One might argue that the trial was a minor one and, since Britain was at war and needed her every man, had the best practical outcome. Further, Phillips had been imprisoned for over three years, hence punishment had been fairly served, although justice had not. The lords themselves might plead distraction by the war effort and annoyance at being taken from it to deal with a trivial matter that occurred years ago and far away.

George understood these things and was further disgusted by them—that powerful men were willing to compromise the most basic principles of their public trust to serve their own ends, if not their own kind. By their decision, the lords of Whitehall failed to consider fully the implications of upholding an inferior's right to work as he saw fit, reason and authority be damned. More brazen unrest and defiance were certain to follow, with mutiny being the inevitable result. There is a tidy irony to Phillips's farcical little trial being held at the Nore, where, in November of 1797, all hell broke loose and every ship in the roads was mutinied—with Phillips there in memory, if not in the flesh.

What Britain failed to learn from the mutinies at the Nore, or indeed from the mutinous American and French Revolutions, is that justice will and does prevail, and if it is not served by the *actions* of the ruling elite, it will eventually be served by their blood. As this is an undesirable means of achieving a desirable end, it behooves all those in power to employ something of George's principles and foresight in conducting their daily business, that fairness might be won within the law. When just laws are twisted and broken by those pledged to protect and apply them, the 'little' people follow their lead, seize these mighty weapons, and respond in kind. Blood will flow; the only question is how much.

There is justice, after all. George knew none in his final years, but he has not died in vain if, by his life and example, we might reflect upon our duty to serve justice—this greatest and most fundamental of needs—and to live by its principles of order, reason, and fairness. This is why I write, and this is why I must resist death's tempting embrace until I have restored what I know of certain vital information to the public record, though it causes me anguish to recollect George's last, miserable, unjust years upon English soil.

I must hasten to add, however, that George's final days were not unremittingly dismal. On November 22nd, the *Macassar* made the Thames, bringing George's remaining officers and men home safe and sound. Finally, he could relax and savour the full satisfaction of having brought all but six of his hands back to England from a voyage of unprecedented length and difficulty. He also had the satisfaction of applying for the prize monies owed him, his officers, and crew for the capture of the *Macassar*; their shared portion could run as high as £30,000. George's percentage would instantly remove his every debt and "put him in the velvet", as he liked to say.

Christmas of 1795 brought particular joy, for our family was whole again, as it had not been in many, many years. George distributed the most singular gifts imaginable, chosen from his little hoard of exotic souvenirs. What astonishment and delight they caused, in adult and child alike! And what misery they spared him, from having to go further into debt to take part in the festivities, for he had not yet received his pay. One week before Christmas, the Admiralty magnanimously agreed to credit him with the monies he had spent out of pocket for his people's extra allowances of grog and slops [clothing held in ships' stores for sale to the crew], while making no mention of *when* they would pay him.

By year end, George's health was little improved. As the Admiralty, ministers of the Crown, and the king himself (who knew George had been personally charged by King Kamehameha to deliver to His Majesty a splendid yellow feather cape) apparently had no need of him at present, in any capacity, he resolved to quit dreary, dirty London and seek a cure at the Bristol Hot Springs. He brought in the New Year there, where he found welcome relief from society's cold shoulder. His peace and contentment did not last long, however.

On January 5th of 1796, George received a letter from the Admiralty stating that a strongly worded complaint had been lodged against him by the Spanish ambassador, accusing him of having refused to pay the costs incurred by the deserters at Monterey. George was surprised and furious; obviously, some troublemaker was at work. He responded immediately by saying that, at Monterey, he had not known under what head to charge the monies owing or on whom to give drafts for the money. Further, he had not carried a sufficient sum with him to liquidate the debt, nor was he authorized to do so, even if he had possessed the means.

George had proposed to Governor Alava that he refer the matter to the Admiralty as soon as he returned to England, to which Alava agreed and which, consequently, George had done. In fact, he had forwarded details of the transaction at *three* different periods for their lordships' information. They were apparently so ready to condemn George at every turn, they conveniently forgot what was under their noses when presented with the Spanish ambassador's trumped-up attack. Damn them, but they were a pack of hounds, determined to overlook all evidence and run George into the ground! They ignored him completely when he was in town; they sent a special courier to harass him when he was away and attempting to convalesce.

George's *fourth* letter to the Admiralty on the subject had the desired effect: Lord Grenville instructed the Navy Board to pay the charges when a demand was received from the Spanish government, although George was uninformed of this action until he returned to London. During his remaining fortnight at Bristol, he received no further word from the Admiralty, which was both a relief and a disappointment. Why, he wondered, must all contact and correspondence be cold and contentious? An invitation to serve their lordships in a cooperative capacity would have done more to restore his good health than a year at the baths, while their studied neutrality and mean-spirited little punishments seemed designed to ensure his continued decline.

He could not believe this was the case, and he resolutely refused to believe it until denial was impossible. My poor, ingenuous brother simply did not understand. Why was a little quiet recognition, a little private support, so impossible? He had perhaps erred a few times on the side of caution, but was that so terrible in light of all that he and his company had achieved? Indeed, his caution had preserved his people's lives, that they might now serve as fodder for war, and his caution had maintained the integrity of the British Crown, now augmented by the cession of Hawaii. He could only conclude that the current crisis was to blame, in conjunction with his illness, which removed him from active service and active consideration.

George had all but forgotten Thomas Pitt, and he was in no position to hear society's spicy rumours about Camelford's eagerly awaited homecoming. Apparently, Camelford had not for one moment forgotten Captain Vancouver, and the mad young lord was expected to arrive soon, roaring and snorting for George's blood. Camelford's mother, a formidable matron in stylish circles, was hard at work setting the stage for her hero's entrance. If the hounds did their job nipping at George's heels, Camelford would have no trouble making the kill.

That George was oblivious of his 'crime' and unsuspecting of future 'punishments' is evidenced by his choice of residence following his departure from Bristol. He moved, of all places, to lovely, peaceful Petersham, near Camelford's family lodge. There, George hoped to perfectly regain his health and, as soon as he was able, to devote himself to preparing his journal for publication.

By March, George was nicely settled in and, although still unwell, convinced a cure was at hand—to be effected when his pay arrived and his increasingly angry creditors were satisfied. The Admiralty ignored his requests for monies owing; George's letters to them on this topic are now, as one might expect, nowhere to be found. He had to find some cash and quickly.

George sought recompense from the Board of Longitude for his work as the expedition's astronomer. Mr. Gooch had been sent aboard the *Daedalus* to relieve George of this responsibility; following his tragic murder at Oahu, George was obliged to continue these exacting duties. He very humbly put his case and his log books before his old mentor William Wales, the astronomer on Cook's second voyage, for consideration. He expected a quick and favourable reply.

By late March, while daily waiting and hoping for word of his pay from Wales and Whitehall, George requested that their lordships release all necessary charts, logs, and journals, that he might begin his public accounting. He also asked what expense monies would be granted for the production of plates to illustrate his work. With surprising swiftness, they sent their permission, followed by the delivery of all charts, journals, and so forth necessary to begin his work.

The Admiralty made no mention, however, of the requisite expense monies, which was disappointing, but far worse, George caught wind of rumours, doubtless being circulated by that eternal busybody, Sir Joseph Banks, that the Admiralty wished George to incorporate Mr. Menzies's journal in his own, for which Menzies would take a portion of the profits. George was livid! Absolutely not; never, never, never!

Before George could address this insult, he learned that his application for payment of prize monies owing for capture of the *Macassar* had been stalled because two other parties had claimed a share: one was Governor Brooke; the other was the captain of an East Indiaman that had been in St. Helena Bay. George was further incensed! Damn their eyes and greedy hearts! Brooke's superior position justified his claim, but the East Indiaman had done nothing, absolutely nothing, to aid in the possession-taking or subsequent manning. In this case, George could clearly see that some person or persons high in office were attempting to do him harm, and worse, to benefit financially by doing so.

Three times George travelled to London, with difficulty due to poor health, to seek an interview with Lord Chatham. Each time, Chatham was in, but unable to see George, who waited as patiently as possible and tried to understand. England was at war, after all.

On April 8th, George wrote to Lord Chatham, still naively expecting him to hear his plaint and to support his plea for assistance—for his officers and crew, if not for himself. With all due apologies for intruding upon his lordship's leisure and his exalted situation, would Chatham consider two things: first, since George's years of distant service left him without connections with persons of consequence or friends in power, would Chatham be so good as to take up his cause; and second, by so doing, would Chatham see that justice was done with regard to the Dutch prize ship?

Foolish questions! Chatham did not respond, of course. The matter was referred to the King's Advocate, who would render a decision after duly considering it. Delay was in order—again! Wait and hope; hope and wait. There was nothing else to do.

In the same letter to Lord Chatham, George disputed the inclusion of Menzies's observations in his journal, with the resultant profit-sharing from its sale. George had been fully responsible for prosecuting the voyage, for which he had not yet been paid, and now he must take full responsibility for the written record, a labour the Admiralty had asked him to undertake without financial support beyond his unpaid half pay. As Mr. Menzies had been paid off, and at more than double George's allowance throughout the voyage, he must be considered adequately recompensed, and his work was now entirely the property of the government and totally at their disposal.

George received no word from Wales, Chatham, the Secretary of the Admiralty, the King's Advocate, or any other official for the remainder of April and the entire month of May. He grew increasingly agitated and despondent, which had a seriously debilitating effect upon his health. His creditors grew angrier and more abusive, till George had difficulty showing his face in public. He grew so desperate for relief from his monetary woes, he could scarcely concentrate his mind upon revising his journal. It was so unfair! So miserably unfair, and that it was all part of a grand plan made it foul beyond words.

At last, on June 11th, the Board of Longitude apprised George of their decision, which was *not* to recognize or pay him as the voyage's astronomer. They reasoned that, as George had not been under engagement to act in that capacity when he sailed, they "did not perceive how they could do anything in the Business." They returned George's log books to him, without so much as a commendation for his years of fine, voluntary service. George had been rejected by no less than his beloved old teacher, the venerable William Wales, *and* he had no further recourse. He was wounded to the quick.

On June 27th, the King's Advocate rendered his decision, and he upheld the East India Company's claim. The prize monies, therefore, would go half to the Crown and half to be divided equally between George, Brooke, and the East Indiaman captain. There was no mention of *when* payment would be made, which could only mean further delay. In the meantime, who knew what inroads might be made upon George's rightful claim, while he waited and hoped, hoped and waited, for the monies to be released?

On July 4th, the Admiralty agreed verbally to finance the production of charts and plates to accompany his journal. Naturally, George wished to have this promise in writing, hence he sent a letter requesting a formal statement of support. Within weeks, their lordships gave George liberty to employ engravers of his choosing; when each plate was complete, they would defray his expenses. Damn them! They still had not paid him a penny-piece owing since mid-December 1790, yet they were so gracious as to allow him to pay the engravers, whose total costs were certain to run above £1,000, after which they would reimburse him! Further, their lordships would decide upon the views to be engraved, once again giving George no voice whatever at their table.

I might add here, that by taking control of the illustrations to be used in the journal, the Admiralty was able to ensure that the tradition of including the commander's portrait on the frontispiece was *not* honoured. One might argue that this is an unnecessary vanity—for George, or for any captain—but still, had he been able to choose the plates, he would have followed tradition and enjoyed a minor, but flattering, perquisite earned by years of hard and daring work. As it was, their preemption and their pointed oversight wounded him, and, I must add, denied the public a glimpse of a great man's face.

The financial arrangement the Admiralty offered was far from satisfactory, but George was beginning to understand that, from every quarter, he was *deliberately* being stonewalled—a seige to the death, perhaps. His only means of vindication might be through his published journal, which he was determined would have no equal (excepting perhaps Captain Cook's great work) in quality, completeness, and worthiness. He would have to bear all costs up front, but it was becoming increasingly imperative that he devote himself entirely to its production, for, apparently, his reputation would stand on the printed record alone.

On August 17th, George's uncertain understanding finally came into sharp focus. A letter arrived, posted from the Dalmatian coast, from Lord Camelford. Its purpose, mired with puerile insults, was to challenge George to a duel at Hamburg on August 5th. A draft for £200 was enclosed to meet his expenses. The date was 12 days past, but that was unimportant. What mattered was that several rumours were confirmed at once: first, Camelford had, indeed, left the China Seas late in 1795 to make his way home; second, he was due in England any day; third, he was madder than ever; and finally, he lived and breathed to wreak vengeance on Captain Vancouver. George was a poor, lone, lame, sitting duck, and deliberately so; Camelford's kin had worked very hard for nearly a year to ensure it.

All London was agog with anticipation of Camelford's imminent arrival. The coffee houses were loud with talk of his glorious service under Captain Pakenham. He had been raised to third lieutenant, a position confirmed by the Commander-in-Chief of the East India station, Admiral Peter Rainier (after whom George had named a majestic mountain on the northwest American coast). Camelford begged his mother to use her every influence—and quickly!—to secure him a post-captaincy before his return. In times of war, this was not unheard of, and if anyone could pull strings, Lady Camelford knew the ropes.

The young, dashing captain would then burst into town, challenge a duel, and thus slay the old, wicked captain—a battle of equals at last. How splendid! Bring on the mad young lord; flush out the horrid old man! There would be blood in the streets ere long—George's blood, and three cheers for it!

28
Camelford Returns

The Honourable Thomas Pitt, Lord Camelford and Baron of Boconnoc, burst into town on September 1st, 1796, as vengeful as the most malicious gossip could hope. He held George accountable for his every failing, the latest of which fuelled his simmering hatred into a frightful cauldron of venomous humours.

He was not a post-captain. His mother had failed to secure him a promotion and command, and for the most infuriating of reasons. His cousin, Lord Chatham, was no longer First Lord of the Admiralty; he had been replaced recently by the high-minded, punctilious Lord Spencer. Lord Grenville had tried to win favour with this impossible martinet, without success. Spencer held that Camelford's appointment as acting lieutenant was on an irregular vacancy, hence the Admiralty could not uphold Admiral Rainier's confirmation of lieutenancy without breaking an invariable rule of the service. Further, Camelford must take the necessary examination, which was also an invariable rule.

He was not a lieutenant, therefore. He was a mere midshipman again, further insulted by a posting to the little sloop *Tisiphone* at Deptford Yard. He was murderously angry at George for this perceived demotion. Where he had intended to challenge George captain to captain, now he would have to throw down the gauntlet man to man.

No sooner was Camelford upon home shores than he posted down to George's house at Petersham, even before seeing his own mother. Lord Grenville and his wife, Anne Pitt—whom George had informed of the challenge to a duel at Hamburg—had urged Thomas to call at their home first, to no avail. Like a mad hornet, he rushed headlong and headstrong to George's door and immediately began spitting a steady stream of abuse at him.

George steadfastly refused to argue, justify, or in any way discuss actions he had taken in an official capacity. If Camelford must place blame, he should look to himself, and if he must seek retribution, he should submit his case to the Admiralty. George offered to stand trial before any flag officer of the Royal Navy, who would undoubtedly rule in his favour. Take that challenge, Mr. Pitt, and be gone!

Camelford was trembling and scarlet with rage. He told George that they were now two men face to face, that he could no longer hide behind his uniform. The thirst for George's blood had kept Camelford alive through so many vicissitudes, and now, by God, the duel must take place, one way or another!

George was shocked that Camelford had nursed his grievances for so long and so passionately. He was scarcely well enough to stand up to such abuse, yet stand he did and admirably so, never once losing his temper or reason. George's measured, fearless response angered Camelford the more, but eventually, the young hound gave up and exited, shouting that no man of honour would turn down his challenge. Watch out old man—and be ready to die!

With Camelford so hell-set on a duel, George felt that a trial must take place and soon, or he would not be safe from Camelford's impulsive, explosive rages. He also wished that his refusal to duel be regarded as honourable, for the illegality of it was little respected. Thus, he consulted a number of people regarding the best course of action to take.

Legal counsel agreed with George that Camelford's trespassing, challenging a duel, and threatening death were, indeed, indictable offenses. Civil charges against a peer, however, were extremely rare and would create a public spectacle. George's best and most discreet course of action would be to seek the protection of the civil courts—also an unusual circumstance that might meet with some difficulty and delay—while he sought to clear his name honourably through martial channels.

George also consulted Lord Grenville, who was greatly disturbed by the growing potential for scandal. He agreed that, yes, George was correct to refuse any discussion of Camelford's difficulties while he served aboard the *Discovery*; and yes, he upheld the general principle "that a commanding officer ought not to allow himself to be called upon to answer personally for his conduct in command."

Bolstered by such legal and personal advice regarding the honourable path to take, George wrote to Camelford on September 7th, reiterating his stand and again proposing to submit himself to the judgement of any flag officer. Charles delivered the letter to Camelford House in London, where he found the scoundrel in residence—and as poisonously possessed as ever.

Camelford took Charles to task as vigorously he had George at Petersham. He threatened to insult George publicly in a coffee house and thus force a duel. If George declined, he would drive him from the service, compel him to resign his commission, and finally, wherever he should meet him, box it out and try which was the better man. Charles was alarmed and made a hasty retreat. George was in grave danger.

The next day, Camelford wrote a note to George—a difficult task, due to his proud resistance to all discipline and schooling, which rendered him nearly illiterate (or so George was led to believe, for Pitt either could not or would not keep a journal aboard ship). In a furious scrawl, he said that "When a man of honor has the misfortune to be embroiled with a Poltroon [a base coward] the line of conduct he ought to pursue is too obvious to occasion him the smallest embarrassment."

George visited Lord Grenville again with this note in hand. Grenville endorsed George's proposals regarding use of the civil and martial courts, and he would speak to Thomas, which was certain to have a calming effect. George believed him; Grenville was a reasonable, decent man, strangely old for his 40 years and very devoted to his much younger, beautiful wife and her wild little brother. If anyone could reason with Thomas, it was he.

Grenville talked to Camelford, and reason appeared to prevail. Grenville reported to George that Camelford looked upon "the whole of the affair to be now concluded, at least for the present." With this, George expected to return soon to his peaceful situation and arduous undertaking.

As George's counsel had guessed, the civil courts were little able or disposed to proceed against a peer of the realm. After wasting a fortnight on this blind alley, he suggested that George take his concerns to the Lord Chancellor, Lord Loughborough, whom George knew well enough to have dedicated, with some personal affection, an impressive waterway on the northwest coast of America to his honour. George urgently requested an audience with Loughborough, therefore, who agreed to see him immediately.

On the morning of September 21st, George and Charles left the Bond Street lodgings to make their way on foot via Conduit Street to Lord Loughborough's home at Bedford Square. No sooner had they turned onto Conduit Street than they spotted Lord Camelford and two of his young cronies idling about there. The instant Camelford saw George, he became a rabid dog, mad for blood. He made directly for George with his cane drawn back, ready to bring it down with all the force his tall, powerful frame could muster.

He managed to land several blows before Charles seized him by the throat and beat him severely about the arm and shoulder. Camelford and his two friends then turned their attentions fully to

Charles, until some passers-by hauled them off. Thus held, Camelford challenged Charles to a duel, which Charles accepted, if no other means of settlement could be found.

Camelford's apparent satisfaction with this arrangement won his release, upon which mad Tom immediately pounced on George and thrashed him with a series of blows. George valiantly wielded his own stick, to some effect. Camelford was eventually stopped from venting his unbridled fury upon a sickly man, but he was determined to have the last, belligerent word. As his bloody, disheveled enemies continued toward Bedford Square, he shouted that he would do the same to both wherever they met.

Naturally, Lord Loughborough was alarmed by the condition of his callers. After reading George's "Articles of Misdemeanor exhibited in his Majestys [sic] High Court of Chancery by George Vancouver Esquire against the Right Honorable Thomas Lord Camelford...", he agreed to do all he could, and instantly, to protect George from another attack. He would speak to Camelford and demand a sizeable peace bond at the earliest possible moment. He sent a note summoning Camelford forthwith.

Thomas, Lord Camelford, appeared at Lord Loughborough's door at ten in the forenoon of September 22nd. His appearance was frightful: clothing awry; hair wild; trembling from head to foot; eyes hot and haughty. After Lady Loughborough saw him into her husband's chamber, she persuaded a visiting friend to stand guard outside the door, ready to leap to his aid at the slightest hint of need. This proved unnecessary, and Camelford emerged willingly tamed by his vastly superior lordship into giving his word of peace, secured by a one-year surety of £10,000 (of which Lord Grenville paid one-quarter).

The sly dog knew that the year began from the date the bond was posted, which gave him a few days yet to continue his wild campaign. The very day he gave Loughborough his word, therefore, he sent Charles a note demanding a duel! Charles did not dignify it with a reply, for Camelford's attack in Conduit Street was certain to be reported in all the newspapers, and the world would then see what a damned fool he was—a damned fool who would forfeit £10,000 should the Devil him possess again.

That very day, also, Camelford was assigned to the prestigious 74-gun *London*, Sir John Colpoy's flagship, at Portsmouth. He would soon be out of town and, if all went well, out of the country as well. The teapot tempest would blow out to sea, and George would return to tending his health and work, both of which had suffered a regrettable setback.

The Saturday newspapers reported the "Caning in Conduit Street", as they called this infamous fracas, and to our initial dismay, George and Charles appeared more to blame than Camelford. How was this possible? Of course, among Camelford's friends were some influential members of the press, whose venal interests were better served by buttering him up, while tarring and feathering a former commander of the Royal Navy. They had obviously consulted only the guilty party, who presented himself as the grievously offended one, whose own honour he had righteously defended.

A refutation of this stinging report was clearly in order, that both sides of the issue might be fairly presented for the public to assess and judge. Charles took up this task, and the *Morning Chronicle* published his report in their next edition. My, my, but Camelford was the crying baby over that! He tattled to Lord Loughborough, whining and snivelling that Charles's attack should not have been published after he had been such a good boy and had given his sureties for good behaviour. He so charmed the old lord, who knew nothing of his latest challenge to a duel with Charles, he won himself the right to issue a public defense of his conduct in return. Would this nonsense never stop?

He had not, in fact, given his sureties at that time, for the promised year of peace did not begin until September 28th. The lords are thick as treacle with one another, however, when push comes to shove, even the reasonable Grenville and venerable Loughborough. A day here, a day there—details, details. Young Tom must be given the benefit of the doubt, for such a handsome, highborn Hercules was the bright hope of the empire and the tight, hard little company that ruled it. Those who were too honourable to break rules had little trouble bending them—for the proper reasons, of course.

Camelford had his say in the newspaper of his choice, and his various friends had theirs as well. Every day, new and malicious accounts and squibs appeared, all at George's expense, and much to the amusement of rich and poor alike. For all their high breeding, Camelford and his lofty scribes got the greatest fun from the basest humour. Their most scathing pun was that the name Vancouver should be changed to "Rear-cover", as if keeping one's backside protected from the likes of them *and* out of the news was a dishonourable thing. The very worst was yet to come, however.

On October 1st, George looked out from his London lodgings to see a jeering crowd gathered round Mrs. Humphrey's print shop across the street. The object of their merriment was a print by the popular cartoonist James Gillray, a recent addition to Camelford's crowd of carousing friends, who were greatly enjoying the lubrication his largesse provided at the coffee houses and taverns of the town—fair-weather friends all, but what did Camelford care? He was using them as well as they were using him, and *they* were more easily bought, dropped, and replaced than he.

Gillray's latest cartoon was entitled "The CANEING in Conduit Street", and it was the nastiest pasquinade imaginable. George went down to look, and he was stabbed through—mortified, shamed, furious, humiliated, damned! Publicly and irretrievably damned! Prints of it were circulating around London and soon made their way throughout the Channel fleets. He was the laughing stock of land and sea, from respected superiors in high offices to scruffy strangers in the streets.

What was the worst part of this horrid depiction? Lampooning his fatness, caused by mortal illness? Charles, acting in his defense, called Chas. "Rearcouver"? Camelford calling him a coward, as if an honourable man would not mind being murdered in the street? The long list of those "disgraced during the voyage"? The implication that he gathered a hoard of "Fine Black Otter Skins" to sell in China for his own enrichment? The grinning street urchins looking on? The tattered feather cape "from the King of Owhyhee to George III, forgot to be delivered"?

Yes, each of these things, of course, but perhaps the latter most of all. George had not forgotten to deliver the long, beautiful yellow feather cape from Kamehameha; he was waiting for an audience with the king, that he might present it personally, according to Kamehameha's instructions. How far away those lovely islands, full of happy, generous 'savages' were, and how impossible for George to return. Any such dreams were instantly shattered with that wicked cartoon. The king would never receive him now; he would never appreciate the treasured islands that George had won for him; he would see nothing but shabbiness. Shabbiness and savages! Only George's memories were left untarnished... but then perhaps, in our dog-eat-dog 'civilized' world, paradise can never be closer than that.

George surrendered the cape to the Home Secretary, Lord Portland, who eventually (some time in 1797) passed it on to the king, without ceremony or explanation of its symbolic import. George's dearest unspoken hopes went with it, reduced by a few strokes of the pen to a ragged old heap of dirty yellow feathers. Dear Hawaii was lost—the finest gemstone of the entire Pacific Ocean, more dazzling by far than the famous Pitt diamond of India that the ancestral Thomas Pitt, a lowly parson's son, had bought from some hapless native in 1702 and sold to France for a fortune, thus starting the Pitt dynasty—and George was a buffoon, which he must protest as long as he had life and breath. He must also redouble his efforts to produce a most singular and serious journal, that his reputation might be posthumously restored. Camelford had had his way. George was done in—a paper mutiny. He welcomed death thenceforward, but prayed it not come until he had adequate time to redeem himself.

I pray for as much now, for I must redeem what was destroyed after George died, to salvage what I can of the continued paper mutiny. I am nearly done in too, but not quite. Hear me out, then hear me no more.

29
Invitation to Glory

For George, all of October, 1796, was a nightmare of gleeful attacks upon his person and upon his command, in answer to
which he had scarcely a voice. Even if he had, it could not have
been heard above the clamorous derision he suffered at every turn.

George wished to publish a defense in the *Morning Herald*, for
which he sought Lord Grenville's approval; Grenville refused his
support and closed his door. George desperately sought a public in-
quiry, but it was roundly denied. The Admiralty refused to set up a
trial, that it might review George's treatment of Pitt, and George
could not call a court martial. He not only lacked the authority to
do so, he also lacked the desire; to his mind, he had fairly punished
and discharged Pitt, hence he had no grievance against his service.
It was up to Camelford to lay a complaint and insist upon a hearing,
but this, he would never do. George had no recourse. Muzzled and

isolated, he read the newspapers[19] and fought back the tears.

George had no recourse, that is, until a rumour began circulating that a mutiny had taken place aboard his ship, apparently in June of 1792, following the incident in which George had removed the barrier between midships and the fo'c'sle. This was the first he had heard of it, and the source of the rumour was never identified. It was a heinous charge, but George seized it as an opportunity to present his case at a full-fledged court martial. He not only wished to defend his own actions; he must also defend his many loyal officers and men, whose reputations would be tarnished by this unfounded charge.

Several former officers, Camelford's once best friend Robert Barrie among them, wrote to George urging him to help clear their names. George immediately sought aid through every possible channel, to which every response was denial and delay. The rumours persisted, gaining some legitimacy as they became old news, leaving George's command further sullied by their lordships' shameful neglect. They would sacrifice the reputations of a dozen worthy young officers to protect one of their kind.

Camelford left London to join his ship in late October, and blessed peace returned to George's fading life. He worked obsessively at his journal, every day pushing himself beyond a sustainable capacity. He could not have sapped his own life more effectively had he written every word with his own blood. When he was too ill to write, he dictated for hours on end to me, until I, too, felt as if I had been writing with *my* blood. What a task it was, and what a tale he had to tell! It would run to some half-million words when it was done, each one winnowed with care from his more lengthy ship's journal and expansive memories.

Christmas came and went again, and George was still without his

[19] On October 24th, the *True Briton* printed: "Captain VANCOUVER says that Lord CAMELFORD cannot *write*. He must, however, acknowledge, that the young Nobleman can *make his mark.*" On October 26th, the same paper printed: "Lord CAMELFORD can boast of a power which rivals that of the First Lord of the Admiralty—He has made Captain Couver *a yellow rear.*" (The rank of Yellow Rear-Admiral was the next promotion to which Vancouver might aspire.)

pay or prize money. The New Year brought no respite from this monetary seige; George so keenly felt Whitehall's frost, along with the winter cold, he slipped dangerously close to death. On February 7th, George was further struck down by news that Lord Keith (Commander-in-Chief of the entire Capetown operation) had claimed a portion of the prize monies for the *Macassar*, although he was far from St. Helena when she was seized, and George was not under his command. George wrote to the Lords of the Treasury, via the Admiralty, for clarification and an expeditious settlement of the matter. Not surprisingly, months of silence greeted his urgent request.

On February 20th—a dismal day—Camelford returned to town to take his seat in the House of Lords, the day after celebrating his 21st birthday. Talk of a supposed mutiny on the *Discovery* began circulating again, and George renewed his efforts to effect an investigation. He was so very ill, he could not have attended one at that time, but he pressed for a future hearing, for which he would certainly have rallied.

On March 12th, his agent, James Sykes (who continued to loan George whatever money and give him whatever supplies he requested) informed him that an investigation was a virtual impossibility, for all the unstated reasons George knew too well. Besides, Sykes continued, George should attend to nothing but his health, which was kindly and just advice, but George responded that "it is highly important, that attention should likewise be paid to the means of supporting that health when acquired: independently of this consideration, the ascertaining & refuting the *falsehood* in Question, is an *indispensable duty*, which I owe to all those, whom at the time I had the honor to command. . . . "

How well I remember those words, which I had the mournful task of penning, complete with the postscript: "As writing is exceedingly pernicious to my present indisposition my brother who is here has been good enough to write this letter for me." George was frightfully near death; had he not some redeeming work to do, he would have slipped away then, grateful for peace from his monstrous cares.

The monster at the root of all, Camelford, had not yet sailed to do his valiant duty in war-torn waters but was idling about the Channel and, occasionally, in town—a cowardice abetted by his lordly kin. Charles had the misfortune of seeing him on March 14th in Mr. Ramsden's optical shop in Piccadilly[20], where Camelford spotted him and instantly came running for blood.

Camelford suggested they step out onto the street, as if Charles would be fool enough to engage in another public caning. Charles calmly said he had pressing business with Mr. Ramsden, but he would listen to his lordship where they stood. In a rage, Camelford shut the shop door and demanded to know if Charles had received his written challenge to a duel, delivered following the fracas in Conduit Street. Yes, Charles said, but he had not replied, because his lordship had pledged his honour to the Lord Chancellor not to take any further steps in the business.

Camelford insisted that Charles should have had the courtesy to reply, for only a dishonourable coward—a poltroon, like his brother—would have ignored it. Charles was unmoved by this puerile barb, hence Camelford issued his challenge anew, this time for a duel to be fought at Ham after his year's surety expired. Charles coolly replied that he would consider it *then*.

That set Camelford to ranting in a manner reminiscent of Fletcher Christian's harangue at William Bligh as the mutineers took control of the *Bounty*. Camelford accused George, and now Charles, of depriving him of all the enjoyments of life, and nothing short of their deaths could appease or quiet the torture of mind under which he existed. To Christian's credit, he expressed his insanity better, in the famous, agonizing words, "I am in hell—I am in hell." Camelford had not half Christian's wit or will, however, and he made puny work of his self-serving madness, as he did everything else.

Charles tried to reason with Camelford, which was pointless, of

---

[20] Jesse Ramsden, F.R.S., a noted instrument maker. Some of the instruments on the *Discovery* and *Chatham* had been supplied by him. He greatly improved the accuracy of the sextant.

course. Camelford took this as cowardice and taunted that, if Charles was concerned about danger or conceived Camelford had some advantage over him, Charles may have two shots to his one! Charles was finding this all rather tedious, although he held his temper and simply declined Camelford's offer for the time being. He promised to answer Camelford's challenge on September 28th next, but not before. With that, Camelford stomped from the shop, hard on his heels like a spoiled child, swearing that he would have his revenge on *both* of his enemies.

April, May, June, July, August... these months passed peacefully, for Camelford finally shipped off to the West Indies late in April. Just prior to sailing, he had witnessed the mutinies at Spithead by seamen demanding just pay. Rumour had it that he trembled in his boots. Could he then understand the measures George had taken to prevent mutiny aboard his 99-foot ship, crowded with 100 men, far from home for nearly five years? Apparently not, in light of the trouble Camelford got himself into in the West Indies, where his fear of mutiny made him truly the tyrant he accused George of being.

Camelford sailed from England with his lieutenant's papers in hand, although they were won by influence, not commendation. His first commander, Captain Riou, refused to sign his certificate for promotion, saying he had done nothing during that year of service to deserve it. Naturally, George was not consulted, which was irregular and distressing, but he found comfort in his belief that wicked men eventually and inevitably fashion their own fitting punishment; Camelford would hang himself when he was given enough rope.

In May, Charles was off to America, where he had agricultural and mercantile interests. It is worth noting here, for I have failed to mention it earlier, that, as a man of many interests and talents, both in the theoretical sciences and practical arts, he was ever disposed to promoting the frontiers of human knowledge and settlement. As such, in early 1793, he had proposed to the Royal Society (Sir Joseph Banks's bastion, an enemy fortification following

George's return home) that a colony be established at Nootka Sound by means of overland penetration, rather than the seaward approach under consideration.

Five days after Charles's proposal was delivered, Alexander Mackenzie arrived at Pacific tidewaters from his base camp at Lake Athabasca, proving the feasibility of this approach. Nothing has come of it yet, but it shows that Charles's interest in the American continent was practical and wide-ranging, and if there was a new and daring idea in the wind, he caught it and endeavoured to advance it.

What business he had in America during his 1797 visit, I cannot clearly recall, but it was undoubtedly something too pressing and exciting to resist. He left George and me, therefore, to our own devices; with Camelford safely away, and likely for several years, the risk was minimal. Nonetheless, he wrote and signed an affidavit outlining his recent exchange with Camelford at Mr. Ramsden's shop, should anything untoward come of it before he returned to England that autumn. He regretted that he had not noted or complained of Camelford's written challenge to a duel the previous September; this time, he would give Camelford no further opportunity to use his gentlemanly silence to unfair advantage.

September came, but no word of pay from any source came with it. George's work was advancing nicely, as was the engravers' work, which meant that George had to borrow yet more money from Mr. Sykes to pay them, then await the Admiralty's grudging repayment. Charles returned in good order, and on September 28th, true to his word, he delivered a letter to Camelford House stating his acceptance of Camelford's challenge to a duel at Ham, at his lordship's convenience.

Lady Camelford opened the letter, and she flew into a frenzy. She immediately informed the Lord Chancellor, who served Charles with notice to pay a large surety as *his promise to keep the peace*, without hearing Charles's side of it at all!

Charles could not raise such a princely sum, and he was forced to retire to Holland. What a bitter parting that was—hounded out of

England by Camelford, when the young devil was not even there! So much for trying to be honourable to a completely disreputable, dishonourable rapscallion, with a nosy, nervous, vindictive old witch for a mother. Damn, damn, damn! George and I were alone—more so than ever before.

In October, the Admiralty finally made an offer to pay George for his years of service. They proposed giving him six shillings, six pence a day, which infuriated George. William Bligh, who sailed the *Bounty* as a lieutenant commander, not post-captain, and acted as purser, as George had, was paid eight shillings a day. Precedent had been set; George insisted he must receive at least equal recompense.

The Admiralty could not deny the legitimacy of his claim, and bless their niggardly hearts, in November of 1797, they released the grand total of nearly £700 of pay owed since December of 1790. Such largesse—while Camelford sat prettily upon his unearned income of more than £20,000 per year! What justice is this, pray tell?

That same month, word came regarding the division of prize monies—a welcome settlement, but alas, too late, for George's spirit was beyond lifting by then. He would receive one third of one half, as originally determined by the King's Advocate. Payment would be made in due time, which meant that George had no cash for comfort as he rang in the New Year of 1798, with numerous creditors still pressing for full payment. At least he had some gratifying news on another front.

Camelford was making quite a reputation for himself in the West Indies, and, true to George's prediction, it was as tarnished as the buttons on his slovenly uniform. In September, he had been appointed acting master and commander of the *Favorite*, based at St. Kitts, over a more senior, capable, and high-born lieutenant, Charles Peterson. To truly appreciate what sort of officer Camelford had become, one must consider his appearance, which had changed considerably from the young dandy about town. I have the pleasure of reporting from no less than *The Annual Register . . . For the Year 1798*, which was published in 1800—too late for George to read, although he heard talk enough of Camelford's peculiar style:

Lord Camelford appears to be a new character in his class. His person is not altogether unlike the late Lord George Gordon, when he was the same age; their whimism is somewhat similar. Lord Camelford provides a table of plenty of good fresh meat every day for the men who are sick in his ship. He is very severe in carrying on duty: seldom ties up a man but he get six or seven dozen lashes, which is a more severe punishment, in this country, than what's produced by giving the same number in a northern climate. Although his lordship is a master and commander, he does not set an expensive example, by wearing extravagant clothes. He makes use of no swabs [gold shoulder knots], but still appears in a lieutenant's uniform. His dress is, indeed extremely remarkable: all the hair is shaved off his head, on which he wears a monstrous large gold laced cocked hat, which, by its appearance, one would think had seen service with sir [*sic*] Walter Raleigh. He is dressed in a lieutenant's plain coat, the buttons of which are as green with verdegrease as the ship's bottom; and with this all the rest of his dress corresponds.

Camelford's singular and unsavoury appearance came to be the talk of London due to his most singular and unsavoury actions. On October 25th of 1797, past midnight, he undertook a forceful attack on what he supposed to be enemy batteries at Charlotte Town in Grenada. With darkened ship, he fought a noble and pitched battle, refusing to answer all hails and messages. When he finally took a broadside hit, he sailed off, with time then to contemplate the meaning of the shouts and notes delivered from shore. He had, if disbelief can be overcome, attacked a British fort! Was he suitably humiliated (for this is the stuff of suicide)? Not a chance! He went ashore in his cutter and demanded to see the governor, to whom he instantly and indignantly insisted the Royal Navy had been insulted by an unprovoked attack on one of His Majesty's ships (damned fool Brits, defending their fortifications, what?), and he soundly berated this astonished official for not joining in the fray.

The governor replied smartly that he had taken a vigorous part and, fortunately, had driven Camelford off before any serious damage was done. He reported the incident to Admiral Harvey at Martinique, who was apparently so awed by Camelford's status and connections, he simply assured the governor that he would instruct Camelford never again to approach the forts without showing a light or sending a boat to make the ship known to the commanding shore officer. Thus, Camelford suffered no consequences for his actions, which were "extraordinary and unprecedented," according to the report that reached the Admiralty, and consequently circulated through London in early January of 1798.

More damning news followed shortly thereafter, for Camelford went straight from one mad encounter to another. He left Grenada and made his way to the Barbados, where he planned to press some merchant seamen into service aboard his ship—a legal action in wartime, but far easier said than done, for any sign of an impending impressment sends every eligible man into hiding, and those who are caught put up a hard fight for their freedom.

Under cover of darkness, in the early hours of November 6th, Camelford directed his boats to slip into Carlisle Bay, where two merchantmen lay at anchor. By surprise and force, Camelford led his men on board and struggled to take whatever men they could capture. The story quickly becomes confused, for there was insistence and resistance on both sides, including numerous wild goose chases ashore. The upshot of all the commotion was that Camelford stabbed and shot a seaman, then did the same to a merchant captain who was lodged ashore. Two men dead—one a commanding officer!—and their blood was all over Camelford's hands. He beat a hasty retreat, with half a dozen or more impressed men, and sailed safely away.

Relatives of the murdered captain quickly made their case known in England, demanding prosecution of the absent, cowardly, mad Camelford. His mother, sister, Lord Grenville, and others were in a wild flap, lining up all possible witnesses and court machinery to ensure he received a 'fair' trial—meaning, of course, that his peers at Westminster be called in to protect his good name, and theirs as well. No wonder, when lampooning George, they were obsessed with making sad puns about rear covering, for it was a frequent and familiar activity to them.

Within months, however, the incident had blown over, and Camelford once again suffered no consequences for his increasingly irrational and violent behaviour. During this time, George struggled ever harder against all odds to live long enough to finish his journal. January was a cold, miserable month, made worse by news that Mr. Menzies, aided by Sir Joseph Banks, was determined to have his journal published before George's appeared—a mean and spiteful effort that would, nonetheless, fail to undercut sales of George's accounting, however deeply it sliced the private man.

The prize monies had not arrived, although George expected to touch the cash any day. It was a sizeable sum and would render George solvent for the first time in many, many years. Despite so many deliberate delays and debilitating setbacks, George still had a dream or two left. In particular, he talked about using his 'fortune' to purchase and improve a small manor at Ealing in Berkshire. He would retire there, secure financially from sales of his journal, which he was certain would meet with wide approval. Equally important, by such means he would regain the honour that had been so cruelly stripped from him.

I could plainly see that this was a pipedream, so close now did death hover, but I encouraged him to embrace it, for neither of us could abandon hope that justice would be done while he still lived. I promised that I and family would move there with him, that we might tend the place together—two country gentlemen enjoying the land and sky through all their seasons.

February, 1798: no prize monies; other disheartening news. The Navy Board decided to pay Joseph Whidbey the astronomer's pay denied George, although the Admiralty had neither authorized Whidbey to undertake this activity in Mr. Gooch's absence nor had George appointed him to the position. George no longer had the strength to raise an indignant voice, at home or at Whitehall. His eyes bespoke his pain...his desolation. How could they? Why?

Why now? He was dying a death of a thousand cuts, and he could take no more. Dear God, how he found the will to drive himself those last months of his life, I do not know.

We pressed forward on his journal every day, doggedly making for Valparaiso, where we both knew he would at last be free to die. Not only had he finished his commissioned work at that port, but all his Chilean notes were missing—the thousand and first cut. He was so close to death, I feared he would not make Valparaiso before he died, hence I contrarily wished to hurry there in all haste, for if he failed to reach that last goal, he would be robbed of his last satisfaction—finishing his journal to the end of his commissioned work—which was unthinkable.

News of Camelford's latest folly reached England in late winter, and shocking news it was! In January, he and his former first officer, Lieutenant Charles Peterson, were each given command of their own little warships. One's superiority over the other was not clear, and Camelford presumed to take the lead. Naturally, rivalry between Camelford and Peterson sharpened, although Peterson alone understood that, whatever their personal animosity, they remained brothers at arms.

At Antigua, some business or other arose by which Camelford chose to press his higher rank. Peterson pressed in return, repeating Camelford's orders back to him, as though Peterson were the superior officer. Camelford could not stand such impertinence, which smacked of mutiny. When the two commanders met, ostensibly to discuss the matter, Camelford placed a pistol at Peterson's breast and challenged him: Do as I say, or else! Peterson refused instant compliance, and Camelford blasted him through the heart.

Murder, and by a fellow officer! At a hastily called trial, Camelford defended himself by raising the spectre of mutiny, swearing that Peterson was poised and ready to lead an insurrection. No proof of this was offered, save Peterson's refusal to submit to Camelford's questionable authority, ironically over the exact same orders. The five judging officers were so fearful of the word mutiny and so cowed by Camelford's formidable connections, they acquitted him!

Unbelievable! They acquitted him unanimously and honourably, and they let him loose again.

No sooner was Camelford back on the streets of Antigua than he grew irritated with the naval officer and storekeeper at English Harbour who was not outfitting his ship quickly or preferentially enough to satisfy him. Camelford hauled this upright citizen, well liked and respected, to the wharf and horsewhipped him. Camelford was arrested, charged, jailed, and was to face public trial for this misdeed. Bail was set at £5,000, which is a pittance (and an appropriate pun) to one of his station; he paid it immediately, then galloped from town at breakneck speed, never to be seen there again.

The Commander-in-Chief of the West Indies fleet finally decided that he could no longer permit Camelford to assault British fortifications, ships, officers, and citizens in those waters. He quietly arranged for Camelford's return to England by giving him command—command, no less!—of the *Terror*, a most fitting vessel, indeed.

While Camelford was running amok in Caribbean waters, George and I worked relentlessly upon his journal. What horribly stressful days and weeks those were, as March and April slowly progressed. Early spring storms streaked the windows with copious sweet-water tears; as the days grew longer, delicate, showy blooms nodded in the clear, bright air, their promises of renewal contrasting sharply with George's grey, painful, plodding, inevitable demise.

On April 28th, George dictated and signed his will. I was to take the bulk of his estate and buy the Ealing manor, that I might walk the grounds with him in memory—two country gentlemen enjoying the land and sky through all their seasons.

The last of the engravers' plates was printed and met George's approval by May 1st, the date all the illustrations bear. Valparaiso was not far off. We had to put in to that port. The *Discovery*'s mainmast was badly sprung and must be repaired—replaced, if possible. If the latter, then George could chart the shoreline from 44° south latitude to the tip of Tierra del Fuego, according to his instructions. How I wished that a good, big stick could have been found somewhere in all of Chile, that George might stay with me, regain his health, and live for years yet. It was not to be, and I knew it. He was so very, very ill that I prayed for his release, and I also prayed that "God spare him many days", as the Spanish say.

I stayed with him round the clock, and often when he sank into irresistible sleep, I studied his face intently, as if memorizing it would somehow keep him with me. We struggled onward each day, him clinging to his notes and I to my copy. May 2nd... 3rd... 4th...

May 10th, 1798: We made the Chilean coast. May 11th: Governor Alava graciously welcomed George to Valparaiso. May 12th: The courier arrived with Higgins's welcome to Chile, his confirmation that no replacement mast was available, and his invitation to George and officers to visit him at Santiago. George penned his acceptance to Higgins on March 28th, 1794. I penned it for him again on May 12th, 1798.

That done, I looked up at George, knowing his commissioned work was now complete. Before my horror-struck eyes, he surrendered to... to death, yes, but to much more than that, and I instantly took courage from him. Peace washed over him, peace that could only have come from the serene knowledge that time was his eternal ally now, by which honour would be restored and justice would be done.

Up, up, and away he went, over the great snowy Andes mountains on an arduous journey to the Chilean capital city, a civilized Spanish outpost, home to more than 30,000 souls. A mile from town, he pulled his care-worn frame and time-worn uniform atop a handsome steed, caparisoned in princely gold and silver. He and his officers slowly paraded to the president's palace, through streets thronged with curious, admiring, cheering crowds. In his hand, he carried his invitation... his invitation to glory.

30
All That Remains

George was buried in the lovely, snug churchyard of St. Peter's Church in Petersham in a quiet ceremony on May 18th, 1798. He was the 20th member of the *Discovery*'s officers and young gentlemen to die since returning to England. Nineteen had been lost in battle; one now died of a broken heart. Time and tide had so turned against George, the state and its ministers played no part in the funeral ceremony, nor did they send official representatives or regrets.

George had willed the bulk of his newly-paid fortunes—£5,000—to me, with which to purchase the Ealing manor. I was not able to do so, as I had worked without pay for several years while tending George, hence I had more immediate and pressing financial concerns; the manor fell to other hands. My unpaid labours continued, as I set to the melancholy task of finishing George's journal alone. All but 100 of nearly 1,500 pages were in type or ready for the printer when he died, and all the charts and illustrations were printed. Nonetheless, producing those last 100 pages taxed me beyond my powers to describe.

I had all of George's notes before me, volume upon volume of them, which I returned to the authorities when my task was done. They were soon gone, vanished. . . . Of the few things of George's that remain, and of the many things that are lost, the disappearance of those notes must weigh most heavily upon all those who seek enlightenment and adventure. They contained numerous observations George had edited for his published journal, some of which he intended to comment upon later, in other publications, and *all* of which had value as a national—indeed, international—treasure.

Of the two dozen officers' and young gentlemen's journals George delivered to the Admiralty upon the *Discovery*'s return to Great Britain, several are now missing, each of which contained references to Thomas Pitt. Joseph Whidbey's is the most serious loss, but they were valuable records all.

The dear old *Discovery* herself has fallen to ruin. She serves as a prison hulk, rotting at the Deptford Yards, as if she were any old barge, with nary a tale to tell. If the sudden demise of George's favourite boat made him weep, then the slow undoing of the *Discovery* would tear his very soul. She is beyond redemption now; she will be dust ere I am. It pains me too greatly to think upon it; I should rather dwell upon what has been gained than what has been lost, although it is the latter that has impelled my pen all these many pages.

Praise be, George's printed journal remains, and in great numbers, various languages, and several editions. It was first published in three quarto volumes, plus a folio atlas, in the early autumn of 1798, and it immediately won the recognition for which George had so dearly hoped. It soon sold out, and I took charge of revising the text for a smaller format, second edition, which was printed in larger numbers than the first.

The 1801 edition consists of six octavo volumes, without the fo-

All That Remains

lio atlas, for the chart plates were all stolen. Stolen! To what end, one might ask? For their copper? Not likely, for no other plates disappeared with them. One can only conclude that it was deliberate, malicious sabotage, which I place squarely at Camelford's feet, as I do the disappearance of George's extensive notes.

Camelford did not act alone, however. His every misstep was supported by family and friends in high and mighty places. I readily confess my bitter hatred for the young blackguard, for he was at the root of George's sad demise, but the blame is more fairly spread over the entire, rotten system of blind privilege and patronage that tended to that bad seed and brought it to full flower. That said, let me tell you what became of Camelford before his death, and, of the Pitt dynasty.

Camelford returned to England in July of 1798 (which means, of course, that he was not able to skulk around Petersham at the time of George's death, although I allude to this early in my writing; we expected Camelford home at any time, and, thus, I had some very real fears of seeing his wicked, gleeful face peeking through the windows—a tall, handsome young madman triumphant at last over an ugly, fat old opponent). No sooner was he in town than he gave assurities to the Lord Chancellor not to pursue his old quarrel with Charles. His relatives quickly looked for a posting for him and, after several months—even their influence was waning, in view of Camelford's West Indies antics—got him the command of a ship bound for the Mediterranean.

Unfortunately, Camelford was still in England by year end, and he had got himself into a fine fix trying stupidly to become a spy in France, where all Britons were forbidden to travel. A recent act of Parliament made any such attempt, however innocently undertaken, a capital offence, and a man had just been hanged for the crime. After Camelford's arrest at Dover, he was brought to trial before the Privy Council, with family members (Lords Chatham and Grenville, Prime Minister Pitt) discreetly absenting themselves. Every newspaper account of his activities branded him "insane", "certainly mad", "mentally deranged", and so forth.

I have accused Camelford of pilfering and destroying as many of

George's papers as he could find, and I have no doubt about the truth of this charge. His actions, however, may not have been as a lone thief rampaging about Whitehall after hours. Camelford's trial before the Privy Council presented the Crown with an opportunity to review his past crimes and punishments, including those under George's command. There is a good possibility that George's notes and letters were compiled as evidence at that time, during or after which they disappeared. This does not remove Camelford as a prime suspect; it simply puts George's work neatly together in a pile, at Camelford's disposal or at the disposal of his legal counsel and 'discreetly absent' relatives, to 'innocently' vanish somewhere in transit.

To no one's surprise, Camelford was granted a free pardon, on the condition that he never again "be intrusted with the command of any ship or vessel in his Majesty's service." At last, at long last, his naval career and all related lofty aspirations had come to an ig-nominious end. How many men had died before truth and justice won out? Perhaps a dozen native warriors on the northwest coast of America at Traitor's Cove; a merchant captain and a seaman at Barbados; certainly others in the West Indies who died from the ill effects of being excessively flogged; Lieutenant Charles Peterson at Antigua; and finally, Captain George Vancouver at home in En-gland, by the cruellest, slowest torture of all.

Camelford was far from finished venting his frustration and anger at the world, however. Several months after being acquitted, he at-tacked a fellow theatre patron and pummelled him rather thorough-ly, although the man was unknown to him and had done nothing to provoke him. The jury at that trial found him guilty and fined him £500. Over the remaining six years of Camelford's life, he regularly and tediously attacked whoever crossed him, and he killed again in duels, although the count from this illegal activity was never tal-lied.

The duel in which he died was over a young married tart, with whom Camelford and his best friend had long had separate and even simultaneous affairs. Somehow, she said something trivial to Camelford's friend that called his honour into question, which, of course, could only be defended by a duel to the death. Death it was then, and slowly too—three days it took for the life to ebb from his body; three days for him to reflect and regret, although I wager not enough to get himself into Heaven. His funeral was a pompous affair and well enough attended, although his passing was little lamented by any but his most intimate family.

The great Camelford wing of the Pitt family came to naught, therefore, for young Lord Camelford had no issue. Prime Minister William Pitt died a bachelor in 1806. The second Lord Chatham, William Pitt's older brother John, left no sons, and Lord Grenville died childless by Camelford's sister Anne. It appears that Lady Justice at last took offence at the Pitt boys' misuse of her and, with God's help, blessedly saved the empire from the continuance of their line. (Let us pray that He does the same for King George's many nasty, self-serving sons, and spare us from their tyranny.)

Enough of Camelford for now—and forever! He is done, and nothing of him remains but his foul reputation and the damage he inflicted. George's reputation, on the other hand, was restored by his published journal and continues to rise as his word spreads. A French translation was published in 1799, and a second edition appeared in 1802. A German translation was published in 1799-1800, a Swedish in 1800-1801, and a Russian just last year [1827]. Several abridgements have been published in English, as well as in French and German.

In time, as the part of the world he discovered is opened by the push of civilization, his reputation will shine through the tarnish of all the societal and political forces pitted against him. The vast shorelines he so meticulously delineated and described await settlement by hardy English souls, and one day, in the centuries to come, that great land shall certainly have its time in the sun. George's good name and great deeds will be celebrated by the industrious colonials who shall build a new, free Utopia at the western edge of this tired old world.

Had George lived, and had his grandest dreams come true, I believe he would have returned to Pacific waters and helped to forge a new society there. His base would have been the Sandwich Islands, from which he could have built British links from the Far East to the Far West, while integrating the best of civilized and 'savage' cultures, to bring comfort, peace, and justice to all.

For years now, his beloved Sandwich Islands have lain torn and untended, regal treasures certain never to fall to British hands, for American missionaries are paving the way for possible American annexation. Since England never gave serious thought to what she might have gained, she will likely never care to ponder what she lost.

The son of King Kamehameha visited England four years ago [1824], with his queen, to seek affirmation of their islands' subjection to the rule of King George IV. The king supposedly said, "Think of that damned fellow [Canning, the Foreign Secretary] wanting me to have the King and Queen of the Sandwich Islands to dinner, as if I would sit at table with such a pair of damned cannibals!", which no doubt caused great merriment in fashionable circles. Fortunately for the arrogant king, he was spared such an indignity; Kamehameha II and his wife soon succumbed to measles and expired in England's chilly embrace.

George's good friend, Kamehameha I, died in 1819, after uniting all the Sandwich Islands under his crown. He had fought many bloody wars to achieve this end, although his initial victories were swift. Within a year of George's departure from the islands, Kamehameha had extended his kingdom as far west and north as Oahu. Kauai and Niihau fell under his control, by peaceful agreement, in 1810. Even now, after so much has changed, the Sandwich Islanders are said to prefer British rule, in large part because they so fondly remember Captain George Vancouver.

George's memory, therefore, remains strong and bright in those paradise isles, where the native people saw and appreciated what a great, good man he was. Something else of him may remain there as well, although I shall die with the riddle of it teasing my mind. In the short time that remains of my life, I cannot discover or guess the answer, despite my own dearest wishes and speculations; I can only hope that my heart shall be proven right when I join George— and soon.

Lieutenant William Broughton returned to the Sandwich Islands in 1796, and there he found much turmoil and fear. The natives' growing hatred of white men, most of whom ill used them, led them to murder two of Broughton's marines on the beach at Niihau (proof that George had accurately judged Broughton's treatment of nátives and was well rid of him, but this is not my point). In Broughton's journal, published in 1804, his greatest attentions are given to describing this event, while making minor, puzzling references to several native persons.

One of the natives Broughton blindly accused of playing an active part in the attack was a man named Tupararo, whom he had met at Kauai before sailing to Niihau. Tupararo offered to provision the ships with yams at Niihau, and he went ahead in his own boat to make arrangements. Broughton followed, no doubt with many native women aboard, although he makes a singular reference to only two of them:

> . . . It was extraordinary that the two women, Rahina and Timarroe (whom Captain Vancouver brought from the N.W. coast) should have come with us from Atooi [Kauai], when Tupararo was the husband of the first, and whose child had been sent on board that we might see him.

Tupararo was Raheina's husband? That is possibly true, for a woman with a child needs a provider and protector, although Tupararo could have been these things without being her husband. One must not presume, as Broughton did, what their arrangement was, especially in light of his very peculiar claim that Raheina had sent her child aboard "*that we might see him.*" Why did no other women, Tymarow in particular, insist that Broughton see their children? Why was it so imperative to Raheina that he see her son? Why?

This is the riddle that teases me, and the one I shall take with me to my grave. I want to believe that George knew the sweet fullness of love in Raheina's arms, and I want to believe he has a strong, healthy, wise son living on his tract of land at Kauai, building the sort of peaceful, just society George had envisioned.

That said, I am spent and can now surrender. I have outlined as faithfully as memory will allow all that I know of what is missing, and I have tried to detail all that matters of what remains. I have railed my last against those persons and forces that fought to defeat George and, indeed, appeared to win over him. Through this recounting, by which I have considered George's life and death in the light of the ages, I can plainly see, in the balance, what George knew when he found eternal peace: there is justice, after all.

RESTORED BY
THE NATIVE SONS OF
BRITISH COLUMBIA,
POST No. 2 (CANADA)
MAINTAINED BY THE LATE
MAJOR J.S. MATTHEWS
AND THE CITY OF VANCOUVER
B.C. (CANADA)

Epilogue

John Vancouver's will is dated December 11, 1828. He died some-time before February 3rd, 1829, when his will was proved in London. He was survived by his second wife, Elizabeth, and four children.

The second of John's two sons was named George. What became of him is not known, although an oil painting purportedly of George Vancouver came to auction at Christie's in 1878. The National Portrait Gallery bought it and displayed it for years as an authentic likeness of Captain Vancouver. There is, indeed, a family likeness to the miniature portrait of John Vancouver in the possession of a direct descendant. Is the larger painting of the captain, his nephew, or someone else entirely?

There are tantalizing reasons for believing that it is a portrait of *the* George Vancouver, but careful review by John Kerslake, Deputy

Keeper at the National Portrait Gallery in the 1950's led to its reclassification: ". . . all we have is a painting of a middle-aged man dressed in mufti, backgrounded by a globe showing the track of Cook's voyage and a few books on voyages of exploration: a painting of an unknown man by an unknown artist".

Captain George Vancouver must, therefore, remain faceless, which is a particular loss, when portraits exist of all the major and many of the minor characters of his times.

What disease killed Vancouver is equally a mystery. Many theories have been advanced; the currently accepted one is proposed by Surgeon Vice-Admiral Sir James Watt, who is confident Vancouver suffered from myxoedema (thyroid deficiency), with or without an associated Addison's disease (adrenal deficiency). Vancouver's condition may have been inherited, or it may have been precipitated by tuberculosis or perhaps by some deadly disease contracted in the West Indies.

Alternately, certain foods such as cabbage are thought to induce the condition in a small number of susceptible patients. It would be ironic if Captain Cook's great reliance on sauerkraut as an antiscorbutic was at the root of what plagued his most devoted disciple. Given that Mr. Menzies's "nutritive diet" rescued George from death's door more than once, there may be something to this argument.

What became of Camelford's body is also unknown. Rumours circulated for many years regarding its supposed disappearance. In 1930, Vancouver biographer George Godwin declared that, "The basket in which the body had been placed mysteriously disappeared and has never been heard of since."

In 1976, Camelford biographer Nikolai Tolstoy wrote that, following 1815, one of Camelford's friends requested permission to remove the body for transport abroad, but was refused. Further, he states that mid-19th century novelist Charles Reade reported that Camelford's remains were yet in the sealed vaults at St. Anne's Church in Soho, in "an enormously long fish-basket, fit to pack a shark in." Tolstoy believes the body is still in the vaults, which now lie beneath a car park, for the church did not survive World War II.

Only disinterment will solve this little puzzle; if any traces of Camelford remain, reinterment might take place, as he wished, in Switzerland.

Captain George Vancouver's simple grave remains well-marked and tended in St. Peter's churchyard in Petersham, which has been called "the most elegant village in England." Not far from the church is "The Glen", a charming stone cottage that is likely the home where Vancouver wrote his epic journal and died. It was a servant's house, the small satellite of a nearby manor. The present owners have renamed it "The Navigator's House"; it has some minor Victorian additions, but one can readily imagine Camelford passing through the gate and generous garden to the front door, there to rave at Vancouver, wildly determined to destroy a dying man and his life's work.

What is missing of the public and private record of George Vancouver is clear enough: the originals of his extensive shipboard journal have disappeared, as have many official and personal letters he wrote during and after the voyage; his volumes of navigational observations, of which both ships' daybooks formed a part, are gone; the journals kept by Robert Barrie, Edward Harris, the Honourable Charles Stuart, and Joseph Whidbey have vanished; several other officers' journals are missing their latter sections; most papers relating to Vancouver's early service are lost.

The few dozen existing papers that bear Vancouver's handwriting are principally in the Public Record Office in London; the rest are in the National Maritime Museum and scattered in private and public collections throughout the world.

Vancouver's published journal has appeared in 11 different editions: four in English; three in French; one in German; one in Danish; one in Swedish; one in Russian. The earliest English edition is extremely rare and valuable, while the second English edition is also rare and relatively expensive. In 1967, Amsterdam, N. Israel; New York, da Capo Press issued a facsimile reprint (Biblioteca Australiana nos. 30-32), which quickly sold out. In 1984, the Haykluyt Society of London published the most informative edition to date, edited by the superlative historian and Vancouver scholar, W. Kaye Lamb; limited numbers are still available. So thorough is Dr. Lamb's edition of Vancouver's voyage, nearly all quotations included in this book can be found therein. The exceptions are as follows (see Sources for the full reference): pages 33, 34, and 247 are from Tolstoy's *The Half-Mad Lord*; pages 59n and 92 are from Beaglehole's *The Journals of Captain James Cook*, vol III; page 93 is from Meany's *Vancouver's Discovery of Puget Sound*; page 147 is from La Pérouse's *Voyage Around the World*; page 255 is from Kennedy's *Bligh*; and page 271 is from Broughton's *A Voyage of Discovery to the North Pacific Ocean*.

Half a dozen biographies of George Vancouver have been published, five of which give a fairly rote description of his life and voyage. One bizarre book, which won the Canadian Governor General's Award for fiction, suggested a homosexual relationship between Vancouver and Quadra, interspersed with discussions of the author's personal difficulties. Obviously, something about Vancouver piques our interest, although what exactly makes him a hero or anti-hero remains an enigma. That he did splendid work is beyond question; that he died under a cloud has spawned ever-new opinions and theories about the man.

His surveys were so accurate that mapmakers continued to incorporate portions of them into their charts until the 1920's, when aerial surveying took precedence. His longitude was often misplaced slightly, but if this is ignored, his latitude is still surprisingly accurate.

The best known and most lasting legacy of Vancouver's voyage lies in the place names he bestowed. He named 388 geographic features along the coasts of northwest America, the Hawaiian Islands, southern New Zealand, and southern Australia. Nine out of ten names have survived in their original or modified form. His own name lives on in British Columbia in the city of Vancouver and in Vancouver Island, as well as in the smaller Washington state city of Vancouver. Lesser known features named for him are: Mount Vancouver (4,830 m) on the Yukon-Alaska boundary; Cape Vancouver, Vancouver Rock, and the Vancouver Peninsula in Western Australia; Vancouver Arm of Dusky Sound in New Zealand; and

Epilogue

Port Vancouver, Staten Island, off the coast of Tierra del Fuego. Millions, if not billions, of people know his name, although few know his work and even fewer have a sense of the man. The Hawaiian people have not forgotten. Most do not know why his name is held in high esteem, but they do know he was a great and good man. This remembrance, more than any other, must embody Captain George Vancouver's dearest wish—that his heart be understood and cherished, for his honourable intentions and just deeds.

Sources

References

1. Anderson, B., *Surveyor of the Sea: The Life and Voyages of George Vancouver*. University of Washington Press, Seattle, 1960.
2. Bathe, B.W., *The Visual Encyclopedia of Nautical Terms Under Sail*. Crown Publishers Inc., New York, 1978.
3. Beaglehole, J.C., *The Life of Captain James Cook*, vol. 4 of *The Journals of Captain James Cook*. Hakluyt Society, Extra Series XXXVII, London, 1974.
4. Bligh, W., *The Log of the* Bounty. 2 vols., limited edition of 300 sets, printed by Christopher and Anthony Sandford, London, 1937.
5. Broughton, W.R., *A Voyage of Discovery to the North Pacific Ocean*. T. Cadell and W. Davies, London, 1804.
6. Burges, J., *A Narrative of the Negotiations Occasioned by the Dispute Between England and Spain in the Year 1790*. London, 1791.
7. Burkhardt, B., McLean, B.A., and Kochanek, D., *Sailors & Sauerkraut*. Gray's Publishing Limited, Sidney, BC, 1978.
8. Cook, W., *Flood Tide of Empire: Spain and the Pacific Northwest, 1543-1819*. New Haven, Conn., 1973.
9. Colnett, J., *The Journal of Captain James Colnett Aboard the 'Argonaut' from April 26, 1789 to Nov. 3, 1791*, with an introduction, notes, and supplementary documents, (ed.) F.W. Howay. Publications of the Champlain Society, XXVI, Toronto, 1940.
10. Efrat, B.S. and Langlois, W.J. (eds.), *Nu.tka: Captain Cook and The Spanish Explorers on the Coast*. Sound Heritage, Vol. VII, No. 1, Provincial Archives of British Columbia, Victoria, BC, 1978.

11. Godwin, G., *Vancouver: A Life, 1757-1798*. Philip Allan, London, 1930.
12. Haig-Brown, R, *Captain of the Discovery*. Macmillan of Canada, Toronto, 1974.
13. Haswell, R., *Voyages of the 'Columbia' to the Northwest Coast 1787-1790 and 1790-1793*. (ed.) F.W. Howay. Massachusetts Historical Society, Boston, 1941.
14. Henry, J.F., *Early Maritime Artists of the Pacific Northwest Coast, 1741-1841*. Douglas & McIntyre, Vancouver, BC, 1984.
15. Howarth, D., *Tahiti: A Paradise Lost*. The Viking Press, New York, 1983.
16. Howay, F.W., "John Kendrick and his Sons." Oregon Historical Quarterly XXIII (1922), 277-302.
17. ─────,(ed.) *The Dixon-Meares Controversy*. The Ryerson Press, Toronto, 1929.
18. Humble, R., *Captain Bligh*. Arthur Barker Ltd., London, 1976.
19. Kendrick, J. and Inglis, R., *Enlightened Voyages: Malaspina and Galiano on the Northwest Coast, 1791-1792*. Catalogue for a display, Vancouver Maritime Museum, Vancouver, Canada, 1991.
20. Kennedy, G., *Bligh*. Duckworth and Company, London, 1978.
21. ─────, *The Death of Cook*. Duckworth and Company, London, 1978.
22. La Pérouse, *Voyage of La Pérouse Around the World*. Biblioteca Australiana Nos. 27-29, N. Israel, Amsterdam, 1968.
23. Levathes, L., "Kamehameha". *National Geographic*, November 1983.
24. Makarova, R.V., *Russians on the Pacific, 1743-1799*. Materials for the Study of Alaska History, No. 6. Translated by R. A. Pierce and A. S. Donnelly. The Limestone Press, Kingston, Ontario, 1975.
25. Manning, W.R., *The Nootka Sound Controversy*. Annual Report of the American Historical Association, 1904; Government Printing House, 1905.
26. Marshall, J. S., and Marshall, C., *Vancouver's Voyage*. Mitchell Press, Vancouver, 1967.
27. Martínez, E.J., *Diary of a Voyage . . . to the Port of San Lorenzo*

de Nuca . . . in 1789. Translation by W. L Schurz, Bancroft Library, Berkeley, California.

28. Meany, E.S., *Vancouver's Discovery of Puget Sound.* Binford & Mort, Portland, Oregon, 1949.

29. Meares, J., *Voyages Made in the Years 1788 and 1789, from China to the North West Coast of America.* J. Walter, London, 1790.

30. Moziño, J.M., *Noticias de Nutka.* Translated and edited by I. Higbie Wilson, McClelland & Stewart Inc., Toronto, 1970.

31. Mourelle, F.A,, *Voyage of the Sonora from the 1775 Journal of Don Francisco Antonio Mourelle,* as translated by The Hon. Daines Barrington, reprint of the 1920 ed. by T. C. Russell. Ye Galleon Press, Fairfield, Wash., 1987.

32. Nordoff, C. and Hall J.N., *Mutiny on the Bounty.* Little, Brown and Co., New York, 1932.

33. Parker, J.W. (author?/publisher), *Sir Joseph Banks and the Royal Society.* London, 1844.

34. Portlock, N., *A Voyage Round the World; more particularly to the North-West Coast of America: performed in 1785, 1786, 1787, and 1788 . . .,* John Stockdale and George Goulding, London, 1789.

35. Quadra, J. F. (de la Bodega y Quadra), *Voyage of the North West Coast of North America . . . in the year 1792.* (University of British Columbia Library, Special Collections holding)

36. Rodger, N.A.M., *The Wooden World: An Analysis of the Georgian Navy.* Fontana Press, London, 1986.

37. Smith, E., *The Life of Sir Joseph Banks.* John Lane Co., London, 1911.

38. Tolstoy, N., *The Half-Mad Lord: Thomas Pitt, 2nd Baron Camelford.* Jonathan Cape, London, 1978.

39. Thurman, M. E., *The Naval Department of San Blas. New Spain's Bastion for Alta California and Nootka 1767 to 1798.* The Arthur H. Clark Co., Glendale, California, 1967.

40. Vancouver, G., *A Voyage of Discovery to the North Pacific Ocean and Round the World, 1791 - 1795.* With an introduction and appendices, (ed.) W. Kaye Lamb. Hakluyt Society, London, 1984.

41. Vancouver, J., *An enquiry into the causes and production of poverty and the state of the poor*. London, 1796.
42. Wagner, H. R., *Spanish Exploration in the Strait of Juan de Fuca*. Fine Arts Press, Santa Ana, California, 1933.
43. Walbran, J. T., *British Columbia Coast Names, 1592-1906*. Ottawa, 1909; facsimile reprint with an introduction by G.V.P. Akrigg, J.J. Douglas Ltd., Vancouver, 1971.

Illustrations: Plates

Abbreviations
BCARS   British Columbia Archives and Records Service, Victoria, Canada

BL   British Library, London, England
BM   British Museum, London, England
ML   Mitchell Library, State Library of New South Wales, Sydney, Australia
MN   Museo Naval, Madrid, Spain
NMM   National Maritime Museum, Greenwich, England
NPG   National Portrait Gallery, London, England
SCL-UBC Special Collections Library, University of British Columbia, Vancouver, Canada

Number
1. *John Vancouver, c. 1753-1829*
   FROM A MINIATURE IN THE POSSESSION OF A DESCENDENT, MRS. CAROLINE BUNDY, NORFOLK, ENGLAND; DETAIL OF A PHOTOGRAPH FROM THE VANCOUVER MUSEUM, VANCOUVER, CANADA)
2. *Captain James Cook, 1728-1779*
   (DETAIL OF A PORTRAIT BY NATHANIEL DANCE, 1776; NMM)
3. *Mrs. Elizabeth Cook, 1742-1835*
   (DETAIL OF A PORTRAIT BY W. HENDERSON, 1830; ML, ZML4304)
4. *William Bligh, 1754-1817*
   (DETAIL OF AN UNFINISHED PORTRAIT BY JOHN SMART, 1803; NPG)
5. *John Meares, 1756-1809*
   (FROM AN ENGRAVING IN *Voyages made in the Years 1788 and 1789, from China to the Northwest Coast* BY JOHN MEARES; SCL-UBC)
6. *Estevan José Martínez, 1742-1798*
   (DETAIL FROM AN ANONYMOUS PORTRAIT; MN/PHOTOGRAPH FROM ROBIN INGLIS)

7. *Spanish Insult to the British Flag at Nootka Sound*
   (FROM A CONTEMPORARY PRINT PUBLISHED IN LONDON IN 1791
   SHOWING A FICTITIOUS IMAGE OF THE SEIZURE OF THE ENGLISH
   SHIPS; BCARS, PDP678/PHOTOGRAPH FROM ROBIN INGLIS)
8. *Elevation of the* Discovery, 1789
   (REPLICA OF ORIGINAL IN THE NMM; AUTHOR'S COPY)
9. *Robert Barrie, 1774-1841*
   (BY AN UNKNOWN ARTIST, 1795; ROYAL MILITARY COLLEGE OF
   CANADA, KINGSTON, ONTARIO)
10. *Sir Joseph Banks, 1743-1820*
    (DETAIL OF A PORTRAIT BY T. PHILLIPS, 1810; NPG)
11. *Archibald Menzies, 1754-1842*
    (DETAIL OF A PORTRAIT BY ETON UPTON EDIS; BY PERMISSION OF
    THE LINNEAN SOCIETY OF LONDON, ENGLAND)
12. *Zachary Mudge, 1770-1852*
    (DETAIL OF A PORTRAIT BY JOHN OPIE; BCARS, HP28286)
13. *Kaiana*
    (FROM AN ENGRAVING IN *Voyages made in the Years 1788 and 1789,
    from China to the Northwest Coast* BY JOHN MEARES; SCL-UBC)
14. *Robert Gray, 1755-1806*
    (FROM *Voyages of the 'Columbia' to the Northwest Coast 1787-1790 and
    1790-1793* BY R. HASWELL [F.W. HOWAY, ED.]; SCL-UBC)
15. *Interior of the* Discovery's *Cabin*
    (PHOTOGRAPH OF A FULL-SCALE REPLICA AT THE ROYAL BRITISH
    COLUMBIA MUSEUM, VICTORIA, CANADA)
16. *Dionisio Alcalá Galiano, 1760-1805*
    (DETAIL OF A PORTRAIT BY AN UNKNOWN ARTIST; MN/PHOTO-
    GRAPH FROM ROBIN INGLIS)
17. *Cayatano Valdés, 1767-1839*
    (DETAIL OF A PORTRAIT BY JOSÉ ROLDAN, c.1847; MN/ PHOTO-
    GRAPH FROM ROBIN INGLIS)
18. *'The* Discovery *on the Rocks in Queen Charlotte's Sound'*
    (SKETCH BY ZACHARY MUDGE, 1792; ENGRAVED BY B.T. POUNCY
    FOR VANCOUVER'S *Voyage of Discovery*, 1798; SCL-UBC)
19. *Friendly Cove, Nootka Sound*
    (SKETCH BY HENRY HUMPHRYS, 1792; ENGRAVED BY JAMES
    HEATH FOR VANCOUVER'S *Voyage of Discovery*, 1798; SCL-UBC)
20. *Juan Francisco de la Bodega y Quadra, 1743-1794*
    (DETAIL OF PORTRAIT BY JULIO GARCÍA, c.1950; MARITIME MU-
    SEUM OF BRITISH COLUMBIA, VICTORIA, CANADA/PHOTOGRAPH
    FROM ROBIN INGLIS)

Sources

21. *Maquinna*
    (1791 DRAWING BY TOMÁS DE SURIA; MN/PHOTOGRAPH FROM ROBIN INGLIS)
22. *Interior View of Maquinna's House at Tahsis*
    (1792 DRAWING BY ATÁNASIO ECHEVERRÍA, 'IMPROVED' BY JOSÉ MARÍA VASQUEZ; CANADIAN PARKS SERVICE COLLECTIONS, OTTAWA, CANADA/PHOTOGRAPH FROM ROBIN INGLIS)
23. *Kamehameha, c.* 1758-1819
    (WATERCOLOUR SKETCH BY LOUIS CHORIS, 1816; HONOLULU ACADEMY OF THE ARTS, HONOLULU, HAWAII)
24. *A Young Woman of Queen Charlotte's Islands*
    (FROM AN ENGRAVING IN *Voyages made in the Years 1788 and 1789, from China to the Northwest Coast* BY JOHN MEARES; SCL-UBC)
25. *Joseph Whidbey*, 1755-1833
    (CAPTAIN D.G. WIXON, HMS DRAKE, HM NAVAL BASE, DEVONPORT, ENGLAND)
26. *Details of a Letter by George Vancouver.*
    (TO HIS LONDON AGENT, JOHN SYKES, FROM NOOTKA SOUND ON OCTOBER 2ND, 1794; VANCOUVER CITY ARCHIVES, VANCOUVER, CANADA)
27. *'The Town of Valparaiso on the Coast of Chili'*
    (SKETCH BY JOHN SYKES, ENGRAVED BY JAMES HEATH FOR VANCOUVER'S *Voyage of Discovery*, 1798; SCL-UBC)
28. *Prime Minister William Pitt*, 1759-1806
    (DETAIL OF A PORTRAIT BY JOHN HOPPNER, 1805 [REPLICA]; NPG)
29. *John Pitt, Second Earl of Chatham*, 1756-1835
    (DETAIL OF A PORTRAIT BY JOHN HOPPNER; ROYAL MARINES MUSEUM, SOUTHSEA, HAMPSHIRE, ENGLAND)
30. *A Caricature of Thomas Pitt, Lord Camelford*, 1775-1804
    (FROM A COLLECTION OF BIOGRAPHIES PUBLISHED BY R.S. KIRBY IN 1805; BM-PRINTS AND DRAWINGS DEPARTMENT)
31. *William Grenville*, 1759-1834
    (DETAIL OF A PORTRAIT BY JOHN HOPPNER, c. 1800; NPG)
32. *Anne Pitt*, 1772-1864
    (DETAIL OF PORTRAIT BY MADAME VIGÉE LEBRUN, 1789; CAPTAIN DESMOND FORTESCUE, BOCCONOC, CORNWALL, ENGLAND)
33. *The CANEing in Conduit Street*
    (BY JAMES GILLRAY, 1796; BM, MS 37920)
34. *The Discovery as a Convict Hulk at Deptford in 1828*
    (NMM)
35. *Captain George Vancouver (?)*, 1757-1798
    (NPG; SEE EPILOGUE FOR DISCUSSION)

Illustrations: Chapter Head Drawings

Where possible, these drawings were made from images contemporary with Vancouver's tale; others were adapted from relevant secondary sources. The original source of each drawing is given, followed by the reference text (by number; see References) in which it appears.

1. *The death of Lord Camelford*, from an engraving in Vol IV of *The Eccentric Mirror, c.* 1804; (38).
2. The King's Lynn Custom House, from a 1986 tourist brochure; HMS *Resolution*, from a watercolour by Henry Roberts, Master's Mate of the *Resolution*; ML/(3).
3. Kealekekua Bay, from an unsigned drawing, possibly by William Ellis, Surgeon's Mate on Cook's *Discovery*; Public Record Office, London, England/(3).
4. The Kamchatka coast, from a drawing by John Webber, Artist on the *Resolution*; BM/(3). Sea otter, from a modern notecard by Pat Wright.
5. *The Lieutenant*, from a drawing by T. Rowlandson, 1799; NMM/(2).
6. Beam ends; (2). Icebergs and sea, from a drawing by Gordon MacLean; (12).
7. Table and globe, from a drawing by Gordon MacLean; (12).
8. *Crossing the Line*; NMM/(2).
9. *A Deserted Indian Village in King George III Sound, New Holland*, sketch by John Sykes engraved by John Landseer; author's original/(40).
10. Matavai Bay, Tahiti, from a watercolour by William Hodges, Artist on the *Resolution*; NMM/(15).
11. The village at Waimea, Kauai, drawing by John Webber, Artist on the *Resolution*; BM/(3).
12. Part of Meares's controversial map; (29).
13. De Fuca's Pillar, 1841, a woodcut engraving of a sketch by Charles Wilkes; University of Washington Library, Pacific Northwest Collection/(14).
14. The Goletas *Sutil* and *Mexicana* in the San Juan Islands with Mount Baker in the background, by José Cardero; MN/(19).
15. *Village of Friendly Indians at the Entrance of Bute's Canal*, sketch by Thomas Heddington engraved by John Landseer; author's original/(40).
16. View of the interior of Friendly Cove, 1791, by José Cardero, 1791; Museo de América, Madrid, Spain/(19).

Sources

17. *The Mission of San Carlos, near Monterrey,* sketch by John Sykes engraved by B. T. Pouncy; author's original/(40).
18. *The Presidio of Monterrey,* sketch by John Sykes engraved by James Fittler; author's original/(40).
19. Mission San Francisco de Asis (Mission Dolores), completed in 1791; from a 1987 tourist brochure.
20. Typical shore camp with observatory tent, sketch by John Sykes at Discovery Bay, 1792; The Bancroft Library, University of California, Berkeley/(14).
21. Kamehameha statue, Honolulu; American Museum of Natural History photograph/*Hawaii* by A. Carpenter, Children's Press, Chicago, 1979.
22. Hula hands, photograph; (23). Hawaiian hills, from watercolour of Kamehameha receiving Russian officers in 1816, by Louis Choris; Bishop Museum, Honolulu, Hawaii/(23).
23. Icy Bay and Mount St. Elias, sketch by Thomas Heddington; 1784, DeGolyer Library, Southern Methodist University, Dallas/(14).
24. Broaching to; (2).
25. View of Santiago, Chile, 1793; Colección Armando Braun Menéndez, Universidad de Chile/*Historia del Arte en el Reino de Chile* by Eugenio Pereira Salas, Universidad de Chile, 1965.
26. The Eddystone Lighthouse, third replacement 1757-1878, Mansell Collection, England/(2) Compass; (2).
27. "The Glen", purportedly George Vancouver's home from 1796-1798, now called "The Navigator's House"; author's photograph, taken with the owner's kind permission.
28. Whitehall from St. James Park; author's photograph.
29. The shooting of Lieutenant Peterson, from an early woodcut; Radio Times Hulton Picture Library, London, England/(38).
30. Vancouver's charts and journals; author's 1801 edition.
Epilogue. St. Peter's Church cemetery, Petersham, England; author's photograph.

Index

prescriptions for health, 46n,
50–51, 211
Cook Inlet [Cook's River],
192–195, 204
Couverden, Holland, V's ancestral
home, 9, 197, 257
Cranstoun, Surgeon Alexander,
Discovery 46, 50, 59, 127
Cross Sound, Alaska, 196–197
Daedalus, storeship to V's *Discovery*
and *Chatham*, 34, 43, 70, 76,
85, 104, 109, 117–118, 120
122, 127, 131, 135, 139, 142,
148, 172, 175, 183, 207, 216,
239
dance/music: European, 51–52,
126, 140–141, 178, 199;
native, 68, 126, 141
deaths: among explorers and
traders, 81, 88–89, 117, 128,
159, 271; among natives, 64,
70, 77, 84, 97, 100–101,
151–153, 167, 198; among V's
company, 52, 111, 146,
164–165, 202–203, 220–221
Decision, Cape, 172, 198,
200–201
desertions, 71, 142–143, 146, 237
Destruction Island, Washington,
88–89, 121
diet/food, 26–27, 44, 46, 46n, 53,
59, 62, 65, 70, 74, 80, 97, 102,
109–110, 120–121, 125–126,
151, 155, 159, 162–166, 173,
195, 199, 205, 208, 211, 214,
271, 274

Discovery, Cook's tender ship, 3rd
voyage, 10, 19–23, 26
Discovery, V's ship: aground,
114–116, 194; damage and
repairs, 86–89, 95, 98,
157–159, 165–166, 192,
194–195, 208, 210, 212, 214,
219, 222–226; description,
26,31, 40, 48–48, 266;
meetings with other vessels, 50,
89–91, 108, 112–113, 117,
120, 139, 143, 159, 161, 172,
190, 193, 195–196, 203,
205–206, 209, 213, 221–222,
224; NW coast surveying
seasons, 87–117, 158–171,
193–199; personnel
additions/losses, 26, 31–35, 39,
46, 48, 52, 71, 77–78, 127,
130–132, 143, 146, 154,
164–165, 183, 202–203, 220;
separated from the *Chatham*,
61–63, 78, 134–137,
158–161, 173–174, 192–194,
211, 220–221, 223–233;
special events aboard, 62,
68–69, 84, 99, 121, 140–141,
144, 152–153, 157, 184–185,
187, 192–194; voyage,
beginning to end, 43–228, 233
Discovery Bay [Port Discovery],
Strait of Juan de Fuca, 95, 108
disease, (see also Cook-
prescriptions, scurvy, and V-
illness): among natives, 58, 84,
100–101, 140, 190; V's com-